SOMEONE
TO
LOVE

Also by Kasey Michaels
in Large Print:

Jessie's Expecting
Marrying Maddy
Prenuptial Agreement
Raffling Ryan

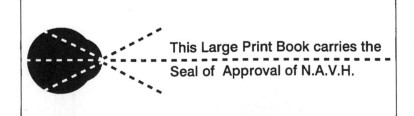

This Large Print Book carries the
Seal of Approval of N.A.V.H.

SOMEONE
TO
LOVE

KASEY MICHAELS

Thorndike Press • Waterville, Maine

Published in 2001 by arrangement with Warner Books, Inc.

Thorndike Press Large Print Basic Series.

The tree indicium is a trademark of Thorndike Press.

The text of this Large Print edition is unabridged.
Other aspects of the book may vary from the original edition.

Set in 16 pt. Plantin by Myrna S. Raven.

Printed in the United States on permanent paper.

Library of Congress Cataloging-in-Publication Data

Michaels, Kasey.
    Someone to love / Kasey Michaels.
       p. cm.
      ISBN 0-7862-3491-1 (lg. print : hc : alk. paper)
    1. Widows — Fiction.   2. Large type books.   I. Title.

PS3563.I2725 S66 2001
813′.54—dc21   2001034664

To Melinda McRae and Ron Henry.
Here's to smooth sailing!

I am about to be married — and am of course in all the misery of a man in pursuit of happiness.

— Lord Byron

Chapter One

The two nattily dressed gentlemen entered Hyde Park through Park Lane, curly-brimmed beavers jauntily tipped on their heads, canes lazily swinging at their sides, their air of sophisticated boredom half-feigned, half–all too real.

One dark and handsome. One fair and more than handsome; almost pretty. Both of them titled, both of them wealthy, popular, self-assured.

Blessedly unattached.

They stopped, posed, sniffed the air like any buck hoping to pick up a scent. Exchanged meaningful glances. Touched assessing fingers to their cravats, shot their cuffs. Proceeded on their way with consciously relaxed saunters, and yet with alert, watchful eyes.

Part predator. Part prey.

Hyde Park had once been a hunting ground, full of deer and boar and wild bulls. Over the centuries, many duels were fought beneath the trees as the morning mist gave way to a watery sun. There had once been fortifications there, military camps had dotted the thick grass.

Footpads had once owned the Park, until Charles II enclosed the entire area with high walls and William III had the happy idea of lining the *route du roi* with over three hundred lanterns hanging in the trees.

Now the Park presented a place of peace, of exquisite landscaping, of bridle paths, carriageways, and quiet walks, the air perfumed with the scent of thousands of flowers. The sun-kissed waters of the large, ornamental lake named Serpentine had been the creation of Queen Caroline, who had ordered the damming of the Westbourne so that she and her family could relax aboard either of the two yachts that had once bobbed on its surface.

Yes, Hyde Park was a lovely, tranquil place.

But, as the two men well knew, it remained very much as it had begun . . . a hunting ground.

"Oh, do cast your gaze over there, Kipp," the dark-haired gentleman prodded, nodding to their left. "Not that I need direct you, for I'm convinced we can both sniff out the desperation from here."

Kipp Rutland did as his friend bade him, lazily cocking his head in time to see a rented hack all but running away with its driver, the always hapless and definitely pocket-pinched Sir Alvin Clarke. The man dressed as best as he could, which meant that his collar and cuffs were probably on their second turning in order to disguise their fraying edges. Obviously a cow-handed driver, he hung on to the reins for dear life as he tried, quite unsuccessfully, to capture the attention of a young debutante and her protective mama.

"You know, Kipp, young Clarke's as much chance of winning a first at Newmarket with that nag as he does of snagging Miss Oliver in his threadbare matrimonial net," Brady James, Earl of Singleton declared, not without some small trace of pity. "Thank the good Lord I've sworn off marriage, or else that could be me making a cake of myself." He shuddered, elegantly.

"If your comment is meant as some sly, backhanded sympathy directed toward me, Brady," Kipp, who was also the Viscount Willoughby, said as they continued along the pathway, "I will accept it gladly, and with both hands. Now, do you see any prospects for your dear friend?"

Brady's grin was wicked. "Me? You expect *me* to pick your bride?"

Kipp tipped his hat as an open carriage chock-full of giggling ladies drove past.

9

"Why not, Brady? I've always admired your taste. Except for that satin waistcoat you had stuck to yourself the other night. I really believe you should have rethought that choice before appearing in public."

"Silk, not satin, and my valet is over the moon with his new gift. Teach me to listen to my tailor's suggestions when I'm half in my cups. But shall we return to your suggestion that I am to select the future Viscountess Willoughby? Just long enough for me to decline the honor, you understand."

Kipp smiled. "And you call yourself my friend? I'm hurt, Brady, cut to the quick. Oh, very well, if you'd rather not. Will you at least bless me with your opinion as we peruse the available ladies?"

"And how shall I peruse the ladies, I ask you? Invite them, oh, so politely, to please throw back their heads and open their mouths, so's that I might inspect their teeth? No, I think not. Besides, I want you to tell me again why you believe it so necessary to bracket yourself this Season."

Kipp's smile faded. He'd already given his friend Brady some silly reason for wishing to marry, something about tiring of bedding women, then having to get up, get dressed, and toddle off home again.

But at least part of the truth he'd told

Brady was that Kipp had promised his mother, on her deathbed, that he would marry before he turned thirty, and secure the title before he reached the ripe old age of thirty-five.

He'd turned thirty some six months past, and his promise to his mother had been haunting him ever since. He didn't personally care if the Rutland name died out, if the Willoughby title went to some deliriously grateful distant cousin in Surrey. After all, he wouldn't be there to watch, now would he?

No. He'd be sitting on a cloud, beside his mother, abjectly begging her forgiveness as she delicately wept into her wings.

So he would marry to keep his promise to his dead mother. That truly was one reason behind his just-begun foray into the marriage mart.

But it wasn't the only reason, probably not the main reason.

"I told you, Brady, I need an heir," Kipp said now, watching as three more open carriages passed by, each with its gaggle of debutantes trying to do their best to appear haughty, and only succeeding in looking as desperate as Sir Alvin had done. "I happened to get a peek at my Surrey cousin," he continued, fibbing easily, "and I must tell you, my friend, I shudder to think of that bovine man sitting in my chair, slopping up my wine. Or feeding it to his hogs as a special treat, which seems more likely."

"All right, lie to me," the earl said affably. "I can accept that. But are you sure you wish to enter into matrimony with anyone I would choose? Because there's this little red-haired dancer in Covent Garden —"

"Upstanding, Brady," Kipp said, laughing. "My wife must be upstanding. Not perpetually horizontal. Horizontal I can and do find on my own, thank you."

"Upstanding. Upright. Passably pretty? I should think you'd want at least passably pretty. And not too deep in the pocket, or too full of her family's consequence, Kipp, or else she'll have a will of her own, and God knows you don't want that in a wife. An orphan. Yes, an upstanding, well-bred, passably pretty orphan. With good teeth, for the sake of the children, you understand. Nothing worse than a peer with teeth like a donkey."

Kipp smiled his appreciation. "Ah, Brady, I knew I could count on you. Now, shall we begin?"

The ladies had been in the Park for thirty-five minutes. Abigail Backworth-Maldon knew that because she had just peeked at the large pocket timepiece she'd shoved into her reticule.

Another twenty-five minutes, and she'd order their coachman to head back to Half Moon Street, as to linger too long in the Park would be much the same as tacking a placard to the back of the carriage, saying: "Purse-pinched: will gladly marry for money."

Not that her current companion and niece by marriage could be said to be without admirers. In fact Miss Edwardine Backworth-Maldon almost always found herself knee-deep in admirers whenever Abby allowed the marriageable miss in public.

That was the trouble.

If a debutante could be too beautiful, Edwardine Backworth-Maldon could be said to be a victim of beauty. Wonderfully small, yet genteelly curvaceous, Edwardine possessed a flawless complexion, pink rosebud lips, a saucy little nose, bright blue eyes as large and wide as saucers, and a golden halo of ambrosial curls.

Shakespeare had written that men had died from time to time, that worms might then have eaten them, but that men have never died for love. That was because, to

Abby's mind, Will Shakespeare had never met Edwardine Backworth-Maldon. Because men would offer to die for Edwardine Backworth-Maldon.

And she'd be flattered enough, and dim-witted enough, to curtsy, thank them very much . . . and then hand them swords to fall on.

Which is to say that Edwardine's mental powers, if not precisely nonexistent, at least spent most of their time hiding behind those ambrosial curls, their feet propped up on velvet footstools, sipping lemonade.

The child was a romantic, plain and simple, and Abby knew there was nothing more dangerous than a romantic female (look at the trouble it had gotten her into!). Romantic females saw life through rose-colored lenses, and Edwardine would, too, if she hadn't steadfastly refused to wear glasses at all. Indeed, Abby lived in fear the shortsighted girl would someday walk up to a statue of Zeus in her hostess's ballroom and begin a lively conversation on the excellence of the musicians.

So, keeping the child's limits firmly in mind, Edwardine naturally was thrilled, positively thrilled, that her presence in the Park, the lending library, wherever she appeared, caused such a lovely commotion among the gentlemen. She was, in her mind, a smashing success, doubly so since she had come late to the Season, thanks to her uncles.

The uncles, yet another subject which Abby felt loath to refine upon on such a lovely, sunny day. The Widow Backworth-Maldon shivered a bit in the warm spring air, just thinking about her much older brothers-in-law, who insisted she refer to them as Uncle Bailey and Uncle Dagwood.

The uncles were the eldest of the universally batty Backworth-Maldon brood, and the only surviving sons. Both dedicated bachelors, either by design or because there were more females in England of good sense than anyone had yet imagined, they had outlived both Edwardine's father and Abigail's husband, who had been an afterthought, born fifteen years after the first three boys.

At five-and-fifty, and as the titular heads of the Backworth-Maldon family, one might believe that Bailey and Dagwood were in charge; the older, stable, rock-solid leaders of the clan. One might also suppose that finches could sing opera, or that St. Paul's Cathedral had been built in a single night. None of these things would be true, but one could suppose them.

Abby mentally slapped herself back to attention, because Edwardine was speaking. Never a good thing, allowing the child to speak.

Not that her adoring suitors would even notice if she said something any sane man could interpret as emanating from a brain inhabited mostly by sugarplums and cobwebs. And especially not this throng of half-pay officers, impecunious second sons, and aging fortune hunters surrounding the carriage, eager men who had yet to discover how very far out their hopes were of gaining more than a few groats from the beauteous Edwardine.

Besides, did gentlemen truly expect to get brains, beauty, and deep pockets, all from the same debutante? If so, they were sillier than Edwardine.

And that was pretty silly.

"Why, Mr. Pickworth," Edwardine was happily chirping, her alabaster cheeks flatteringly pink with easily summoned emotion, "how above all things wonderful of you to invite me. Of course I shall allow you to escort me. I have never seen Vauxhall Gardens, you understand. Abby says the gardens are past their prime, and too racy by half. But you will protect me, I am sure of that."

"Edwardine," Abby said, smiling at Mr. Pickworth, a grinning fool who looked very much, at the moment, like a hound just gone on-point, "I believe Mr. Pickworth spoke out of turn. Didn't you, Mr. Pickworth? After all, your mother and guardian is not here with us today, Edwardine, which leaves me to act in her stead and at her request. Mr. Pickworth, you may repeat your invitation, this time addressing it through me, if you please, and I will decide whether or not Miss Backworth-Maldon may be allowed an evening with you at Vauxhall Gardens."

"Oh, fiddle," Edwardine said, rather collapsing herself against the plush seat of the carriage, her entire posture one adorable pout. "You're cutting up stiff now, aren't you? Just the way Iggy says you do when he wants something totally innocent and you see his simple request as being worse than asking to jump off the roof to see if he can fly. You'll never say yes, will you, Abby?"

"Nonsense," Abby responded, watching with barely disguised glee as Mr. Pickworth ran a finger inside his suddenly tight collar. "We would be most happy for an evening at Vauxhall. Your uncles, your brother, Ignatius, your mother, your mother's inseparable companion, Cuddles, myself. I should think we'd be a most jovial assemblage, walking the walks, partaking of dinner, and all as Mr. Pickworth's guests. You're too kind, Mr. Pickworth, truly you are."

Mr. Pickworth's complexion paled noticeably. In fact, if he had had one, his tail would have been drooping onto the ground. "Um . . . that is . . . I, of course . . . how many was that? Six — *six* of you?"

"And Cuddles," Abby added, reminding the fellow of her sister-in-law's impossible poodle. She wondered, just for a moment, if young men of no more than three-and-twenty could possibly be felled by an apoplexy. But then, being basically of a good heart, if at times a fairly facetious one, she cut line — allowing herself to mix her metaphors — and let Mr. Pickworth escape with the hook still attached to his suddenly slack lip.

"Unless that would be too much of an imposition?" she questioned him with fairly well feigned concern, and immediately saw a flicker of hope dawning in his fearful eyes. "After all," she went on kindly, "we are a rather *large* family, are we not, and I imagine the expense of an evening such as you would have planned might cause an undue burden on you, sir. Then it's settled. My conscience

18

cannot allow this. No, no, Mr. Pickworth —
please do not insist, for I truly must refuse. I
could not live with myself, else."

Mr. Pickworth, who had not so much as
opened his mouth to protest (indeed, Abby
had momentarily worried that he might
have swallowed his tongue), nearly wept in
his gratitude. His hopes of getting
Edwardine alone on the Dark Walk and
stealing a few kisses might have been
dashed, but at least he'd eat more than stale
crusts until his next quarterly allowance
came due.

"And now, gentlemen," Abby announced,
as at least three of Edwardine's inappropriate suitors eyed her with transparent
malice, "I do believe it is more than time
Miss Backworth-Maldon and I returned to
Half Moon Street. You will forgive us, won't
you?"

"Which one was Mr. Pickworth?"
Edwardine asked with her usual block-
headed innocence as the carriage drove off.
She had moved sideways in her seat, and
was squinting back at the group of gentlemen now standing very much alone together beside the carriage path.

"Was he the one in blue, Abby? Yes, I
think he has to be the one in brightest blue. I
couldn't quite make him out, although he

19

did have the most lovely voice. Was he heartbreakingly handsome?"

Abby rolled her eyes. "He had a wart the size of a button on the end of his nose, and three teeth. Green ones; they clashed badly with his jacket," she told her niece, who she knew could not contradict her.

"Now, turn around and sit properly, Edwardine, while I tell you one more time how fruitless it is to encourage these very fine but very poor gentlemen, as you are in London to make a brilliant match. And, just because we have nothing else with which to occupy ourselves on our way back to Half Moon Street — as you could not see the sights even if I were to point them out to you — perhaps we can also take this time to again discuss the difference between being courted and being seduced, ruined. I do not believe you have yet quite grasped that difference."

Lecturing Edwardine on any subject of the least complexity, to Abby's mind, ranked straight up there with banging one's head against a stone wall. But it remained better to concentrate on Edwardine's social education than to refine overmuch on the tall, blond-haired gentleman she'd seen very obviously eyeing Edwardine measuringly as they drove out of the Park.

That man, that obvious gentleman of means — that incredibly handsome creature with the intelligent gaze and proud, natural strut of a walk — was definitely what Abby had in mind when it came to a young lady's most hopeful matrimonial prospects.

She just had never entered Edwardine into that particular equation. . . .

The lush redhead stretched, breathed a purring sigh, then sat up, holding the pink-satin sheet to her bare bosom. She watched as Kipp moved about the candlelit bed-chamber, locating the clothing she had stripped from him earlier.

What a magnificent animal he was, his tanned skin glowing in the light from the candles, his muscles rippling as he stepped into his smallclothes, slid his arms into his shirt. As handsome in the buff as when rigged out in London's best tailoring.

She sighed once more, this time with true regret. "*Must* you go, darling? It won't be dawn for hours and hours."

Kipp patted a fold in his neckcloth and tipped his head as he inspected his appear-ance in the mirror.

He also took a moment to glance at Roxanne's reflection in the background. He examined her expression, read the faint hint of apprehension in her eyes. A single word sprang into his mind: *clinging*. Yes, after all her promises to the contrary, dear Roxanne was about to become clinging.

How unattractive an attribute in an otherwise beautiful woman.

Kipp shrugged into his jacket, feeling a sudden need to escape the pink, perfumed bedchamber before he smothered. "As I much prefer leaving by the front door rather than to scramble over the rooftops, yes, Roxanne, I really must shuffle off now. Or do you forget what happened the last time you told me dear Sir Olney wouldn't push himself away from the card table before dawn?"

"Oh, pooh," Lady Skelton said, plumping up a half dozen pillows before subsiding against them. "You're no fun anymore, Kipp," she chided him, then smiled, showing her small, faintly carnivorous-looking white teeth. "But you are a marvel in bed. An absolute *marvel*."

Viscount Willoughby — as Kipp looked much more the viscount now that he was back in his evening clothes — turned to bow to the gloriously in the nude Lady Skelton. "I appreciate the endorsement, Roxanne," he said lightly. "We will, however, keep that our secret."

"Ha! Who would I tell who doesn't already know? Or is there some poor lady in Mayfair you *haven't* yet bedded?" Lady Skelton asked. A blond god, that's how she'd heard him described, and the description fitted him very well. Taller than the average gentleman, leanly muscular, with a face kept from womanly beauty only by its more angular shape and the cleft in his well-defined chin.

And very good in bed.

Kipp had been her lover for almost six months, but he was slipping away from her. She could feel it, sense it. She'd lasted longer than most of his mistresses, but her time was coming, and she struggled to understand why.

Was she too old? He'd known her age, only two less than his own thirty years. He'd known she was married to the dull, weak-chinned, but comfortably wealthy Sir Olney Skelton.

Her marriage, she believed, had only added to her attraction as Roxanne had most certainly heard the gossip, the rumors. Viscount Willoughby did not consider himself to be the marrying sort, much preferring to romance lonely wives. They were all, she'd also heard, immensely grateful for his attention and spoke fondly of him even after their liaisons were over.

Roxanne, although she had entered into this affair with no intention of falling in love — and was not in love now — had begun to believe herself the exception to Kipp's notoriously transitory affections. She actually had begun dreaming of bills of divorce and the sound of "Viscountess Willoughby" being called out as she entered a ballroom.

But now the object of her ambitions was preparing to flit off like a butterfly, to scent out another flower, sip the sweet nectar from another bud.

The bastard.

"Will I see you at the Selbourne ball?" Roxanne asked, wincing inwardly at the hint of desperation she heard invading her voice. No wonder he couldn't wait to leave her — she was entirely too transparent.

"I mean, not that it matters one way or the other, darling," she amended quickly, "but as Olney will be visiting his atrocious mother in Dorset, I thought perhaps . . ."

She allowed her suggestion to finish itself as she sat up in the wide bed, letting the sheet fall to her waist as she used both hands to lift her burnished curls high on her head. Would a fish — especially a male fish, as males were notoriously lazy — really struggle to evade such a well-baited hook just to see what delicacies might await him on the other side of the pond?

Kipp felt himself being tempted. He liked Roxanne, liked her very much. She was beautiful and eager, and they'd actually enjoyed a few reasonably intelligent discussions over the past months.

It would be easy, so very easy, to slip out of his clothing and return to the inviting pink-satin prison of her bed. Kipp even stole a glance at the mantel clock before mentally shaking himself back to what he knew to be the most reasonable plan, that of slowly but surely distancing himself from Lady Skelton.

After all, he was soon to become a married man. The very moment he found himself a suitable bride . . .

"You sorely tempt me, Roxanne," he said honestly, bending to pick up the cane he'd propped against a chair, then giving it a graceful twirl before tucking it beneath his arm. "But I have a full day tomorrow, and probably should allow my head to become at least marginally acquainted with my own pillow sometime before the cock crows."

Roxanne bit her bottom lip as she smiled, decided to be naughty, if naughty might bring Kipp back to bed. "I believe that manly bird has already sung out the dawn tonight, darling. Twice."

Kipp's laugh came out clearly, unaffected by her innuendo but definitely appreciative of her attempt at risqué wit. "Shame on you, Roxanne," he scolded as he walked around the bed, bent to kiss her smooth white forehead. "I believe you might be trying to corrupt me. Good night, my dear, sleep well."

She scampered to the end of the bed, then caught herself in time, before she actually grabbed at his sleeve. "Until the Selbourne ball, Kipp?"

Kipp took a short breath, stopped himself from sighing, and turned a dazzling smile on Lady Skelton. "Until the Selbourne ball, Roxanne," he agreed. He then let himself out of the bedchamber, delved into his purse for a generous tip to the yawning underfootman patiently waiting in the foyer, and slipped away into the night.

Chapter Two

The Cocoa Tree Chocolate House, located at Number Sixty-four St. James's Street, had its beginnings as an innocuous coffeehouse in the seventeenth century. But it hadn't stayed that way. Now a private club, and known for its strong spirits and gaming tables, its main appeal to Kipp at the moment was the fact that the place could be counted on to be nearly deserted until the sun set.

He rather slouched in his chair at the back of the room, contemplating the universe and his place in it — or at least as much as could be seen in the bottom of a wineglass. "Well, that was a waste, wasn't it? May as well have been hunting up mares' nests, for all the good that uncomfortable little sojourn in the Park did us yesterday. I don't think I have the heart to return there today, Brady, I truly don't."

"True, true, Kipp," Brady said after a moment, nodding sagely from his place across the small, round table. "I can't see the point of it myself."

Then he went in for the kill — carefully — because Kipp was his friend, and he knew

27

the man was hurting. "But I sense that your heart isn't precisely in this matrimonial hunt, Kipp. Still nursing that broken heart, aren't you? Not that I've mentioned it, if you've got any thoughts over bloodying my nose for my impudence. No, you just think you heard me mention it. Didn't even say her name, now did I?"

"You're a true friend, Brady," Kipp agreed, knowing what his friend was attempting, but not about to help him along as Brady tried to pry into his heart and mind. "Now why not stick your fine, aristocratic nose in that glass and let me drink in peace?"

"Done and done, friend," Brady answered with a wink, then contradicted himself with his next statement. "I do so love to watch and listen as you morbidly refine upon your woefully unhappy past, however. You get such a remarkable frown upon that toohandsome face of yours. A few wrinkles on that smooth brow might ugly you some, which the rest of London, save the ladies, would take as a gift from the gods."

Kipp took another sip of wine, gave up trying to avoid the subject Brady obviously refused to let drop. "Merry and Jack are in Philadelphia, you know, and have been for nearly a year," he said, staring into his glass.

28

"Cheerful as crickets and totally oblivious to my pain. No," he added, shaking his head, "that's not true. Merry knows now. Jack, I believe, has always known, ever since we three were all children together. God, Brady, what a damned gentleman I am, wishing them happiness and even helping them, in my small way, to gain that happiness."

"Jack Coltrane has been your best friend since childhood, Kipp," Brady pointed out, for he'd had the story from his friend once before, when Kipp had been deep in his cups, and his sympathies were all with the man sitting across the table from him. Still, he felt Kipp had to air his past one last time before he could truly get on with finding himself a wife, and a future. "You had no choice, I'd say, considering how you told me Merry had never seen anyone but Jack from the time she was in leading strings."

Kipp emptied his wineglass. "All right, Brady. Since you'll nag at me until I tell you anyway, I might as well get it all out in one sitting."

"Me? *Nag* at you? Well, I'm insulted, Kipp. Yes, definitely insulted." Brady grinned, pulled his chair closer to the table, propped his elbows on the scarred surface. His dark brown hair glinted with gold in the circle of candles hanging above the table, his dark brown eyes all but danced in his head. His lean, ruggedly handsome face took on the slyly delighted expression of a successful Piccadilly pickpocket. "Now, please go on."

"You know, Brady, you're good for me. Either that, or I keep you around to punish me for my lifetime of mostly enjoyable sin."

"We do it well, though, don't we? Sinning, that is."

Kipp grinned, the mischievous archangel showing his appreciation to the playfully roguish devil. "Yes, I suppose so. Now, if you'll just shut up for a moment I can tell you that I received a letter from Jack just last week. Took nearly three months to reach me."

"Is that so?" Brady took another sip of wine, saw how the skin around his friend's lips had compressed into a tight, white line. "Wrote to you of the flora and fauna, the interesting characters they've met, how they plan to bring you gifts of maize and tobacco and woven blankets upon their return?"

"Hardly. They've asked me to stand as godfather to their first child, a child probably born by now, as they were expecting the birth at any time."

"Ouch." Brady winced, sat back in his

chair, waited for Kipp to continue his story.

"And I'll do it. Because I do wish them both all the happiness they deserve. There has never been any question of that, Brady. But I do believe Jack and Merry both will be even happier to see me married before they return from America, in the next month or two. It has to be uncomfortable for them both to believe that I'm pining away on my estate, only a stone's toss from their happy home, the selfless victim of an unrequited love. You —" he called out to the barmaid, "another bottle, if you please!"

Brady remained silent, caught between guilt over goading Kipp into speaking and congratulating himself that he had forced his usually secretive friend to confide in him. "Ah, so now I have the answer I already knew, don't I, and even more I didn't. No matter what lies you've so glibly told, both to me and to yourself, you're really looking for a wife because Merry will be happier when she believes you to be happy."

"Something in that vein, Brady, yes. And, as I can only think of this one solution, I now have only a few weeks in which to find myself that wife," Kipp agreed, and then fell silent once more.

Brady, being a good friend, knew he had said enough, that his friend had, thank God, at least the wish to finally put the past be-hind him.

So thinking, he set out to lighten the somber mood that had enveloped them at the table. "Now, friend, about that little blond angel we glimpsed in the Park yesterday. The one with the huge blue eyes? I'm going to do you the great favor of discovering her name, learning a little bit about her. Then, with any luck, I imagine we'll see her again tomorrow night, at the Selbourne ball. Even if we don't, at least we know Sophie and Bram will provide an entertaining evening. Bram told me just last week that there's now another flea-bitten monkey running tame about the house — just to keep Giuseppe company."

"Ah, yes, dear Sophie and her menagerie. I still don't know what she sees in our friend Bram, do you? As I keep telling him, it's a good thing their daughter resembles Sophie. But I sincerely hope you don't waste too much time searching for a creature as perfect as our little duchess, Brady, because I don't think another such female exists. I'm not even convinced I'll want anyone too beautiful, although I will admit to admiring the small blond confection in the Park."

"But she might be too pretty? Is that what you're saying? Now I really don't understand you, old fellow. All right, not too pretty, if that's what you want. But with good teeth, remember," Brady slid in, grinning so that his own straight white teeth all but twinkled in the candlelight. "I'm afraid I'm going to have to be adamant about that one. But are you sure you wouldn't like a raving beauty? I mean, as long as you're so hot to put your neck in parson's mousetrap, why not?"

"Because I'm not interested in another Sophie, or another Merry, for that matter. And I most certainly am not holding out for a love match, even for a beauty. I just want a wife who will give me the heir my mother seemed to believe necessary, then mind her own business and leave me to mine. I think that's enough, don't you?"

"If you say so, friend," Brady murmured, immediately nominating himself as the one person in all of England who might reasonably believe he could act as Cupid to Kipp Rutland and his pragmatic view of marriage. The man might think he wanted a convenient wife, a conformable, pliant, barely invasive wife, but Brady knew differently.

What Kipp needed, Brady decided, was a woman who would put him through hoops, drive him to the brink of insanity, and make him fall madly, passionately, hopelessly in love with her in spite of himself.

Now all he had to do was discover who the beautiful young blonde could be, toss Kipp at her probably vacant head, prove to him that he was looking for his bride in all the wrong places — then figure out where the right place . . . the right young woman . . . actually was located.

The earl of Singleton, his course now set, lifted the bottle the barmaid had brought and tipped another measure of wine into both of their glasses. From that moment forward, it was onward, into the future, where Kipp — Brady ever ready and willing to help — would finally find another woman worthy of his love. The unpalatable subject of Jack and Merry Coltrane and their connubial happiness would not be raised again.

"Abby? Abby, dear, is that you out there? Well, of course it is. Has to be. Unless you're a housebreaker, and if you are I must warn you there's nothing here to steal worth more than a groat. Abby? Come in here — come, come! Your uncles have just had the most splendid idea!"

"Oh, no, not another splendid idea, please God. Heaven save me from the uncles' 'splendid ideas,' " Abby complained under her breath as she handed her pelisse and bonnet to an oblivious Edwardine, who then happily drifted up the stairs to gaze myopically in her mirror.

"Coward," Abby halfheartedly called after her niece, then ran a hand over the thick blond hair she'd ruthlessly swept back into a matronly bun before their drive to Bond Street, squared her slim shoulders, and entered the rather shabby drawing room that, unfortunately, had to be considered the highlight of their small rented house in Half Moon Street.

The uncles were there, of course, their balding, gray-fringed heads all but pressed together as they sat side by side on the fraying, garish pink on sickly lavender striped sofa, congratulating each other on their latest burst of brilliance.

They were also ignoring her, even though Uncle Dagwood had summoned her only moments earlier.

This was typical. The Backworth-Maldon twins lived inside their own rather bizarre cosmos, always had. Abby should only feel fortunate — depending upon who was making the judgment — that they even remembered her existence.

While the two gentlemen variously grinned, and giggled, and happily completed each other's whispered sentences, Abby resignedly sat herself down on the matching sofa on the opposite side of a lilliputian, lopsided round table. She poured herself a cup of cold tea, and lovingly observed her brothers-in-law cum courtesy uncles.

The "two peas in a pod" cliché did not precisely apply to Dagwood and Bailey Backworth-Maldon, but it came within three feet of it.

Firmly entrenched in their fifties, the twins always dressed themselves entirely alike from head to toe. This was unfortunate as, between them, they had all the sartorial taste of a boiled turnip.

They also shared their mostly bald pates and monklike fringes of thin, graying hair, their rather short stature (which measured only two inches taller than Abby's own five feet, three inches). They were woefully pigeon-toed, had a tendency toward runny noses, and both favored the same sickeningly sweet perfume, which they must daily pour over themselves from a very large bucket.

But Dagwood was the heavier by at least three stone, which was the only reason Abby could tell them apart with any certainty. How strange that one twin would have such

a love of sweets, while the other much preferred vegetables and what he termed a
"laudatory diet for the bowels and the ex-
pulsion of ill humors and suchlike."

One pudgy, one slim, instead of being as
alike as two coins they were, to Abby's mind,
a personification of "in for a penny, in for a
pound." Dagwood was the pound, Bailey, in
his turn, the penny.

Which was, alas, about as much as either
of the Backworth-Maldon twins, the entire
Backworth-Maldon family, was worth in
real, spendable coin.

The Backworth-Maldons, never more
than a whisker from genteel poverty in their
best times, had fallen on the very worst
times four years ago. This was shortly after
Abby had married the twins' brother Harry
and at approximately the same time as
Edwardine's father, Chester, had lost his
battle with a putrid summer cold.

It was all Harry's fault, the loss of what
little fortune the family had. Abby had spent
the past four years, more than three of them
in widowhood, feeling the responsibility
Harry had left — that of making up for his
idiocy.

Not that Abby had anywhere else to go,
anything else to do. Twenty-three-year-old
widows with no other family aboveground

and no prospects, either matrimonial or economic, seemed fated to be supporting props to families as inept as the one she had married into with such high hopes and blind eyes.

Besides, Abby loved them. She loved them all: Edwardine; her hapless, helpless brother, Ignatius; Chester's widow, Hermione; the twins. Oh, all right, so there was one exception. She detested Hermione's poodle, Cuddles. But, then, anyone of any sense would do the same.

It had been Abby who had seen the potential for economic revival in the rapidly growing, beautifully ripening Edwardine. The child could marry well, without much effort. (Please, God, don't let it require effort, because Edwardine only existed in this world. Heaven forfend, she did *not* participate.)

Even with its pitfalls, it remained a good, hopefully workable plan. An advantageous marriage to a man solidly respectable, and respectably wealthy, would help refill the Backworth-Maldon coffers. Which, in turn, would, with any luck at all, deter Dagwood and Bailey from their four-year-long campaign to recapture their lost fortune.

A fortune which, if Abby knew these men at all, constituted the reason she had been summoned to the drawing room in the first place.

Abby set down her empty teacup and politely cleared her throat, hoping to gain the uncles' attention.

Such subtlety rarely worked, and it didn't work now. The uncles were deep in their own conversation, totally oblivious to her presence.

"I tell you, Dagwood, this will work. I'm sure of it. Enough of these intrigues, these failed schemes, all our efforts to shame the man into doing the right thing. An all-out assault, that's what's needed."

"He took it away . . ."

". . . and we will take it back."

"Nighttime, rags muffling the hooves, masks on our faces . . ."

". . . a coin or two pressed into the right hand, a head turned in the correct direction . . ."

". . . preferably toward the wall, say what?"

". . . and, *bam,* we're in and out . . ."

". . . come and gone . . ."

". . . safe and dry . . ."

". . . and hanged at sunrise!" Abby ended for them, finally gaining their attention. "Are you two out of your minds? You plan to boldly *steal* your so-called fortune back from Sir Thurston? This is why you consented to come to London? This is why I'm all but killing myself trying to get your niece popped off before anyone accidentally shakes her and finds that her angelically lovely head is so empty it rattles? So that you two can steal a *horse?*"

"Not just a horse," Bailey mumbled into his rather crushed cravat, which bore evidence of his usual noon meal of carrot soup. "Backworth's Prize, and don't you forget it, little girl. Brother, tell her."

"Won Newmarket — twice!" Dagwood pointed out for, oh, about the thousandth time in the past six months, the millionth time in the past four years. But those were only approximate numbers. In fact, if Abby were to count up all the times she had heard the story of the great Backworth's Prize, if she refined on all the times she'd had to sit and smile and listen sympathetically, she just might have to do away with herself.

"Beautiful wins, going away," Bailey put in, his watery blue eyes beginning to glaze. "Put him out to stud, we did, and ate off him for three years. Lined our pockets well, that horse did."

"Until Harry . . ."

"Yes, yes, I know," Abby said, sighing. "Until my late husband gambled him away to Sir Thurston Longhope. Who, according to you, cheated him at cards, not that you can prove it, allow me to remind you."

"Doesn't matter. Harry was swimming in gin, not thinking straight, and Longhope took advantage of him."

"Too true, Bailey," Dagwood agreed. "Everybody knew what a bloody sot Harry was — sorry, Abby. And Backworth's Prize wasn't Harry's to lose in the first place. He was ours to lose, as the eldest, and we didn't sit down and gamble with the man, now did we?"

"Not that Longhope cared a whit about that, no, he didn't. He just up and sneaked himself into Backworth House, and took our fortune while we were busy burying Chester as Hermione drove us all half-mad with her fits and hysterics, not that Chester ever cared a hoot for her . . ."

". . . and while we were all trying to live down the mountain of gossip attending poor Harry's unfortunate demise. Don't forget that."

"Too true, Bailey. Hanging himself by his cravat like a chicken whilst escaping down a drainpipe from Lady Stanton's boudoir. Imagine the sight as the good citizens of Mayfair woke the next morning to see Harry swinging in the breeze like a flag, his tongue doubtless all purple and protruding, his breeches still at half-mast," Dagwood ended for his brother, then looked sheepishly at Abby. "But we won't mention that, will we?"

"No, of course not," Abby answered with a tight smile. She could no longer feel embarrassed by her late husband's conduct, his so depressingly public end. She was only angry that, at the tender age of nineteen, she had been silly enough to believe the man wonderful — right up until he'd gambled away her small dowry and figured out that she was no longer worth a groat to him. "We won't mention that. But we will mention that stealing a prime stud horse from Sir Thurston's Wimbledon stables —"

"And any progeny he has in those stables," Dagwood interrupted. "They're all ours, by blood. Not that long a ride to Wimbledon, and no one to see us since Longhope's camping here in Berkeley Square for the Season. Could be there and back in a twinkle, then off home to Syston the next morning."

Abby looked at the twins levelly, her expression warning them to silence. "As I was saying," she continued, her chin lifted, her jaw set, "you can't do this. For one thing, it won't work. For another, if it did work, Sir

Thurston would immediately know who had robbed his stable, now wouldn't he? Steal the horse — horses — at midnight, bring them back here, and be in the guardhouse by breakfast time. Is that what you want? Are you trying to outdo Harry in harebrained stupidity?"

"So? We start for Syston straight from Wimbledon, smack in the dark of the night, wend our way north . . ."

". . . couldn't be simpler, now that you pointed it out to us, Abby, thank you so much. Always said you had a good head on your shoulders."

"And I intend to keep it there, above an *un*stretched neck." Abby jabbed a finger in the air toward one uncle, then the other. Wagged that finger a bit for emphasis. "I said, *no*. You're not stealing that horse. Now, promise me you won't even consider it, and let's get back to concentrating on the fortune you do have: Edwardine. Agreed?"

The twins exchanged what the two men surely must have believed were conspiratorial glances Abby could not intercept, shrugged, and apologized profusely.

"We'll drop the scheme, Abby dear," Dagwood then promised as Bailey nodded solemnly. "We'll drop it, never think of another one, and be patterncard uncles in town to enjoy the Season and marry off our beloved niece."

"Liars! Of course you won't stop this nonsense," Abby declared, rising to her feet so that she could glower down on them — not that she expected to impress them a whit with her fierceness. "I'd be a fool to believe otherwise. However, I will ask you to promise that you will inform me of your inspirations as they occur to you, all right? At least then the rest of us might all have the luxury of a head start before the law comes pounding at our door, ready to clap the lot of us in irons."

"Such a dear girl . . ."

". . . so caring, so . . ."

". . . wonderful. Definitely wonderful. And yet, it would be such jolly good fun to —"

"No," Abby interrupted firmly.

". . . black our faces, ride across the countryside at midnight . . ."

". . . sneak up on the stables . . ."

"Uh-uh-*uhh!* Stop that."

". . . tippy-toe inside, find our Prize . . ."

"I said, no, gentlemen! N-O, *no!*"

"As we said, such a dear girl . . ."

". . . always so concerned for our welfare. Come here, Abby, give your uncles a kiss."

Abby shook her head, smiled, gave in to the inevitable. She kissed one round cheek, one lean, and allowed herself to be similarly saluted in return. Then she became stern once more for, heaven knew, someone had to be stern or else the entire family would already be halfway to Hades in a handbasket.

"Now, gentlemen, you may recall that we all have been invited to a small dinner party this evening, the first and, to date, only invitation we've had since coming to town. I don't believe I have to tell you how important it is that we all make our very best impressions on Baron Hundley and his wife, in the hope this one invitation might lead to others. It's crucial, gentlemen, if we are to successfully launch Edwardine into Society."

"Hundley," Dagwood grunted. "He'll probably be asking for that hundred pounds you borrowed from him last year, Bailey. Man has no sense of proper behavior, the right time, the right place. Try not to let him corner you. You know . . ."

". . . stay on m'toes . . ."

". . . and stick close to the ladies . . ."

". . . easy enough to hide behind Hermione's skirts, eh what?"

Abby sighed, wondering what great crime she'd committed that she could be punished this way. "I ask three things of you, dear uncles, and three things only. One, be prepared to leave on time, so that we do not have to lay out more blunt than necessary to our hired driver. Two, if Sir Thurston Longhope is in attendance, and I most sincerely pray he is not, neither of you is to call him a thief to his face — or behind his back! Do I have your promise?"

Bailey, never able to boast of being a top scholar when it came to arithmetic, nodded his agreement.

Dagwood, however, frowned, then asked, "But you said three favors, Abby. I believe you missed one."

Smiling as she prepared to sweep out of the room and head upstairs to coax Edwardine into her bath, Abby said, "Oh, that. Just the usual, Uncle Dagwood. And I do believe it is Iggy's turn to lock Cuddles in a cupboard so that his *mother* can't drag the yapping little water can along to dinner."

Chapter Three

Brady propped up a pillar as he watched his friend Kipp bowing over the hand of a freckle-faced debutante who'd been cooling her heels at the side of the Shelbourne ballroom.

Viscount Willoughby, Brady knew, was every hostess's dream. Rich, handsome, affable, witty, and always wonderfully willing to partner all the poor wallflowers usually left to sit on the edge of the dance floor.

And he wasn't just being nice, being polite. Kipp truly enjoyed London Society, its fits, frolics, and foibles, and had spent as much time as possible in the Metropolis over the years. He was known everywhere, thought to be an affable fellow, if at times a bit of a loose screw, and if he were a bragging man, his friend could easily declare that Kipp did not have a single enemy in this world.

Why? That was simple, Brady knew. Kipp had long ago discovered he was much happier being happy. It was also easier to choose to be happy; easier, certainly, than if he'd been born a rat-catcher's son. Kipp was very forthcoming about how mightily grateful he was for his title, for his wealth, for his comfortable estates, his mansion in Grosvenor Square, even his good looks.

Society saw Kipp as a well-dressed fribble, a man who laughed easily and angered slowly. A born flirt, he flitted from woman to woman, never forming a serious attachment, never leaving a teary eye behind him when he danced away from one woman, waltzed into the waiting arms of another.

In short, Society saw Kipp Rutland, Viscount Willoughby, exactly as he wished them to view him.

Brady knew differently, knew the real man as well as anyone might ever be privileged to know him. He knew that Kipp was quite the contradictory character, even to his own mind. Yes, he was basically cheerful, born chock-full of natural optimism. And yet, he had also been born skeptical and had never been anyone's fool, even if he occasionally allowed people to think so.

Half-happy, half-sad, half-frivolous, half-serious. Part-foolish, part-wise. Capable of playing the clown, equally able to be the philosopher. Highly interested in other people, although he gave little of himself away, and then only to his closest friends — and sometimes not even then.

Indeed, Brady thought, quizzing glass to his eye as he hunted out the petite blonde they'd seen in the Park, his dear friend could safely be termed the most complicated uncomplicated person in the Selbourne's ballroom that evening.

Except for himself, that was. . . .

Abby had been silently congratulating herself for the past half hour that she had not once looked up at the grand, vaulted ceiling of the Selbourne ballroom and cooed: "Ah, can you believe it!"

For, while the country bumpkin in her sat, jaw agape, taking in the painted ceiling, the stuccoed walls, the elegant lords and ladies posturing and preening, the sober, sensible, even conniving side of her recognized the ballroom as being the definitive marriage mart, a chamber fit as the perfect setting in which to showcase the lovely Edwardine.

The invitation to the Selbourne ball had come only that morning, delivered by a smiling young man in well-cut livery and accompanied by a handwritten apology from the duchess herself that she had not sent the invitation sooner.

As if Abby could possibly feel insulted to have this grand chance tossed into her lap.

The small dinner party the Backworth-

Maldons had attended the previous evening could not be considered a success. Not with the baron making references to the high cost of food each time anyone dared to put a bite in their mouths, then looking at Uncle Bailey owlishly, asking if that might be a new jacket the man had on.

Embarrassing, that's what it had been. And, quite obviously, the only reason for the invitation in the first place had been so that the baron could dun Uncle Bailey about that dratted hundred pounds.

Which was a pity, as the baron's invitation had been the only one to hold the place of prominence on the Half Moon Street house's cracked marble mantel.

Until, that is, the duchess of Selbourne had summoned them to her ball.

What a madhouse there had been in the tall, narrow house in Half Moon Street. Abby had an awestruck Edwardine in a tub, scrubbed her golden curls until they shone, then sent her off for a lie-down. Meanwhile, she, in the role of ladies' maid, pressed the child's best gown and begged, without success, for the uncles to please not decide to wear the rose-colored satin jackets and breeches.

Hermione, in her turn, had taken to her bed for two solid hours, pouting because

Abby had put her foot down, quite firmly, as to where the dear Cuddles would be spending the evening.

All her running, and fussing, and general organizing of her very unorganized family had left Abby less than an hour for her own bath in less than tepid water. She had even less time to worry that her very best gown — three years old if it was a day — was still packed in one of the trunks and was doubtlessly sadly crushed.

In the end, wearing her dowdy, sallow yellow, definitely crushed gown, her still-damp hair scraped back in a bun, Abby had still managed to have them all standing in the foyer ten minutes early, waiting for their hired coach.

Now the uncles were off in one of the card rooms, doubtless in hopes of borrowing more money from any poor, unsuspecting soul who had yet to hear of the scandal that had lost them their "fortune."

The woefully useless Ignatius, his blond hair pomaded, his wasp-waisted evening coat setting off his small, slim figure, could be spied out following the comelier female servants about — as his highly amorous interests always seemed to lie in that direction.

And Edwardine sat at the far end of the

ballroom somewhere, hidden within a dense circle of gentlemen admirers. Abby felt no burning incentive to wade through them, elbows jabbing, excuses dribbling from her compressed lips, in order to listen to the inane compliments undoubtedly already piled three feet deep at her niece's obscenely expensive evening slippers.

Yes, she did worry that Edwardine would say something silly and totally inappropriate but, then, from the looks of the assembled gentlemen, none of them would even notice. Besides, the uncles had already taken a quick inventory and declared none of the love-struck young suitors to have enough blunt between them to mount a matrimonial crawl, let alone a charge.

Which meant, according to Uncle Dagwood's whispered nuggets of insight earlier, that the young men, who probably had already learned that the Backworth-Maldons were less than solvent, were after Edwardine's body, yes, but not necessarily her hand.

"Remember trying as much myself in m'salad days," Uncle Dagwood had confided, his breath smelling not all that unpleasantly of peppermint mixed with gin. "The desperate ones were always ever so willing. But not to worry. Nothing untoward can happen to her here — just don't let her out on the balconies, understand?"

Remembering Uncle Dagwood's words, and not much comforted by them, Abby knew she really should bestir herself and go check on her niece. Even if she'd rather try to forget, just for one evening, that she was in the Selbourne ballroom as ape-leader, not debutante.

Not that Abby wished to sit alongside her sister-in-law for another moment, as that woman complained of her aches and pains and sipped what she swore was water but what Abby knew for a fact to be gin. Hermione might only have married into the family, but she shared her late brother-in-law Harry's fatal flaw when it came to her taste in liquid refreshment.

Dress it up, pour it into crystal, call it Hollands or Geneva, Cobbler's Punch or Heart's Ease, but it was still the same spirit favored by those unfortunate souls living in squalor in the bowels of London. Those less fortunates referred to gin as the Last Shift, Crank, Diddle, and even Strip Me Naked as they bought it for a halfpenny a glass. Potent stuff, and Hermione drank it as if it really were water, and seemed to have a tolerance for the strong drink equal to that of an elephant being sat upon by a very small ant.

"I miss Cuddles," Hermione declared, pouting as she sighed. That sigh unleashed a cloud of gin vapors in Abby's direction, so that she felt forced to open her fan and begin waving it furiously in front of her nose even as she dug in her reticule for a peppermint she could offer the woman.

"Cuddles will be fine at home, Hermione," Abby said, deftly handing over the mint.

"That's what you say. I don't see why she couldn't accompany us this evening. Such a good little baby, my own dear love. I'm sure Lady . . . Lady . . . um . . . well, whoever she is, she wouldn't have minded a bit."

"Our host and hostess are the duke and *duchess* of Selbourne, Hermione. Selbourne. *Sell,* as in what we'll have to do with our only home if Edwardine isn't successfully bracketed within the next few weeks, and *bourne,* as in, oh, dear me, the troubles I have borne and continue to bear. Please do apply yourself to remembering their names. And you're absolutely right," Abby then added bracingly. "I most certainly understand how Their Graces would have rejoiced at dearest Cuddles's presence as the vicious little monster bit them, then piddled on their feet."

"Oh, for shame, Abigail! I am sure I

cannot help it if Cuddles has taken you in such dislike, but she is normally a mild-tempered sort." Hermione narrowed her eyelids, looked at Abby assessingly. "Dogs are quite good judges of character, I've heard it said. God's own sweet creatures. Perhaps Cuddles sees something base in you, Abigail, something we mere mortals have not discerned."

Abby looked at her sister-in-law dispassionately, this remarkably homely, horse-faced woman with the unfortunate blue hair and the too small, too deep-set, beady brown eyes.

Edwardine had taken every bit of her looks from her dead father, and her brain-power, such as it was, from her mother. Imagine the catastrophe if things had been reversed. A fairly intelligent young lady with the jaw of a dray animal and a complexion that could only be called muddy by the charitable. Imagine trying to pop *that* Edwardine off this Season!

Poor Hermione. Another woman married for her money, brought into the family in order to shore up the always tottering Backworth-Maldon fortunes. She'd produced two remarkably handsome children who didn't care a fig for her, had been all but deserted by her husband, and had found her comfort in a bottle of Heart's Ease and a nasty little scrap of fur and bone who loved her unconditionally.

"You're right," Abby said at last, feeling in some sympathy with Hermione, for she, too, had been a discarded Backworth-Maldon bride. "Cuddles is a good dog. A good, good dog. Precious as a peach. It is I who am evil, and Cuddles senses that. I apologize profusely, Hermione, and promise to mend my ways and sin no more. In fact, I will go now to check on your dearest daughter, if that is all right, apply myself to doing my best to redeem myself in Cuddles's discerning eye?"

Hermione looked at her through her small, beady, and somewhat bleary eyes as Abby stood up, then nodded her approval, as, if Abby could count on little else in this life, she could count on the fact that sarcasm would always be lost on a Backworth-Maldon. "Good. You do that. And you are in my prayers, Abigail."

"I am so blessed," Abby said, bending to kiss her sister-in-law's painted cheek before turning away, rolling her eyes heavenward. She then headed off in the direction she'd last spied out Edwardine holding court over an assemblage of gentlemen she couldn't see, speaking words she didn't really understand, and probably reciting the tale of the time she and her brother, Iggy, had been caught out by the vicar, bathing in a local stream, stark naked, and wasn't that just the most delicious story?

"Oh God, why did I ever start this? I must have been out of my mind," Abby berated herself as she pushed through the clutter of peers and peeresses congregating in the Selbourne ballroom, locked in their insular groups and eyeing her dismissively as she slipped past them.

Not that she could blame them for looking at her, looking straight through her, then pigeonholing her instantly as someone of no consequence.

Because Abigail Backworth-Maldon knew she had no consequence. None whatsoever. She wasn't rich, she wasn't titled, and she certainly wasn't beautiful. Not when plunked down beside Edwardine, who soaked up all the light, leaving Abby very much in the shadows.

Abby had long ago inspected herself, compared herself to the blossoming Edwardine, and firmly believed herself to be more ordinary than extraordinary.

Yes, her hair was thick, and long, and a rather lovely, almost golden-blond. It was also as straight as a poker at a time when curls were all the rage.

She believed her clear complexion to be her best feature, but not all that important, as whoever heard of a man tumbling head over ears in love with a complexion?

Her eyes were fairly remarkable, a deep, mysterious, heavily black-fringed violet. There was that.

But nobody really looked at her eyes, so they missed the spark of mischief in them, the appreciation for the ridiculous, the love of life that would, if she let it, explode in ways that could be considered dangerous in a widow of three-and-twenty who was very firmly on the shelf.

She should put on her caps once and for all, and have done with dreams. She knew that, but she had ruthlessly shoved them in a drawer and left them at home in the country, figuring that if she was to be in London for the Season she should at least be able to *pretend* that there might be a chance she, too, could snag herself a husband.

For all the good that had done her in the past two weeks, since arriving in Half Moon Street. She might as well have been wearing a shroud, or tripping about the town stark naked, for where Edwardine went all eyes followed, and she had immediately been relegated to precisely what she was — and that wasn't much, by her own measuring stick.

Abby, supposedly Edwardine's companion to Hermione's chaperone — the woman couldn't successfully mind mice at a crossroads, let alone be a competent chaperone to a silly young girl — had found herself to be in London precisely what she had been in the small manor house just outside Syston.

Reliable. Dependable. Practical. Unobtrusive. Sane. Sober. Levelheaded.

And bored to flinders.

Her adopted family believed they knew her, but they didn't. They had only seen the nervous, neglected bride, the unnaturally young widow and — forced into the role these past years — the commonsense despot who ruled all their lives, held the purse strings, and bullied them lovingly but firmly into, for goodness sake, behaving themselves.

But in her mind, in her heart of hearts, Abby was a very different person. Perhaps a dozen different people. Practical, yes. But quite devoted to the ridiculous, with a sense of humor out of the ordinary and based very much on her sharp wit and a true love of nonsense, the ridiculous.

Otherwise, how could she exist, year after year, in a house crammed with bacon-brained, self-centered yet somehow lovable Backworth-Maldons?

But, oh, how she longed to escape! To settle all her dear relatives, see them safe and happy and solvent, and then perhaps sail off to tour the world, or at least those bits that interested her most.

How she longed for adventure, for the sort of delicious excitement of, say, the beauteous Lucinda Pomeroy, the heroine of Aramintha Zane's most recent novel, who had been captured by pirates and rescued by the greatest, most handsome, dangerous corsair of them all.

She had a face now for that handsome corsair, had seen it fleetingly in the Park and been unable to forget it. Tall, blond, handsome as the most delicious sin, the man had the carriage of a confident hero, the smile of an angel . . . and he had been smiling at Edwardine.

Abby stopped short, reeling in her wandering mind even as she used two fingers of her right hand to help shut up her jaw, which had unexpectedly dropped to half-mast a moment earlier.

The crowd of admirers around Edwardine had gone, disappeared into the smoke.

And no wonder.

Even idiot half-pay officers and younger

sons knew when they were being out-classed, cast as far into the shade as Abby had ever been when in her niece's sunshiny presence.

Edwardine had only two gentlemen hovering over her now, and Abby immediately recognized them as the two gentlemen she had seen in the Park.

One tall, dark, ruggedly handsome, with an air of amused boredom about him that could in no way be feigned. Interesting. But not really to Abby's taste when it came to heroes capable of toppling her off her reluctantly sensible feet.

The other was also tall, but blond, a fallen angel, a dream come true, a man so beautiful he could scarcely be real. And he was bowing over Edwardine's hand as that silly girl giggled, and simpered, and desperately tried to focus her wide blue eyes.

Abby sighed, shrugged, and realized that handsome did not translate to intelligent — Iggy certainly bore witness to that! — and told herself she didn't care a fig if the blond Adonis had made a dead set at Edwardine. No. She didn't care at all.

Really, she didn't.

But that didn't mean she couldn't walk up to them, politely interrupt, and establish herself as Edwardine's companion.

★ ★ ★

"Mrs. Backworth-Maldon. Charmed, I'm sure," Kipp said after cursory introductions had been made by a giggling Edwardine.

He bowed over the young widow's hand — he knew she was a widow because the chattering Miss Backworth-Maldon had earlier, in the five short minutes of their acquaintance, given away nearly every family secret he could hope, or fear, to hear.

His lips did not quite touch the widow's gloved hand as his gaze discreetly assessed her, seeing her as Edwardine's young chaperone, a woman he most certainly should impress, but not one who particularly impressed him. Although her gown most certainly did impress him, being quite the ugliest creation he'd ever seen, poor thing.

"Are you, my lord? Charmed, that is. And why is that?" Abby responded, neatly withdrawing her hand, and immediately causing Kipp to take a second look at her, see the quick flash of humor in her eyes.

Interesting.

But he was not in the market for a widow, even if interesting.

"Ha! She's got you there, Kipp," the Earl of Singleton said, clapping him on the back. "You know, we mumble this stuff by rote, but what does it really mean? Are you charmed, Kipp? Are you really? Or are you simply polite? I think you're simply and rather mundanely polite. I, on the other hand, am highly amused, on many levels. Madam," he ended, lifting Abby's hand to his lips, "amused to meet you, I'm sure."

"My lord," Abby answered, still looking at Kipp, who suddenly had the uncomfortable feeling he had been judged by the lady, and found wanting in some way . . . and that the lady was mightily disappointed in him.

Well, no matter. He was here for the innocuous little Miss Backworth-Maldon, not some faintly drab spitfire who had probably haunted her husband into an early grave.

Annoying woman.

"Am I to understand, madam," Kipp then went on, undeterred, and once more looking at Edwardine, who had the most wonderful blue eyes — almost dreamy as they gazed at him, or at least in his general direction — "that you are Miss Backworth-Maldon's chaperone?"

"I don't think so, my lord," Abby answered, at last able to withdraw her fingers from Lord Singleton's grip. Still flustered by her initial verbal slip, she answered Kipp honestly, much too honestly. "Her mother is here in London with us. I am her aunt by marriage, and more in the way of her keeper. Aren't I, Edwardine?"

The child giggled, gave Abby's forearm a playful slap. "Oh, you're so droll, Abby! And oh, my, yes, she is my keeper, my lord. I am so dreadfully incapable of keeping myself. Everyone says so. In fact, that's why we're here, isn't it, Abby? So that we might find someone else to keep me and you can leave off feeling like a — ?"

"Isn't she delicious? Such a droll sense of humor!" Abby interrupted just as the young lady, Kipp was sure, had been about to repeat her aunt's bound-to-be-embarrassing description of her role as bear leader.

He watched as Mrs. Backworth-Maldon snagged a glass of wine from a passing servant. She nearly jammed it between her niece's rosebud lips — all as she glared at the two men who had just heard the young beauty announce that she was shopping for a protector, which couldn't possibly be the case. "Your voice is sounding dry, poor dear. Here, drink this. All of it."

"But, Abby, this is —"

Kipp put a hand over his mouth, knowing that laughing out loud was not quite the thing he should be doing if he seriously wanted to get past this small but fiery

64

dragon to the beautiful Miss Backworth-Maldon.

"It's a special evening, Edwardine, dear," Abby pronounced tightly, quite painfully aware she had just invited her niece to take her first taste of anything stronger than a sour lemonade. What was wrong with her? Asking rude, pointed questions, allowing herself to point out Edwardine's flaws when that child was innocent and undeserving of such treatment?

Was she so easily knocked off her perch of sober respectability by the touch of the viscount's hand, the sound of his voice, the sight of his smile? Was she that jealous of Edwardine's beauty, of her ability to draw the viscount to her side like a bee to honey?

Well, shame on me, Abby thought, *and shame on him for being here in the first place, allowing me to make a complete cake of myself.*

Had she really believed herself attracted to the man? Why? Because he was pretty? Of all the stupidity! Harry had been pretty — had she forgotten that? If so, she wouldn't forget it again, just as she wouldn't forget that Viscount Willoughby was not what he appeared, but only another human who looked at her, looked through her.

And what was he doing now? This was worse than looking through her. He was smiling at her now, *laughing* at her with his warm brown eyes, even as he reached out to Edwardine.

Annoying man.

"May I?" Kipp neatly removed the glass from Edwardine's hand, passed it over to Brady, who obediently downed the contents in one long swallow. "Mrs. Backworth-Maldon, if I might have your kind permission to be Miss Backworth-Maldon's partner in the set just now forming?"

"Oh, go, go," Abby told him quickly, making shooing motions with one hand as she rubbed at her forehead with the other, for she was feeling the beginnings of what promised to be a crushing headache. "I'll just stay here and amuse Lord Singleton. Won't I, my lord?"

"It is my great hope, madam," Brady responded cheekily, smiling as he watched Kipp watch Mrs. Backworth-Maldon. "Well, are you going to stand there all night, Kipp, looking as if you'll tip over if you take a single step? Go on, please, the two of you. Get out there on the dance floor, and let the oohing and aahing commence as you two uncannily beautiful people dim the blazing chandeliers above our heads with your combined brilliance."

"Abby? What did he say?" Edwardine

asked, her beautiful face made even more so by her maidenly confusion. "Did His Lordship mean me? Does he really think I outshine the chandeliers? Should I thank him?"

Abby tipped her head, looked inquiringly at Kipp, waited for him to speak, to make some comment, even just some facial expression that told her that he knew her niece to have about as much sense as an infant. Or was beauty all he cared for, all he needed?

Kipp refused to accommodate her, even though he already was well aware he had made a mighty error in judgment in believing that youth and good looks were enough in a wife. He'd at least like to have one who could be relied upon to know how to count to ten without having to stop and ask for assistance. So much for allowing Brady to select possible contenders for the next Viscountess Willoughby.

Not that he'd want to exchange the empty-headed Backworth-Maldon for the irritating Backworth-Maldon, a woman with a real ability to get under his skin . . . rather like a splinter, he told himself.

No, all he wanted to do just then was to partner the young Edwardine in the dance, and then go somewhere and try to forget that he stupidly had made it his mission in life to secure himself a wife.

"Come along, Miss Backworth-Maldon," he said when Abby didn't answer her niece. "We don't wish to be late for the set, now do we?"

Abby mentally patted herself on the back for not pulling a face or sticking out her tongue at the viscount as he and Edwardine glided away.

Chapter Four

"Pitiful, aren't we?" Abby asked Lord Singleton, no longer caring a whit that she had made a complete fool of herself with Viscount Willoughby, or even that Edwardine had seemed to go out of her way to display the depth of her wit, which was approximately six inches less shallow than a mud puddle.

"On the contrary, Mrs. Backworth-Maldon. I find both you and your niece delightful," Brady told her honestly, feeling certain that the astute young woman would see through the smallest lie.

Big lies, however, whopping great clankers of the sort that were by then all but standing in line inside his brain, pushing and shoving to be told, were seldom seen by anyone . . . even his good friend Kipp.

How wonderful fate's little tricks could be. Brady had managed the Backworth-Maldons' invitation to the ball to once and for all show Kipp the error of his ways, hoping to prove to him that the beautiful Miss Backworth-Maldon and others of her ilk were not for him.

But he hadn't planned on finding the perfect woman for his friend at the same time — and in the same family, no less.

Sometimes the best brilliance was really only a happy accident. Now, with Kipp occupied for at least the next quarter hour, he could hopefully decide whether Mrs. Backworth-Maldon was, indeed, the answer to his rather lighthearted prayers.

"Truth be told," he continued, "I find you and your niece to be the least pitiful persons present here tonight. Your niece, because she seems to be happy simply to exist, and yourself because you are obviously such a clearheaded woman. Although I feel I must warn you, madam, in this small circle of Society, too much sanity can be dangerous."

Abby smiled, tried to compose herself. All she *really* wanted to do was to run back to Hermione and hide her burning cheeks behind her fan.

"Thank you for that warning, my lord," she replied after a moment, believing herself to be back under control. "I am always careful to surround myself with enough gentle *insanity* to keep my head balanced quite nicely on my shoulders. But, I hope, not stuck there too tightly, as nothing should be taken to extremes, even sanity."

"Ah, a practical woman."

"As practical as I have to be, my lord."

"Here to launch your niece at the head of the nearest eligible bachelor?"

Should they be speaking so frankly? Abby wasn't sure. Still, the earl was a man of the *ton,* so how wrong could she be in following his lead? She certainly hadn't read anything about being so familiar with the opposite sex in any of the books she'd purchased to help her learn how Edwardine should go on in Society. But then, for all she knew, there could be an entire separate list of rules for dowdy, on-the-shelf widows than there were for dewy-eyed debutantes.

She looked at Brady levelly, dared to be blunt. "Isn't that the usual plan, my lord?"

"But with no hopes of your own, Mrs. Backworth-Maldon? No dreams of your own?"

Abby straightened her shoulders. She might not know all the rules of polite conversation, but she hadn't spent her three-and-twenty years dug *that* deeply into the country! "I feel we have moved from bantering to a highly personal inquisition, my lord. May I ask why?"

Brady offered Abby his arm, and she took it, so that they began a lazy circuit of the ballroom. "I'm not known for my tact, madam. Forgive me. But, as you had earlier been so wonderfully honest about your hopes for your lovely niece — do you see them out there together? They hurt the eyes, don't they? — I thought perhaps I could be equally blunt as to my own quite similar intentions. Thinking of you as a kindred spirit, and all that sort of thing."

Abby, who had been looking at Edwardine and the viscount, wishing herself in Edwardine's place and then feeling ashamed of herself for thinking any such thing, responded, "Excuse me? I'm afraid I wasn't quite attending. Did you just say what I thought you just said?"

Brady smiled inwardly as he saw the hint of longing in Abby's eyes. He'd already seen a hint of confusion in Kipp's, when he'd looked at the woman. This could be fun. *He* certainly was enjoying himself, that was for sure. "If you think I just said that I'm here tonight in hopes of popping someone off, then, yes, Mrs. Backworth-Maldon, you did hear me correctly."

"Oh. A sister?"

"No, madam, not a sister," Brady said as he neatly plucked two glasses of wine from the tray of a passing servant, offering one of them to Abby. "Care to wager another guess? You might begin by thinking blond, and obscenely handsome."

"Hand— *handsome?* Not beautiful? I mean, Edwardine is beautiful. But to call a female handsome . . . well, I should think if you were serious about helping the young girl find a husband, then . . . oh." She looked up into the earl's eyes, saw the mischief in them as he watched realization dawning in her own.

"Oh," she repeated hollowly. "How — how very unusual, my lord."

"And our little secret, Mrs. Backworth-Maldon," Brady told her as the duchess of Selbourne approached them, her arms outstretched so that he could take her small hands in his, lift them to his lips one after the other. "Sophie, you become more beautiful every day."

"Liar, I grow *larger* every day, and the sillier gossip birds are twittering all over this room, saying I should be hiding myself away in an attic somewhere, as if pregnancy is a quite horrible disease, possibly even *catching*," the duchess said, withdrawing her hands and rather lovingly cupping them around her pregnancy-enlarged abdomen. "Bram swears I look just fine, but I really look ready to explode, yes?"

She turned her attention to the curtsying Abby. "And you're Mrs. Backworth-Maldon, if I remember correctly from when my husband and I greeted you earlier in that absurdly long receiving line. We're so pleased you were able to accept our very rude, last-moment invitation and could be with us tonight. I feel such a ninny for not knowing you were in town until this morning. You will forgive me, yes?"

"There's nothing to forgive, Your Grace, as we were honored that you'd even heard the Backworth-Maldon name, let alone considered inviting us here tonight."

Abby was beginning to feel like a particularly homely duck suddenly thrust into the pond with a collection of swans. Not just Edwardine. Not just the viscount and the earl. Was everyone in London blessed with such physical beauty?

The duchess was even more than simply beautiful, exquisitely formed, and blooming with health. Standing next to the duchess, even Edwardine would be nothing more than a sweet, too-young, still-unformed nursery darling.

As the earl and the duchess teased each other, bantering lightly back and forth, Abby surreptitiously performed an inventory of the vision standing before her.

Yes, the duchess was a petite scrap of perfection in glowing silk, flawless from her head of tousled curls to the tips of her small feet. Winsome, almost childlike brown eyes, but eyes unwilling to hide the intelligence behind them. A single mole kissing the upper edge of her right cheekbone. Pregnancy, rather than distracting from her beauty, seemed to enhance it. The duchess was dewy, she positively glowed.

Abby longed to hate the woman on sight, except that she couldn't. The duchess's smile was too genuine, her behavior too gracious, her manner refreshingly candid. Instead of allowing jealousy to influence her, Abby felt herself wanting very much to be this woman's friend. Not because she was a duchess, but because she sensed that Her Grace could be nothing less than a kind, loving person.

After winking at the earl in answer to something he'd just whispered in her ear, the duchess turned to Abby once more, saying, "Your niece is such a lovely child. I remember her from the receiving line. Edwardine, isn't it?"

"You remember correctly, Your Grace," Abby told her, curtsying yet again, as gracefully as she could while holding the wineglass. "And I thank you again for your generous invitation. We had not been expecting such kindness."

"I can imagine what you *were* expecting,

my dear," Sophie whispered, leaning toward Abby even while playfully shooing Brady a few steps away. "I shall be blunt, yes?"

Abby felt herself being dazzled, dazzled by the woman's smile, her soft brown eyes, her obvious concern. "All right," she offered, trying not to sound too wary.

"You were expecting, my dear, to be at the least laughed at and, at the most, discreetly shunned by most of the starched backs littering Mayfair. Because of your late husband, and his rather *public* demise? In fact, if it weren't that you have hopes of settling your little niece, you probably would never have dared to leave the country, yes?"

Abby looked at the earl, wondering if he could overhear this whispered conversation, have so much as a glimmer of what was being said. The man was just standing there, smiling, and still looking as smug, as self-satisfied, as he'd looked before the countess arrived.

Something was going on here, some sort of conspiracy between the duchess and the earl. Abby felt sure of it, even as she knew she had no explanation to offer herself.

Perhaps it was only that these London Society people seemed absolutely to *thrive* on their own cleverness, and delight in making

76

as many startling statements as possible.

But, even if that were true, why on earth had they picked *her?*

Sophie's hand came down on Abby's wrist, squeezed it. "It's all right, Mrs. Backworth-Maldon," she said bracingly. "Truly it is. I know scandal; both my husband and I are well acquainted with it. I assure you that the whispers fade if you keep your chin high and refuse to allow the gossips to see you have felt their stares, heard their whispers. Which is why I told Bramwell — the duke, you know — that we simply must invite you and your family to our ball, the moment I heard of your presence in town."

"Really?" Abby didn't know what else to say. Although, as she looked at the earl, who was looking at his nails, she wondered just *how* the duchess had learned of her presence in town.

But, no. That couldn't be right. Because how would the *earl* have learned of her presence in town? And if he had, why would he care, and why would he share his knowledge with the duchess of Selbourne?

Abby began to wonder if she'd drunk too much wine. Either that, or perhaps she had not drunk enough.

"Oh, yes, yes indeed — *really,*" the

duchess was saying earnestly, so that Abby pulled herself back to attention. "We were very definitely a scandal when first we married, living through the resurrection of another very public scandal concerning our parents, but we survived. No, we triumphed! I am ever so popular now, much to my own amusement, and an invitation to my ball assures all who attend that they are accepted by the *ton*. You will see, Mrs. Backworth-Maldon. After tonight, you will be invited everywhere. That is what you'd hoped for your niece, yes?"

Abby was feeling increasingly dizzy. She really didn't have the faintest idea what the duchess was prattling on about so cheerfully, as she had never before left the country, and had no connections with anyone in town, nor with any old gossip concerning the Selbourne name.

But if the duchess was saying that she'd invited the Backworth-Maldons to her ball *because* of Harry's scandalous demise, well, it was the first time Harry had ever done anything even remotely helpful for his family.

"Thank you, Your Grace," Abby said at last, truly at a loss to utter anything more than the simplest statement.

"Sophie," the duchess corrected her,

kissing Abby's cheek. "I am Sophie to all of my friends. Although I admit to being selfish in granting such informality. But if you were to call me Sophie, I shall no longer have to twist my tongue around Backworth-Maldon, and that could not be seen as anything other than a blessing when next we meet, yes?"

"Abby," Abby answered, smiling, relaxing in spite of herself, and well aware of the social award the duchess had bestowed on her. "I would be honored, Sophie, more than honored, if you would call me Abby."

"Am I now allowed to stop pretending to be deaf and blind, and rejoin the conversation?"

Abby looked at the earl, remembering that he had been telling her something she probably didn't want to hear. Or perhaps she wanted too much to hear what he had been trying to say. "Oh, very well," she said, tapping him on the arm with her folded fan, and feeling much more an unencumbered young girl than she did a widowed bear leader, "if you promise to be good, I suppose you may rejoin us."

"No, no, Abby," Sophie declared, winking. "He may only rejoin us if he promises to be his usual wicked self. Are you feeling your usual wicked self, Brady? You were certainly looking the part as I came to join you. But now I must leave again, I fear," she went on before Brady could answer. "I am a hostess, you know, and must gracefully float from group to group, making most certain everyone is enjoying my ball. And then, as I have promised the worrying Bram, I will retire to a chair beside the dowagers and rest my swollen feet on a footstool."

She sighed, touched a hand to one side of her abdomen for a moment, then spoke once more. "Abby, my dear new friend — don't believe a word this man tells you, and promise we'll see each other again soon. Brady, I will hold you to it — promise me you'll bring Abby to see me soon. Definitely soon," she added, winking, "as I believe I may give birth before the week is out, perhaps before this night is out, which would be nice, as I've grown rather disenchanted with my profile when I catch sight of myself in a mirror."

"You — you think the baby is coming *now?*" Abby looked at the earl, who finally looked human, and rather endearingly helpless.

Sophie giggled. "Oh, don't be alarmed. Babies take a lot longer to be born than most people think. I'll make it through the ball, I promise. As a Selbourne, my baby knows not to interrupt the annual ball. Do you like babies, Abby? I adore them, and would be pleased if I could show off *both* my children to you when Brady brings you to visit. You'd like that, yes? But don't tell Bram what I'm supposing at the moment, Brady, or else he will toss everyone out on their ears, order straw put down in the street outside, and once more become the most endearingly silly, worried man I've seen since our Constance was born."

"If you don't tell him, Sophie," Brady warned, "he'll be the *angriest* you've ever seen him."

"Oh, pooh, Brady. Now I'm off. Brady, don't forget to bring Abby to me," she said, standing on tiptoe to kiss his cheek, then stepping back, winking at him once more as her back was turned to Abby. "And thank you so much for introducing me to our new friend."

"What a strange and wonderful woman," Abby said as she watched the duchess glide away, a vision in soft honey-colored curls and that butter yellow gossamer gown that could have been fashioned by fairies. "And what a *nice* woman. Have you known her long?"

"Long enough to know that my friend

Bram is probably going to be caught between kissing her and strangling her before the night is out," Brady said, shaking his head. Then he took Abby's arm, led her toward two empty chairs beside an open door to the balcony.

The evening breeze coming through the doorway was welcome, as the ballroom was fast becoming overheated by dancing bodies, the sheer crush of humanity Society felt necessary to call any social event a success.

"I've known her husband, the duke, for many years," he continued as they sat down. "Fine man. But marrying Sophie was the making of him. Why, they even can be seen taking the air in the Park with their small daughter, a vision of domestic bliss. It's almost frightening, to see such a change in a man, but he appears happy. Downright delirious, at times."

"Although you wouldn't wish the same fate for yourself," Abby slid in, beginning to believe she could read this man, at least a little bit. "You would, however, wish the same fate on this *handsome* person we were speaking of a minute ago?"

Brady smiled, arched one well-defined brow. "How considerate of you not to have forgotten what we were discussing before

Sophie blew herself into our midst. But tell me, Mrs. Backworth-Maldon, can you envision the dear viscount in the Park, pushing a miniature blond-haired image of himself as he and his lady wife bow and smile to the populace?"

Abby looked out onto the dance floor, saw the viscount still going through the motions of the country dance, trying to keep the myopic Edwardine from floating off toward entirely the wrong partner.

He was a kind man, she supposed, or else he would have deserted Edwardine at his first possible chance, and then run screaming from the ballroom. After all, Edwardine was a beautiful child, who could only really appeal to another child. The viscount was a man, experienced, older. He couldn't possibly be entertained by Edwardine's nonsense prattlings or amused by her shortsighted missteps.

But yes, she could see him walking his child in the Park. Their child in the Park. . . .

"I don't know, my lord," she answered, measuring every word, every protective fib. "Surely you, as his friend, are the better judge? I'm afraid I haven't really considered the viscount — in any way."

"Ah, Mrs. Backworth-Maldon," Brady said, sighing. "And here I thought we had cried friends. Very well, I'll take my gloves off now, tell you precisely what is on my mind, stop this enjoyable but slow-moving dance of words."

Oh, dear lord! He *was* going where she thought he was going! "Not on my account, my lord, please," Abby responded quickly. "I think I'd much rather retreat to banal, courteous conversation, frankly. I could quite happily discuss the weather at some length, truly I could."

"Kipp — Viscount Willoughby — believes himself in need of a wife," Brady went on doggedly, knowing full well that he had Abby's undivided attention. "Because he was disappointed in love a few years ago, he is not holding out for some romantic dream, just a wife. A woman to bear him children and mind her own business, to be coldly precise about the thing."

"My lord, really —"

"No, no, don't interrupt, please. As I said, the viscount is wife-hunting. I'm here because he begged my assistance in the matter, which we can both clearly see he needs if he, even for a moment, considered your niece to be a candidate in his marriage stakes."

"That's cruel," Abby said, automatically defending her niece. It was one thing for her to say that the child had the brains of a flea, but quite another to allow Edwardine to be insulted by strangers.

Brady apologized at once. "I did not mean to be disparaging to your niece, Mrs. Backworth-Maldon —"

"Oh, please, call me Abby, my lord, if you so desire. It may be a horrendous breach of etiquette, but I do believe our conversation has moved us both beyond concern for such niceties. Besides, the duchess was right when she said it would be much easier to be more informal."

"I thank you, and hope you return the favor, as we stand to become co-conspirators, and friends as well, I hope, and very much to your benefit, Abby, if you take my meaning," Brady said, agreeable to abandoning the subject dearest to his heart in favor of relaxing Abby Backworth-Maldon enough that she didn't jump up, slap his face, and run away from him as fast as she could.

She turned in her chair, looked at the earl closely, finally said what was on her mind. "Coconspirators, my lord? And to *my* benefit? Surely, as Edwardine is so clearly out of the running in your opinion, you can't mean that I should believe you see *me* as a possible wife for the Viscount Willoughby. Because, if you *are* —"

"You'd hate the thought?" Brady interrupted, taking hold of Abby's arm as she shot to her feet. "Swoon at the prospect? Rather die than even so much as consider becoming a viscountess, marrying a man who is, even to your discerning eye, I'm sure, one of the most odiously handsome creatures ever created. Oh, and he's nearly drowning in his own wealth, in case you didn't know that. So, yes, of course, you couldn't possibly consider marriage to the man. Whatever could I have been thinking?"

She sat down again.

"Good," Brady said, smiling. "I thought so. Now, as the set is concluded and Kipp and your niece are heading in our direction, we'll not continue this most interesting conversation for the remainder of the evening. Just follow my lead, if you please, while I arrange for the four of us to meet again tomorrow, when you and I will speak again."

Chapter Five

Kipp awoke in a poor humor the morning after the Selbourne ball and unable to hide that fact, which was greatly annoying, as he prided himself in almost always being able to present himself as very much a good-humored fellow.

He *was* almost always a good-humored fellow, damn it!

He was also a polite fellow. Polite to a fault.

Which unfortunately explained why he had allowed Brady to go prattling on and on last night about how delightful it would be to meet with the ladies Backworth-Maldon this afternoon at Hatchard's.

Which most definitely explained his poor humor, his very bad mood, his wish to invent some minor emergency at Willoughby Hall in order that he could escape to the country.

What could he have been thinking, to have allowed himself to be convinced that he could casually pick one of the dozens of debutantes from this Season's crop at random, romance her a little, and then marry her, bed her, put her in charge of running his several households and all necessary things domestic — and then blissfully ignore her?

He did not really wish to become a husband. He most certainly did not harbor aspirations of becoming a *keeper*.

That's what Mrs. Backworth-Maldon had become, had admitted she was, and he could certainly see the necessity of running herd on Miss Backworth-Maldon at all times.

The child was . . . a child! Helpless, hapless, giggling, smelling of nursery bread and butter, incapable of thinking a single thought past the end of her own nose. And years too young.

She'd be run by his housekeepers, not the other way round. She wouldn't know the first thing about setting up menus, or supervising servants, or hostessing a ball. She'd giggle inanely, her conversation would stun a charging ox and put him straight into slumber, and she'd most probably expect him to make love to her while she kept her nightclothes on and herself buried beneath the covers.

Oh, yes, that would be delightful, wouldn't it?

Still, as Brady had so gleefully pointed out

as they'd bolted from Bram and Sophie's ball and headed for White's, young and innocent Edwardine Backworth-Maldon was precisely what Kipp had declared he wanted when he'd first begun his search for a wife.

And more than he wanted. Young, impressionable girls tended to fall in love. Messily, sloppily in love, most especially with the first man who bedded them.

And *that,* Kipp knew, was the very last thing he wanted in a wife.

So why was he drawing on his gloves, accepting his curly-brimmed beaver from Gillett (and ignoring the man's frowns), and heading off to Hatchard's, to meet with the ladies Backworth-Maldon and the sure to be still-snickering Brady James?

Because he was a good man, that's why. A kind man. Considerate. Unwilling to hurt anyone. A bona fide idiot.

And desperate.

Hatchard's was situated at Number 187 Piccadilly. The establishment had the honor of holding the Royal Warrant, which gave the place no end of cachet. It also meant that the place was always hip-deep in lords and ladies who might never read more of a book they bought there than its cover, but who nonetheless made damn sure they bought that book at Hatchard's.

The inaugural meeting of the Royal Horticultural Society had taken place in the reading room behind the shop. Staunch antislavery advocate William Wilberforce also was allowed use of the reading rooms for his meetings.

William Hatchard, the owner, endorsed a firm Christian ethic, and published *The Christian Observer* as well as various publications of the Society for Bettering the Conditions of the Poor, many political pamphlets, and even an assortment of children's books.

Every day, the London papers were spread out beside the fireplace for the lords and even the ladies to peruse. The servants accompanying their employers to Hatchard's were privileged to take advantage of the benches Mr. Hatchard provided for them outside the shop.

In short, in long, Hatchard's was quite the respectable, farseeing, upstanding establishment.

It was also, as was nearly every bit of park or shop or ballroom in Mayfair, yet another prime hunting ground for the marriage-minded ladies and gentlemen of the *ton*.

Just the thought made the hair on Kipp's

nape stand up on end as he entered the building.

Because he knew what could happen, would most probably happen. If he kept attending balls, partnering debutantes in more than the occasional dance to satisfy his hostess, if he showed up in all the recognized marital hunting grounds like Hatchard's day after day, someone would be sure to conclude correctly that he was at long last on the search for his viscountess.

And if he allowed that to happen, if hostesses and conniving mamas got wind of what he was about, he would be a doomed man. Doomed.

No. He had to do this quickly. He'd seen a possible candidate. Picked her — as unsuitable as she'd turned out to be — and her alone, from the crowd of eligible young ladies parading in the Park like pigeons hoping for crumbs. He was not about to look further, as the whole thing really didn't matter all that much to him, either way. He needed a wife. That's all he needed. After all, he had to wed her, bed her. Nobody said he'd have to *listen* to her.

Still, with self-preservation so firmly fixed in his mind, he had to squash a flinch as he espied Brady waving frantically to him, the Backworth-Maldon ladies flanking him behind a table littered with tomes on Greek history.

Proceeding with all the joy and low expectations of a man climbing the steps to the gallows, Kipp smiled, waved, and began making his way toward the small group.

As he weaved his way through the many tables he visually examined the two ladies, hoping his gaze looked nonchalant, not measuring, all while doing his best to ignore the smug, self-satisfied smirk on Brady's face.

Edwardine Backworth-Maldon was as lovely as she had been at the ball, as she had appeared in the Park. Except that her eyes no longer looked soft and dreamy to him. Just young, and fairly vacant.

As vacant as her aunt's intelligent eyes were full, nearly to brimming, with what he told himself could not possibly be interest in him, his walk, his clothing, the set of his shoulders, even measuring him as for the depth of his character. Very unsettling.

Lord save me from intelligent women, Kipp prayed automatically, then realized that the Lord had been listening all too closely lately, if He had put Edwardine Backworth-Maldon in his path.

All right, so maybe he did want an intelligent woman. Maybe, just maybe, it would be an intelligent woman who could meet his criteria, and have enough interest in the rest of the world, in her own pursuits, to be the sort of wife he most desired. An unromantic one, with no thought to tying him up in ribbon and giving him her vulnerable heart.

That thought in his mind, the mind he no longer trusted quite as much as he had done these past thirty years, he stopped for a moment, pretended interest in a book of maps, and thought about Abigail Backworth-Maldon.

Intelligent, yes. Independent; she had to be. Resourceful? Did she have a choice in the matter, saddled as she was with her late husband's reputation, the remaining Backworth-Maldon menagerie, and with a pretty, purse-pinched, dull-witted debutante to settle?

And drab. The woman was drab. Beyond drab. A figure too boyish, slim-hipped, small-breasted. Blond hair and skin as pale as the moon. Only those violet eyes were at all distinctive, at all interesting.

Although her posture was commendable. And, remembering Brady's criteria, her teeth were good.

Now, if the lady only knew how to dress. . . .

Kipp dropped the book of maps back onto the table, disgusted with himself.

He'd thought he would do best with an innocent debutante.

Now he was looking at a sharp-tongued widow.

Did he have any idea what he wanted? What he needed?

Yes. Yes, he did. He wanted Merry. Had always wanted Merry, and had always known she was not for him.

And, if he couldn't have Merry — and he couldn't — did it really matter all that much whom he chose?

"Kipp? Are your feet stuck to the floor? Come here, and say hello to the ladies."

Dredging up yet another hopefully happy smile, the depth of his hypocrisy amazing him, Kipp made his way to the ladies, bent over two gloved paws, and refrained from kicking his good friend in the shins.

"Am I late?" he asked, trying to ignore Edwardine's giggles as she picked up a book, opened it, and all but plastered it against her nose as she looked at the pages.

"A thousand pardons. And," he continued quickly, still smiling, "before you ask me if I truly am offering you a thousand pardons, Mrs. Backworth-Maldon, may I correct myself, please? A thousand pardons could only be seen as being overdone. Would you settle for one, heartfeltly given?"

"You haven't forgiven me for being so flippant last evening, have you, my lord?" Abby countered, still eyeing him levelly, looking not in the least intimidated by him.

Kipp realized with a bit of a start that, among all that he had already found to dislike in her, the dratted woman also had a very annoying way of answering his questions with questions of her own.

No, he'd do better to stick with the pretty and brainless one. The widow could be dangerous, more than simply an annoyance. Because he'd pick one of the two of them before the week was out, or he'd know the reason why. There could be no incentive he could think of that would force him back into the hunt, to run the gamut of matchmaking mamas and yet more inane debutantes. It just wasn't worth it.

"Abby!" Edwardine shrieked, slamming the book shut with a loud snap, and gaining herself the attention of everyone within a twenty-foot radius. She dropped the book to the tabletop, then pointed at it as if she'd discovered a snake stuck inside the pages. "The people in here aren't wearing any *clothes!* They're *naked!*"

Three young bucks who had been passing by paused, looked at each other, grinned evilly, then nearly fell into a fistfight trying to be the first to grab up the book Edwardine was backing away from, her blue eyes wide as saucers.

Brady, who had been watching Kipp watching Abby, and enjoying himself almost as much as he had done all last night — as he had finalized his inspiration into what he believed to be a very workable plan — mentally patted himself on the back for his brilliance. The comely Edwardine was a twit. A perfect twit!

As Abby was occupied in attempting to console her niece, it was left to Kipp to deftly retrieve the book before it could disappear. He handed it, unopened, to the Widow Backworth-Maldon, who accepted it with some alacrity, and only a small apologetic smile on her face.

"Thank you, my lord." Opening the book, paging through it, Abby then sighed, shook her head, and said, "Statues, Edwardine. This book is full of sketches of Greek *statues*. And, yes, many of them are not wearing clothing. Most of them also don't have arms, or heads, if you happened to notice that. In other words, dear, this is a book of ancient *art*."

As the trio of young bucks melted away in disillusionment, Edwardine stood very still, her cheeks a becoming pink, and peeked into the book. "Oh," she said at last, as Kipp leaned forward, interested in spite of himself at what the foolish young girl might say next.

She didn't disappoint.

"But, Abby, if that isn't above everything silly of those Greeks. How could they remember to put on *bosoms,* and forget arms and heads?"

Brady averted his head, coughed. Choked a time or two.

Abby rolled her eyes, part-amused, part-resigned.

And Kipp, who wanted to do nothing more than to fall across the table, kicking his feet and howling in mirth until he cried, manfully suggested the four of them leave the stuffy bookshop to stroll over to nearby Berkeley Square for a visit to Gunter's, to sample some ices.

Chapter Six

Gunter's Tea Shop on the east side of Berkeley Square was a half hour's leisurely stroll away on that warm, sunshiny day that seemed to have all of Mayfair out taking the air.

Kipp and Edwardine led the way, the young girl's hand tucked most endearingly and trustingly around his elbow. And making Kipp feel very much like an older brother, even a father, but most definitely not a suitor.

Abby and Brady followed behind, careful to linger as far behind as necessary to hold a private conversation.

"Not too far back, my dear," Brady warned facetiously, gesturing toward his friend. "I have to feel confident I can stop him if he decides the only sane solution left is to throw himself in front of a passing carriage and end it all."

Abby bowed her head, tried in vain to control a giggle. "Did you see the expression on his face when Edwardine so innocently said 'bosoms'?" she then asked him. "Although it *was* funny, wasn't it?"

"She'll make someone a fine wife, Abby, have no fears about that. As long as he's rich, madly in love, and as silly as she is, of course. Luckily for your niece, the type of gentlemen I've just used as an example always lie quite thickly on the ground here in London."

"How you comfort my mind," Abby said, wondering how to ease back into the conversation the two of them had danced around last evening, the memory of which had kept her awake half the night. "But you still don't see Edwardine as the answer to the viscount's cold-blooded hunt for a suitable wife?"

"Do you?"

"That's not the question, my lord. I am barely acquainted with His Lordship, and could scarcely know his possible *preferences*, now could I? Other than that silliness you were waving in front of me last night, which I'm sure is fair and far out, because he couldn't possibly be interested."

"Silliness? Interested? Ah! You mean my suggestion that *you* would make my friend a nearly perfect wife?"

"Yes, yes," Abby said quickly, looking about to see if anyone could overhear them as they walked along the crowded flagway. "Now here's a thought, my lord. Why don't you climb to the top of St. Paul's, and shout your suggestions to the populace?"

"Forgive me, dear madam," Brady told her, squeezing her fingers as they lay on his well-tailored sleeve. "Secrecy is, of course, of the utmost importance, isn't it? Especially since the last person who should hear of my plan is Kipp himself. He'd run for Willoughby Hall in a heartbeat — right after he broke my interfering nose, that is. You see, he might *say* he wants my help, but he's never meant it. Now, have you given any more thought to my proposal?"

She had. She most definitely had. For nearly all of last night and most of this morning. "I do have some more questions, my lord, I cannot help but admit that."

"Good, then you haven't rejected my inspiration out of hand. Go on."

Mentally reviewing the few conclusions she'd been able to draw, Abby began, "Sophie — that is, the duchess of Selbourne knew all about my late . . . about our family. I suppose it wouldn't stretch credulity too far to believe that you also know all about them, would it? Not just some small snippets — but everything? That both you and the viscount knew all about the family scandal before you so much as introduced yourselves to Edwardine last night?"

"The curse of being in Society, Abby, my dear," Brady responded as kindly as he could. "Can't take more than two steps in any direction without hearing all the gossip. That said, I imagine I should belatedly offer you my condolences on the loss of your husband."

Abby gave a small wave of her gloved hand, silently accepting Brady's condolences and dismissing them at the same time. "And my brothers-in-law, the rest of the family? You know about them as well?"

"Casually, yes. Although the Backworth-Maldons have not appeared in town in some years, I remember enough to feel sure that they must be . . . *interesting,*" Brady admitted. "But, to be truthful, none of that mattered all that much to me until I met you last night, Abby. Before that, my primary concern had been, frankly, to simply parade your niece under my friend's nose so that he'd see the error of his judgment in believing that he wanted a young, innocent wife."

"How very *calculated* of you."

Brady smiled at her. "Calculated? I prefer brilliant, but I'll have to settle for calculated, I suppose. But, to continue. The fact that a young lady in your niece's position would probably grab at someone like my friend with both hands was, of course, not lost on either of us. Your niece was thought to be perfect for his needs, and is now, happily, perfect for my own plans. Especially since the viscount wishes to have the entire matter settled quickly, probably within the week. Remember, my dear, the viscount sees this entire project as one of business, not pleasure."

"Really? How cold-blooded of you both, my lord. Do you know what? I don't like you. Neither of you," Abby said, stiffening. "I thought I might, but I now know I don't."

"Now there's a pity, for I find myself liking you, Abby, more with every word you speak. I think we could be great friends."

"Oh, really? How unflattered I am by that sentiment, my lord. Now, as you've admitted that you know about my family's . . . foibles . . . can you tell me if they had anything at all to do with our last-moment invitation to the Selbourne ball? Are *you* how the duchess found out about us, why she invited us to her ball? Even though I'm sure I already know the answer. I did see the duchess wink at you, you know."

"Gloves off?" Brady asked, smiling what he hoped was his most ingratiating smile.

"Gloves off," Abby answered, glaring at him.

"All right, my dear inquisitor. First, I will reiterate. We — Kipp and I — saw your niece in the Park, and the viscount decided to begin his hunt for a bride by pursuing her. Cold-blooded enough for you so far?"

"I saw you in the Park as well," Abby admitted. "And I saw the viscount measuring Edwardine with his eyes. Go on."

"There isn't much more. Yes, I went straight to Sophie after I'd found out your niece's name, and begged her to invite you and your family to her ball. Which wasn't difficult to do, as Sophie is, well, she's just Sophie. The best of good fellows, you understand, and always willing to help. Especially when I told her your family's sad story."

"She already told me there is some hint of scandal attached to her and the duke, if that's what you're trying not to say," Abby told him.

"More than a hint, Abby, but that's all in the past now, although I admit to shamelessly recalling the Backworth-Maldon scandal for her, to gain her sympathy — and your invitation. Anyway, I had hoped that Kipp would meet with your niece, dance with your niece, and be bored to flinders by your niece, at which time he would begin to listen to me, and *my* notions of what he needs in a wife."

"Because *you're* to choose his bride for him? What utter nonsense!"

Brady shrugged. "Perhaps. But only because I was asked, Abby, only because I was asked, even if he wasn't being completely serious about the thing. And now we come to my most recent inspiration, the one I alluded to last evening. I'm sure you remember it."

"Oh, yes, I remember it. How many *inspirations* do you usually have of an evening, my lord?"

"Ah-ah, *Brady*. Even if you do detest me at the moment." He grinned at her. "Three, at the very least," he then answered easily. "You see, I have some very firm opinions of just what my good but obtuse friend needs in a wife, opinions quite opposite from his, although I do believe he's already questioning those opinions. And you, madam, are all I have been looking for and everything he has sworn to avoid, although he'd never see that, as he's still too busy sunk in a funk, pitying himself and what he sees as his unhappy fate. It's perfect!"

"Perfect," Abby repeated hollowly, shaking her head at this insanity. "My lord — Brady — have you at least considered that you might have drunk too much wine last evening?"

"No, no, to the contrary. I was blessedly sober when my inspiration hit me. You're the perfect bride for Kipp. And I believe I can — or *you* can — convince him that you are just the bride he needs."

"Me, convince him? Are you out of your mind? Besides, I am anything but perfect, and we all know it."

"All right, Abby," he agreed, patting her hand. "Perhaps you're not perfect, not in the way you believe perfection is calculated in Society. But you are perfect in ways you don't yet understand."

"And will never understand, don't wish to understand," Abby told him, withdrawing her arm from his as they turned yet another corner, heading toward Berkeley Square. "I think we're done talking now, Brady, if you don't mind."

But Brady wasn't about to let it go, let *her* go. Not when he knew he was right. "He doesn't want your niece, but if he gets you, Abby, he still gets the entire Backworth-Maldon clan. All those *interesting* Backworth-Maldons. Think about it, Abby. He would have his hands full, even as he believed he wouldn't, even as he believed all his problems to be solved. He wouldn't be able simply to keep going along as he is now, skimming through life, not really feeling,

105

not really enjoying that life. He needs to be shocked, shaken up — perhaps even to the point of falling in love again."

"Falling in love," Abby repeated, slowing down, taking Brady's arm once more. "Would that be possible?"

Brady immediately knew he had gone too far, said too much, set one too many dreams to dancing in her head. "Anything is possible, Abby. Although he won't see it that way at first, of course. And not that you, being a practical sort, would even wish it, correct?"

"Of course," Abby parroted, her head beginning to spin. "And, if you can't convince him of my, um, suitability by throwing me at his head, then you propose that *I* do? You propose that I *propose?* Is that what you said? How could you think I could do that?"

"Abby, my dear, dear Mrs. Backworth-Maldon," Brady said with a grin, taking her hands in his, "I may have only just met you, but I believe you could tell the devil himself how warm to keep Hell. Now, if you don't confide to me your heart has been given over to some country squire, and if you truly aren't interested in my plan, my inspired brilliance . . ." He let his words fade away as he pretended an interest in a passing coach and four.

She looked at him levelly, and for a long time. "Your brilliance. Your plan, you mean. Your plan to have *me* married to the viscount, because he needs a wife he can't possibly love to produce children he probably doesn't even want and then leave him alone to do whatever it is he was doing before he married. Is that your plan, my lor—Brady?"

Brady scratched at the side of his head, trying not to wince as he looked at her, saw her deathly pale cheeks. Had he really worried he had been making his proposition too appealing? "Hearing it all stated so baldly, Abby, I suppose I should be ashamed of myself. But my plan is still new, just born, so you will please oblige me by not becoming too insulted as I do most of my thinking out loud. Forgive me, please."

"Don't worry, my skin is necessarily thicker than most. Besides, I've heard that lunatics often speak their every raving, rambling thought to the masses, and should be excused for their lapses," Abby told him, relaxing slightly at his apology, yet still more wary than could be considered comfortable.

"Oh, you're perfect, Abby. Perfect! That said, I'll insult you again, as I push home my point while you feel in some charity with me. You failed to mention that, as a widow with little money, your matrimonial hopes can't be much higher than a flea's kneecaps, Abby. Which means you will be left to tend to your remaining Backworth-Maldon relatives after you've married off your niece. Tied to them, slave to them, keeper to them, the lot of you constantly sunk in debt."

"My, what a cheerful person you are, Brady. I shall probably remain awake all night tonight, giddily recounting all the blessings in my life as you've pointed them out to me. Does the entire world know this much about us, about *me?*"

"Not everyone, Abby. I imagine there are a few who are still tottering along in happy ignorance. Like those drooling little boys who keep flitting about your niece, too stunned by her beauty to ask any of the important questions. But, yes, I am very much aware of the Backworth-Maldon finances, or lack of them, I should say. I was present, you see, the night your late husband recklessly gambled away the family's small town house, his carriages, even his horseflesh. If he hadn't passed out from drink, right there at the table, I daresay he would have wagered his valet on the next hand."

Abby held up a single finger, stopping Brady from speaking further, as she had a question of her own now. Damn the uncles, she was beginning to look for reasons to believe them. "You were *there?* You were there the night Harry lost everything to Sir Thurston Longhope? You *heard* him wager his horseflesh? *All* the Backworth-Maldon horseflesh? I mean, did Harry actually *say* that he was wagering *all* of the Backworth-Maldon horses? Not just the ones he kept here, in London?"

Brady frowned, not quite understanding Abby's sudden intensity, the sudden change of subject, but knowing his answer was important to her. "*Which* horses did he wager? I don't think he was specific, Abby, to tell you the truth. I think we all just assumed he meant those useless, showy nags he kept to pull his curricle, and his saddle horses, those he kept in town. After all, everything he'd wagered was connected to his town house, to London."

Brady rubbed at a small, suspicious itch that had begun just beneath his nose. Had Sir Thurston overstepped, claiming more as his winnings than the drunken Harry Backworth-Maldon had wagered? Was that why the Backworth-Maldons had been too purse-pinched to appear in town for the past few years? Interesting. "This is important to you in some way, isn't it, Abby? If I ask how, will you tell me?"

"No," Abby said, shaking her head. "I don't think I will. In fact," she continued, thinking of the uncles and what they would do with such information, "if I possess so much as a single smidgen of brainpower, I will never mention what you just said to *anybody*."

Brady considered himself to be nothing else if not obliging, and very obligingly dropped the subject from his conversation, if not from his mind. "Then, as we're nearly at Gunter's, we shall quickly return to the matter at hand. If you'll allow me to state my case in a nutshell?"

Abby sighed. "If I said I wasn't interested, that I was more insulted than I am intrigued, you'd know me to be a liar, so you may as well say anything you like."

"Frank and honest when you want to be, aren't you, Abby? Good, I like that. All right, to go over this one last time — my friend needs a wife. You would do well to consider finding yourself a husband. And, if you'll allow me to continue assuming a few things, there could be nothing that would make you happier than to be safely married, blissfully solvent, and yet unencumbered with having to ride herd on anybody for quite some time to come."

Abby sighed again, wistfully this time. "There is that . . ."

"Exactly. Neither of you is looking for some heart-pounding love match, unless I miss my guess and you have a romantic bent I've not yet discovered on top of your wonderfully pragmatic view of life. And, even better, your advent into his orbit — your family's advent into his orbit — works yet another small miracle. Merry could scarcely be able to believe Kipp would take them on without being madly in love with you. It's the perfect solution, for both of you."

"Merry? That would be, I assume, the woman who scorned Ki— your friend?"

"No, that would be the woman he grew up alongside, knowing full well she could never love him, had eyes only for his best friend. She and her husband, Jack Coltrane, will be returning from America shortly, and Kipp wants to be firmly bracketed by then, believing his friends will be more content if they believe him to be happily wed. Sounds something like a romantic novel, doesn't it?"

Abby nodded. "Aramintha Zane, my favorite."

Now Brady did have to bite his lip, to keep from laughing out loud. "She's your favorite? Really? Well, there's something I didn't count on. So you *are* a romantic at heart. Perhaps that's good."

Abby decided she was giving too much of herself away to this man who seemed to see her as a solution to the viscount's problem, as a pawn in a game he was playing. "I don't think you have to be a silly romantic to read Miss Zane. She's always so amusing, with all the comedies of errors and mistaken identities and such in her novels. Although, now that I think of it, there's usually a measure of intrigue, sometimes even bloodshed included along with the romantic . . . um . . . nonsense. Such fun to read, to dream about, but I don't think I'd like that if it were really happening to me."

"No bloodshed involved in my plot, I promise you. And you've already heard about all the intrigue that will be involved. But, if it makes you feel more comfortable, why don't we think of what we're about to do as being just another amusing plot twist in one of the illustrious Miss Zane's books? All that's needed now is to keep putting you in Kipp's company over the next few days. If he doesn't come up with the obvious solution to his problem on his own, then I trust I can rely on you to point out that solution to him."

He looked at Abby, smiled. "So, are you

game, Abby? Does my proposal interest you at all? Because we must act quickly — forgive me — before Kipp runs screaming from your niece's adorable but definitely mind-numbing presence."

Abby looked toward the viscount and Edwardine as they stopped in front of the confectionery. Edwardine was beaming, absolutely angelic in her delight in the warm spring day.

The viscount, on the other hand, seemed to be smiling only because it was expected of him.

Could she do this? Could she cold-bloodedly pursue the Viscount Willoughby, watching, waiting, and then proposing the cold, impersonal solution to both their problems that Brady had suggested?

Could she do nothing, let him go, let him walk out of her life before he'd really been in it?

Could she give up her chance to be a viscountess, to have her own household? To have children of her own, a life of her own? Could she, knowing what she knew, protect her heart while she was about it?

Abby looked at the viscount. Saw his handsomeness, yes. Saw the nearly invisible strain around his eyes. If this was how he reacted to a simple walk with Edwardine, she could only imagine he would, as Brady had said, be running, screaming, from London within a week of sporting Edwardine or any of the current gaggle of giggling debutantes around town.

Could she let him get away? Did she want him to get away? Did she really have a chance to capture him?

Could she live with herself if she didn't try?

"I don't think we have more than two days, Brady, three at the outside," she whispered matter-of-factly as they approached the shop. "You arrange the meetings, but leave everything else to me. Agreed?"

Brady relaxed in his skin, feeling all the self-righteous pleasure of a man who had just thrown his unsuspecting friend's life into a turmoil. "Oh, very much agreed, Abby, my dear. I have the greatest confidence in you, almost as much as I have in my own judgment. Now, my dear Aramintha Zane heroine," he said, "shall we begin?"

Chapter Seven

Kipp descended the staircase in his Grosvenor Square mansion, his step light, a smile on his face, his thoughts his own, the conclusion those thoughts had led him to definitely not to be shared. "Good morning, Brady, old friend. Lovely day for a picnic, isn't it?"

Brady, who had been holding up one of the large white pillars in the square entry hall, favored his friend with a dirty look, then moaned, as the simple act of frowning had set off an anvil chorus inside his skull.

"Look at you," he said, pushing himself upright, wishing his head didn't feel as if it had somehow grown two sizes overnight. "Happy, clear-eyed, all but bouncing with good health. You are the same fellow who dropped me off in Portman Square at four this morning, aren't you? I'm not sure, old man, but I think I have grounds to call you out."

Kipp walked past his friend, accepted the gloves, hat, and cane offered to him by his butler. "Thank you, Gillett."

"My lord," Gillett answered, bowing imperiously, his old bones creaking. The butler was a tall man, his shoulders refusing to bend to age, his thin frame clad in well-tailored black and white. He had a full head of snow-white hair, the physical presence of a duke, the acumen of the most accomplished majordomo, and a bunion on the big toe of his left foot that seemed to have taken on a life of its own. He might have looked a well-preserved sixty, but Gillett was seventy if he was a day. "About that conversation we had a few days ago? Generous as you are, my lord, I still think . . ."

Kipp sighed, cut the man off with a wave of his hand. "Must we, Gillett? I really am in a rush. Off to see the ladies, and all of that. Perhaps tomorrow? Or next week?"

"As you wish, my lord," the butler said, bowing once more, then turning on his heel and walking away, leaving Kipp to feel more dismissed than dismissing.

"What's with old Gillett?" Brady asked as the two men exited the mansion and climbed into the crested carriage waiting just outside the door.

"He wants to leave me," Kipp said, settling back against the cushions. "He says he's too old, says I don't need him, says he longs to live out the few remaining days of his life in some ungodly place in Wales, if you can believe it. I doubled his wages last week, thinking that would give him reason to reconsider, but I'm guessing it didn't work. Silly me, believing where forty years of loyalty to the family failed, greed would win out. I suppose I'll allow his retirement, once this Season is over. But I will miss him, can't imagine London without him, frankly."

Brady sat on the facing seat, which he hadn't planned to do, considering that his stomach was still faintly queasy and riding backwards couldn't possibly help his situation.

"You know what, Kipp?" he said, tipping his head to one side. "I think you have a difficult time parting with the past, with anything or anyone from the past. Let the man go, for God's sake. Although you're right about Wales. I can't imagine why anyone would want to live there."

"Perhaps he has a woman stashed away there all these years," Kipp suggested, grinning wickedly. "You never know, do you? Old Gillett, spending his three weeks a year tucked away in a little love nest, billing and cooing with some wild Blodwen or Lilybet. Lord, Brady, there's a picture I'd like banished from my mind."

"Agreed. Although I can't quite believe that mind of yours is functioning all that well these past days. This is our third outing in as many days with the totally inappropriate Miss Backworth-Maldon. I know, because I've been keeping count. You can't really mean to make her your viscountess, can you? And, if you do, would you then explain why you seem to leave her presence each night and then drag me off somewhere to wash the memory of the dear little twit out of your head? I don't think either of us has poured so much wine down our gullets since — well, in a long time."

"Since I returned from the country after standing up for Jack when he and Merry repeated their vows, believing the first ones hadn't quite taken? Yes, I know. Amazing how the very thought of marital bliss can send an otherwise fairly sober man diving headfirst into a bottle, isn't it?"

"Then you are serious about the twit — that is, about Miss Backworth-Maldon? I don't believe it."

"That's what I like best about you, I think, Brady. You're so unfailingly astute. Of course I'm not going to bracket myself to the child. She was amusing, at the start of it, but I think I'll probably have to choke her if I'm in her presence after today, a meeting which, if you'll recall, I had nothing to do with arranging in the first place."

Brady pinched the bridge of his nose, avoiding Kipp's gaze. He'd warned Abby that her time was running out. "Yes, well, meeting Miss Backworth-Maldon and her aunt at today's picnic seemed such a good idea at the time. Forgive me for proposing it, and for not intercepting your signal that I should not."

"You're going to stick with that nonsense, aren't you, Brady? That you didn't see me standing behind the two women, all but jumping up and down, pretending to choke myself, so that you'd stop asking them to please, please be our guests today? Would it be too insulting to tell you I don't believe you? Would it unduly strain our long friendship if I were to tell you that I think you've some sort of *plan* that has something to do with that young lady, and everything to do with me?"

"Such intrigue. Plotting another book, are you, Aramintha, darling?" Brady asked cheekily as the carriage slowed, having arrived at the picnic site just outside the city. "Never mind — I apologize for even hinting at your secret hobby. Ah, and here we are. Five hundred people and as many servants having a cozy pic-a-nick in the country, complete with tables, comfortable chairs, gobs of linens and fine silver, and musical entertainment thrown in for good measure. How I adore the bucolic life as envisioned by the ladies of the *ton*."

"You love it, and you know you do, you idiot." Kipp didn't wait for the groom to open the carriage door, but pushed it open himself, hopping lightly to the ground and waiting for Brady to follow after him.

"I think I know what you're doing, you know. You're pushing Miss Backworth-Maldon at my head, knowing she is fairly well representative of most of the dewy debutantes we'll see here today, and hoping that — if I don't run mad in the meantime — I will come to my senses and give up my determination to marry. Confirm myself a bachelor evermore, as you've done. Is that it, Brady? Because if it is, it won't work. I've made up my mind to — oh, damn. Roxanne."

Brady turned and looked behind him just in time to see Lady Skelton bearing down on them, the low bodice of her green-and-white-striped gown setting her up for quite a sunburn if she didn't soon unfurl her parasol, her small, caninelike teeth bared as she circled in for the kill. "I thought you were backing away from that one," he whispered to Kipp. "If so, I don't believe the lady has quite taken the hint."

"I know. I've been giving serious thought to celibacy, as a matter of fact," Kipp answered, then pinned a smile on his face as he bent over Roxanne's gloved hand. "How delightful to see you, Lady Skelton. And your dear husband, is he joining us here as well?"

Roxanne slid her gaze toward Brady, then sniffed, dismissing him as either being of no account, or figuring he would not betray his friend. "Olney? Yes, he's here, back from seeing his mama in record time, more's the pity. Worse, his mother has ordered him to father a son, if you can believe even a loving mama could want to see Olney's all but nonexistent chin reproduced."

She stepped closer to Kipp, actually nudged at him with her hip. "We need the increased allowance you understand, so I suppose I'll have to oblige the old harridan and produce *someone's* offspring. Will I be seeing you tonight, darling? I feel as if I haven't seen you in *years*."

"We danced at the Selbourne ball, Roxanne, if you'll remember," Kipp said, glaring at Brady, who had begun to choke into his fist. "Now, if you'll excuse us, I'm afraid the earl and I have promised to be part of a small party I've just now spied out walking this way."

"The Backworth-Maldon chit, of course.

Kipp," Lady Skelton said, her usually well-modulated voice very much resembling the growl of a she-wolf protecting her young, "if you mean to replace me, for God's sake find someone more suitable than that vacant-faced confection˙ you've been squiring around town the past few days. She couldn't be more than seventeen. It's insulting. Or are you, like Olney, under some sort of order to set up your nursery? If so, darling, I do believe you've got it all the wrong way round. You're supposed to father the infant — not *marry* it."

Kipp watched as Roxanne moved away from him, her well-shaped derriere waving like a red flag to a bull — if the bull was in the mood to mate. Then he turned to Brady, smiled. "I should have thought of this months ago," he said. "Chase a debutante, insult a mistress. Why, with any luck, Brady, I could end up bracketed to a ninnyhammer and stabbed in the back by a spurned woman, all in the same week."

His smile faded and he shook his head. "I had no idea getting married was such a dangerous business. It's a wonder any of us do it."

"If I could perhaps brook a suggestion . . ." Brady began, believing he couldn't find a better time to tell Kipp of his plan. After all, he hadn't *promised* Abby he'd keep his mouth shut, now had he? Kipp might cut up stiff at his interference, but once he saw the beauty of the plan he'd relent. Brady would just stay out of his way until Kipp recognized his brilliance.

"Not now, Brady," Kipp said, stepping forward reluctantly as the Backworth-Maldon women approached. "Ah," he said, easily slipping into his usual role, that of delighted and faintly silly gentleman, "now the sun is truly out, ladies, shining down on your beauty, even envious of it. Please, allow us to secure a table and comfortable chairs for you in the shade. Otherwise, you will blind all these lesser lights who pale to insignificance in your presence."

"What did he mean, Abby? We're brighter than the sun? Well, if that isn't above everything silly, as we'd burn up if we were that bright, wouldn't we?" Edwardine whispered, a girl who had never quite mastered either the nuances of empty flattery or the notion that whispers were to be a good octave or two lower than hers.were prone to be.

While Brady choked on another cough, and Kipp pretended not to have heard Edwardine's questions, Abby squeezed her outspoken niece's hand, warning her to silence.

On this, the fourth day of what Abby liked to privately think of as their acquaintance, Viscount Willoughby continued to work his silent marvel on her — becoming more handsome, more intriguing, with each succeeding meeting. Was that because he simply was a beautiful man, or because Brady's suggestion that the two of them might make a successful, civilized marriage had brought back memories of the times Harry had come to her bed?

Harry had been quite wonderful in bed. He must have been, as he had been invited into so many of them. He certainly had been a revelation to Abby, his virgin bride.

And she didn't think she would be wrong if she concluded that the viscount's bedroom performance would be just as educational. Not when she had seen that tall, redheaded woman looking at him as if she would like nothing better than to drag him into the bushes and beg him to ravish her.

"How flattering you are, my lord," Abby said at last, through gritted teeth, mentally slapping down her own thoughts, her own vision of the viscount, some concealing shrubs, and herself lying on the sweet, cool grass.

Her embarrassing thoughts were all his fault, and she would do well to remember that. "I fear I won't be able to eat a single one of the many delicacies my niece and I have seen spread out as we toured the picnic grounds. My stomach is already so . . . *full* of your kind words."

"Ouch," Brady said, leaning toward Kipp, his whisper no less audible than Edwardine's. "Mrs. Backworth-Maldon has a fine way with an insult, don't you think? She said *full,* but what she meant was —"

"I know what she meant, Brady," Kipp said, cutting him off even as he glared at Abby, who was glaring right back at him. She and her niece couldn't be more different. He considered that to be the widow's greatest asset, perhaps her only asset.

Still, he'd made up his mind. What had Will Shakespeare said? "If it were done when 'tis done, then 'twere well it were done quickly." The bard might have been speaking of assassination, but the sentiments behind the statement seemed much the same to Kipp as he applied them to his plan for the afternoon.

"Mrs. Backworth-Maldon," he then said, stepping forward, putting out his crooked arm, "I would very much like to show you a lovely hidden stream you may have missed as you first walked around the picnic area."

"Is that so, my lord? I'm sure my niece will be delighted."

"But then who, madam, would secure us a table in this crush?" Kipp countered smoothly, fairly certain that the dratted woman was being purposely obtuse. "And we won't be long, I promise. The earl, I'm sure, will be more than delighted to shepherd Miss Backworth-Maldon, do all the little domestic chores he so delights in performing, as he prides himself so much on his ability to organize everyone. Don't you, Brady?"

Abby looked at Brady, who just smiled, shook his head. Did that mean he had nothing to do with this, she wondered, that he was as much at a loss as was she about whatever it was the viscount was planning? Worse, was the viscount about to corner her, ask her to rate his chances of success if he applied to the uncles for Edwardine's hand in marriage?

Good God, what a depressing thought!

As Brady made small nudging motions with his hands, Abby reluctantly accepted Kipp's offered arm and, with a prosaic warning to Edwardine about watching where she stepped, as this sweep of land was normally occupied by cows, allowed him to lead her away.

This was only the second time she'd touched the man, and her reaction to him seemed to have intensified by half and half again, so that her knees nearly buckled beneath her when he smiled down at her.

The wren and the peacock, that's how she saw the two of them, how the people they passed undoubtedly saw them. Why had she never noticed that three-fourths of her scant wardrobe was brown? Mud brown. Really ugly, unfashionable, mud brown. Not that it mattered. If she were dressed in the finest silks and smothered in diamonds, she would still be the same unremarkable Abigail Backworth-Maldon.

"Have you heard the good news?" Kipp asked, sensing that Abby was lost in a mood that was anything but carefree.

Not that it mattered, not that he felt insulted by her marked lack of excitement at being alone with him, which was highly at odds with the usual female reaction he'd grown so weary of these past years. In fact, she was reacting just as he'd hoped she might. Independent to a fault. Almost standoffish. Definitely not the clinging sort. It made things easier all around, to his mind.

"Good news?" Abby repeated, waiting for Kipp to pull back a low-hanging branch, so that she could pass ahead of him, leaving the sunny meadow for the cool shade of the trees. "And what would that be, my lord?"

"Her Grace, the duchess of Selbourne presented her husband with a fine, healthy son the morning after their ball. I received a scribbled note from the duke this morning, apologizing for not notifying me sooner, as both Brady and I are to stand as two of the at least dozen godfathers the new heir is bound to have hovering around him at the baptismal font. Brandon Winstead Cecil Seaton, already blessed with a string of lesser titles, and one day to be the tenth duke of Selbourne. Bram — His Grace — said he's still recovering from the excitement, and finding it very difficult to keep his dear wife in her bed, where he believes she belongs."

Abby smiled, genuinely delighted. "So she did it? Just the way she warned she might. A successful party and a new baby, both in the same night. I must talk to Br— to the earl, as Sophie asked if he would bring me to visit once she could show off *both* her children to me."

She looked up at Kipp questioningly. "A silver cup, perhaps? Would that be a suitable gift? And a small doll for his sister, young Lady Constance? Yes, that would be good, as I wouldn't want the child to think she is forgotten now that her brother has arrived on the scene."

"How very thoughtful of you, madam," Kipp said, mentally tucking away her verbal slip, the one in which she very nearly addressed his friend as Brady. And her second slip, in which she so easily spoke of Sophie, rather than "Her Grace."

Something was going on, something Brady had a lot to do with, Kipp was sure. This wasn't like him, missing so much, allowing any bit of intrigue to go sailing over his head, unnoticed.

His inattention probably had something to do with Miss Backworth-Maldon and the constant pressure he was under to think up something to say that she might, just might, understand. Not politics, certainly. Not art. Not literature. Not horseflesh or the theater or even the safest gossip.

In fact, his last conversation with the girl had been one in which he'd listened with a stunned brain as she prattled on for twenty minutes about the day she and her mother had searched every shop in London for precisely the correct shade of blue ribbon to secure the bonnet she'd been wearing at the time. He had amused himself, ten minutes into her monologue, by fantasizing about ripping the ribbon from the bonnet and stuffing it down the girl's gullet.

And he'd thought he could marry one of this Season's crop of young, bread-and-butter debutantes, then just go on about his business? He must have been out of his mind.

Luckily, that mind had not deserted him totally, which explained why he now followed after the more friendly, relaxed Mrs. Abigail Backworth-Maldon, mentally assembling the speech, the offer, he would soon make to her.

Chapter Eight

Abby stopped, feeling the sun on her once more as she stepped out of the trees, stood on a grassy bank beside a quite small, quite lovely stream. "Oh, this is beautiful, my lord. However did you find it?"

Kipp looked around the small clearing, remembering all too well how he had discovered the place, and the woman he'd brought there. How long had it been since he'd said his farewell to dear Alicia and moved on to Lady Fairchild? No, not Sheila. She came after Belinda Masters, and before . . . God! What did it matter?

Kipp mentally shook himself, knowing he was having one of his infrequent bad moods that could lead to an all-out sulk, and knowing he'd picked a damn fool time to indulge himself.

"How did I find this place, madam?" he asked, stripping off his gloves and shoving them into his pockets. He eyed her consideringly, pretending to measure her capacity for secrecy. "Dare I trust you?"

Abby caught the hint of mischief in Kipp's expression, and relaxed. Seating herself on the grass, she picked a bouquet of the tiny wildflowers growing there. Better that than to fall down, as her knees were becoming increasingly wobbly.

"I imagine, my lord," she said, looking up at him, "that you would *dare* almost anything. Please, continue. I promise to take whatever secrets you reveal to my grave. Or must I first cross my heart and spit?"

Kipp laughed in genuine enjoyment. What a wonderfully unaffected woman, even if she had shown him, time and again, that she thought him to be a useless fribble she really couldn't like. That was her most endearing quality, along with the obvious fact that she didn't much like him. "Cross your heart and spit? I haven't heard that since . . . well, in a long time. All right, madam, I'll trust you."

"Oh, how blessed I am, truly," Abby said, still picking flowers one at a time, hoping he didn't notice that her hands trembled slightly. "Now, if you'll just wait until I search in my reticule for some paper and pencil, so that I can repeat everything verbatim as I write my titillating exposé for the London papers . . ."

Kipp laughed in appreciation of her wit, feeling better about his decision with every moment that passed. She might not be a beauty, but at least he could *talk* to her. He sat down on the ground, not caring if he rose again later, grass staining his pantaloons. "Once upon a time . . ." he began.

"Ah," Abby interrupted. "A fairy tale."

Kipp feigned surprise. "Fairies, yes. Then you've already heard the story?"

"Now you're being silly," Abby said, slapping at his arm with her small bouquet. She'd always made friends easily, both male and female, back in the days when she had time enough to spare in which to be sociable. Still, she was amazed at herself, how she was relaxing, bit by tiny bit, feeling more at ease in the viscount's company than she ever could have imagined.

Which was a good thing, considering that she had chosen today to offer him her proposition. She really had no choice, feeling certain that today would be the very last time Brady could maneuver the viscount into another meeting with an increasingly reluctant Edwardine.

"Here," Kipp said, extracting part of her bouquet from her unresisting fingers. "Do you know how to make a daisy chain?" He began slitting the stems of the flowers, working each bloom into the next. "I consider my own expertise in the area to be one of my finer accomplishments."

"You either have rather low standards for personal accomplishment, my lord, or you've led a very sheltered life," Abby said, then almost slapped herself. Is this how she had planned to lead up to presenting him with her outlandish offer, by insulting the man at every turn? "I'm sorry, my lord. But you do seem to bring out the worst in me, and I'm told my tongue may be clever at times, but it is nearly always too quick to move. Perhaps if you told me why you brought me here?"

Kipp bent over his work, neatly finishing the daisy chain, then reached up and slipped undone the bow holding the atrocious, limp-brimmed straw bonnet on Abby's head. He removed the bonnet as she looked at him, her eyes wide enough that he noticed, not for the first time, that they were actually a quite lovely shade of violet. Placing the chain on her ruthlessly swept-back hair, he gave himself one last chance to come to his senses (and run for his life), then told her the truth.

"I've decided to marry," he said, watching her closely for her reaction.

That reaction came quickly. "No," she said, shaking her head. "No, I can't believe it. I've *tried* not to believe it. I kept telling myself, all right, Abby, he's handsome. But that doesn't mean he's *silly*. His eyes are too intelligent, for one, his wit is no accident, he tries almost too hard to show himself as just one more rich, titled gentleman in a society littered with much more beauty than it is brains. And to think that I had actually —"

She clapped both hands to her mouth in horror, trying to stuff the words back inside her head. Had she really said all of that? All of those awful, revealing words that now hung in the air between them?

"My lord," she said, shakily getting to her feet, brushing at her skirts that could only be improved by a hint of color, even if that color was a grass stain. "You will have to appeal to my uncles, as I am not the one you should be addressing. Although I am convinced Edwardine will be more than pleased to know that you hold her in such high esteem . . ."

Edwardine thinks you're too ancient for her by half, she added silently, her heart not breaking, but feeling considerably bruised. No, it wasn't her heart that was bruised, but her pride. Four days. Four days and nights of being all but *pushed* at his head by Brady, and the man didn't even *see* her, hadn't the faintest idea that she was even female.

And what had *she* been thinking? That he had brought her to this pretty place, away from the others, in order to talk to her, learn more about her . . . show an *interest* in her?

Was she out of her mind?

Kipp had risen to his feet along with Abby, and took hold of her arm as she turned, ready to run back through the trees — and about to head off in entirely the wrong direction.

"You misunderstand me, madam. I wish to marry, but your niece is not the one I've chosen."

He couldn't help a small, one-sided smile. "In fact, although it is highly impolite to say this, after your own frankness of a moment ago, I now feel free to tell you that your very lovely niece would be my *last* possible choice."

Now here was a dilemma. Abby felt relieved to know the viscount had forgiven her her rude outburst. Still, she probably should reprimand the man for spurning Edwardine so coolly.

She should also probably bite the inside of her cheek in hopes that would remove the grin from her face.

And she should, most certainly of all, ask this infuriating man what he wanted from *her.* Surely he didn't think he needed her to break the news of his disenchantment to Edwardine, so that the poor romantic child wasn't crushed by his defection? Ha! Besides being too old for her, the poor romantic child thought the viscount was also the dullest stick in nature because he had politely declined to take her to view Madame Tussaud's traveling waxworks exhibition.

"Now," Kipp went on as he thought he might actually be able to hear the wheels whirring in Abby's brain, "you probably believe I've brought you here to beg you to understand that I meant no harm in paying Miss Backworth-Maldon such highly individualized attention these past days. Although I do recognize that I may have raised her hopes, your family's as well, and for that I do apologize."

"So why have you been courting Edwardine so fiercely, my lord?" Abby felt forced to ask, knowing that not even Brady's attempts to throw them all together would have worked if the viscount hadn't allowed them to work. Besides, when she was old and gray, and sitting in her attic chamber in some shabby Backworth-Maldon establishment, it probably wouldn't be a good idea to allow herself to be driven batty by not knowing the answer to that question.

"Truth?" he asked, pulling her back down onto the grassy bank, where they could sit and talk, and he could catch her before she could run away once he'd screwed his courage to the sticking point.

"Unless a fib would make me happier? I have the feeling, my lord, that you are probably quite an accomplished fibber," Abby answered, pulling the daisy chain from her head and throwing it into the stream, where it almost immediately became caught up on a small rock.

There it was. Her life, or at least her image of it — stuck against a rock, rapidly wilting, going nowhere.

Because, no matter what else she had decided in the past few moments, she'd firmly closed the door on Brady's suggestion that she should lay the business of a purely self-serving marriage in front of the man she'd gone to sleep thinking of these past nights. She just didn't have the courage. Not that he'd ever know how close she was to bursting into stupid, maidenly tears.

Watching Abby, trying to read her expression, and for some reason he didn't feel he had time to investigate, Kipp suddenly realized he was enjoying himself. Perhaps it was because Abigail Backworth-Maldon didn't flinch, didn't bat an eye, didn't give an inch. She just took whatever he said, whatever he did, and tossed it straight back at him.

He scratched at his left ear, seeking a way to make his confession amusing, his intention lighthearted. No, there was no way to do either thing. So, much as it went against the grain, he decided on the bald truth. No jokes, no grins. Just the truth, even when the truth would probably end with him getting his face slapped for his pains.

"As I said, madam, I am, for reasons that will remain my own, most seriously on the hunt for a wife. You may realize that my heart has not been in the chase, which it has not been, is not now. That said, I still feel I have come to a time in my life when I should be settling down, thinking of my heir, as my friend the duke has just done."

Knowing he sounded dry as a day-old muffin, he took refuge in a bit of nonsense, where he felt most comfortable. "I began my search with your niece, believing one debutante to be very much like another, and after three days of hot pursuit I've decided that if one debutante is much like another, I probably would be well served to give away my lands, my money, and hot foot repair to some high mountaintop in Asia, there to freeze in my underclothing while I contemplate the futility of life."

"You have such a way with words, my lord," Abby interrupted, picking up a smooth stone and sending it skipping across the surface of the stream. "But I think I may understand what it is you're saying. If I were to believe that all men were like my late husband, Harry, I should be happy to join you on that mountaintop, where I could sing songs and let my hair grow until I could weave it into a warm blanket."

"But we wouldn't become opium eaters; only a little judicious wine, to warm us," Kipp told her, thinking of the tales he had read, had even written about as Aramintha Zane. Because Abby had all but directly quoted his own words to him as she spoke of growing her hair long enough to weave into a blanket. How odd. He wouldn't have thought of her as being a fan of the romantic novel.

Then again, he'd just today noticed that her eyes were quite lovely, as well as intelligent.

He looked at her, really looked at her. Drab gown, sensible shoes sticking out beneath the hem. Hair drawn back so tightly her forehead seemed to pucker at the roots. But very good skin; clear, creamy, without blemish, without so much as a freckle on her small, ordinary nose.

Nice bones, too, with high, well-defined cheekbones, a firm, no-nonsense chin.

Straight white teeth that would pass Brady's muster easily. Pleasantly sized, slimly rounded if slightly angular. Perhaps a pleasant if not breathtaking shape beneath the shapeless gown?

God, now he *was* reaching, hoping for more than he really wanted. He was looking for a wife, not a lover. Cold-blooded, he knew, but true.

"Yes, well," Kipp mumbled, pulling himself back to the matter at hand, to the proposition he was about to make to this woman whose finest quality remained, to him, the fact that she probably could run her own life without his help.

"Yes, well?" she repeated meanly, picking up another smooth stone, massaging it between her thumb and forefinger. "You were saying, my lord, that you are on the hunt for a wife, and that my niece is now quite out of the running. Is that right? So, is that why you brought me here? I imagine it is, that you wish for me to bring Edwardine down gently, for she must be all but giddy with the prospect of becoming your bride. Well, don't worry your head another moment, my lord, I shall handle everything."

She threw the stone into the stream with more force than finesse. "Besides," she added, her treacherous tongue running ahead of her yet again, "if I may be as blunt as you are being, my niece will probably be much relieved, as she thinks you're entirely too ancient for her."

"Ancient, is it?" Kipp threw back his head, laughed. "I'm crushed, madam, positively laid low, brought stumbling to my knees. Do you think I shall go into a sad decline, wither away? Or perhaps I'll just totter off now, leaning heavily on my cane, looking forward to mashing gruel with my toothless gums this evening before being tucked into my bed at eight."

"You're *insulted*," Abby declared in genuine surprise, turning to look at him closely. "It's true, isn't it? Because I've noticed, my lord. I've noticed that you are always most lighthearted when you feel most vulnerable. I become rather snide, myself, whenever I feel threatened. Perhaps your way is better?"

Kipp cocked his head to one side, narrowed his eyelids in the way his old tutor had done when his student had said something reprehensible. "Have I turned transparent, then, madam, that you purport to see through me so well?"

Abby relaxed even further. "Now you're trying to frighten me into apologizing for speaking the truth. Much as it pains me to tell you so, my lord, that won't fadge either.

I remain totally unimpressed."

In truth, she was near to shaking in her shoes, appalled at how she'd been goading him. But something told her that his lordship would much prefer that she continue to give as good as she got, that he somehow *wanted* her to react this way.

Sure enough, Kipp's scowl resolved itself into another broad smile, and he said, "Touché, Mrs. Backworth-Maldon. Touché."

Strange, wasn't it, Abby considered as she bent her attention to choosing another good skipping stone. By now she had been calling the earl by his Christian name. In less time, she'd been invited to address the very important duchess of Selbourne by her Christian name. And yet she felt in no great rush to suggest that she and the viscount, sitting there together on the ground just as if they were childhood chums, might consider such an easy, friendly relationship.

That probably should convince her, if she had not been already convinced, that the last possible thing she should ever have considered was the ridiculous notion of sitting down with this man, placing her cards face-up on the table, and suggesting that a loveless marriage between them would not only be convenient, it would be highly logical.

". . . so, that said, Mrs. Backworth-Maldon, and with the firm understanding that ours would be a most sane, civilized marriage, one based on mutual need, convenience, and individual hopes, including that of an eventual heir, I would be honored if you would consider becoming my wife."

The stone fell from Abby's suddenly nerveless fingers. She turned her head slowly, looked at His Lordship, repeated his words inside her head. She had missed a few, intent on her own musings, but she believed she'd heard enough to understand what the man had been saying, what he had been asking.

"Mrs. Backworth-Maldon?" Kipp prompted, noticing how her cheeks had paled, wondering if the woman was about to disappoint his assessment of her character and slip into a missish swoon. "Did you hear me?"

"Yes," Abby said huskily, then cleared her throat, said it again more strongly, so that she could hear herself through the sudden ringing in her ears. "Yes, I did. I heard you. But, under the circumstances, my lord, perhaps you should consider addressing me as Abby?"

Chapter Nine

How surprising. The world had not tipped on its axis. He'd proposed marriage to a woman he barely knew, a woman who scarcely knew him — and her only answer had been to invite him to address her more informally?

Kipp looked at Abigail Backworth-Maldon for long moments, trying, and failing, to understand her at all. She hadn't gone all missish. She hadn't fainted at his feet. She hadn't slapped his face, burst into tears, or even asked him if he had lost his mind.

All in all, she'd barely reacted at all.

Granted, he had chosen her mostly because he didn't believe her to be the hysterical sort. A woman with a very level head, a cool, controlled manner. An independent, nonclinging woman. But he'd thought his proposal would have made *some* sort of impact on her.

Well, that was lowering.

"And I will address you as Kipp, as the earl does, all right? Don't you think that best?"

Her pleasant, matter-of-fact tone sounded eerily like his mother's when she had sat him down to discuss something like how much better her dear son would behave in the future rather than to continue resting his elbows on the dinner table, or climbing trees in his new breeches. No yelling, ever the lady. Kind, and loving, yes, but she'd always been able to make him feel as if he should crawl out of her presence on his belly, for he was low, lower, than a worm.

And that's what finally warned Kipp, niggled at the corners of his brain, whispering that he may have bitten off more than he could comfortably chew. He had underestimated the little mouse with the secrets in her eyes. This was a strong woman, a woman who wouldn't suffer fools gladly. Their children would grow up strong, and straight, and loving their mother dearly even as they remained very much in awe of her.

God, she was perfect in so many ways.

Unless she ever decided to take charge of *him,* that is, and he frowned, reconsidered his plan.

Not really trusting himself to speak, he spread his hands, nodded his head in agreement to whatever it was she'd last said to him. Oh, yes, she'd invited him to call her Abby. How condescending of her.

"Good," Abby pronounced, brushing off her skirts as she rose, began to pace. "Now, my — Kipp, if I heard you correctly, you have just proposed what I gather is a marriage of convenience between us? Is that correct?"

Kipp remained where he sat, watching her pace. "I think I'm beginning to regret some of my phrasing but, yes, that is exactly what I have just proposed. Not that you've answered my question, may I point out, if I have been given permission to speak?"

Abby was amazed that her legs worked, that they kept her to a slow, measured pace, that they didn't either buckle beneath her or send her running straight into the trees.

"There's more?" she asked, stopping, pivoting, looking down at him. "I thought you explained yourself quite well. I may have lived in the country, but I am well aware of what a marriage of convenience entails. Lords and ladies do it all the time, either for prestige, or money, or other considerations."

"We're a vile lot, us lords and ladies," Kipp agreed, rubbing at the back of his neck. "Mercenary, society-crashing, selfish. But the system has worked for centuries, although Prinny probably wouldn't recommend the procedure too highly, now that I think on it."

"How encouraging. So, allow me to tell you my understanding of what constitutes a marriage of convenience, why you have come to this point, why I'm considering your proposal, and we'll see if our conclusions concur."

"I'm hanging on your every word, Abby," he told her, wishing he had that paper and pencil she'd spoken of earlier, so that he could record her every stilted, outrageous word. After all, someday he might even find some humor in them.

"Now you're being facetious. You want a wife so that you may produce an heir, one of the most common incentives for such marriages. You want a woman capable of living her own life so that you might continue to lead yours as you please. A *convenient* marriage. All because you have looked at Edwardine and decided she, or others of her age and ilk, are not suitable, then looked at me and thought, my goodness, she's ideal for my needs. Fairly self-sufficient, for a female. Dowdy enough to fade into the background, young enough to bear children, and poor enough to think that even a marriage of convenience is more than she could ever have hoped to achieve. And, lastly, a woman definitely in no way able to refuse you if she wants to get away from her encroaching family. Am I right so far? Have I missed anything? What else could there be?"

Kipp got to his feet, held out both his hands as if applying the brakes to Abby's suppositions . . . and to the truths she so baldly stated, so that he knew himself beginning to feel pretty much like a cad. A rotter. Even an opportunist. Certainly a man of no heart, no feelings.

She'd held a mirror up to his plans, to him, and he didn't like what he saw. No wonder she had momentarily reminded him of his mother. His mother would have been appalled at his heartlessness, his selfishness. His motives.

"Forgive me, Mrs. — *Abby*. Please. I retract my offer, and beg your forgiveness."

"Oh, no," Abby said, stepping closer to him, hoping she sounded clearheaded, and not desperate. "Oh, no, no, no. You've made your offer, sir, and it is up to me now either to accept or reject it. And I accept."

"You . . . you *accept?*" Kipp nearly smiled, then stopped himself, narrowed his eyelids, looked at her assessingly. How had he gone from feeling so full of himself, so very generous in making his clearly magnanimous offer, to feeling so relieved that she'd accepted him? "Well, damme, woman — why on earth would you want to do that?"

"Why would I want to do that?" Abby put her hands on her hips, tipped her head, returned his look. Her violet eyes twinkled. "You *do* know that you're a viscount, don't you?"

Her answer was as honest as a splinter jammed beneath his fingernail. He threw back his head, laughed. "Well, there goes any thought that you might have tumbled head over ears in love with me in these past few days, doesn't it?"

"Would you want me to be in love with you?"

"Dear God, no! That's the last thing I want. Wouldn't be much point in a marriage of convenience, would there, if anything as disquieting as love entered into it."

Abby picked at the ends of the ribbons tied beneath her bosoms. "I don't think we have any fear of that, my — Kipp. After all, you don't wish to marry for love, that's plain enough. I imagine you may have been disappointed in some matter of the heart, and have soured on the subject. Which sounds highly romantic, but was probably quite painful for you at the time. For me, I also have learned, to my sorrow, that love isn't quite the mindless, amorous nonsense those who write about it so blithely believe that state to be. If I can offer you any solace, I can at least tell you that a one-sided love does not thrive, cannot survive."

"Your late husband," Kipp said, nodding, feeling embarrassed for the entire male sex, even as he flinched inwardly, remembering his own one-sided love for Merry. He shouldn't be surprised by Abby's practical, pragmatic reasoning. After all, it mirrored his own. He was just surprised that she had seen through him so quickly, correctly recognized *why* he'd even considered a marriage without love, not that he'd admit the truth in her deductions.

"Yes, Harry," Abby said, twisting the ribbons in her fingers, looking down as she watched those fingers begin to unravel the end of one of the ribbons that had begun to fray. "There is that. Once bitten, twice shy, isn't that what they say?"

She forced herself to stop playing with the ribbons, and looked straight at Kipp. She'd had days, days and nights, to think about how she would approach the man, offer herself to him in a mutually beneficial bargain. He didn't know that, but she did, and she had come to a few conclusions during those days, definitely during those long, sleepless nights.

Abby took a deep breath, looked straight into Kipp's eyes. "Now that we understand each other a little better, may I propose a few — not restrictions or rules, surely — but a few considerations? If we're really going to do this, that is."

"I don't know, Abby," Kipp said easily, still amused that he was, for the most part, still amused. Because this woman seemed full of surprises. "What sort of considerations?"

She took a deep breath, let it out slowly. "I would rather, sir, that you have no mistresses. Not so that anyone would notice, at least."

"Because of Harry."

"Because of *me*, sir. There will be enough people twittering about, wondering why on earth you chose me over Edwardine, over anyone else in London. To have us wed and then to see you running about town with another female? No, I couldn't do that. I really couldn't. I don't have much pride, but I do have some."

"I see your point," Kipp answered sincerely. "I agree. No noticeable mistresses, if I should ever decide to take one. Although," he told her warningly, "that does not mean you can expect me to answer to you every time I leave the house, just to be sure I'm living up to my end of our bargain. We are both to maintain our independence, Abby.

That's a large part of what I'm proposing along with this marriage."

"Agreed." Feeling that she had made a small inroad into his, she felt sure, innate good manners, she rushed to push home her points before she lost her nerve. "Now, ours would be a marriage of convenience, yes, but children are included in the bargain, as you'll need an heir. You've already said so, and I am agreeable to your plan. I had thought children would be denied me, and look forward to holding my own babes. So, in return for your not openly keeping a mistress, I feel I should point out a few things I can offer to you in return for that . . . um . . . sacrifice."

"Ah, a bargaining list? So soon? Why do we men remain ever amazed at the ingenuity of women?"

"I'll ignore that, as the answer is so very obvious," Abby said, grinning to disguise her nervousness. She'd almost given herself away earlier, speaking of an unrequited love in Kipp's past. If he were to know of Brady's involvement, her prior knowledge, she might as well don her caps, return to the country, and consider raising cats . . . and eating them, if the Backworth-Maldons didn't soon discover some way to replenish their pocketbooks.

A home of her own. Children. Security. Freedom. So very many reasons to marry the viscount. And still such shock that he had seen benefits to *him* in their marriage on his own. . . .

She blinked, just once, then looked at Kipp levelly, daring every honesty. "To continue. One, I am not a virgin, and that can only be a good thing, as I already know what to expect from marriage, from the marriage bed. I won't run from you screaming, or tell myself that you must be in love with me in order to enjoy bedding me. I understand that men have . . . needs. I do as well, above that of wanting children of my own. Besides, you don't have a head like a molting cabbage, you know. It would not be any great sacrifice to have you . . . um . . . make love to me."

"Abby, I'm beginning to think I'm not good enough for you," Kipp broke in, taking her arm and heading them back toward the picnic area.

"Now I've embarrassed you into joking, haven't I? I'm sorry for that, but I really feel we should talk about this now. Openly. Frankly. With our gloves off, as I've heard it termed. So, yes, I will embarrass myself by being horribly blunt just this one time. You see, having been married, I can tell you that

I honestly do enjoy the . . . the act. Harry was quite good at it, or at least several dozen other women seemed to have been pleased with his performance out of the marriage bed."

"I can only hope I'll live up to your expectations," Kipp drawled, lifting a branch out of her way even as he wondered how old he'd been since the last time he'd felt a hot blush invade his cheeks. A long time ago, he was certain of that.

He let go of her arm so that she could precede him along the narrow path, following after her closely, trying to urge her along. He really did need to get back to their table, in the hope Brady had commandeered at least two bottles of wine. After all, a man could take only so much honesty before he could be considered justified in searching out some liquid sustenance.

"I'm not all that worried about your amatory prowess, my lord," Abby said, finding herself somehow unable to keep calling him Kipp, or even sir. Such informality felt too intimate with him, even as it hadn't felt at all uncomfortable with Brady. How strange, almost bizarre. And definitely ridiculous considering how intimate their conversation, her conversation.

But, since she'd felt like she'd been in a

dream ever since he'd first made his offer, perhaps she should continue to feel that way. She had always been braver in her dreams. Besides, the worst was already over, and she could now concentrate on more mundane, less embarrassing matters.

Kipp watched Abby walk ahead of him, still amazed at what he'd done, all she'd said, how he had come to this point. Her step was firm, her voice even, and he knew that he remained as off-balance as she appeared to be calm, collected.

They'd nearly reached the end of the path when Abby stopped in a spot wide enough for them to stand together. "I have no idea why I allowed you to shepherd me back here, when we still have so much to discuss. Or have I been too blunt? Are you reneging?"

Kipp pressed both spread hands to his chest. "Me? Reneging? Perish the thought! I think I'd be afraid to cry off now, as I've seen more histrionics from a potted plant, and can only think I've somehow found myself the only sane, levelheaded woman in England who would suit my plans. I doubt, at this moment, that I could refuse you anything."

"How splendid, my lord. Have I mentioned money?" Abby asked him, a small smile tickling the corners of her mouth. Gracious, but she was having fun now that the worst was over! Rather like a child kept in the schoolroom for three-and-twenty years, repressed in mind and body, finally being let out to play. "We really should speak of it, don't you think?"

"Money," Kipp repeated hollowly. "From the bedroom to the bank vault in less than a blink. Madam, surely you don't wish me to consider *you* my mistress?"

Abby looked up at him, startled, then grinned. "Well, my goodness. I hadn't thought of that. I *would* be very much like your mistress, wouldn't I? How deliciously decadent!" Her grin widened. "Very well, let's talk terms then, shall we?"

Kipp spread his arms wide. "By all means. Shall I go first?"

"By all means," Abby repeated, nearly dancing where she stood. Alive. She felt so *alive!*

"I shall settle an allowance on you. A most generous allowance. Although you," he added, winking, "may think of it as a fee for service, if you so desire, as I believe you are enjoying the idea of seeing yourself as faintly wicked."

"I'm so obvious, my lord? Shame on me. But, much as I intend to enjoy my allowance

— you have no idea how tedious life can be without one — I shall require other monies as well. A dowry, paid to the uncles — my brothers-in-law — so that they and Edwardine's mother can exist somewhere above abject poverty. A dowry for Edwardine follows most naturally, and perhaps a small party for her or some such thing in order to sort out a suitable husband for her. An allowance for Ignatius — a small one, as the boy gets into enough mischief as it is."

"Is that all? Is that it?"

Abby bit her bottom lip, running down her mental list of conditions as they had occurred to her during those late-night sessions spent trying to convince herself that the viscount could do worse than to marry her.

"Well, if we could perhaps engage a *manager* or some such thing for the uncles? You see, my lord, if I am to manage your houses, be your hostess and all that sort of thing, I really must be free of worries concerning my family. They're quite thoroughly helpless on their own, you understand. So, helping them is actually helping you." She peered up at him, frowned. "You do follow my reasoning, don't you?"

"I believe I do, Abby. You want your

family out from underfoot. I don't blame you."

She felt hot color running into her cheeks, blushing for the first time since they'd begun this bizarre discussion. "I love them dearly, my lord, truly I do." She shrugged her shoulders, sighed, closed her eyes. "But, oh, how I long to spread my wings, enjoy myself." She opened her eyes, looked at Kipp. "Is that so selfish?"

"No more selfish than my desire for a wife, a family, and all without entanglement, I suppose," he answered honestly.

Abby looked out over the picnic ground, at the hundreds of ladies and gentlemen who were gossiping and flirting and stuffing their faces. At their fine gowns, their handsome suits, their confidence in their own worth, their own selves.

She could be one of them. She *would* be one of them.

All she had to do was to marry this man, and not fall in love with this man.

She could do that. She *had* to be able to do that.

She stepped out onto the closely scythed lawn, slipped her arm through Kipp's. "We're quite a pair, my lord, aren't we? It seems almost logical that we've found each other. I think we're going to be *great* friends," she said as she spied out Edwardine and Brady, both of them waving to them, attempting to get their attention.

Edwardine daintily waved in their general direction, doubtless without seeing them. Brady continued to wave his upraised hand over his head, in the manner of a ship-wrecked sailor who had just seen a rescue ship on the horizon.

"But now," she said, trying not to giggle, "I think His Lordship would like us to rejoin him, as he has been amusing Edwardine long enough, I believe."

"And how does one go about that, Abby, amusing your too-young niece?" Kipp asked. "I scarcely think Brady came here today, his pockets loaded with spinning tops, a jack-in-the-box tucked under his arm."

"Poor Edwardine," Abby said, returning Brady's rather pathetically desperate wave. "I should have known sixteen was too young for her to have a successful Season. But my defense is that we could not afford to wait another year. If she only knew how she has soured you on all but plain, no-nonsense ladies of independent ways. What do we tell His Lordship, to explain our long absence?"

Kipp stopped walking, so that Abby had to as well, and he made a business out of inspecting the bottom of his boot.

"Step in something, did you?" she asked, momentarily diverted.

"Not yet, my dear lady," he answered as she looked down, saw the clean sole of his boot as he bent up his leg. "I'm merely pretending, so that we have a moment more to ourselves, and so that I can step in something else. That something, Abby, is a condition I hadn't thought of until this moment. I'll want us to show the world a love match, if you can bear to do so. It will make things easier around Brady, you understand."

Abby looked up at Kipp, then to Brady, to the one other person she knew would understand precisely why she and the viscount had agreed to wed. Why would Kipp want to have even his good friend think otherwise, after he had all but commissioned him to find him a convenient wife? What did it matter?

And then, belatedly, the penny dropped in her brain, so that everything became clear to her. She understood. Kipp didn't care a fig about what Brady thought, about what anyone in Society thought. His concerns were for one person, and one person only. Merry. The woman who had married his best friend.

Abby wasn't just to be a convenient wife, a handy repository for the seed of the next Viscount Willoughby. She was to be a foil, a shield, Kipp's protection and Merry's peace of mind.

How on earth had she forgotten that? And why did she hurt, just the tiniest bit, inside her chest, just thinking about it now?

"That — that would probably be best, my lord," she said at last, agreeing to honor his request. "For both of us."

"Good," Kipp said, relaxing at last, knowing the worst was finally over.

Now it was time to have a little fun at Abby's expense. He tucked her hand back into his elbow and proceeded across the picnic area once more. "Oh, and I will be obtaining a special license yet today, as I've already inquired into the matter, so that we can be married by the end of the week. Friday, to be precise about the thing"

Abby stopped dead, pulling Kipp to a halt as well. "The end of the week? The end of *this* week? Five days from now? Surely you're not serious? You can't be serious!"

"I try not to be, Abby, as I've been told my silliness is most endearing. But, sad to say, I am most definitely serious. I've already planned a rather large party . . . oh, all right, a *ball* . . . in Grosvenor Square for Friday night. Annual institution and all of that, everyone looking forward to it. So I thought, why not have us marry in the afternoon, announce our marriage at the ball? What could be simpler?"

Abby felt herself inwardly exploding in a sudden, full panic. "What could be simpler? Your *brain*, if you truly believe I can be ready for a marriage in five days. *That's* what could be simpler," she all but spat at him.

She didn't wait for him to answer. Any thought of tact, or anything even vaguely resembling feminine politeness blew off to the four winds as she spoke aloud, but only to herself. "I have no gowns, no shoes. And my nightgowns? Good Lord, how could I possibly come to him wearing one of those awful — never mind," she abruptly ended, snapping her jaws shut as she realized what she'd just said.

"Friday, Abby," Kipp told her, knowing he was probably going to go to Hell for what he was thinking, the uninspiring mental images his mind had just conjured up for his review. Abigail Backworth-Maldon in an old, probably ears-high and toes-low nightgown. Abigail Backworth-Maldon in a diaphanous white-silk dressing gown.

Did she really think it made a difference to him?

He took refuge in the most honest statement he'd made all day. "Not a day later, my dear, or we shall both probably lose our nerve. Besides, you must remember that I have fallen so thoroughly in love that I cannot wait to make you my bride. At least that's all Society is to know."

Abby sighed, silently agreeing with him, then nodded her acquiescence. "And to think," she said quietly, "not six months ago I thought my life would continue to be one long, continuous yawn, interrupted only occasionally by some diverting Backworth-Maldon bout of idiocy. And why does that very ordinary life suddenly seem so appealing?"

Chapter Ten

A weak sun still shone down somewhere in London, but it didn't even bother attempting to penetrate the narrow, sooty windows of the shabby drawing room in the rented house in Half Moon Street.

That might have been a good thing, Abby thought distractedly as she raced about, an oversize apron tied around her, covering her second-best gown, dusting the scarred tables, raising new clouds of dust as she punched and plumped the thin cushions on the matching couches.

She adjusted a vase full of the faded, leggy flowers she'd discovered in the small back garden, centering the display on the low table between the couches. Stood back. Tipped her head. Squinted, hoping that would help.

It didn't. Picking up the vase, which took up too much room anyway, so that she'd have no place to set the tea service if anyone wanted refreshments, she walked around the room holding the thing, hunting for somewhere to place it that wouldn't look too outrageous. Or too pitiful.

The mantel. Yes, that could work. She placed the vase directly at the center, obscuring most of the depressing painting of a red-eyed beagle clutching some poor dead game bird in its jaws.

Tugging a small footstool in front of the single chair in the room, she positioned it over a threadbare spot on the carpet, then finally stood back, pushed an errant lock of hair behind her left ear, and surveyed her handiwork.

"Well," she said, jamming her fists against her hips, "if this doesn't give the viscount pause about my abilities to run his household, I can't imagine what would. I'm willing to wager the debtors' quarters in Newgate are furnished more lavishly, and with considerably more flair."

She reached into the pocket of her apron, withdrew the large timepiece she'd placed there. Consulted it, then frowned. She'd lost so much valuable time, trying to explain to the uncles — mostly in words of less than three syllables — what would be happening in this room in less than thirty minutes.

"Viscount Willoughby will be stopping by to speak with you, Uncle Dagwood," she'd begun, once she'd corralled them in this very room. "Uncle Bailey, are you listening? He's coming to see you, too, even if Uncle

Dagwood is the oldest by five minutes. Please, if you would, put that mess aside for a moment and attend me. Ah, thank you. Now, did you hear what I just said, Uncle Bailey."

"Never a mess, little girl." Bailey Backworth-Maldon had given his snuffbox one last look, then laid down the small funnel he'd been using to fill the thing with his own homemade sort. He brushed at his clothing, knocking snuff everywhere, sneezed twice, and looked up at Abby, his expression doing a grand impression of pained innocence. "And of course I did, my dear. Listened very closely. I heard every word, *hung* on every word." He winked broadly at his brother. "But don't feel you can't repeat yourself, if it soothes you to do so."

"I said," Abby told him, looking him straight in his watery blue eyes, "that the house is on fire. The roof is gone, but we may still have sufficient time for you to finish filling your snuffboxes before the flames roar down the steps and overtake us."

"Did not," Bailey objected, throwing his bottom lip out in a pout. "You said something about a willow tree. Didn't she, Dagwood?"

"Willoughby," his twin corrected him, spitting on one corner of a large white handkerchief, then rubbing at an orange stain on his cravat. "Don't know why you bother to lie, brother. She always finds you out. Nasty piece of work, our Abby is, when she puts her mind to it."

"Thank you, Uncle Dagwood, I'm sure," Abby had said, stepping forward and deftly removing snuffbox, funnel, and pot of snuff from Bailey's reach. "I can only hope you don't feel it necessary to recommend me to the viscount in such glowing terms when he arrives."

"Viscount?" Bailey repeated, then looked to Dagwood. "Willoughby? Viscount Willoughby?" He sat back in his chair, grinning until Abby felt sure she could see all of his molars. "Well, damme, Dagwood, we've done it! We've popped Edwardine off to a viscount. Do you know what that means?"

"She won't be needing any more dresses and gewgaws and furbelows, costing us the earth . . ."

". . . won't be forever underfoot, asking us those silly questions of hers . . ."

". . . and never listening to our answers, mind you. Will she be taking Iggy with her, d'ya think? Could only be a blessing, that. Boy's never here anyway, but when he is, his hand is always out."

"And Hermione . . ."

". . . and Cuddles."

Abby had made a great business out of yawning into her fist, knowing that to interrupt, try to get the uncles back to the subject at hand, would only prolong her agony. Besides, they were nearly there now. A few more mutually completed sentences, and they were bound to find a way to their favorite topic.

The uncles didn't disappoint.

"Brother, I think my heart is racing. Yes, yes, definitely. My heart is racing like a, like a —"

"Backworth's Prize after winning the Derby? Brother? Do you think? Can you even suppose?"

"Yes, yes, he could help, couldn't he? Invite us to his home, set us down beside Sir Thurston, get us to rubbing elbows with the man while we look for his tender middle, his most vulnerable spot. Hazard, do you suppose? Perhaps whist?"

"Two against one, three with the viscount. Our original plan, gaining with cards what Harry lost with cards. Best him . . ."

". . . beat him. Put him under the hatches . . ."

". . . then suggest a final wager, a chance to recoup. All he has to do is put up Backworth's Pride —"

"— any progeny he might have in his stables —"

"... and presto! We've won our fortune at last!"

And the long-suffering Abby had waited silently through the whole of it, tapping one foot against the shabby carpet, her arms folded beneath her breast.

"Are you quite done now, Uncles?" she had asked at last, when they'd finally run down. "And, if you are, would you consider it rude of me to point out that the only fortunes won during your practice at hazard, or whist, or even our single game of blind hookey, were won by *me?* That's why you abandoned the plan, remember?"

"Too true ..."

"... gel's got a point."

"We'll think of something soon, Dagwood, I promise you. Something brilliant."

"Well, good," Abby had interrupted, taking another step forward, so that she blocked one twin's vision of the other. "And now, as I was saying? Viscount Willoughby will be stopping here anytime now, to speak to both of you, hopefully to gain your permission in asking for my hand in marriage."

"*Your* hand?"

"*Her* hand?"

Dagwood and Bailey began to laugh.

They gulped, they snorted, they choked. They slapped their knees in mirth. They wiped at their streaming eyes with their matching handkerchiefs — Dagwood's free of carrot-soup stains.

Abby had stood very still, staring at a spot above the door to the minuscule entry hall. At last, her uncles had subsided, their laughter dying away slowly, escorted by more than a few lingering, high-pitched giggles. A single loud hiccup from Uncle Bailey.

"Ah, Abby girl, you're a wonder!" Bailey had managed at last, sniffling, as his nose had begun to drip. "Lift our spirits no end you do. Ask for *your* hand in marriage? Not that you aren't a great gun, my dear — but *why?*"

"Yes, thought we was here to pop off the idiot."

"Edwardine is *not* an idiot, Uncle Dagwood!"

"No, no, o'course not. Just silly. Like her mother. So you threw Edwardine at the viscount's head, and he picked you instead? Is that what you're saying? Well, I'll be damned."

"Yes, you will, if you bollix this up, Uncle," Abby had warned him, then skewered Uncle Bailey as well with her most daunting stare.

They'd listened then. Possibly understood. Now they were off upstairs, fighting
over which of their matching outfits went
best with playing guardian to a widow of an
independent age, a woman who needed
their permission to marry as much as she
needed another hole in the sole of her evening slippers.

She'd sent Edwardine and Hermione off
on an errand to Bond Street, then given Iggy
a five-pound note she'd been saving for a
rainy day and watched him skip off to some
cockfight, knowing that the uncles were
more than enough for His Lordship today.
Too many Backworth-Maldons in a single
go, and the man would be heading straight
to that Asian mountaintop!

The knocker went at the front door, and
Abby nearly jumped out of her skin.

The apron strings had knotted behind her
head, and she had to struggle to pull the
dratted thing up and over her hair, ruining
what was left of her severe coiffure.

She ran her hands down the front of her
mud brown gown, took a deep breath, and
headed for the entry hall, wishing she'd had
enough expendable income to provide for
an underfootman who could perform this
service for her. The slatternly woman they'd
hired to cook and clean for them wouldn't

think to answer the knocker, even if someone was outside, doing his level best to beat it down with a battering ram.

Then again, what did it matter? His Lordship knew of their straitened circumstances. In fact, those straitened circumstances seemed to be one of the things that had most appealed to him when he'd considered her for the role of his wife.

Only a role. She would do well to remember that.

Taking a deep, steadying breath, her hand on the latch, she flinched visibly as the knock came again. With one last, short but impassioned prayer that nothing had happened to change Kipp's mind, she threw open the door, blinked into the slowly setting sun that had finally found its way across the rooftops to Half Moon Street.

"My lord?" she asked, squinting, not really seeing anything past a tall body, some rather grand tailoring, and a curly-brimmed beaver that threw a shadow over her visitor's face.

"Abby," the earl of Singleton returned affably, stepping past her and into the house. "You've got a smut on your cheek, my dear," he offered kindly, drawing off his gloves and handing them to her. Brady then took her chin between his fingers and wiped at her face with a pristine white handkerchief. "Ah, that's more the thing. So, are we going to stand here, playing at statues, or will you invite me in?"

"I — I — of course. Of course you may come in." Abby extended an arm toward the narrow entrance to the small drawing room. He didn't move.

"You first, my dear, and I shall follow," he told her, bowing. "But not to worry. You'll pick up the niceties in no time, I'm sure, now that you're to become Kipp's viscountess. Have I yet told you how extraordinarily proud I am of you? How very flattered I am that I was right to invest so much confidence in you?"

"I didn't ask him, Brady," Abby told him, sitting down on the edge of one of the couches, stashing the discarded apron behind one of the loose cushions.

He paused in the act of splitting his coattails, preparing to sit himself down on the facing couch. With his hands behind him, his coattails sticking up much like bird wings, he said, "You *didn't* ask him? Then how — ?" He sat down with a thump. "Well, I'll be damned. . . ."

"We both will, Brady, if you ever let him know that you'd told me about his plan to marry Edwardine, or any young woman he

174

thought wouldn't be too much trouble. If you ever tell him that you've been deliberately throwing both Edwardine and me in his path these past days. If you ever let it slip that I knew a single thing about Merry. If you ever say one *single,* solitary word. Because he thinks this marriage of what he terms mutual convenience is all his idea."

"Bloody hell," Brady breathed, then quickly apologized for his profanity. He rubbed at his mouth, squeezed his eyes shut as he tried to gather his thoughts. Then, at last, he smiled. "But I was right, wasn't I?"

Abby sighed the sigh of one who has spent several years of her life bolstering the good feelings of people who really had no great grasp of the finer points of any remotely serious situation. "Yes, Brady, you were right. Even brilliant. Now it remains to be seen if you can keep your mouth shut and enjoy your brilliance in prudent silence."

She then stood up, signaling that he, too, should rise. "Now, go away, please, before His Lordship gets here and wonders why you're here, all right? I don't think I'd have any explanation for him, and you're looking entirely too pleased with yourself for my comfort. I'll show you to the —"

"Willowtree! That you, boy?"

"Oh, God, why do You keep doing this to

me?" Abby whispered, her shoulders slumping as Uncle Dagwood bounded into the room, his hand outstretched, his grin as wide as his considerable waistline.

"Not Willowtree, Dagwood — Willoughby. Don't you listen to the gel?" Uncle Bailey corrected, munching an apple as he followed his twin into the room, took up a seat on one of the couches. "Prompt one, ain't he? Must be in some hurry to speak to us, eh what?"

Abby longed for the floor to open up and swallow her. Brady's delighted smile did nothing to change her mind, either, as she knew he had to be thinking what she was thinking. How would Viscount Willoughby react to such a scene?

By running as far and as fast as he could, she concluded, wondering if she'd left it too late to dose both her brothers-in-law with laudanum, roll them up, and lock them in a cupboard. Still, if nothing else, she was beginning to see benefits in marrying the man before he had time to really get to know her family.

"This is the earl of Singleton, Uncle Dagwood, Uncle Bailey," she said, forcing out each word through gritted teeth as Brady waggled his eyebrows at her, then stepped forward and completed the introductions.

"How delighted I am to meet you both," he said in all sincerity, knowing that the two men could not be dismissed by anyone, ever, with any hope that they'd have the good sense to then go away. Oh, yes. Kipp wasn't just getting himself a convenient bride. He was getting the whole Backworth-Maldon family and all their fits and foibles. Served the fellow right, thinking he could just pick out a suitable female, marry her, and then go back to his life as if marriage had not made so much as a ripple in the tenor of his days. Spend the rest of his life pining for Merry Coltrane? Ha! Not after he bracketed himself to Abby and her family. The man wouldn't have the *time* to sulk!

"Singleton?" Uncle Bailey repeated, looking Brady up and down. "Not Willoughby? Well, what do you want? Looks much too smart to be here for the other one. Don't he, Dagwood?"

Dagwood looked at the earl, measuring him, it seemed, for brains. "Possible. Possible. But still, if we could get two shot off in the same Season . . ."

Brady's left eyebrow rose nearly to his hairline. "Mrs. Backworth-Maldon? May I please see you in another room for a few moments? Gentlemen," he then added, bowing, hoping he could hold back his hilarity another ten seconds, "it has been a most distinct pleasure."

Abby all but raced back to the entry hall, solidly shut the doors to the drawing room behind her, then thrust Brady's gloves and hat back at him.

"You've got to get out of here, Brady," she told him, wishing he'd stop leaning against the wall, rather weak-kneed, and laughing like a loon. "*Please*, Brady." She raced to the front door, opened it wide, "if His Lordship were to see you here, he'd —"

"Why, I could be wrong, but he'd probably say, hullo, Brady, what the devil are you doing here?" Kipp said, stepping inside the doorway.

Abby let go of the door handle and sat herself down on the small bench that crowded one short wall. Plopped herself down on the bench. "I'm having a nightmare, aren't I? None of this is really happening. I'm at home in Syston, asleep in my own bed, and I'm having a nightmare, some sort of warning from Above that, no, I shouldn't even *think* of taking Edwardine to London."

"I can see why you tumbled into love with our dear Mrs. Backworth-Maldon," Brady all but purred as he drew on his gloves. He might not be able to take credit for his brilliance, but that didn't mean he couldn't have himself a little fun. "She's entirely unique, a breath of honest, refreshing air in our jaded London town. A woman without wiles, without guile, devoid of ulterior motives. Such a pair you two will be, as you're so alike. A true love match of kindred souls. How I wish I could tarry, Kipp, listen to your speech as you confront her quite delightful uncles, tell them of your great affection and regard for the lady, beg their kind permission to —"

Both Abby and Kipp interrupted at the same time: *"Brady."*

"Ummm?" he answered vaguely, knitting his brow, doing his best to look bemused. And almost carrying it off. Almost.

Kipp looked down at his brand-new fiancée, then turned to his friend, and said, "We both thank you so much, my friend, for all your kind words. Now," he ended, indicating the open door with a slight tilt of his head, "as I believe you were just leaving?"

"Oh, yes. Yes. I was, wasn't I? Just leaving," Brady agreed quickly. "Only popped in to ask Mrs. Backworth-Maldon here if she'd accept my offer of assistance in searching out a good modiste — you know how knowledgeable I am in that area, Kipp, old friend. Tomorrow at ten, wasn't it, Mrs.

Backworth-Maldon? Yes, I'm sure that was it. Well, I'm off."

"And I'll talk to you later," Kipp warned his friend quietly as he stepped to one side, let him pass. "Count on it, old friend."

"Oh, cut line," Abby said, recovering at least some of her badly shaken confidence as she stood up, closed — quite nearly slammed — the door behind Brady's departing back. "He only came here to convince me that I needs must have a new gown for your ball on Friday night. Or do you think he came here to beg me to reconsider marrying you, plead his case that I should marry him instead? Perhaps we leave for Gretna Green tonight?"

Kipp slowly worked off his gloves, finger by finger, set them on the small table, beside his cane, his curly-brimmed beaver. "Now here's a dilemma," he drawled, watching Abby as she watched him, feeling certain she would like nothing better than to conk him over the head with the small brass horse that was the table's only other ornament. Wasn't it strange, how very much he enjoyed his efforts to set her off, how very much he enjoyed watching her struggle not to strangle him.

"If I say, yes, I do think Brady came here this afternoon to entreat you to elope with him, then I should have to call my very good friend out, challenge him to a duel. Messy business, duels. Up before dawn, tramping through damp grass, perhaps getting a hole blown into my new coat. But if I say, no, I highly doubt my friend came here today for any such amorous pursuit, I will have gravely insulted my fiancée, implying that she is not the most dazzling creature in nature, capable of wresting Brady's loyalty away from me in order to satisfy the cravings of his tender, smitten heart."

Abby stood quite still, appraising Kipp where he stood, keeping the table between them — to protect him or her, she wasn't sure. "Are you quite finished?" she asked at last, her fingernails cutting into her palms as she clenched her fists at her sides. "If so, the uncles are awaiting you in the drawing room. Five minutes with them ought to be enough to wipe that supercilious smirk off your face."

"Certainly, my dear. I'm ready as I'll ever be. Lead the way. Oh, and I'm not quite convinced I approve of your new hairstyle, although it is an improvement over that scraped-back bun you seem to favor."

Abby raised both hands to her head, pushed back the few stray strands of poker-straight hair that had come loose of their moorings. "This isn't going to work out, my lord," she said, pressing her back against the closed doors to the drawing room. "I don't think we like each other."

"On the contrary," Kipp told her, reaching out to tuck one last errant lock behind her right ear. "I like you very much, and I think you like me, too. But I don't think I care for the thought of Brady sharing my opinion."

"Jealousy, my lord?" Abby asked him, startled, too startled to argue with him about how much she did or didn't like him. "I hadn't thought you to be that sort of man."

"And I'm not, Abby. And I thought you were going to call me Kipp."

"Oh, really?" she countered, feeling herself becoming angry. Angry enough to call the whole thing off, much as the thought pained her. "Let me see if I understand you, *my lord,* as we said so much earlier this afternoon that I may be confused on a few points. You could, if you wanted, discreetly keep a mistress, but I am not to take a lover? Is that it? Is that the part that remained unsaid? Do you think that's fair?"

"Fair?" Kipp stepped back a pace, considering her words, weighing them. "No. I don't suppose it is, even if *I* remember *you* offering me that option. Men have been living their lives, taking mistresses, since the beginning of time, and I never saw the harm in it, to tell you the truth. Until now. And you did say that you're more than willing to partner me in bed, didn't you? Have I told you how flattered I was by your frank effort to assure me on that head?"

"God, but you can be insufferable! I cannot believe we're even having this conversation." Abby longed to clamp her mouth shut, but there was something about this man that seemed to bring out every hidden flash of fire she'd been tamping down all these past years. He might infuriate her, but he also made her feel so very, very alive.

"Insufferable? Yes, I've always considered insufferableness to be one of my finer qualities. However, I also believe you're right. An addendum to our bargain is most definitely in order."

He lifted his right hand to his chest, made a business out of crossing his heart. "I hereby promise not to take a mistress, and would only ask you to show me the same courtesy in not finding yourself a lover. You will, however, be free to flirt to your heart's content, as I will be as well. I am rather fond of flirting, and am quite good at it."

"As long as we both remember to show the world a love match," Abby said, shaking her head. "I don't see how that will work, my lord, do you? Are you sure you've thought this whole thing through? You may be losing more than you think you'll be gaining."

As Kipp knew all too well what he was gaining, how he planned to use Abby as his shield to hide his bruised heart from Merry and Jack Coltrane, he adjusted his conditions once again. Besides, did he really want to go through the trouble of finding himself another woman he could trust to understand the parameters of a marriage of convenience? Abigail Backworth-Maldon had all but dropped into his hands like a ripe plum, but could he count on being twice lucky?

"No flirting," he agreed sadly, shaking his head. "Lord, woman, we've only been affianced for a few hours, and I feel married already. You certainly are taking to your part of our bargain with a vengeance."

"I'm only protecting myself, my lord, and you as well."

"Meaning?" he asked, narrowing his eyelids as he peered at her.

Abby winced as she realized she probably didn't have to worry about Brady opening his mouth, saying too much. She was doing it all on her own. "Meaning," she said, speaking even as she fought to think her way through her damning faux pas, "that you have your reasons for this marriage, as do I, and as much as I would like the world to think I am your choice and not just a convenient *object* you seem to need . . . and believing that you have a very good reason to want the world to see the same thing about you, I —"

She nearly fell backwards as the doors to the drawing room opened behind her and the uncles tumbled out of the room. They were talking nineteen to the dozen even as they stopped in their tracks, the small entry hall too crowded for them to pass through it to the stairs.

". . . and if we stay in town, with all the new connections we'll have thanks to Abby . . ."

". . . we're bound to run into the rotter every time we turn around!"

"Right you are, Bailey. Now all we need do is figure out a new plan, some brilliant scheme . . ."

". . . and maybe study the cards some more, figure out trumps. I say, who's this one?"

Uncle Bailey peered up at Kipp, who was a good half-foot and more taller than the twins. "Willowtree? That you? Good. Want our Abby, do you? Well, you've got her! Now, excuse us, we've got work to do . . .'"

". . . plans to make." Uncle Dagwood made small shooing motions with his hands, so that Abby stepped back, allowed them to pass.

"Nice waistcoat," Uncle Bailey remarked to Kipp as he passed in front of him.

And then the twins were gone, still jabbering to each other as they went up the stairs.

Abby looked at Kipp for long moments, then pulled a face. "My brothers-in-law — the uncles Dagwood and Bailey Backworth-Maldon. *Now* do you wish to cry off, my lord?"

"Conversely," Kipp asked her, the corners of his mouth twitching with amusement, "are you sure you want to ask that question? And I'll never again question *why* you were so agreeable to my proposal."

Abby sighed, ended on a giggle in spite of herself. "Oh, this isn't good. Now you must be thinking I see you as the answer to all my prayers."

"And I'm not?" Kipp countered incredulously, deftly slapping his curly-brimmed beaver on his blond head at a jaunty angle. "I can only wonder what all you're asking of the Lord when you go down on your knees at night. May I hazard a guess? A fast wind and a strong ship, both heading toward the opposite end of the world?"

Abby laughed out loud. "For me, my lord, or the uncles?"

"Touché! As you said earlier today, Abby," he said, drawing on his gloves, swinging his cane up and under his arm, "I think we're going to be great friends. Until tomorrow, then? I'd like you to visit Grosvenor Square, inspect the premises as it were, before Friday. Have Brady bring you by, after he drags you through the shops."

"Until tomorrow then, my lord," she agreed, opening the front door and watching as he lightly danced down the few steps to the street.

Then she closed the door behind her, leaned against the solid wood as she counted slowly to ten before picking up her skirts and heading for the staircase, calling out, "*Uncles!* If I might have a word?"

Chapter Eleven

"His Lordship wishes for me to tell you that he has been most unavoidably detained elsewhere, madam, sir, and to offer you refreshments until he returns."

"Thank you, Gillett," Brady said, taking hold of Abby's pelisse as she slipped it from her shoulders, then handing it over to the butler. "I see your cruel master still has you locked up here against your wishes. Tell me, have you ever thought of simply running away?"

Gillett stiffened his already poker-straight posture, looking at Brady in a way he hadn't seen since he'd been called in front of the headmaster after throwing a roll at Willie Wilkins after matins and bloodying the idiot's nose. He'd never forgive Whiny Willie for not having the sense to duck, even if the fellow was a marquis now.

"Forget I mentioned it, old fellow. I should have stopped at 'thank you,' I imagine."

Abby, who had been looking up at the high ceiling, the enormous, glittering chandelier hanging from a decorative stuccoed ceiling done in shades of gray-blue and mustard gold, brought herself back to attention. "Yes, indeed, thank you. I should think a pot of tea would be quite welcome?"

"As you wish, madam," Gillett agreed, bowing, then leading the way toward a pair of carved wooden doors covered in thick, rich, ivory paint. He opened the doors with a flourish, then stood back as Abby and Brady entered ahead of him. "Oh, yes, forgive me. His Lordship also told me that I should offer Mrs. Harris's services, if you should like a tour of the premises, madam."

"Uh-huh," was all Abby could manage in answer as she stopped in her tracks and looked around the immense drawing room, then walked forward again slowly, trying to drink it all in at once, knowing that to be impossible.

She'd never seen a higher ceiling, or one so heavily decorated with painted stucco. Curlicues, sprays of leaves, intricate borders deeply carved, a bevy of angels circling each other as they danced above her on a clear blue sky dotted with small, puffy white clouds.

And chandeliers. Chandeliers all over the ceiling.

And pillars. Golden-veined marble pillars marched along three of the papier-mâché scrolled walls, the combination creating regal frames for paintings so large the figures depicted were life-size, seemed almost real.

Were they looking down their aristocratic noses at her?

A fireplace that could have heated the entire Backworth-Maldon house in Syston stood against the far wall. The mantel and chimneypiece reached nearly to the high ceiling, painted that same thick, creamy ivory, the whole of it intricately carved to look like a flower-filled trellis.

The half dozen windows overlooking the street rose from floor to ceiling, topped by grilled fanlights set deep into the walls. They let in light, sun, a feeling of space, of unlimited space.

Making Abby feel very small.

An Aubusson carpet woven of mustard gold carrying a design of soft green trellised squares joined at the corners by fragile clusters of delicate orange flowers stretched almost from wall to wall. A near square mile of carpet, to Abby's mind. She stood at the edge of another world, and with no bridge to safely take her there, just the shock of having been transported into an alien land without warning.

In truth, the room could be called a

garden. The drawing room resembled nothing more than it did an enormous, indoor garden. Abby felt as welcome as a slug the gardener found hiding beneath the roses, and as sure to be found out as an intruder.

What on earth was she doing here?

The room's size was so considerable that three separate groupings of chairs and sofas, tables, and even chaises still left ample room for two card tables and their accompanying chairs, several delicate wooden chests, a pair of gilded, half-moon tables spaced along the wall of windows and, lastly, a gigantic glass-fronted chest twice as tall as Abby and half again as wide as itself, displaying an array of Chinese art that had to have cost the earth — and most of the moon.

Beautiful. The room could only be termed beautiful. And this was just one room in the mansion. This huge mansion, whispering of riches beyond her comprehension, and more than capable of chewing her up, swallowing her down, making her disappear forever. A nonentity, overshadowed, overpowered, most definitely out of her depth.

Icy panic gripped Abby, held her.

I can't live here, she thought.

She held up her hands in front of her,

began backing toward the door to the entrance hall as she tried to push the room away from her. "No," she said weakly, shaking her head. "I can't do this, Brady. Really, I can't. I don't belong here. God, Brady, does *anyone* belong here?"

"Rather intimidated, are you, Abby?" Brady suggested, putting his hand at the small of her back and propelling her forward into the room, out of Gillett's earshot. "And here I thought nothing fazed you, my dear. Certainly not Kipp, or a marriage of convenience to a man you've just met, or staring down Madame Lucille when she dared to quote you that outrageous price on the pink tulle. I think the woman has probably taken to her bed, frightened that you'll wish to shop in her establishment again."

Abby whirled about to face him. "This isn't amusing, Brady. What was I *thinking?* I'm not cut out for this. A widow, an orphaned daughter of a simple country squire — a woman of *no* consequence. I don't have the background, the knowledge, the . . . oh, Brady, what am I going to do?"

He took her hands, led her over to one of the couches, gently sat her down. "It's just a house, Abby. Floors, walls, ceilings . . ."

"No," she interrupted, wishing her hands weren't shaking, that she didn't believe, just a little bit, that she might actually become sick all over the priceless Aubusson carpet. "This is so much more than a *house*, Brady. This — all of this — represents who the viscount is, what his viscountess should be. I'm Abigail Backworth-Maldon, Brady. The household staff at Syston is comprised of our cook, two female servants, and a gardener older than the dirt he scrabbles in while pretending to work. The staff here will run roughshod over me, as well they should, for I haven't the faintest notion of how to go on in such a place."

She hopped to her feet, began to pace. "I polish the silver myself, and it takes one short afternoon. There's enough silver in this single room to keep a half dozen servants busy for a week!"

Brady sat back, crossed one elegantly clad leg over the other. "Well, then, that's settled. You set a half dozen servants to polishing for a week. See how well you're coping already?"

Abby balled her hands into tight fists. "That's not the point! I was using the silver as an *example*, Brady, and you know it. I'm supposed to be in *charge* here, at His Lordship's estates, easing his life, contributing *something* to justify my position. I can't just make pretend puppy eyes at him in public, produce babies, and then say, oh yes, I've lived up to my end of the bargain, my lord, now may I please go traveling in Italy for the summer?"

She was panicking, and not without reason. But that didn't mean Brady would help her out of her predicament. Not when he knew in his heart of hearts that this endearingly odd young woman would be the making of his good friend Kipp.

Brady decided on a strategy.

He picked at a piece of lint that had settled on his knee. "I confess to not knowing you that well, Abby, but in our short acquaintance I had never thought you were a coward. I do believe you have disappointed me."

Abby stopped pacing, slowly turned to look down at him, glare down at him. "Aren't you supposed to stand up when a lady stands up? But don't bother, please, as the last thing I'd wish to do is to discommode you in any way when you're so obviously enjoying yourself at my expense, as you've *been* enjoying yourself at my expense, at His Lordship's expense, since first we met. However, don't try to insult me into believing I can do what I cannot possibly do, either. Or do you actually think I don't know what you're doing? I — who have used just the same sort of strategy a million times on my family."

"Forgive me, Abby. I imagine I'm still wallowing in my own brilliance, and have not really considered things from your perspective. What do you wish me to do?"

She sighed, spread her arms, then let them drop to her sides. "Be my friend, I suppose. Be my friend, Brady, and *help* me!"

"Oh, if *that's* all . . ." he said, turning toward the doorway as Gillett rolled in a refreshment table laden with, God forbid, even more silver. "Gillett? Mrs. Backworth-Maldon is to wed His Lordship this Friday, do you know that? Become his viscountess, come here to live, be his hostess, run his household. All those quite lovely things you must all have missed since your master's lady mother passed away. Isn't that nice?"

"*Bra—dy* . . ." Abby willed him to shut up, to stop "helping" her.

The butler set the small brake on the refreshment table, dusted his gloved hands against each other. "Yes, my lord. We are all aware of that fact, although I was not aware that I was to appear aware, if you take my meaning. However, I am now pleased, madam, to offer you my best wishes and those of all the staff. We look forward to serving you, madam."

Brady smiled at Abby, who had sunk onto the couch beside him, moaning softly under her breath. "Splendid, Gillett, splendid! And, lucky, lucky you — you won't have to look too far forward to find a way to serve the next viscountess. Will he, my dear?"

"I could cheerfully kill you, you know," Abby whispered, then smiled up at the butler, who looked very much like a prince and not at all like a servant.

He did, however, look like he could be her friend. She'd never had much trouble making friends. Why should it be so different when she was a viscountess? And why couldn't her servants also be her friends? If such things weren't done in Society, she didn't really want to know. Not when her entire future depended on the rightness of her instincts, the results of her own initiatives.

"Gillett," she began formally, "thank you for your kind words. Truly. But His Lordship is correct, even if he's the only one who really understood what he just said. I have absolutely *no* idea as to how to go on in an establishment of this size, I fear. None. And so," she said, then paused to look at Brady, who nodded his agreement, "I would therefore hope to fling myself on your mercy, Gillett, yours and everyone on the staff, hoping that you may be able to assist me, to *teach* me all that I should know in order not to interrupt what I can only see as the absolutely flawless running of His Lordship's household."

"What do you say, Gillett, old man?" Brady asked as Gillett poured two cups of tea, a hand held steady for more than fifty years now trembling slightly in his sudden excitement. "Still want to run away? No, I didn't think so. Now, why don't you sit down here — right here — have yourself some refreshing tea and a nice little coze with the future viscountess, and I'll just trip over to the drinks table and find myself something a little more familiar to my palate."

"Sit down, sir? I couldn't!"

Abby sensed that she had one chance, and one chance only, to make an ally of the proper, straitlaced butler; one chance to establish herself as mistress of this mansion while still gaining the help and respect, and, yes, the friendship, of the staff.

And she took it.

"Gillett" she said, rising to her feet, taking charge of the conversation, taking charge of her life so that she might gain the life she wanted, needed. "I may not know much, but I do believe I feel somewhat cheered in supposing that my lord Singleton here seems to know even less than I. May I please have that tour of the house you suggested earlier? With Mrs. Harris, is that correct? Although I do believe I should like to begin in the kitchens, the heart and soul of any good house. And, as in any good kitchen, I imagine there is a pot on the boil? I'm sure the earl can find something to do to amuse himself while we're gone."

"Yes, indeed, madam, there most certainly is, His Lordship most certainly can," Gillett told her, almost but not quite smiling as he stood back, motioned for Abby to precede him into the foyer, walk toward the baize door she'd seen when first she entered the house.

Within ten minutes, Abby was seated at the large pine worktable in the vast kitchens, sharing a pot of tea and some fresh scones with the most powerful man in the Grosvenor Square mansion — including the viscount.

Within a half hour, she had met every member of the staff, carefully repeating each of their names inside her head so that she would never forget them. She offered them all scones, pastries, bread and butter, thick slices of ham — every delicacy the astonished and flattered chef had put on the table for her delectation.

Within an hour, she had the entire staff eating out of her hand, both literally and figuratively.

She couldn't believe she'd been such a coward, that she'd been so frightened, so ready to tuck her tail between her legs and run away, give up her dream.

From now on, when it came to deciding who ran the viscount's households, it would be Abby and the staff who would be completely in charge, and he would simply have to muddle through as best he could, trying to remember that this was what he'd wanted.

The thought made her smile.

The special license at last tucked safely in his pocket after a long morning of cajoling and nearly downright begging, Kipp entered the Grosvenor Square mansion and inquired of the young underfootman the whereabouts of his guests.

"His Lordship is corruptin' Henry in the billiards room, my lord, Mr. Gillett said to tell you. And the nice young lady is off somewheres abovestairs with Mrs. Harris and a clutch of the maids. Heard some scrapin' a while ago. I thinks they're doin' somethin' to the furniture up there, begging your pardon, my lord."

Kipp looked at the pimply-faced underfootman for long moments, long enough to wipe the smile off the boy's face. "Very well, thank you, George."

"Not a bit of it, Your Lordship. I mean, it's your pleasure . . . *my* pleasure, Your Lordship. That is . . ."

With a wave of his hand, Kipp walked past the flustered boy, remembering that he was new to his position, having served the last two years as potboy in the kitchens at Willoughby Hall. Gillett had made great strides with George, but there still were some raw edges he might want to smooth. And the man wanted to leave him? How could he!

Kipp sought out Brady first, preferring not to think about what might be going on upstairs now that the managing Mrs. Backworth-Maldon was actually in his house. Rearranging the furniture, was she? The woman certainly didn't waste any time, not that he hadn't known that the running of his houses would soon be in her hands. He simply hadn't expected her to jump in so fast, and with both feet.

The billiards room had once been his mother's private study, a room she'd repair to in order to plan menus, make up invitation lists, interview prospective servants, consult with tradesmen, pen letters to her friends. Her stamp had been all over the room, from the light, flowered draperies on the tall windows to the watered-silk Chinese wallpaper, to the rose-colored couches and delicate white furniture.

He opened the door, quietly stepped inside, wishing, just for a moment, that he would see those watered-silk walls, his mother's delicate white-and-gold writing table.

His mother's private study had since been painted a dark, grass green, with the wooden floor bare of carpeting, racks of cues nailed to the walls, and an enormous, green-felt-covered billiards table eating up most of the remaining space. The optimal retreat for the wealthy bachelor.

The earl of Singleton was bent over the table, stripped to his shirtsleeves, employing a bridge as he balanced a cue in his right hand, squinted at the balls arrayed on the green felt. His right foot was awkwardly raised in the air behind him, for balance, and a lock of dark hair had fallen over his forehead, partially obscuring his vision.

"Brady?" Kipp ventured, amused by the sight in front of him. "How go the wars?"

"Not now, friend, I'm about to sink that lovely orange ball and win myself five million pounds. Right, Henry?"

"Just right, my lord," the footman agreed. "Just about make you even, too, sir, by my reckoning."

"Ha! Your lack of prowess at a most simple game never ceases to astound me, Brady. And not the orange ball, you idiot. Go for the blue. At least you have a chance of pocketing that one."

Brady drew back the cue, shot it forward to send the cue ball moving, then cursed as he watched the orange ball seem to leap high in the air in reaction to being struck. It bounced away across the floor, banged into a corner before Henry gleefully retrieved it.

"The devil," Brady said, standing up once more, still looking at the tabletop, wondering if the thing were possessed, and had cast a spell of ineptitude over him. He handed over both bridge and cue to Henry, who also accepted the five-pound note Brady shoved into his hand, then exited the room.

"Oh, well, Kipp. My performance is so very exemplary at so many things. It's only fitting that there's one small something in this world I have yet to conquer. Otherwise, I might become bored, don't you think?"

"You'd give your eyeteeth to be able to play billiards, Brady," Kipp told him, going to the drinks table and pouring them each a glass of wine. He handed one glass to his friend, then leaned a hip against the side of the billiards table. "How did your morning go with Mrs. Backworth-Maldon?"

Brady finished shrugging back into his coat, swallowed down the wine in one long gulp, then grinned at his friend. "She's given me permission to call her Abby, much to my delight. And the morning went splendidly . . . somewhere in London. Unfortunately, not in Bond Street, although I thank you for asking. The morning most especially did not go well at Madame Lucille's, where you told me to take Abby so that she might choose a proper gown for Friday. No, most especially not at Lucille's, although she may still send you a bill."

He held out his empty glass for Kipp to refill, grinned. "I'd pay it if I were you."

Kipp drank his own wine, then went to pour them both another glass. He'd known it. Before he'd even asked Brady, he'd known it. He didn't know why he knew it, but that didn't really matter all that much. What really mattered was that his plan to have a convenient wife who politely stayed in the background, leaving him free to do as he wished, now seemed to have been a castle he'd built on rapidly shifting sands.

His initial impression had seemed so logical. Quiet little mouse of a widow of good but not exceptional birth. Common-sensical, able to run a household of fairly unmanageable people without so much as turning a hair. Honest, forthright, desperate enough to be agreeable to his fairly cold-blooded proposition, her head not stuffed with nonsense thoughts of undying love he couldn't return, and unlikely to run off with some other man who'd been struck love-blind by her great beauty.

Rotter that he was — for his motives and conclusions did have the power to embar-rass him — he still believed she was perfect in so many ways.

Besides, it was too late to back out even if he were to have second thoughts. He had the special license. He had personally written out and delivered the wedding no-tices to all the papers, set to be published on Friday morning. He had read the latest note from Roxanne, pleading with him to come to her tonight, so that they could "talk." Burned the note in the fireplace in his study.

Besides, he didn't want to back out, cry off, renege. Not really. Because that would mean starting over, heading back into the marriage mart, suffering through inane con-versations with dewy-eyed debutantes, running the gamut of matchmaking mamas who all but tripped him as he walked by . . . looking pathetically alone and unloved when Merry and Jack returned from America in a few short weeks, a month at most.

"What happened at Lucille's?" he asked now, motioning for Brady to precede him out of the room, back to the drawing room. "All I asked you to do was to please steer Abby toward a suitable gown, any of the three Lucille had already personally assured me she could have altered and hemmed in time for the ceremony, the ball. How difficult could that be?"

Brady plopped himself down on one of the couches, balanced the wineglass on one knee as he turned it about in his hand. "How difficult? Not at all difficult, if your fiancée were a moneygrubbing, fortune-hunting vixen, that is. As it turns out, the little dear has scruples. Nasty thing, scruples; I try to avoid them at all costs, myself. She refused to even look at anything until Lucille promised her the bill would come to her — not that it needed to, as she brought all of her funds with her, more than prepared to pay down her blunt on the spot. Twelve pounds six, as a matter of fact. All the money of her own that Abby has to her name."

"Oh, God," Kipp groaned, knowing he really didn't want to hear any more.

"Yes, I believe Lucille did call on the Man for assistance at one point. *Mon Dieu, madame! Alors!*" Brady told him, enjoying himself very much, thank you. "Anyway, once Abby had been pinned into a most lovely gown, and when she started in inquiring as to prices . . ."

"Don't tell me."

"Oh, but I must. Please, it's too delicious to keep to myself. And what I can tell you, friend, is that the morning pretty much slid downhill after that, with your dear affianced bride pointing out that robbery is robbery, no matter how one tries to dress it up in fine linen or, in this case, quite expensive white silk. Yes, upon reflection, I suppose you should be expecting some sort of bill from Madame Lucille. Oh, and did you know our dear Madame Lucille speaks a quite remarkable cockney when she's overset?"

Kipp ignored his friend's banter, to zero in on the crux of the matter. "So she didn't come away with a gown? That's what you're saying, isn't it? No gown, no evening slippers. No shawl, no fan, no gloves. Does she really expect to greet our guests on Friday night dressed in one of the muddy gowns I've seen entirely too much of these past days? No, don't answer me. I already know the answer. Lord, Brady, the *ton* will eat her up."

"Yes, I pointed that out to her. And you know what? I don't think she cares, at least not enough to accept anything as personal as a gift of clothing from a man not yet her husband. Those pesky scruples again. Prickly little thing, when she puts her mind to it."

"Even when she's barely trying," Kipp ruminated quietly, then stopped his pacing to look up at the ceiling as a loud thump sounded above him. "And now, according to my source, she's upstairs, pushing furniture around, for reasons I don't think I want to understand. Christ, Brady, what have I done?"

"Well, old friend, if I were gullible enough to believe what you expect the world to swallow whole, you've tumbled into love with the dear girl."

"No wonder so many of your friends still long to bloody your nose," Kipp remarked, running a hand through his hair, not caring that he disturbed its already windswept style. "This is your way of telling me I was in entirely too much of a rush to have this marriage business settled, that I should have allowed you to pick my bride, isn't it, or at least consulted you before proposing to Mrs. Backworth-Maldon . . . Abby. Do you really think you could have made a better choice?"

Brady averted his eyes, coughed into his fist.

"At least you can pretend to know when the safest thing you could do is remain silent while I admit what a fool I am," Kipp said ruefully, as Gillett entered the room and politely asked if he could speak with His Lordship on a personal matter.

"Oh, please, not now, Gillett," Kipp told him, feeling very much put upon for a man who had only a day earlier believed he'd successfully settled all of his problems. "I don't think I am capable of hearing another well-prepared speech listing all the reasons you think will excuse your defection. I've got a wedding in three days, a ball that same night, and I won't even begin to consider muddling through either without you. If you hold me in any affection at all, can't this wait for another time?"

"I'm sorry, Your Lordship, but I feel I must speak. I've come to retract my request to leave your service, my lord," Gillett said as Brady snorted into his wineglass. "Having met the young lady, and having most thoroughly approved of her, I can only consider it a favor to your late mother if I were to be of any and all assistance possible to the future viscountess for as long as she should require it. Sir."

"Well, there you go, Kipp. Gillett approves. You can't hope for more than that, can you?"

Kipp looked at his butler, to his friend. His friend who looked as if he was in the midst of appreciating a very fine, very private joke.

Something was going on. Kipp didn't consider himself a brilliant man, but neither did he think himself so thick that he couldn't sniff out a conspiracy when it stared him straight in the face.

And then it struck him. If Abigail Backworth-Maldon could run herd on her eccentric brothers-in-law, on her scatter-witted niece and supposedly difficult to handle but so far blessedly unseen nephew, on the rather hazy-looking woman who was her sister-in-law . . . then managing his household, his servants, his friends — perhaps all of England and parts of Wales and Scotland — couldn't possibly be easier for her.

That was one of the reasons he'd picked her, after all.

But, being a woman, it would not be

enough for Abby to "handle" them all. She would need to conquer them, just as she'd damn well better not hope to conquer *him*.

The woman was amassing allies, that's what she was doing. Brady, Gillett, probably everyone belowstairs from the lowest serving maid to the housekeeper. She was making herself indispensable, even as he hadn't had any great need for her management before she came onto the scene.

She was going to make damn good and sure that, once she became his viscountess, she *stayed* his viscountess, even if he had a change of mind.

She was going to be everything he wanted of her. And, being an intelligent woman, she had enlisted his good friend Brady to help her succeed, even brought the defecting Gillett around her thumb. She was smoothing out his life even as she inveigled herself into every last inch of it.

Was this a good thing? Was this a bad thing? Would marriage to Abby make his life easier, as he'd hoped? And, if it would, as he still felt sure it would — hoped it would — why did he feel so uneasy? So threatened. Maybe even vulnerable.

And, at the bottom of it, did it matter?

"I don't want to know what's going on here, do I, Brady?" he asked at last, his temples starting to pound.

"No, old friend, I don't think you do," Brady answered, chuckling. "Oh, and Gillett? You've got a few crumbs on your jacket," he ended, before throwing back his head and laughing as the so-proper and so-shocked Gillett brushed away the evidence of his tea party with Abby, bowed, and quickly left the room.

In fact, Brady kept right on laughing until Kipp stomped out of the room, on his way up the stairs, his teeth gritted, knowing he had been left with no other option than to commend Abby on whatever havoc she'd been wreaking in his life in the name of helping him.

He halted on the second stair from the top, suddenly realizing that he was feeling rather angry with Merry for having gotten him into this mess.

Chapter Twelve

My dear Mrs. Backworth-Maldon,

Good morning. You will find, within the accompanying packages, the gowns you are required to wear for this afternoon's ceremony and tonight's ball, including accompaniments for same. May I suggest the obvious — the rose for this evening, the ivory for the ceremony. Whichever you choose, please bring the remaining gown with you to Grosvenor Square as, in any event, you will not be returning to Half Moon Street.

I do not, I believe, have need to reiterate here the terms of our agreement, or that I need further explain my justifiable demand that you appear dressed for both your new position in life and how your appearance in Society reflects upon conceptions of my regard for you.

The cost of the above will be deducted from your first quarter's allowance, as I understand you are concerned about propriety. After the ceremony, you are free to bleed me dry, up to the limits of that allowance.

My carriage will be at your family's disposal at two this afternoon.

Please be prompt, so that we may both get through these mandatory formalities as expeditiously as possible.

Yr. Servant,
Willoughby

Abby read the note through twice, caught between wanting to hang and quarter the man . . . or simply to shoot him and have done with it. She certainly didn't want to fall on his neck, kiss him for his kindness. Not when that *kindness* was only for himself, his appearance, how *he* would look if she showed up at the ball in one of the two half-presentable gowns she had already worn into Society.

Then she realized something. Something about herself she couldn't quite like. That something was that it was becoming increasingly easy for her to fall in with His Lordship's plans, and that she was even looking forward to "bleeding him dry" as she indulged herself in spending her allowance.

Not that she should have been too surprised. She'd spent too many years pinching pennies until they squealed not to have seen the advantages to her in the plan Brady had first outlined, in the offer the viscount had made to her.

It was feeling as if she had been bought by

the viscount, willingly bought, that niggled at the back of her conscience. That, and his not knowing that he had unknowingly acted according to her and Brady's plan.

Now there was something he could never be allowed to find out, not if she valued her own skin!

Such a shame she didn't love the man. She would feel much less guilty if she loved the man.

Or even more guilty.

"Oh, look, Abby — they're positively gorgeous! Isn't the viscount the most wonderful man in creation? Aren't you the luckiest thing?"

Abby turned to look at Edwardine as she sat on the bed beside the opened boxes, tissue paper billowing onto the floor as her niece brought out two of the gowns Abby had tried on at Madame Lucille's ridiculously expensive Bond Street establishment.

"And petticoats. And shoes. *Hose.* And look, Abby, a fan. You adore fans. How the viscount must love you!"

Abby looked down at the note, read it over one last time, balled it in her fist. "Oh, yes, Edwardine," she said tightly, tossing the crumpled note into the small fireplace. "The man positively adores me."

And then she sat down, remembering the

viscount's mention that she would not be returning to Half Moon Street. No, she wouldn't, would she? Not that she had any great affection for the place.

Except that it felt a lot *safer* than the mansion in Grosvenor Square.

She wore the ivory.

She'd been comforted by the modesty of the gown when first she saw it at Madame Lucille's. Constructed of finest percale, it had a high neck, triple shoulder ruffles, and a full, banded mameluke sleeve with pleated cuffs that fell nearly to her fingertips.

The skirt was fairly narrow in front, drawn tightly below her bosoms by a moss green velvet ribbon, and quite without other decoration. More than a dozen full-length pleats gave fullness to the back of the gown, with the pleats allowed to fall freely from her shoulders, to end in a demitrain.

There was more. Ivory silk stockings, butter-soft, moss green slippers that fit her perfectly, even softer ivory kid gloves that almost did. A small reticule that was little more than a rectangle cleverly covered in pleated fabric of moss green velvet intercut with ivory percale, suspended from a thin golden chain.

She looked considerably more expensive

than twelve pounds, six.

Only her hair, freshly washed, straight and flaxen as ever, disappointed her. She'd been utterly defeated in her attempts to curl it, to arrange the thick mop in anything more than its usual tight bun.

Still, she was gratified that the viscount had sent her the gown, both the gowns. Not just because claiming that he was marrying a dowdy, plain widow for "love" would be so transparent to the *ton,* but because she now felt better armed to meet him, to stand beside him, to recite her vows with him.

And not that she was without the protection of her family. The uncles Dagwood and Bailey, dressed alike in grass green satin of an earlier time — Dagwood's jacket mightily strained at the seams — were beside her. Hermione, and Cuddles, and Hermione's small silver flask that she always kept tucked up in her reticule, marched behind.

And Edwardine, led by her brother Ignatius, brought up the rear. As they arrived at the mansion Edwardine looked around in her shortsighted way, saying, "Is this a church? Looks like a church."

"Welcome, madam," Gillett said, bowing as the Backworth-Maldons all congregated in the large foyer. "And may I say how well you are looking today. The viscount awaits you in the drawing room."

"Thank you, Gillett," Abby said, then winced as her words came out as little more than a croak. "Is the minister or whoever also here?"

"He is, madam, as is the earl of Singleton. If you'll follow me?"

Abby meekly followed after the butler, because she couldn't think of any more questions that might delay the inevitable, and because her uncles had fallen into a small dispute as to whether or not Dagwood was wearing one of Bailey's shoes or if Bailey was wearing one of . . . well, it was an argument that could be waged either way.

Ignatius, an only slightly more masculine-looking copy of his sister, sidled up to Abby for a moment, his smile wide and gorgeous, and only partially covered by the perfumed, lace-edged handkerchief he held to his mouth.

"Hold up there a moment, Gillett, whilst I have a word with my auntie. Thank you, old fellow. I say, Auntie —" he always called Abby Auntie, even though he was only two years her junior — "are you really going to *live* here? Quite a deep gravy boat you've tumbled into. My congratulations. I didn't think you had it in you."

217

"Thank you, Iggy," Abby replied sweetly, knowing that her nephew was being as sincere as he was able. Besides, she already knew what was coming next.

He didn't disappoint. Iggy never disappointed, if one always considered him, then decided on the worst possible thing a person could do or say, then stood back and waited for him to do or say it.

"So I've been thinking, Auntie," he continued, his sky-blue eyes as guileless as a child's — a deceptive appearance Abby had long ago learned to ignore. "Being that I'm such a good nephew, loving and all of that, and considering that you'd probably want to reward me in some way for taking over, as I must, the care and herding of our idiot-witted relations . . ."

"You want an allowance, don't you, Iggy?" she asked as he paused, raised his eyebrows, looked at her expectantly. "You can't have one."

"Now, Auntie, don't be mean. You probably won't like what happens if you're mean to your favorite nephew."

Abby motioned for Gillett to step away from the doors to the drawing room without opening them. Then she grabbed hold of the grinning Iggy by the elbow and dragged him to the far corner of the huge foyer.

"Are you threatening me, Iggy? I wouldn't like to think you're threatening me."

"Threatening you, Auntie? Whatever do you mean? That I should be so low, so base, as to *threaten* you?" His grin was maddening. "Well, actually, I guess I am, now that you mention it. How about that?"

Abby remained silent, knowing her nephew would get to the point sooner or later.

"Do you remember the day of the picnic you and Edwardine attended, Auntie?" he asked her after a moment spent fiddling with his dripping lace cuffs, patting at his ridiculously high shirtpoints. "I was there, you know. Frolicking with the other young bucks, taking the air, sizing up the ladies as we young, randy gentlemen are wont to do."

Abby refused to blink, to wince. But her mind was racing along, wondering what Iggy would say next.

And then he did disappoint her, for she had, foolishly, actually hoped the boy could, just this once, resemble in spirit his angelic good looks.

"As the only man in the Backworth-Maldon family to be in attendance — as the only *real* man in the family, now that I think on it — I felt it my duty, when I saw you and the viscount go tripping off on your own, to

219

follow you. Couldn't have my auntie compromised or any of that rot, now could I? Found myself a cozy spot beside the stream, turned up my ears so that I could catch every word, be ready to rescue you if necessary. But you didn't need rescuing, did you, Auntie?"

Abby felt her stomach drop to her toes. "You heard?"

"Every wonderful, wonderfully wicked word." He threw back his head, laughed out loud. Then he leaned close to her, his voice dropping into a whisper. "How did it go? Oh, yes. Something like, 'I'm not a virgin, and that can only be a good thing.' Was that it, Auntie? Should I go on, cudgel my brain for more examples? And can you imagine, just *imagine,* the laughingstock the viscount would become — if I were to do that cudgeling in public?"

"I could tell the viscount," Abby offered rather desperately, wondering how affronted the stately Gillett would be if she grabbed Iggy by both his ears and pulled on them until the boy squealed like a pig caught in a grate.

She had to hand it to the boy, grudgingly. He'd waited, bided his time, then selected just the right moment to approach her. She couldn't tug on his ears, slap his face, ask

Gillett to order two of the footmen to haul her nephew outside and toss him into the gutter.

She was powerless to react.

And Iggy knew it.

"You could say something to His Lordship, I suppose, if you felt at all certain about the man. But you don't, so you won't. He wants you to make his life run smoother, Auntie, not ruin his reputation. Now, we'll leave discussion of the actual figure until another time — the amount of the allowance, a few other small favors I might ask of you from time to time. After all, you don't want to keep your groom waiting, now do you?"

"I will revenge myself on you, you know," Abby told him unemotionally, tugging at her slightly too loose gloves. "I don't know when, I don't know how, but your day of reckoning *will* come, Iggy. You have my promise."

"And I'm shivering in my boots, Auntie. After all, you and your great beauty — and your willingness to climb into his bed — might soften His Lordship's heart enough that he declares his undying love for you. *Then*, Auntie, you could probably confess how you have complicated his life rather than easing it, and even have your revenge," he told her in reply, bending to give her a kiss on the cheek before leading her back to the rest of the small group.

As Gillett threw open the doors to show the glory of the drawing room, announced their arrival, Iggy succumbed to something very close to a giggle. "However," he told Abby, "in the meantime, as I wait out the years for you to conquer His Lordship's heart, I do believe I'm going to enjoy myself very, *very* much."

Abby said nothing. She simply ground her left heel down hard on Iggy's instep, then left him where he stood and entered the drawing room.

Kipp, who'd been waiting for Gillett's announcement with all the enthusiasm of a dreadfully in pain man awaiting the arrival of the tooth drawer — either way, he was going to be hurting — walked across the room to greet his guests.

"My dear, how well you look," he told Abby, taking both her hands in his as he drew her farther into the room, giving her fingers what he hoped was a reassuring squeeze. "I see you got my note."

"Not really, my lord," she snapped, feeling edgy as a sharpened dinner knife. "It must have been very dry, as I fear the thing crumbled to dust in my fingers before I could read a word of it."

Kipp felt his jaw muscles tightening. He'd known his note had been terse, but it had been the best of the three he had composed. He simply had no experience in dealing with a fiancée who was more of a business partner, a woman he would soon be fathering children on without a mention of love, even the illusion of affection. "Please, allow me to make the introductions. We'll begin with the Reverend Peake?"

Decades spent in sailing the waters of social protocol behind him, Kipp was able to make the introductions, say the right words, smile the right smiles, and all while taking inventory of his soon-to-be-bride.

The gown had been a good choice. Modest, without being dowdy. And Madame Lucille had been right; she'd taken sufficient measurements the day Abby had been in her shop to be able to complete the gown without another fitting.

But the hair? Damn. His bride might have been dressed up to look the part of a young London matron, but her hair, when combined with her straight, almost rigid posture, still put him in mind of a nanny, or a governess, or the headmistress of some girl's school.

Would that shiny, blond hair tumble around her shoulders in curls once it was freed of its moorings? Would it cascade over her breasts, breasts he could only hope were as creamy white as her complexion? Did the woman *have* breasts? He certainly had seen little evidence of them, not in the gowns she'd been wearing, and not in this gown either, whose ruffled bodice could hide a multitude of glories or enhance what could only be a paucity of the same.

Why had he promised not to take a mistress? Had he been out of his mind? Or just that desperate to be safely married and still mostly unencumbered before Jack and Merry returned from America?

"Abby, my sweet, you look wonderful," the earl of Singleton proclaimed as he stepped in front of her, raised both her gloved hands for his kiss. "And it's not too late to back out, you know. Because he's not worthy of you."

Abby held on tightly to Brady's hands, willing herself to begin this plan as both she and the viscount had vowed they were prepared to carry on. "Oh, but I couldn't, Brady," she told him, her chin held high, her smile at first wobbly, but then firming, even as her will firmed, became solid. "I love him so, you understand."

Kipp's head swiveled toward his fiancée, he'd been amazed by her calm voice, her firm declaration. And then he remembered why he had chosen her in the first place, why yes, this thing could by damn work. Mrs. Abigail Backworth-Maldon was imperturbable. Practical. Strong. Independent. And, obviously, fairly adept with a fib.

Now, if she only had breasts . . .

"Your Lordship?"

"Hmmm?" Kipp answered, frowning at the interruption, just as he was wondering if he might be the most base, selfish creature in London — and there existed a plethora of competition for that particular dishonorable title.

"I was saying, my lord," the Reverend Peake continued, his expression rather pained, "that this was all so last-moment that I can only remain above another few minutes before rushing off to officiate at Lady Haver's funeral. So, if we could get on with the ceremony, if it pleases Your Lordship?"

"Just so long as you don't mix up the words between your two duties for this afternoon, Reverend," Kipp heard himself say, then smiled as both Abby and Brady — and only Abby and Brady — laughed in appreciation of his joke.

Because Hermione Backworth-Maldon

was at that moment hiding behind a potted plant that was, unfortunately, not quite tall enough to hide the fact that she was in the midst of tipping back her head and sipping at something out of a silver flask.

Some small white dog with nasty black eyes stood at her feet, lifting one scrawny leg as it watered that same potted plant.

Edwardine Backworth-Maldon, still such a pretty girl, even if the light in her eyes would never be much more than a reflection from the nearest candle, had sat herself down on one of the couches, somehow having spilled an entire dish of sugared candies in her lap — and was in the process of cleaning up the mess by popping the candies into her mouth, one at a time.

The uncles Backworth-Maldon stood close together in the very center of the large room, all but holding hands as, rather slack-jawed, they admired their surroundings. They reminded Kipp of a pair of defrocked friars with their stringy fringes of hair — and somewhat of a penny cartoon depicting a pair of country bumpkins, their pet chickens at their feet, as they attended their first London party.

The nephew — Ignatius, wasn't it? — was quite a piece of work, Kipp decided as he watched the young man saunter around the room, seemingly appraising each piece of furniture as if planning to make bids on them at a sale. His long, narrow fingertips grazed each tabletop as he passed, lingered to caress a figurine, pat at a piece of silver. Dressed in the highest of fashion — a height of affected dandyism to which Kipp had never aspired — the boy was tall, slim, as well-favored as his sister, and nearly as feminine-looking.

The only real difference between the two blue-eyed blonds was the very obvious intelligence in Ignatius Backworth-Maldon's eyes. Intelligence, liberally mixed with craftiness.

The boy might bear watching.

"I'll ring for Gillett to fetch the staff," Brady suggested, interrupting Kipp's quick inventory of the faintly bizarre collection that were, any moment now, to become his relatives. "You did say you wanted them here, to serve as witnesses?"

"Yes, yes I did. It was Gillett's suggestion, and a good one," Kipp told him, taking Abby's hand in his as they then both followed the Reverend as he made his way toward the immense white-stuccoed fireplace, the spot earlier chosen for the ceremony.

"Nervous, my lord?" Abby dared to ask him, as she suddenly, and for no reason she

227

neither could nor even particularly wanted to understand, realized that she was calm. Deadly calm. Rather like a prisoner who had given up her last hope of rescue and just *accepted* her fate.

"Petrified," Kipp answered her honestly as the Reverend picked up a thick, black-bound book and began paging through it. "You appear calm enough. Does it get easier with repetition, do you think?"

"After I've buried you and gone on to my third husband, my lord, I'll let you know," she answered, earning herself a small chuckle from Kipp, and another squeeze of her hand.

And then the servants entered the room, led by Gillett, and lined themselves up, two rows deep, in front of the windows.

Brady came to stand beside Kipp, ready to hand over the Willoughby family wedding ring, the one Kipp had personally removed from his mother's finger the day she died, the same day he'd promised her he would marry and produce an heir. The same day he'd promised her that he would stop looking back, hoping for old dreams to come true.

He'd never said a word to his mother about his feelings for Merry, the child who had all but grown up with him, sometimes living under the same roof. But she'd known. Somehow his mother had always known.

He wondered now if his mother was watching, if she would approve. He rather hoped for the former, and didn't really want to think about the latter.

With the first words from the Reverend Peake, Hermione withdrew a large handkerchief from her reticule and began weeping into it copiously, and quite vocally.

"Do you take this woman . . ."

The words swirled, rose and fell, were accented by Hermione's hiccuping sobs, Edwardine's whispered "step back, Iggy, so I can see," and Ignatius's snapped "you can't see your own nose, Eddy."

They were joined by the rumble of undertones from the uncles Dagwood and Bailey that had something to do with plans, and prizes. And, lastly, by a few nasty, little dog growls from Cuddles as Gillett set one of the underfootmen to extracting a small silk-tasseled pillow from the dog's jaws before removing him from the room.

And then it was over. Ten minutes, and Kipp knew his life to have been changed forever.

The Reverend Peake pronounced them married, and Brady, ever the mischief-maker, suggested that Kipp kiss his bride.

"Oh, that's not necessary," Abby blurted out before she could stop herself.

"On the contrary," Kipp corrected her. He knew what Brady was up to, why his friend was daring him to kiss Abby. Brady wanted him to make the initial, intimate physical contact so that, if either he or Abby had not yet fully understood the gravity of the step they'd just taken, there could be no confusion left to them now.

They were married. For richer for poorer, for better for worse, for whatever motives they had, spoken or unspoken, they were married.

As the Reverend stood by impatiently, obviously eager to be on his way to Lady Haver's interment and the hope of being invited to a meal after the services, Kipp turned to his bride. Smiled at his bride. Wondered if his bride might faint.

"My lady Willoughby," he said to her as he lifted her chin with his finger, watched her curiously attractive violet eyes grow dark in her ashen face, then flutter closed.

"My lord," she whispered so quietly he sensed the words rather than heard them.

Her mouth was warm, remarkably pliant, easily molding to his own. This was a woman who had been kissed before. This was a woman who enjoyed being kissed, who responded instinctively, oblivious to maidenly shyness or any need to pretend she didn't know what was going on.

Abby forced herself to breathe, willed herself to stand very still. Not to run. Not to fall forward, melt into his arms, pull him to her, hold on with all her might.

How long had it been since she'd been kissed, since she had still believed herself in love with Harry, and had actually welcomed his kisses?

These had to be carnal fires springing to life inside her, fires that had been banked too long, bursting into flame with just a single small application of fuel from His Lordship's touch.

With their bodies not touching, with only the power of his fingertip to hold her where she stood, Kipp intensified the kiss. He felt her lips opening beneath his, allowing him entry. Giving back as good as she got.

Abby's mind might have forgotten, but her body remembered. Remembered, and responded. She felt herself nearly liquefy as Kipp's tongue touched hers, as she responded naturally, setting up a duel both seemed to be winning.

Behind him, and through the unexpected buzzing in his ears, Kipp at last heard

Brady's laugh, his almost mocking applause, and he stood back, collected himself, tried to compose himself.

He watched as Abby — as his *wife* — politely thanked the Reverend, then accepted Edwardine's teary hug, calmly told Hermione to hold her breath and count to twenty, shook her head and smiled at her uncles.

So easy to run hot, so easy to run cold, and all without a blink. So calm. So matter-of-fact. So in control, when he knew he was not at all in control, his male body having betrayed his supposedly rational, detached mind.

The woman was a wonder, a born general, and yet with all the willing surrender of a woman who knew what she liked, and she liked being kissed.

Had he really ever considered her mouth to be ordinary? Had he really ever considered Abby to be ordinary?

And *now*, having leapt so far after only looking a few inches into the distance, what in God's name was he going to do with her?

Chapter Thirteen

The bedchamber was composed of three adjoining rooms of varying sizes. Cavernous room for the bed. Smaller dressing room. Rabbit-hutch-sized maid's room.

Furnished in white-and-gold furniture that probably came from France — Abby was only guessing, but there were plenty of curlicues and gilt to make her believe the pieces were French — it had once been the viscount's mother's room, and her personality still permeated it.

A feminine woman, a woman who appreciated beauty. Serenity. Order. Peace. Mrs. Harris earlier had pointed out Her Ladyship's life-size portrait in the drawing room, and Abby had immediately recognized the viscount's elongated brown eyes and the sweep of darker brown brows, the same shade of blond hair. Only the softness around the mouth was missing. No, the viscount had taken his full-lipped mouth and strong chin from his late father, whose portrait flanked that of his wife.

Not wanting to think about her new husband's mouth, or her earlier reaction to it,

Abby returned her gaze to this second, more thorough inventory of her new bedchamber.

Soft rose watered silk on the walls. A high ceiling dotted with puffy clouds, chubby cherubs. Three Aubusson carpets scattered on the parquet floor, faded gardens of rose and yellow and a lovely moss green.

White-satin coverlet on the bed, topped by at least two dozen pillows of varying size and color. Filmy white drapes on the floor-to-ceiling windows. Vases and figurines and fragile bowls. An ornately carved white-stuccoed fireplace that mimicked the one in the drawing room.

And a connecting door to the viscount's bedchamber.

She wouldn't think about that, either.

Abby felt quite pampered now, sitting in the painted tub in front of the fireplace, indulging in her second bath of the day, sunk to her neck in bubbles this time instead of rushing through her tepid two-inch-deep bath so that everyone else could have a turn.

Mrs. Harris had led Abby upstairs after she'd finally been able to say good-bye to her relatives and see them off, on their way back to Half Moon Street to prepare for the ball. Abby had nearly to *peel* an almost hysterical Edwardine from her, promising that, yes, yes, she would always be near, always be available to talk to her niece, assist her if she had a problem, any problems at all. Her door, the door of the mansion in Grosvenor Square, would always be open to her.

Edwardine had sobbed, and thanked her profusely, and Abby had been freed at last, wondering to herself when it was that Edwardine had ever experienced a problem. Certainly none that Abby could remember, not unless she considered being Hermione's daughter a problem.

Abby knew she'd consider it a problem if *she* were Hermione's daughter, if she would be dependent on Hermione to guide her through the remainder of the Season. Hysterics, in fact, wouldn't have begun to cover Abby's reaction to that particular fate.

But she hadn't thought Edwardine that deep. The child had always gone on so well, living in her myopic, rose-colored world, oblivious to her surroundings, seemingly unaware of their shrinking finances, totally unfazed by any thought so mundane as wondering where her next meal might spring from if somebody like Abby wasn't counting every penny.

But then, just as the Backworth-Maldons had been leaving, Abby had caught a glimpse of Iggy, seen the gleam in his eyes, and wondered if he had put his sister up to her small bout of hysterics. Had he deliberately frightened his sister? And if he had, why?

How would upsetting Edwardine help Iggy? Because the boy never did anything unless it served him in some way.

She wouldn't think about that, either. There was too much to do between now and tonight's ball, her introduction into society as the Viscountess Willoughby.

Not to mention coming back into this chamber *after* the ball . . .

Sallyann, Abby's new maid — the only maid she'd ever had to herself — poured another bucket of warm, fragrant water into the deep, highly ornamented tub. Abby watched the steam rise, allowing her worries to disappear into that steam as she leaned back and luxuriated in what could only seem the height of decadence.

She could become very easily and happily accustomed to decadence.

"Thank you, Sallyann," she told the young maid, a small, plump redhead with a tendency to giggle whenever she spoke. "This is lovely."

"Yes, ma'am," Sallyann answered, giggling into her hand, her freckled face coloring a deep, not entirely attractive pink. She fetched a blue-glass bottle from a nearby table, held it up for Abby's inspection. "Would you be wanting me to wash your hair now, ma'am?"

Abby touched a hand to her most vexing feature, the thick, straight mop of blond hair now tied up in a wide ribbon, to keep it out of the water. "Oh, I think not, Sallyann. I doubt it will ever dry in time, if we were to wash it."

She swiveled slightly in the deep tub, looked up at the maid, whose touseled, shiny red locks were so naturally wavy they seemed to have a life of their own. Abby would give a year of her life for curls like those, any curls at all. "Sallyann? Do you know anything about *arranging* hair? I'd be so appreciative of your help, any assistance you might be able to give me."

"His Lordship has already ordered up a hairdresser for you, ma'am," Sallyann told her. "He'll be here anytime now, as a matter of fact, so I suppose you should be getting out of your bath now. Here, I've warmed a towel for you."

Abby allowed herself a moment's pleasure at the thought of having her hair arranged by an expert, and a moment was all she got before Sallyann's words fully penetrated her brain. "His Lordship ordered a hairdresser for me? Isn't that so very — condescending of him."

Sallyann nodded, giggled, blushed yet again. "Oh, yes, ma'am, it's true, he surely did. Alfie — he's one of the underfootmen, I'm stepping out with him these past weeks, you understand — well, he told me all about it. How His Lordship said he couldn't have you showing up at the ball tonight with your hair all scraped back like some old-maid schoolmistress. Alfie took the note round to Mon-shur Parfait himself, just this morning."

"Just this morning, you say," Abby said through clenched teeth, momentarily wishing Kipp underground for having allowed his servants — *their* servants to hear such a remark. "Imagine that." She stood up in the bath, felt an immediate chill against her heated skin, and allowed herself to be wrapped in the large, warmed towel. She stepped out of the tub and began drying herself, rubbing at her skin with an unfocused angry energy that had her dry in rapid time.

What really bothered her, she decided finally, was that Kipp seemed to consider her as a *project* in progress, and not his wife at all.

Which she wasn't, not really.

That thought unexpectedly made her sad, which, following quite naturally, made her more angry. Irrationally angry, because she knew she should be thanking him. He was only trying to be kind, after all. So perhaps she wasn't really angry. Perhaps she was *hurt,* her feelings battered by the thought that she needed so very much work to become presentable, and that Kipp knew it.

She really wasn't sure what she felt, except that she no longer felt happy, or deliciously decadent, or independent. And it was so very important to her that she remain independent in any small way she could. She needed something to remind her that she was still a person in her own right, and not just a convenience Kipp was now fixing up the way he would order an old couch refurbished for company — all in exchange for an allowance and the rest of it.

She waved aside Sallyann's assistance and climbed into her underclothes by herself, just as she'd been taking care of herself for three-and-twenty years, then stabbed her arms into her old dressing gown that had been brought to Grosvenor Square along with the rest of her meager wardrobe.

"Sallyann?"

"Yes, ma'am?" The maid, who had been piling towels into one arm as she picked up the blue bottle, turned to her, curtsied, smiled. What a happy sort she was. Open, talkative, endearingly pleasant and unaffected. Abby wished her on the other side of the moon. That way, she could be alone to scream, shout — throw something. He'd *ordered* her a hairdresser? Planned to dress her and primp her, like she was some *doll* he'd purchased, just as if she had no idea as to how to do any of those things for herself?

The devil he would!

"In my trunk, at the very bottom if I remember correctly, you'll find a chocolate brown taffeta gown with long sleeves, a simple white collar. I would appreciate it if you could bring it me."

The maid's forehead puckered. "Now, ma'am? But I was just going off to press the pink while you have yourself a little lie-down on the bed and wait for Mon-shur Parfait. You know, ma'am, the one you brought in the big white box? Such a pretty thing. Then I'll bring you a small plate of sandwiches, as you'll probably be too excited to eat much of the dinner later, at least that's what Mrs. Harris said."

Abby tied the sash of her dressing gown, pulling it nearly tight enough to cut off her air. "I really don't feel in the need of a nap, Sallyann. I do, however, wish to have a few words with His — with my husband, and as it's too early to dress in my new gown, the brown will do me just fine," she told her sweetly. "Besides, I'll need to be wearing something more substantial than this when Monsieur Parfait arrives, now won't I?"

The maid opened her mouth, closed it again. Wrinkled her brow. Shrugged her shoulders, shook her bright red curls. "But . . . but — yes, ma'am."

Twenty minutes later, with the sound of her husband's whistling coming to her through the closed door — she'd opened it a crack, just to be sure he was in residence, just to assure herself he was alone — Abby knocked on the wood three times, then swept inside his bedchamber.

She'd seen his rooms before, when Mrs. Harris had conducted her tour, and knew the suite of rooms to mimic hers in design, if not in decoration.

The viscount's chamber was done in dark cherry woods, heavy pieces that matched the massive cherry mantel, that contrasted well with ivory flocked walls, deep burgundy drapes. A shiny brass hip bath sat in front of the fireplace, a few damp towels draped over its edge.

Thick ivory carpets dotted with gold fleur-de-lis covered the floor. The huge, four-poster bed was hung with burgundy velvet, the bed a wide sea of burgundy satin. Three enormous armoires held His Lordship's clothing, and the wall decoration leaned more toward dark portraits and a goodly supply of huge brass wall sconces.

This was a room that could swallow her, devour her, much as she admired the bold colors, the sharp contrasts. She would much prefer the viscount in her rooms, hopefully as intimidated as most men would be surrounded by so much feminine lace and satin and delicate furniture.

Except for now. Right now, she'd prefer the man in Hades, singed to his eyebrows.

Her husband was sitting at his ease in one of two matching burgundy-leather chairs placed in front of the fireplace. He sat low on his spine, his stockinged feet balanced on a matching footstool, his long body wrapped in a navy-and-burgundy dressing gown. A thick lock of damp, blond hair hung low over his lazily hooded eyes. He held a half-full glass of deep red wine in his hand, dangling over one arm of the chair, held by two fingertips.

If she had never been married, if she had never seen a man in a dressing gown and stockinged feet, she might have felt intimidated. As a matter of fact, she *did* feel intimidated.

Which only made her angrier, more determined.

"Comfortable? Perhaps even complacent? Smug and satisfied with yourself?" Abby asked when her husband didn't notice her entrance. She slammed the connecting door so that the sound echoed in the large room.

Kipp nearly dropped the wineglass as he cursed, pushed himself to his feet, stared at the intruder.

She was wearing one of those damn brown gowns, so heavy it barely moved as she walked — no, stomped — into the room. Her slim shoulders were squared, her eyes were narrowed slits, and her rounded chin seemed high enough to knock her off-kilter and send her reeling backwards on her heels. Her hair was still in that ridiculous scraped-back bun, which told him that Monsieur Parfait had not yet arrived to work what Kipp sincerely hoped would be a miracle.

And her expression? Well, that was very much like that of his old nanny, the one he had secretly called Miss Ironbottom. That woman had seemed to enjoy rapping his knuckles when he couldn't button his shirt correctly, and had delighted in telling him there'd be no pudding until he'd done it right.

So, of course, thanks to that memory Kipp immediately went on his guard, put there even more so by Abby's damnably tipped-up chin that warned him he'd be listening to a blistering lecture in a moment, if he could not defuse or at least redirect her obvious anger.

"Wife," he drawled, bowing in her general direction. "Don't you look well. Come to scrub out my tub?"

There was a slight, almost imperceptible hitch in Abby's determined forward movement, but she didn't flinch, didn't blink. She just kept on coming, an advancing army of one, now with one hand stuck out in front of her, one accusing finger pointed straight at his chest.

"We had a bargain, my lord. We marry for mutual convenience, we share children, we leave each other *alone*. Do you remember that?"

"Vaguely," Kipp said, sitting down once more, looking up at her, smiled. "Perhaps we should have thought to write it all down, record the terms for posterity? Then, perhaps, you would have remembered that I also asked you to please, for the sake of my very thin skin and woefully immense pride, show Society a happy couple, a happy marriage. I hesitate to point this out, wife, but you aren't looking in the least happy at the moment."

Abby longed to choke the man. "What does posturing in public about our undying love for each other have to do with my hair, my lord? Or my gowns? Are you saying you're so shallow that you could not be believed if you said you loved me as I am now? Is that what Society thinks of you?"

Kipp pretended to consider this, knowing he could not tell Abby the truth — that everything else he'd said to her had woven no more than a convenient web of fairly plausible lies, that he really had married her because he couldn't have Merry and so it didn't matter whom he married. It only mattered that Merry believed he had married for love. Not that he was about to tell his new wife that particular truth.

So he smiled again, hopefully maddeningly. "Well, yes, now that you point it out. I do think I am that shallow, that Society correctly sees me as being that shallow. A pity, but there it is, especially as you've had this small, unsettling epiphany of yours a few hours too late, *after* this afternoon's ceremony."

Abby bit her tongue to keep silent about the truths she knew, the real reasons behind the viscount's proposal that had gratefully rescued her from her own precariously lived but frankly boring life.

She had to remain angry with him, which she was, in order not to pity him for his loss at love, which she did. "And you now expect me to be dressed and primped and *shown off? Paraded* in front of the *ton?* Like — like some pet horse?"

"My, but you're the astute one," he said, standing up again, as he had motioned for Abby to take the facing chair, and she had pointedly ignored him. His smile disappeared as he looked at her mouth, remembered the kiss they'd shared — yes, *shared* — after the ceremony two hours earlier.

"However, I do appreciate this show of independence. I'm impressed, truly. I apologize for believing you might want some feminine armor tonight. I go down on my knees — figuratively, of course — to beg your forgiveness for believing you might wish the services of a hairdresser, or to wear the jewels I handed over to Gillett a few minutes ago in the hope you'd wear them this evening."

"Jewels?" Abby repeated, then mentally kicked herself for her weakness. What a rotter he was, tempting her this way, almost as if he knew the only jewels she'd owned (a garnet ring and matching necklace Harry had given her on their wedding day), had gone the way of Harry's gambling debts years ago.

"Yes, jewels. Lovely things, if ancient. Handed down from bride to bride for generations. But if you feel your independence would be compromised if you wore them, well, who am I to argue? Do as you wish, wife. As you've just reminded me, we most certainly did promise not to interfere with each other's lives, didn't we?"

He was giving in? What was he doing? He wasn't supposed to give in. He was supposed to fight, perhaps even threaten, and then apologize, so that she could gracefully accept his apology — and the gown, and the services of Monsieur Parfait. And the jewels. Heaven forbid she could forget that mention of his mother's jewels, the way he had dangled them in front of her as he smiled so smugly.

He was being so kind, and she was being so very unreasonably ungrateful for all that kindness.

Damn him!

Abby's eyes shifted to the left, to the right. She looked down at her toes. He had called her at her own game, turned the tables, made her appear silly, and shallow, and ungrateful. Still, she pushed at him one more time, just to see if he could hold that facade of a smile, and not flinch. "So you wouldn't mind if I went down to the ball wearing my own gown, looking like this? If I told you I felt I could only maintain some semblance of independence by deciding on my own gowns, my own hairdresser, my own judgment in outfitting myself?"

"Would I mind? Not in the slightest," Kipp told her calmly, lying through his teeth. If he presented Abby as his bride, dressed as she was now, they'd both be the laughingstock of all of Mayfair by morning. He didn't care, not for himself, but this strange little woman would be destroyed. As well she knew. All for the sake of her most commendable, admirable, but, in this case, badly applied pride.

"You're lying," Abby declared, her chin coming up once more, even as a clutch of butterflies took wing in her stomach. She couldn't go downstairs looking like this. She wouldn't be downstairs two minutes before one of the arriving guests handed her a cloak and told her to hang it up somewhere, or asked her to please show her the way to the ladies' withdrawing room.

When he didn't answer, she pushed harder. "You'd stand beside me, introduce me as your wife?"

Kipp stepped closer, bent down, whispered into her ear. "Try me," he cooed, flicking a finger at her thick bun before moving away from her once more.

"Although," he said, giving her an out, because he was not by nature a mean man, "if you were to wear the gown I ordered, and avail yourself of Monsieur Parfait's services, I believe my mother's diamonds will be shown to better advantage. You might have noticed her portrait in the drawing room? She wore them for the portrait, commissioned on her own wedding day. It would please me very much if you'd wear them tonight, Abby, in her memory."

"Diamonds?" The word came out as little more than a squeak as she remembered the magnificent necklace in the portrait, and Abby knew she'd been beaten. She'd thought pearls. She really liked pearls.

But she adored diamonds, not that she'd ever owned any. Was she really that hungry to wear beautiful things, to show herself to her best advantage tonight as she faced the *ton* for the first time as Kipp's bride, that she'd compromise her principles for a few shiny stones?

Of course she was, of course she would.

Hadn't she already compromised those principles, marrying this man for her own convenience and, yes, for his great wealth as well?

Of course she had, and they both knew it.

In fact, now that she looked at it all clearly, she had just been about as ridiculous as any woman could be — taking everything he offered with both hands, and then complaining that she was somehow losing herself in his generosity. That wasn't what he wanted from her. He really didn't want much from her at all.

Perhaps, she thought, her stomach doing a small flip, it was she who wanted more from him? Not gowns, not jewels. Just *more*. More of his smiles, more of his attention, more of him.

And that, she knew, was not only stupid, it was impossible! No wonder she had gotten so angry with him. It was much preferable to being angry with herself. Mentally kicking herself for her own foolishness, she then quickly applied herself to being the convenient wife and comfortable companion he wanted . . . which was all that he wanted.

Taking the wineglass from Kipp's unresisting fingers, she sat herself down on the chair he'd just vacated and grinned up at him. It took everything that was in her to do so, but somehow she managed.

"Well, then, that's settled, my lord," she said, lifting the wineglass in salute, then downing half its contents. "I accept your gifts."

"I've won? How gratifying."

"And how untrue. You've won nothing, my lord Willoughby. I've simply changed my mind, that's all. I am allowed to do that, aren't I, when presented with a convincing argument? After all, I wouldn't want you to think I'm pigheaded, too stubborn for my own good."

"Of course not," Kipp said, appreciating her logic, twisted as it might be.

Abby relaxed in the chair, feeling marginally better about herself, *knowing* herself a little more than she had an hour earlier. "I wanted to punish you for your rather high-handed attempt to gain control over my wardrobe, my hair, my *life*. I wanted to let you know, in no uncertain terms, my lord, that I may have agreed to this marriage, but that I did not turn myself over to you entirely, that I would remain my own woman. As I believe I've made my point, I believe I am now also allowed graciously to accept a reasonable compromise."

"A gracious compromise? Yes, I can see it clearly now. No one won, no one lost. You simply changed your mind. And all on your own, too, I imagine?"

"Would you wish to take credit for my mind now, too, my lord?" Her smile was pure sugar, so sweet he could nearly taste it. The almost prudish-looking nanny with the unremarkable features had a coquette's smile.

Very unnerving.

"Take credit for the workings of your mind? Not in this lifetime, my dear. But you did make your point, madam. Shall I deduct Monsieur Parfait's services from your first quarter's allowance? The man is still here, I most sincerely hope?"

"He is. I've set him to cutting Sallyann's hair, as he protested at standing about, having nothing to do. And no, you shall not deduct his fee from my allowance. I've decided to graciously accept his services as your bride gift to me."

"How gratifying," Kipp said as he walked her back to the connecting door. "We've been married, we've had our first kiss, and now we've had our first argument — which neither of us has won, because you just changed your mind. We've covered quite a lot of ground in a few short hours, a few short days. And I find I'm growing increasingly content with our arrangement. Do you feel the same?"

Mention of their kiss made Abby stumble over her dragging hem, and she stopped, took a deep breath, then looked up at her husband. "I am quite satisfied thus far, my lord, yes. And, if you're asking if I enjoyed our kiss, which I am sure you are — no doubt in the hope of unsettling me — allow me to tell you that I enjoyed it very much. In fact, I believe you will probably make quite an interesting lover."

She smiled when she had finished, letting Kipp know she could give as good as she got. Hot color ran into his cheeks, which greatly gratified her, for, if she was to be outspoken and brazen, she might as well enjoy watching the effect it had on him.

She hadn't asked if he had enjoyed their kiss, as if she simply *assumed* he had. Now it was Kipp's turn to feel uncomfortable, and he knew she'd wanted him to feel this way. What a strange, brave little creature. It was as if she enjoyed saying outrageous things, liked to remind him, over and over, of the conditions of their marriage . . . and that she was more than prepared for all of them.

"You enjoyed our kiss? How exceedingly gratifying, my dear," he purred, opening the door that separated their rooms. Her maddening imperturbability in the face of such an intimate discussion goaded him into asking another outrageous question. "Are you then perhaps saying that, if our single kiss serves as any indication, I may yet measure up to your late husband in my love-making abilities?"

"That remains to be seen, my lord," she told him, tipping her head to one side as she examined his expression. She was beginning to know him, know how to read him, understand him — how to put him off-balance. She knew he was always at his most maddeningly droll when he was most upset. The thought that she might have some small power over him, was able to affect him in some way even if that way was not within one hundred miles of love, was as heady as fine wine.

At least, she believed, she would not now be sharing her bed with an absolute stranger.

"You see," she told him as she began moving through the doorway, putting some distance between them, "I've been thinking about Harry these past days, comparing him to you, as you've just now suggested. And, frankly, I'm hopeful that you will probably outshine Harry in this area. Because, my lord, I believe you truly *like* women, whereas Harry probably didn't, now that I've had time to reflect on the thing. So, yes, this afternoon's kiss was most definitely gratifying."

She shut the door behind her, leaving Kipp to stare at the dark wood, her last words to him repeating themselves in his head.

Mocking him.

Daring him.

Just when he thought he understood her, she changed into another person. Sometimes modest and unassuming. Sometimes witty and insightful. At times prudish. Quick to anger, just as quick to relent. Sometimes a tease, pretty damn close to a temptress for a woman with the physical presence of a country mouse.

He'd thought he'd found himself a sensible paragon. Now he wondered if he hadn't gotten himself bracketed to a maddening paradox. A woman who changed her mood, even her personality, a lot more often than most Society ladies changed hats.

He poured himself another glass of wine, sat down in his chair once more, splayed his long legs out in front of him.

He laughed deep in his throat as he conjured up a mental image of Abby's delight and dismay at his mention of the Willoughby diamonds, reacting much like a child offered an unexpected treat, but only if she first ate all her unwanted porridge.

He frowned into his glass when he wondered just how good the late Harry Backworth-Maldon *had* been in bed.

And he stared into the fire for a long time as he asked himself the most important questions of all: Who *was* this woman he'd married for such selfish reasons, and why did he suddenly believe he might just be interested enough to find out?

Chapter Fourteen

Abby didn't come down to dinner.

Kipp had knocked on the dividing door when the second chime had gone, only to have a very harried-looking Frenchman pull the door open, then glare at him rather evilly before collecting his emotions and performing a rather elegant bow for a man holding a pair of scissors in one hand and a hank of golden hair in the other.

The hairdresser was a tall man of about forty, thin as a whip and dressed all in rather flashy blue satin, as if expecting to be called to the French court at any moment. Lace foamed at his throat, at his cuffs. A narrow brown belt stuffed with scissors, combs, slid halfway down his hips.

The man was laughable, but he didn't know that.

"My lord," Parfait said at last, in highly accented English. "Thees es the interruption necessary? Eet es *I* who am necessary, I do think."

Kipp suddenly found himself somewhat intimidated by the hairdresser, which was above anything ridiculous, for he was a viscount, damn it, and this man was only holding a huge amount of his wife's hair in his hand.

Still, the workings of flamboyant artistes like Parfait were a mystery to Kipp, and he'd rather keep things that way. He decided to tamp down his temper and attempt to look more concerned than outraged. He certainly knew he didn't want to enter the room, see what the fellow was doing to his wife's head!

"I only came to inquire if Her Ladyship is ready to go down to dinner." Kipp pointed at the scissors, then added, "I imagine not."

"You do the imagine correctly, my lord," Parfait told him regally, and then closed the door again.

Leaving Kipp to realize that he hadn't been in charge of his own household for more than a moment since Abby had first walked through the door and done whatever in blazes it was she did that had made him feel an interloper in his own home.

It was true. Abby Backworth-Maldon — no, Abby Rutland, Viscountess Willoughby — hadn't been in residence more than five hours, and his household, the one he believed would now run more smoothly than ever before, was already topsy-turvy.

How had that happened? It wasn't supposed to have happened.

Turned away at his wife's bedchamber door. Dismissed by a hairdresser.

How lowering.

As Kipp walked down the hallway, he met Sallyann coming toward him, trying her best to curtsy without tipping the heavy silver tray in her hands.

Kipp lifted one of the two identical silver lids, saw what he vaguely remembered as the second course of the evening's planned dinner. Slices of fine, rare roasted beef and a few simple accompaniments.

"And the second serving?" he asked the maid, already knowing it had to be for Monsieur Parfait. That would be just like Abby, making sure the man was properly fed — then wondered why he knew that.

"For the Mon-shur, my lord. They're very busy, my lord," Sallyann told him, keeping her nervous gaze on his evening slippers. Then she looked up at him, giggled. "It's grand fun we're having, my lord, if you don't mind my saying so. Her Ladyship is just the nicest lady. You got yourself a good one, that's for certain."

"How gratifying to have your approval," Kipp said, then smiled as gently as he could, for the maid was turning a rather unbecoming shade of puce and he began to worry for his hose and evening slippers. "Carry on, and please inform Her Ladyship that I shall most definitely require her to be downstairs in one hour. All right?"

Sallyann swallowed down hard on whatever had been attempting to rise from her stomach, then curtsied yet again, so that Kipp had to remove the slipping tray from her hands until she righted herself.

"Excuse me, my lord. So sorry, my lord. Must be going, my lord," the young woman muttered rapidly, her words tumbling over themselves as she retrieved the tray and went on her way.

Leaving Kipp to go downstairs on his own and explain to their only dinner guest why two gentlemen, one of them a bridegroom, would be dining on their own this evening.

"Convenient, uncomplicated. Live our own lives, don't bother each other. A sane, sensible solution, a perfect bargain at both ends." He stabbed his fingers through his hair as he turned the corner in the large entrance hall, headed for the drawing room to collect Brady and by damn eat something before he started chewing on the woodwork. *"Hah!"*

Gillett waved the servers out of the large dining room after the main courses were served, then took up position to the left of the sideboard, in case he was needed. Kipp had wondered, more than once, if Gillett were prepared to spoon-feed him if that became necessary, although why it might become necessary still eluded him.

"Locked in her rooms, is she?" Brady said after a long silence, his deep brown eyes twinkling. He'd tried to bring Abby into the conversation several times, only to be rebuffed, but he was nothing if not persistent. "Isn't that interesting. What did you do, old friend, scare her half to death with your husbandly ardor? For shame."

"Eat your peas, Brady, or there'll be no dessert for you tonight," Kipp commanded, pretending not to hear Gillett's suppressed snigger. Gillett. Yet another traitor in his midst! "As I've already told you, my lady's toilette is taking considerably longer than she had anticipated. Although I will admit to you that I await her eventual entrance with some trepidation, considering the wild-eyed appearance of her hairdresser."

"Parfait? You did get him, didn't you? Of course you did, as he's the best. Wild-eyed, you said? Parfait? Well, he is French, isn't he, although I've heard it said that he's an artist with the scissors. Do you think Abby may have stabbed him with them?"

"And why would she do that?"

"Because you sent him, Kipp," Brady responded, popping a small bit of buttered bread into his mouth. He couldn't remember when he had last so enjoyed a meal. "You sent the gowns, too, and we both know Abby only accepted them under duress. I believe your new wife, if I've read her correctly at all, is not much appreciative of charity. Or," he ended on a smile, "the idea that you might think she needs refurbishing."

"How perceptive of you," Kipp grumbled, pushing his plate away, his meal barely touched. "Perhaps you should have married her, as you seem to know her so well."

"Ah, but I'm not head over ears in love with her and about to proclaim that fact to the world in a few minutes, now am I?"

Kipp eyed his friend levelly. "Why did I invite you here for dinner?"

"Because you needed an ally, I suppose. A buffer between you and your new bride as you begin your first evening as man and wife. A supporting prop to get you through the evening as smoothly as possible. A friend who will remind you, lest you forget, of the very solid reasons you've chosen this particular route to, if not happiness, at least some sort of harmony and — dare I say it? — *protection*."

"Really? All that?" Kipp sat back as Gillett personally poured him another glass of wine. "What a sterling fellow you are, Brady."

"Yes, I am, aren't I? Simply sterling. And am I being at all helpful?"

"No, Brady, you're not."

Brady threw back his head and laughed out loud until the look on Kipp's face alerted him that his friend had just suffered at least a minor shock. "Kipp?" he asked, then turned in his chair, to see what it was the man was looking at that had served to put such a bemused expression on his face.

"Good God!" Brady jumped to his feet, cursing himself for letting that surprised exclamation escape him. And then, because he was Brady, a man never afraid to insert his expensively clad foot into his mouth when the spirit moved him, he added, "Abby? Is that you? You look wonderful. Kipp, doesn't she look wonderful?"

"I look *better,* which is no great accomplishment, considering how I looked in my old gowns, with my hair the bane of my existence. It would have been difficult to make me look *worse,*" Abby said, before Kipp could find his tongue, which he'd, just for a moment, believed he might have swallowed. "Monsieur Parfait vows I'll become all the

263

rage. But he's a rather volatile man, and I believe he likes me — did you know he once created Marie Antoinette's wigs, helped his father with them, I should say — so I can't take his words as truth without adding a few healthy spoonfuls of salt."

Kipp's ears were buzzing, so that he barely understood her. "Where's your hair?"

Then he winced as he heard what he'd asked, as the words hung in the air as Brady looked at him, shook his head sadly, as if highly disappointed in him. But then, Kipp also knew, Brady had probably not wondered how Abby's long blond hair might look spread across his pillow. Because Kipp *had* thought about that. Now he'd never know.

"That is," he went on quickly, coming around the table to take Abby's hand in his, "I hadn't imagined Parfait would cut off quite so much."

"Sheared me like a sheep, didn't he? I can't tell you how *freeing* it is not to have that mountain of hair pressing down on my head," Abby said, withdrawing her hand as she sat down in the chair Gillett had pulled out for her. "Am I too late for dessert? Sallyann told me there'd be strawberries. I've never tasted strawberries."

Abby was trying her best to appear calm,

somewhat normal — if sitting down to dessert with her new husband and the man who had conspired to bring them together in this marriage of convenience could be considered even marginally normal.

But she knew how she looked, and she certainly did not look or even *feel* like the same woman His Lordship had proposed to, had suggested a convenient marriage to only a few short days ago.

That woman had worn an ugly gown. Her hair had been scraped back from her face, tortured into a tight bun.

Tonight, the viscount's bride wore softest rose silk against her very white skin, and diamonds around her throat, in her ears.

Tonight, his wife's hair couldn't be more than two inches long all over her head, most all of it combed toward her face, to end in carefully ragged wisps in front of her exposed ears, on her brow, with more wisps hugging her nape.

Tonight, his wife felt as if she just might be able to hold her own when he introduced her to the *ton* as his bride.

What a pity that her husband made her so very nervous.

How gratifying that he seemed as nervous as she.

"You really do look splendid, Abby," Kipp

told her as Gillett raced to place a bowl of strawberries in cream in front of her. "Really."

Kipp gave himself another mental kick. Lord, why didn't he just go into his study and shoot himself? What was the matter with him? His tongue might not be silver, but he'd always been quite adept with a compliment, real or simply polite.

So why couldn't he say anything even halfway sensible to Abby?

And, although she certainly looked better than she had — as she had said, how could she not — he couldn't really say his bride had somehow turned into a raving beauty. He'd seen his share, bedded his share, of raving beauties.

So why couldn't he take his eyes off her?

And, as long as he was cudgeling his brain for answers to unanswerable questions, when had her violet eyes grown two sizes, all but filling her face?

Kipp lifted his wineglass, drained it.

"Thank you, my lord. You were right to insist, you know. Monsieur Parfait was just what I needed," Abby told him, then closed her eyes as she took her first taste of strawberries. She let a small moan of pleasure escape her, then self-consciously licked a bit of cream from her upper lip. "Oh, this is so *good.*"

266

Kipp put his wineglass down with a thump.

Brady, who had been standing by silently, watching the exchanges between husband and wife with all the interest of a patron at a first-rate play, coughed into his hand, then made a quick excuse to leave the room.

"Sophie sends her love — from her, to Bram, to me," Brady told Abby as the two of them walked around the perimeter of the ballroom, Abby having at last been released from standing in the seemingly endless receiving line with Kipp. He'd been drawn off into some discussion of horseflesh by a florid-faced man Abby vaguely recalled being introduced as the duke of someplace or other.

She smiled now at the memory of the friendly duchess of Selbourne. "She does? What a nice woman. So friendly and caring. I sent her a note congratulating her on the birth of her son, and she sent one back telling me how lucky His Lordship is finally to have someone to watch out for him. I'm supposing you told her about the marriage? She's very protective of her friends, isn't she?"

"Some might call it interfering, or even managing," Brady said, smiling, "but protective is a much nicer word. I'm to watch over you tonight, you know, and then report back to Sophie tomorrow, to tell her about every moment of the ball. Bram would have been here as her eyes if she'd had her way, but he refuses to leave her until she can be out and about again herself. According to Sophie, that will be any day now. She's really champing at the bit, Bram says, telling him that she's a mother, not an invalid, and only a man would think he had to take to his bed for a month if he gave birth, yes? That's Sophie, for you. She says exactly what's on her mind."

He shook his head, smiled again. "Needless to say, Bram's looking a little ragged."

Abby smiled, the smile suddenly freezing to her face as she watched an absolutely *stunning*-looking redhead approach Kipp, lay her hand on his arm, smile up into his face. She'd seen the woman before, the day of the picnic, the very day Kipp had proposed to her.

"Brady?" she asked quietly, indicating with a quick tilt of her head that he should look across the ballroom to the place she had indicated. "A name, if you please."

Brady pretended to squint into the distance, although he had already seen enough to know the answer to Abby's question.

"Lady Skelton, my dear," he told her, "and of no consequence. She was already on her way out the door before you ever walked in."

"Does *she* know that?" Abby asked, as Kipp smiled at the woman, patted her hand. "Does *he?*"

"Oh, never mind that, Abby. Kipp's a born flirt. I doubt he can help himself. But that's all. If he made you a promise, he made you a promise, and he'll live up to it. *Did* he make you a promise?"

"We made promises to each other," she told him, deliberately turning her back on the sight of her husband laughing as Lady Skelton whispered in his ear. "And if you're wondering if my heart is in the least involved, let me tell you now that it is not. My pride, however, will not allow for my husband *flirting* with his lover on the very day of his marriage. I'm having enough difficulty trying to look convincing enough in my new role to have Society believe our marriage is anything more than a sham. Oh, and if I haven't told you lately, thank you very much for all you've done for me. I do appreciate it, even if I don't sound very appreciative. Now, will you please go over there and remind my husband that he is a married man? Just for this evening, at least."

"Your wish will always be my command, Abby," Brady told her, bowing. "Are you sure you want to be alone? Lots and lots of sharks swimming in the waters tonight, just hoping for the scent of blood."

"I'll be fine, Brady, I promise. In fact, I see Edwardine over there, and really do want to speak with her, see if she has recovered from her hysterics of the afternoon."

She watched Brady walk away, then sighed in relief as she slipped out an open door, onto the balcony, believing she had earned herself some blessed solitude.

Really, her head was spinning, and she doubted she'd remember a single name if anyone should ask her.

She'd had an itch on her shoulder for the past five minutes, but had fought the urge to scratch it until now, knowing that everyone in the ballroom was looking at her, *gawking* at her, whispering about her, trying to figure out why His Lordship had married her. In God's name, why had he married *her*?

No, not a time to indulge herself in some healthy scratching — not unless she wanted the gossips to conjecture that the viscount's country wife had fleas.

And then there was her family, the gaggle of Backworth-Maldons who were busily circulating among the members of the *ton,* telling anyone who would listen that, yes indeed, they were the viscountess's closest relatives, and what would you like to know about her anyway?

Swearing that bunch to silence would be about as helpful as trying to catch rainwater in a sieve.

Abby leaned against the balustrade, enjoying the feel of the cool stone against her hips. For as much as she longed for this ball to be over, she knew she was also dreading the remainder of the evening, the moment the viscount opened the door dividing their rooms and claimed his rights.

His kiss that afternoon had shocked her to her toes. She'd been kissed before, several hundred times, but obviously Harry wasn't quite as proficient at the procedure as she had believed him to be.

Or maybe she had been widowed too long, rather like a sailor too long at sea, so that any port she landed in seemed like Paradise.

She knew, from Hermione, from her late mother, that ladies of any quality weren't supposed to enjoy the marital act she had bluntly, recklessly told the viscount she herself enjoyed very much.

But she had enjoyed it, saw no shame in it and had not looked forward to living the remainder of her life chaste as a nun. Not if it was to be a very *long* life. . . .

Because he was young, and handsome, and clean, and rather nice in his own arrogant way, she could only suppose that the viscount would make a very nice lover. Considerate.

But to be able to evoke such unexpected passion in her with a single kiss?

She obviously had not given the man enough credit.

Something else bothered Abby, the knowledge that, to date, she had not done much to make her new husband's life easier for him. He had asked, and she had agreed, that they should not infringe on each other's lives more than necessary, that they each should go their own way as much as possible.

The only problem was that she couldn't feel comfortable simply living in his house, occasionally warming his bed. Not if she didn't want to feel like a kept woman, a well-recompensed whore. She had to make his house hers as well, but her befriending the servants, asking for their help, seemed to have upset His Lordship for some reason.

Just as his interference with her wardrobe, her hair, had upset her.

She'd hoped they could rub along fairly

well. Now she wondered if they were more likely to set off sparks from each other, arguments that should not be fought over situations that should not mean so much to either of them.

She closed her eyes, vowing to herself that she would be less intrusive in future, mind her own business, and stay out of the man's way. That was all he'd asked in return for giving her his name, his protection.

"If you're contemplating jumping, please allow me to assist you over the rail."

Abby turned at the sound of a woman's voice, rather husky, unnaturally melodious even in sarcasm, tinged with the vitriol of a very real hate.

"Lady Skelton," she said when she saw the woman, recognized her. "Is there some problem?"

"Problem?" Roxanne repeated. Her well-plucked eyebrows rose toward her hairline as she mocked Abby's attempt at innocence.

Roxanne approached more closely as Abby stepped away from the balustrade, walking clear around her, sizing her up, sneering as she judged her gown, sniggered at her short crop of hair.

Abby returned Roxanne's scrutiny, measuring the woman's worthiness as an opponent.

For they were opponents.

They each recognized the other as the enemy in the way women could, without really speaking, without knowing more about each other than their names. Their instincts told them they didn't like each other, not by sound, not by sight, not by association.

Like cocks set at each other in a sawdust ring, more than ready to peck and claw, draw first blood.

"Yes, a problem. Perhaps something a plate of prunes might fix?" Abby suggested, still trying to keep some sweetness in her voice, letting the sugar drip freely, turn to acid on the air.

"He's using you, you know," Roxanne said, ignoring Abby's insult. "Using you to protect himself against all the insipid little girls who thought they'd be his viscountess."

"And from all the married women who saw him in much the same way?" Abby asked, a flash of feminine insight bursting inside her skull. She watched as a flush of anger crept up Lady Skelton's throat and invaded her cheeks.

Good gracious, the woman had actually harbored aspirations of someday becoming Kipp's wife? She'd considered the scandal of divorce in order to do so? Would have expected him to go along with such a scheme?

Clearly Lady Skelton didn't know Abby's new husband as well as Abby did, and Abby knew him not very well at all.

Perhaps the viscount did know what Lady Skelton had planned for him, had hoped from him. Was Lady Skelton another unspoken reason he had decided to sacrifice himself to a marriage of convenience, just to be shed of her? Perhaps showing Merry and Jack Coltrane a happy marriage wasn't the only hidden reason for Kipp's proposal. No wonder he had hunted down what he thought was the least intrusive solution to his various dilemmas, then married it.

My, she *had* solved a multitude of problems for him, hadn't she? And he had just landed a new problem square in her lap in the form of his discarded mistress!

Abby suddenly saw herself as one of Aramintha Zane's beleaguered heroines, caught up in a web not entirely of her making, and she didn't believe the reality lived up to the romance of fiction.

Still, if she had to play a part, being a heroine wasn't all that depressing.

When Lady Skelton remained silent, Abby pressed home her point. "That is how you saw yourself, isn't it, Lady Skelton? As having the title I now hold? Such a shame. Another matronly dream dashed against the rocks. You must be devastated, not to mention mortified. To be replaced is one thing. But to be replaced by *me,* an insipid little nobody? Yes, definitely mortifying."

"You'll never hold him."

Abby reached down deep and grabbed for all her courage, then dared to be profane. All the best Aramintha Zane heroines could, when sufficiently goaded by the Evil Monster, be quite wonderfully profane at times. "Hold him? I haven't yet, no, but the evening is young, isn't it? Perhaps you'd care to check back with me in the morning?"

"Whore! My God, the country drab is nothing but a *whore.*" Roxanne lifted her hand, intent on slapping her enemy's face, only to find herself somehow turned around, her right arm pinned behind her. She felt herself being pushed toward the balustrades as Abby whispered into her ear.

"If you're contemplating jumping, please allow me to assist you over the rail. Isn't that how you said it, how you *threatened* me?"

Abby let go of the woman's arm, stepped back, smiling. My goodness, she hadn't had to resort to physical violence since the last time Harry had come home drunk and tried to push her into bed. It was nice to know she wasn't all that much out of practice.

Roxanne took one step forward, rubbing

at her shoulder, then seemed to think better of it. "I don't know why he married you, but I'm going to find out. And then, *my lady*, I'm going to see you *destroyed*."

Suddenly Abby felt weary, bone-weary. Had she thought this was going to be a convenient marriage? It had been markedly inconvenient so far, and she'd been married less than a day. She brushed past the woman, heading back toward the ballroom. "If you say so, Lady Skelton. You're certainly free to try."

She stepped into the ballroom just in time to see Iggy walking away from her very swiftly, like a man very much not wanting to be noticed.

"Damn," she said under her breath.

And she had thought this marriage would give her peace of mind, some independence? So far, all it had given her was something else to worry about, someone else to protect.

Had she been born to take care of people?

Had anyone been born to take care of *her*?

Chapter Fifteen

He'd danced with her three times. Two impersonal country dances.

And one waltz.

Abby floated around her bedchamber. Her eyes closed, her arms held out as if still within his embrace, her feet barely touching the floor as Sallyann chased after her, doing her best to undo the buttons of her gown, convince Her Ladyship that it was late, very late, and she really should be in bed.

"You should have seen me, Sallyann," Abby said, at last coming to a halt in front of her four-poster bed, her arms wrapped about the white-and-gold-painted wood, her cheek pressed against its coolness. "Oh, I was rather unsure of myself at the beginning of it, but His Lordship is quite proficient at the steps, and within moments I forgot to be nervous."

"Yes, ma'am," the maid said, releasing the last of the buttons, then coaxing Abby into letting go of the bedpost so that the rose-silk gown could slide to the floor. "Now, if your ladyship were to just *step* out of her gown? One foot, then the other. Ah, there's a love."

Freed of her gown, Abby commenced to dancing once more, oblivious to Sallyann's sigh, to Sallyann's rather worshipful smile.

"Round and round and round," Abby told the maid as she spun across the floor, kicking off her evening slippers, whirling about in her petticoats as violins played in her head.

"Their lordships, the Viscount Willoughby and his lady wife. Everyone watching, everyone whispering, everyone impressed all hollow in spite of themselves. I'm a lady now, Sallyann — a *lady*," she told the maid as she came to rest beside the bed once more, then used one of the bedposts for leverage as she all but threw herself up onto the mattress, flopped onto her back to smile up at the draperies.

She spread her arms and legs on the slippery satin coverlet, moving them about the way she had done as a child, making angels in the snow. Giggled.

And then suddenly came to her senses.

"Sallyann!" she exclaimed, sitting up, sliding her body toward the edge of the bed. "His Lordship. His Lordship could be here any moment, and here I am, in my underclothes. Quickly, help me find my night rail."

"Now there's a thought I'd never have on

my own," Sallyann teased, tittering in girlish delight as she held up Abby's best nightgown — which wasn't saying a lot, for her night wear was nothing if not practical.

Abby looked at the thing for long moments, then shrugged. "It will have to do, I suppose. But I promise you, Sallyann, tomorrow you and I will make a positive *assault* on Bond Street. I have an allowance now, you know, and I have decided to magnanimously accept His Lordship's generosity."

"And not a moment too soon," her husband said as he advanced into the room, which sent a red-faced, giggling Sallyann scurrying out the door to the hallway.

Abby looked to the night rail now heading out the door with her maid, then down at her new underclothes, a strapless, ankle-length affair that covered her bosoms — well, *half* covered them — and a second thin petticoat worn over it and tied tightly at the waist.

She shrugged, thinking she probably looked better as she was, and then smiled at her husband, feeling a sudden need to engage him in conversation. "I had a most pleasant evening, my lord. I do hope you're satisfied with my performance. And you, gazing so adoringly into my eyes as we waltzed? Although most of Society probably now believes me a witch who slipped a love potion into your wine, I think you may have convinced just as many that ours is truly a love match."

"That was the purpose of the exercise, I believe," Kipp said, doing his best to keep his gaze at eye level, not be so crass as to do an inventory of Abby's slim body as she made no attempt to cover herself. Not that he believed her to be at all shy. No, there was a lot to be said for marrying a widow, a woman already bedded, already pleasured.

And then he felt a small tic begin along his jawline, as he realized that if he did nothing else tonight he'd damn well teach this infuriatingly imperturbable woman the real meaning of pleasure.

"Would you care for some wine?" he asked her, half-turning toward his own bedchamber.

"Hmmm?" Abby hadn't been paying attention. She'd been much too busy coming to grips with the fact that her husband was standing in her bedchamber, clad in the same dressing gown she'd seen earlier, but now with his feet and legs bare, probably indicating that the rest of him was as well. The butterflies nesting in her stomach, previously in bed for the night, woke up and began to swarm.

"I said, would you care for some wine?"

She shook her head. "No, my lord, I don't need it. But if you —"

"I don't *need* it either," Kipp said, cutting her off before she angered him past all endurance. How dare she attempt to calm *him?* She could probably take all of her experience with the miserable Harry, stuff it in a thimble, and still have room for Gibbon's five-volume *The History of the Decline and Fall of the Roman Empire.* "And when are you going to stop calling me *my lord?* You're more informal with Brady, which is rather insulting, now that I think about it."

"I'm sorry, my lord — Kipp. It's just that we really don't know each other all that well, do we?"

"And you know Brady *better?*"

Abby thought about that for a moment, her brow furrowed as she sat down on the side of the bed — didn't realize she'd sat down on the side of the bed. "Brady, well, Brady's not too difficult to understand."

"And I am?" Kipp walked over to the bed, sat down beside her. Noticed, not for the first time that evening, that she smelled most delightfully of violets. "Shall I take that as a compliment, that I'm *deeper* than Brady?"

She shook her head. "No, not deeper. Brady has some twists and turns to him, I think, some secrets he keeps hidden behind that smile of his. Yours are just better hidden, I suppose."

Abby turned, looked him square in his bottomless brown eyes, decided to try extracting a secret or two from him. "For instance, I find myself having some trouble believing that your reasons for marrying me are no more than you've said they are, grateful as I am that you chose me, for I do believe I'm going to quite enjoy being a viscountess. In fact, so far, I feel that I'm really the only one benefiting from this marriage, and I know that can't be true."

She dropped her gaze, saw that their thighs were pressed close together. Amazing how easily she accepted physical intimacy from this man. She wondered why. "Perhaps that's the reason I can't yet feel as relaxed with you."

Kipp placed his hand on her knee, and she didn't flinch. "You seem fairly well *relaxed* to me."

"I've long ago learned to accept the inevitable, my lor— Kipp." She just hadn't realized how much she'd been looking forward to tonight's *inevitable*. She did, however, realize that he was teasing her again, and that he had neatly deflected her question, which also kept her from telling him about her uncomfortable interlude with Lady Skelton.

"Is that why we're here, Abby? Because it's inevitable? How very civilized. Very well then, wife, shall we get on with it?" Kipp took her hand as he drew her to her feet, kept hold of her hand as he bent to turn the covers back a little more, gestured that she should climb back up on the bed so that he could join her. Dared her to get into the bed, make good on her bargain with him, give evidence to her claim that she enjoyed "the act" very much.

Damn her if she didn't do just as he'd asked, climbing into the bed after untying her overslip, letting it drop to the floor. Leaning on his arm as she did so, still making use of his support as she climbed into the bed, giving him a very interesting view of her well-shaped bottom beneath the clingy white muslin.

She made her way to the middle of the bed, slipped her legs under the covers, folded her arms across her waist, and waited. Waited for him to join her. *Dared* him to join her. Willed herself to keep looking at him, not flinching, not showing any sign of nervousness.

Of eagerness. God help her, of eagerness.

Kipp blew a short burst of air out of his nostrils, shook his head. "I must be out of my mind," he said, more to himself than to her. He left her, walking around the room, blowing out candles until only two burned in a wall sconce, with only the glow of the fire for additional light.

And still she sat there, propped against the pillows, waiting for him in the near dark.

He didn't desire her. He really didn't. He couldn't get around her coolness, her imperturbability, her acceptance of this most intimate part of their bargain.

And he didn't like the notion that he might be judged on his performance, measured against the damnable Harry, possibly found wanting. Stung by the thought, he sent up a silent apology to every woman he'd bedded over the years, finding all of them wanting, wishing all of them had been Merry.

For he'd bedded woman after woman, longing for someone to love, someone who loved him for himself, and not because of his title or his fortune or even the prowess of his lovemaking.

Oh, yes, he was very good at making love, at pleasuring a woman. It was a talent, come to him naturally, that he hoped wouldn't desert him now, as he slipped out of his dressing gown, slid, naked, between the sheets.

And then Abby surprised him again.

"If you were to help with the laces," she said, sitting up beside him, turning her back to him, "I believe I can slip out of this contraption without further assistance."

Abby held back a sigh, knowing it had taken every last grain of courage for her to say what she'd just said, leaving her with nothing but jangled nerves as he reached for her, as she felt his fingers against her spine, as he undid the satin laces. Now, holding the opened material protectively against her breasts, she wondered where she'd ever find the courage to let go, slide the material down past her hips, leaving herself naked, and vulnerable, and suddenly without any emotion save a maidenly fear she hadn't experienced since her first wedding night.

Still, the only thing worse would be to have *him* undress her.

Kipp bit back a laugh as Abby all but dived under the covers, watching as the satin coverlet began to move up and down — the poke of a knee here, the stab of an elbow there. Then his smile disappeared as Abby reappeared once more, very neatly keeping her breasts concealed as she extracted a white bundle of cloth from beneath the covers, then flung it toward the floor.

She folded her hands on the covers, tipped up her chin, and looked straight at him. A slim, almost too-thin woman with rather remarkable shoulder blades and creamy white, unblemished skin; with the hint of an intriguing shadow between her breasts, a mop of badly mussed hair, and her violet eyes wide and panicked even as the defiant chin tipped a fraction higher.

She lifted her shoulders, dropped them. Wet her lips with the tip of her tongue. Blinked once; then said quite primly: "I'm ready."

That tore it. Kipp couldn't contain himself any longer. He threw his head back against the pillows and laughed . . . and laughed . . . and laughed.

Until she hit him, of course.

Punched him, actually, square in the chest.

"This isn't funny," she warned him, feeling near to tears. She punched him again. "This is very, *very* serious. We're consummating a marriage here, remember? Sealing our bargain? God, but you're insufferable!"

He caught her fist with one hand, pulled her against him. Pulled her close, still laughing, even as she still fumed, her violet eyes turned nearly black with passion.

What a pity that her passion seemed to be directed at hurting him, possibly maiming him for life.

She squirmed against him, mindless of their nakedness, trying to get away, trying to free her hands — he'd gotten hold of both of them somehow — so that she could pummel him into a jelly.

And then something odd happened.

She noticed his smile. The little crinkles at the edges of his eyes.

He wondered if her eyes would glow like deepest amethyst when she became aroused with passions other than anger.

They both shifted their bodies slightly, neither of them able to pretend they weren't pressed together, chest to knees.

Kipp looked down to where their chests met, to where the covers tangled around them. Two pale, soft mounds were molded against him, twin hints of pink visible for a moment, then hidden as Abby took another quick, shallow breath.

She'd stopped fighting him, her fists relaxing as he kept hold of her wrists. Only her breathing betrayed her, buoyed him.

He looked up at her again, his smile entirely gone, his head feeling slightly woozy as all of his blood had seemingly decided to leave it, to travel to more southerly regions.

She returned his gaze, not blinking at all now, the centers of her eyes wide and black, her breath coming rapidly from between her slightly parted lips.

She said nothing. She thought nothing.

She felt everything.

Kipp let go of her wrists to bury one hand in her short mop of blond hair. He drew her down, drew her closer, and she didn't resist.

Still looking at her, still not saying a word, he lifted his head slightly and caught her mouth with his own.

Somewhere, in the darkness above the canopied bed, fireworks exploded, the bright light and white fire raining down on them both, igniting them, making them hot to the touch, setting off smaller explosions that rocked them both to their cores.

Whatever inhibitions Abby thought she had been feeling, whatever nameless fears she'd had, were blasted into tiny bits as Kipp ground his mouth against hers hungrily, as his free hand found her buttocks, pulled her tight against his definitely aroused manhood.

He let her go for a moment, looked at her with a curiosity that baffled her, then rolled her onto her back, his mouth once more against hers, his tongue slipping between her lips.

She reached up, slid her arms around his shoulders, splayed her fingers against his skin, as eager for his closeness as he appeared to be for hers.

Kiss after drugging kiss. Their hands moving, their breaths mingling, their bodies separating slightly, so that Kipp could trail kisses down her throat, across her chest. Claim her breasts with hands and mouth and tongue.

Abby arched her head back, lifting herself to him, her hands now gripping his head, urging him to further intimacy as her nipples puckered beneath his touch, as she felt hot shafts of pleasure tracing from her breasts to her belly, and lower.

Kipp adjusted himself slightly, moved one hand lower, trailing his fingers across her flat belly, sliding them in between her legs, finding her center.

He couldn't believe himself, couldn't believe her. She was liquid beneath his fingers, she was fire, she was demanding, she gave and gave and gave.

Her slim body had more angles than he'd been accustomed to, but those angles intrigued him. The jut of her pelvic bones, the narrowness of her hips. But she was also soft, so soft. Her long waist intrigued him, the slit of her navel as he moved lower, flicked at it with his tongue even as she all but sat up somehow, so that she could still hold him close, nearly brand him with her short, rounded nails.

There was nothing calculated about the way this woman gave herself to him. Took from him. No false modesty, no protestations against the intimacy his seeking, searching hands had found. No posing, or posturing, or words of love that couldn't possibly be believed.

Just this urgency, this so sudden and overwhelming passion, this mind-searing *heat* between them.

And then she pushed at him, so that he was caught unawares as he half fell onto his side, as she looked at him with those deep violet eyes, as she reached for him, cupped him in her hand, weighed his heaviness against her palm.

Without a word, she drew him to her. Without a sound, she opened her legs to him. With only a single soft sigh, she closed her eyes as he entered her, filled her, began to move deep inside her.

His passion grew, fueled by hers, encouraged by the way she lifted her slim hips to him, as she wrapped her legs around him, high on his hips.

And she was right. They'd already traveled eons past any thought of gentle seduction. Not tonight. Not when their passion burned this hot, this urgent.

Two strangers, come together for convenience, using each other, and not the least bit apologetic.

Sharing their bodies if not their lives.

Kipp began to move inside her. Drawing back, plunging deep. Moving more quickly, going deeper as she seemed somehow to relax her body even as her arms and legs held him tightly.

Allowing him every intimacy.

He held her, held her tightly, and kept moving as she adjusted each movement of her own hips to the pace he had set, then stepped up the pace on her own.

He felt her nails begin to dig into his back, and he raised his head to see that her eyes were open once more. Open, and full of wonderment. A dawning realization. Surprise liberally mixed with pleasure.

He smiled as he captured her mouth once more, as their tongues began a duel that mimicked the thrust and parry that seemed to lift them both, make them weightless as they rose and fell together, faster and faster, heading toward the completion that rushed toward them with equal force.

Take that, Harry, old boy, Kipp screamed inside his brain as Abby stiffened in his embrace. She held her body very still for a moment, precipitously balancing on the threshold of ecstasy, before he felt her throbbing against him, a rhythmic clutch and release that seemed to go on forever and ever, even as she moaned softly into his mouth.

And then she turned frantic in his arms. Pulling on his shoulders, her heels digging into his back as she moved beneath him, urging him on, and on, and on. Sensing that he needed her with him as he climbed his own crest, leapt off the edge, spiraling down into the valley beneath. Giving back, allowing him to take, moving with him, against him, as he gave in to his own passion. Riding her hard, riding her deep, finding his own pleasure.

And when it was over, when they both lay there, their breaths ragged, their bodies still shuddering, the impact of what had just happened, how it had happened, slowly seeped into their combined consciousness.

They both, at some unspoken signal, rolled away from each other, lay back, looked up at the silken canopy.

"Well," Kipp said at last, having had some

difficulty finding his voice, "that certainly was . . . was *interesting*."

The only sound from the other side of the wide bed was that of the satin cover being pulled tight to the bottom of Abby's chin as she sank lower in the bed.

That was good. No excuses, no reproaches, no — thank God — ridiculous requests that he say something wonderful, no gushing declaration that, my goodness, she hadn't known herself to be in love with him, but now she did.

Still, when Abby did speak, he found himself wondering if having her tell him she'd fallen in love with him might not have been better.

"You aren't intending to sleep here, are you?" she asked him, her question more of a statement, actually more of an order than a request.

He had been, actually. The thought of waking up beside his new wife, finding out if she could be as passionate in the morning as she could be in the dark *had* crossed his mind.

"No, of course not," he answered quickly, throwing back the covers and slipping from the bed, looking at her as he slowly, deliberately bent to retrieve his dressing gown, slipped his arms into the sleeves. "Good night."

"Good night," Abby said, then watched as he walked away, tall and strong, the man who had just shown her soaring heights of physical pleasure she hadn't known existed.

But had that pleasure changed her feelings for him? Did she actually *have* feelings for him?

What sort of depraved creature would she be if she could take pleasure from him, give pleasure in return, and *not* have feelings for him?

Yes, she did have feelings for him. She desired him. Definitely. More now than ever. She'd known from the very beginning that it would be no hardship for her to lie in his arms, feel his hands on her body. But desire was not love. Which was a good thing, for he'd probably run from her, screaming, if she did betray their agreement and fall in love with him. If she began making emotional demands on him, the man who was still in love with another man's wife.

No. She'd be his convenient wife. Pretend to believe he had married her because a marriage of convenience was simpler than dealing another single moment with the marriage mart that was London Society. Help him in his as-yet-unspoken desire to make his good friends believe him happy, in love with his new bride.

And more. She'd give him children to fulfill his deathbed promise to his mother.

She'd love those children with all of her heart, and pray they be blessed with at least a half dozen of them.

She'd see her relatives settled, secure, for the first time in their lives.

And she'd enjoy being a viscountess. Very much so.

She'd do all of those things.

But she would also protect herself. She would *not* fall in love with him.

Kipp had slept like the proverbial log, a realization that surprised him when he finally woke, just after nine, to see his valet bringing in a tray holding his breakfast.

He dressed with more haste than care, eager to get himself downstairs to confront his wife who, his valet had told him, had been up at dawn and had partaken of her own breakfast downstairs an hour earlier, at the least.

Telling his valet that he, too, would be taking his breakfast downstairs in future, Kipp headed for the stairs while still smoothing down the sleeves of his jacket, wondering how Abby would react to seeing him. Would she be shy, ashamed of her passion of the previous night? He rather

296

thought so. He almost hoped so.

And he was about to be disappointed.

"Good morning," Abby said cheerfully, as they met in the entrance hall, both of them headed for the main drawing room. She looked quite animated, dressed in the same gown she'd been married in, her creamy skin a shade pinker in her cheeks, her eyes bright and glowing. "I hope you slept well. I know I did. Such a lovely mattress, not in the least lumpy, and a far cry from the one I slept on in Half Moon Street, or in Syston, for that matter."

Damn her! Was she really going to act as if nothing had happened between them? Pretend she hadn't moaned her pleasure into his mouth, that her hand hadn't held him, urged him on — that he hadn't aroused her, driven her nearly crazy with desire, and then satisfied that desire?

Yes, it appeared that was just what she was going to do.

But he wasn't going to let her get away with dismissing him as if he were nothing more than a convenience.

He took hold of her arm at the elbow just before she could enter the drawing room, spun her about, brought her up against his chest. "Is that all you have to say, Abby? Is your new mattress the *only* reason you slept so well?"

Abby whispered through gritted teeth, "What are you *doing?* Can't you find some other time and place to torment me for not falling at your feet, thanking you for whatever you think I should be thanking you for? There are three footmen standing behind you, do you know that? And Edwardine, she's —"

"We're married now, Abby, and the footmen can go hang," he told her, all but growled at her, then slid a hand behind her head and pulled her close for his kiss.

Abby's kneecaps melted. Melted clear through, so that she had to take hold of his jacket lapels and hang on for dear life or else crumple ignominiously to the floor, which would delight him no end, she was certain.

He tasted so good. His body was so firm against hers, one of his thighs actually insinuating itself between her legs.

She longed to have him take her in his arms, carry her upstairs.

She longed to strangle him.

"Abby? *Abbbb-eeeee!*"

Kipp pulled back, startled, but still holding his wife close to him. "What in blazes? What a squawk. Have you a parrot you didn't tell me about? Sophie has a parrot, but he's been banished to the country for conversation unbecoming to a

298

polite society. Abby?"

Abby took a deep breath, mentally beat herself back into sanity, and succeeded in extricating herself from Kipp's embrace. "It's Edwardine. I tried to tell you —"

Kipp looked over Abby's head, peered into the drawing room. "Tell me what? That's she's stuck herself with a hatpin? And what's she doing here in the first place?"

"She's crying, mostly," Abby told him, sighing. The dratted child had arrived almost an hour before, and she'd not stopped crying since — except to remind Abby a half dozen times that she'd promised to be of assistance if she ever needed her. *Promised!*

"Crying? That's crying? Good God." Kipp felt instantly uncomfortable, as most gentlemen did around crying females.

"Crying *and* unhappy, Kipp. That's louder."

"Well, pardon me. Thank you so much for that clarification. I, in my simple male stupidity, thought she might be *delighted* and crying. Why the devil is she crying and unhappy?"

"*Abbb-eee?* You said you'd be *right back!* I hear voices. Are you out there? I'm sure you're *out there!* I'm coming out there *right now,* see if I don't!"

The sound of a table tipping over and the

crash of breaking glass was followed by another hysterical shriek from the drawing room.

Abby winced. "That was probably the china shepherdess on the table nearest the spot where she was last sitting, hopefully not a piece for which you have some emotional attachment. Edwardine can't see more than five feet ahead of her nose at the best of times, you know."

Kipp swore low in his throat. Had he really come downstairs hoping for a pleasant morning?

"Now, with that river of tears she's shedding," Abby continued doggedly, "I'm surprised she doesn't think I'm one of the portraits on the wall, and just shriek to it. On second thought, that might be better. She could shriek, and I could go into the morning room, put up my feet, and have another cup of tea."

"I'm gratified to see that I was right, Abby. You don't ruffle easily. However, if I may repeat my question, already dreading the answer — why is your niece crying? Even more to the point, why is she crying *here?*"

Abby sighed, knowing she was about to put a rather large ripple in the calm pond Kipp envisioned his new life as being, then

300

said, "Why is she crying, Kipp? She's crying — sobbing, actually — and unhappy because she's sixteen. Sobbing and being unhappy is what sixteen-year-old girls do best. Although I will admit that this is the first time I can remember Edwardine showing such overt signs of melancholy. Now, please, if you don't mind, I'd like to go to her before she knocks over that lovely blue vase on the table beside the satin chair."

"Oh, I could *die*, Abby! I could just *perish!* And nobody would *care!*"

"There she goes again," Kipp said, wincing as Edwardine's hysterics threatened to shatter all the windows in the house. "Were you like that at sixteen?"

Abby shook her head as she recalled, just for an instance, exactly how she had been at sixteen.

Where she had been. Married to a man who drank his meals and wagered away her entire dowry in a single throw of the dice. Learning that young love was a dream easily shattered by reality. Learning quickly that tears and regrets got her precisely nowhere. Learning to take the crumbs she was offered as she buried her single surviving parent within months of her marriage and doggedly made the best of a bad situation.

Abby smiled up at her new husband, refusing to let him see that his question had bothered her. "No, not at all. I believe I was extremely levelheaded, without a dollop of hysteria to be found anywhere. I should also imagine that I'm the exception that proves the rule. Now, please —"

"*There* you are!" Edwardine had somehow made her way to the doorway and was now leaning against it, pointing a finger in Abby's general direction.

She was dressed all in palest blue, her blond curls in quite attractive disarray, her blue eyes looking much like drenched flowers. A man with fewer years and much less sense than Kipp would have been instantly struck to the heart and promised her anything to make her happy. He, however, only found her to be very much in the way, not that he had any crushing need to have his wife to himself like some ardent bridegroom or anything like that.

Edwardine looked in Kipp's direction for a moment, not bothering to say hello to him, then turned on Abby, pouting. "I have *nobody* now that you've deserted me, Abby. *Nobody*. The uncles care only for themselves and their schemes, Iggy is a selfish, heartless brute, and Mama cares only for Cuddles. I'm not loved as much as a . . . as a *dog!*"

"Poor thing," Abby whispered to Kipp as

she held out her arms to her niece. "She has a point."

"Several, I'd imagine," Kipp said, wondering if he'd appear a complete cad if he just turned on his heels and left the house until Abby had everything back under control.

Edwardine, still looking as beautiful in hysterics as she did when smiling as she myopically made her way through her usually happy life, stumbled into Abby's arms. "You promised, Abby. You *promised.*"

"Abby," Kipp asked warily, "what exactly did you promise her?"

"And Iggy . . . Iggy *swore* you'd let me move in with you. He said a promise is a promise, and you'd never break your promise to me. Oh, Abby, I don't know what I'd *do* without you."

"Her brother said *what?*"

"Iggy put this idea into your head, Edwardine? Oh, isn't that just like him — straight down to his nasty, conniving toes. But he's right, drat him. I did promise to help you if you ever needed my assistance."

Kipp raked a hand through his hair. "You're not thinking — you *are,* aren't you? Oh, sweet Christ! Abby —"

"Go away, Kipp. I'll handle this."

"How? By moving her in here?"

Abby looked at him over the golden curls that tickled her nose so that she felt a sneeze coming on. She hadn't really thought about this particular solution before now, but having Edwardine in Grosvenor Square, just for a little while, might not be a bad idea. At least then she wouldn't be *alone* with her new husband. "I don't know. Perhaps, but only for a few days, until she and Hermione come to some agreement."

"Never!" Edwardine shrieked into Abby's badly abused ear. "She threatens not to go *anywhere* if Cuddles isn't *invited.* I won't be able to go *anywhere,* Abby. Not *anywhere! Never again!* I'll die an *old maid!"*

"Really?" Kipp asked, not commenting on Edwardine's dire predictions on her fate, but on Abby's consideration of moving the inane little watering pot in with them. "And if I forbid it, will you listen?"

"What?" Abby asked, believing Kipp may have said something. "What did you say?"

Gillett appeared, seemingly out of no-where, and offered Kipp his hat, cane, and gloves.

Abby relaxed as best she could with her niece clinging to her like a very damp limpet. "Oh, good. Thank you, Gillett. It is perhaps better if His Lordship could escape until I have this settled."

Slapping his hat onto his head, Kipp turned for the door, muttering. "Yes, very good of you, Gillett. Seeing as how I believe I'd be best served by going off to find the earl of Singleton — and murdering him."

"If you must," Abby called after him as cheerfully as possible, not really having heard a word he'd said.

Chapter Sixteen

The many clocks in the mansion had all struck ten, the London skies had gone dark, and the viscount had still not returned to Grosvenor Square. He'd sent home a note, addressed to Abby, informing her that "pressing business" would keep him away until the evening, and that she should dine without him.

Abby had read the note, wondering, if only for a moment, if her husband had run away from home. If she had chased him away.

It had been a rather heady thought, actually, until she'd realized that she'd miss him.

Edwardine was tucked up in one of the guest chambers — one situated on an entirely separate floor from Kipp's and Abby's bedchambers, sleeping the sleep of the content and well fed.

She'd been comforted. She'd gone along to Bond Street and been treated to a new bonnet, as well as a parasol she had to have or else *wither and die*.

She'd sat in the drawing room before dinner, smiling rather smugly, as footmen

Abby had dispatched to Half Moon Street returned with a small pile of luggage and Edwardine's own note, this one from her mother alluding to the poor abused woman having unknowingly nursed a snake at her bosom. There was even a postscript, asking Edwardine if she had by chance seen Cuddles's favorite toy, one of Bailey's cast-off bedroom slippers. This addendum, Edwardine had declared feelingly, had only served to prove her point. If she could walk on all fours, bark, and drool, and perhaps soil a few carpets, *then* her mother would love her.

Still, the child wasn't crying anymore. That could only be considered a good thing. All that was left to do was to figure out how to eject the transplanted and very quickly rooted Edwardine out of the house. That could take some time, but Abby felt sure she'd think of something.

So far, unfortunately, that "something" had involved the arrival of yet another pile of luggage and another Backworth-Maldon in Grosvenor Square. Not that Abby wanted to think about that right now.

Abby and Sallyann had finally finished with putting away Abby's rather extensive purchases, including several quite fetching nightgowns Sallyann had vowed were the cat's whiskers and bound to drive His Lordship into going down onto his knees and thanking his Creator for also having created seamstresses with clever needles.

That's how it stood with Abby and Sallyann. They'd become friends, because Abby really didn't quite know how to be lady of the manor, and she really didn't want to learn. What she needed was friends, allies. Besides, Sallyann filled a void Abby hadn't known existed in her life, that of a confidante who truly seemed to understand that a new bride in a strange household might be very much in need of a friend.

Sallyann had helped Abby with her bath, then had chosen the nightgown and dressing robe she considered her own personal favorite, a sheer white creation with puffed sleeves and decorated with tiny, pink-silk rosebuds at both neckline and hem. She'd then wadded up the last of the tissue-paper wrappings and left her mistress to sit beside the fire, her slippered feet resting on an embroidered footstool, a cup of tea on the table beside her.

Abby sat there for some minutes, sipping her tea, wondering if Kipp would ever come home, and if he'd visit her in her bedchamber when he did.

Would this be best — letting him find her

sitting here, looking very much like she'd been waiting for him, perhaps ready to ask him for some explanation of his daylong defection of his new bride.

No. Probably not.

She'd be wiser just to get into bed, feign sleep. That way, if he did enter her rooms, he would be caught in a dilemma. Would he be a gentleman, and simply tiptoe away, closing the door behind him? Or would he be a boorish, randy goat, waking his bride and demanding his husbandly rights?

Yes. She found the thought of his confusion, his possible frustration, quite comforting.

Besides, what she had to tell him could most certainly wait until morning. Especially since she already knew he wasn't going to like what she had to say, not one bit.

Swallowing down the last of her tea, Abby stood up and began walking toward her bed, snuffing out candles as she went, already untying the satin ribbons of her dressing gown.

But, before she could hop into bed, there was a knock at the connecting door. She hesitated, half-in, half-out of her dressing gown, debating whether or not to quickly snuggle beneath the covers and pretend she was asleep.

She couldn't. She'd made a bargain, and if the man wanted to make love to her, well, that was part of their bargain. Even if they hadn't spoken to each other all day. Even if his kiss of that morning had embarrassed her as much as it had thrilled her. Even if he only wanted to bed her so that he could father a child on her, then probably parade her and her swollen belly in front of his friends to prove that, yes indeed, he was a happy, happy man.

Even if she'd been hoping for the past hour that he'd come home, that he'd knock on the door, that he'd want to be with her tonight. Hold her, kiss her, take her back to those never-before visited heights of carnal pleasure, the memory of which had haunted her all day long, so that she'd found herself smiling at nothing, lost in thoughts that had little to do with Edwardine or any of her problems.

Shrugging back into the dressing gown, Abby turned toward the door, and called out, "Come in!"

A moment later the door opened, and Kipp entered the room, still clad in the clothes he'd left in that morning. "Hello, wife," he said, openly admiring her new nightclothes. She really had cleaned up well, with that mop of hair gone, with decent clothes on her back. And he rather enjoyed the new shyness in her eyes, shyness mixed with expectation. Yes, she was becoming more *human* by the hour, and he liked that. He liked that very much. "Don't you look lovely."

"I should," she answered, avoiding his gaze as she walked over to the pair of chairs flanking the fireplace and sat down, arranging her skirts about her. Then her violet eyes twinkled, and he remembered how she had looked last night, as he had stared deeply into those eyes, and seen the passion there. "I believe I've put you very seriously in debt today."

"And not a penny of it badly spent, I'm sure," Kipp returned politely as he disappeared into his own rooms for a moment, then took up the facing chair, sitting down and placing a quite large square box on his lap. He felt rather like an idiot schoolboy hoping the paltry gift that was all his allowance could afford might please his adored parent.

That thought unnerved him slightly, and he rushed into speech. "I've been spending too, wife. Would you like to see what I've bought for you? Answer quickly please, as it's very heavy."

Abby looked at the box, tied up so nicely

with a broad blue ribbon. It was so wide, so tall, that she could barely see his twinkling eyes overtop the lid. She began to relax. Enjoy herself. "Why?"

"Why? Why is it heavy? No, I somehow doubt that's your question. Why did I get you a gift? Because I believe it is customary for a groom to give his bride a gift, that's why. I wasted most of the day with Brady as he tried to talk me into jewels, or furs, even your own curricle. Although we did spend a few interesting hours at Tattersall's before I decided against that last one. I finally sent him away and made my own choice. Don't you want to see it, or would you rather we both sit here until we can hear the sound of my knee bones breaking?"

Intrigued in spite of herself, Abby motioned for him to put the box on the floor between them, then went to her knees beside it and pulled open the ribbon. She lifted the lid and the sides of the box fell open, exposing a large, mahogany chest inlaid with a rather intricate oriental design picked out in ivory.

"What is it?" she asked, smoothing her hands over the wood, tracing the design on the lid. "It's beautiful, but I haven't the faintest notion —"

Kipp gave in to his own excitement. He'd

never bought a gift like this before for a woman, certainly no woman he'd taken to his bed. But this gift had seemed somehow right for Abby. He didn't know why he knew this, didn't want to investigate his reasoning, but he'd been pleased with himself ever since he'd first laid eyes on the thing.

He joined her on the hearth rug, comfortable as any child in the relaxed atmosphere of the nursery, one leg caught up beneath him, the other outstretched, bent at the knee, all his consequence forgotten. How long had it been since he'd seen anything but avarice in a woman's eyes? How long since he'd felt such pleasure in giving a gift?

His cravat was coming undone, Abby noticed as she tried to avoid his smile, his very open, boyish smile. My, but the man appeared pleased with himself!

"Here, I'll lift the lid," he said, then did so, all while watching her face, waiting for her reaction. She had the most mobile, expressive face.

Even if he did sometimes wonder if he might have somehow married more than one woman — all of them housed in this slight, slim creature who could never be called beautiful but whose face and form intrigued him, seemed to draw him to her because he wanted to know what she might be thinking, what she might be feeling. What she might next decide to do, or who she might next decide to be.

As Kipp raised the hinged lid Abby noticed that the side of the box facing her was actually composed of two doors, behind which were a half dozen drawers holding, of all things, game pieces.

Abby's smile was wide and immediate as she reached inside the box, first opening the drawer that held six small lead horses and jockeys Kipp quickly explained were pieces used in something called the game of the race.

She held up two of them, marveling in the detail of the pieces, the bright colors. "I don't see a wind-up key. How do they race?"

"They don't," Kipp told her, scooting on his haunches until he was sitting beside Abby and could reach into the drawer to extract the ivory dice used in the game. "You advance them across the board yourself with each roll of the dice. I remember playing the game with my father as a child, and people in Society still play it, sometimes for ridiculously high sums of money."

But Abby wasn't really listening. She was much too busy opening the other drawers, inspecting their contents. There were five bell and hammer cards, a hammer, and the eight dice used for the game. A fascinating set of double-six dominoes constructed of bone. A cribbage board. A bezique, and two whist markers. Several beautifully decorated decks of cards.

And then she lifted the second, inner lid — having already noticed that the first held a chessboard tied inside it with leather straps.

"Oh . . . oh, they're *beautiful!*" she exclaimed as the chess pieces were revealed. Carved in ivory and jade, they were more art than game pieces, and she lifted out a delicately formed knight and his horse resting on a vaselike base, the entire piece being at least eight inches high.

She would have removed one of the much larger kings, the queens, but she was too awed by their fragile beauty even to touch them.

"And this is for me?" she asked at last, blinking back sudden tears. "All of this is for me?"

Kipp took the knight from her nerveless fingers and replaced it in its velvet-lined compartment. "Unless, of course, Brady's right, and you'd rather have jewelry?"

"Brady couldn't be more wrong," Abby told him as she replaced the horses and jockeys, closed up the drawers and doors, lowered the lid back into place. She put her hands on the lid once more, rubbing her fingers across it, all but caressing the wood. "Thank you, Kipp, from the bottom of my heart. I'll treasure this for all of my life."

He helped her to her feet. "But you won't lock it away to keep it safe, now will you? Because I thought we could spend some time together with the games, get to know each other a little better. Do you know how to play chess? I could teach you."

Abby tipped her head to one side, lifted a hand to stroke Kipp's face. How wonderful it felt to feel so free to touch him. "You really are a nice man, aren't you?" she said, marveling at how lucky she was, how very lucky she was. "And, yes, I do know how to play chess," she ended, playfully tapping her fingertips against his cheek, "and I will thoroughly enjoy beating you all hollow."

"Ha! A challenge. Would you care to make this interesting, my lady?" Kipp asked her, very much in charity with this woman who might possibly become his good friend. "A small wager, perhaps?"

Abby stepped back, wagged a finger at him. "No, you cannot toss Edwardine out on her very pretty little nose if you beat me. That *is* what you have in mind, isn't it?"

Kipp's smile faded, as did his thought that

they might take the chessboard to bed with them, then improvise penalties for the loss of each piece.

Damn, but he'd forgotten about the niece. "She's here, then? I'd thought you'd be able to settle things without going to that particular extreme."

"So did I," Abby answered honestly — but not completely. "I mean, I know that you want your life to remain as much as it was before our marriage, and I know that I wanted to see my relatives settled and most definitely out of sight, at least for most of the year . . ."

"But neither one of us is going to get our wish. Is that what you're saying?"

"No, that's *not* what I'm saying," Abby answered, suddenly feeling out of sorts with this man who had just pleased her with his thoughtful gift. "*You* will go on as always, living your own life just as if you are not now a married man. That was our bargain, wasn't it? That's just what you did today, isn't it? Going off with Brady, not giving a thought to the half dozen invitations we might have accepted for this evening. It's *I* who has just figured out that I won't be shed of my Backworth-Maldon relatives until I do more than simply toss your money at them in hopes that will solve all their problems."

Kipp grinned, amused by her chagrin. Because, although he'd never let her know it, he wasn't all that certain he had gotten everything he'd wanted out of their bargain. Perhaps he had gotten *more* than he bargained for . . . and liked it, even if he didn't know quite what to do with it. "So everything isn't all sweetness and light for you yet, my dear viscountess? What a pity."

"With that remark, I imagine it would be fruitless of me to appeal to you for help in any way?"

Kipp bobbed his head a time or two, smiling evilly. "We each go our own ways, wasn't that what we said? So, no, I don't think I'm going to help you. If we're yet again recalling my motivations, I believe one of the reasons I proposed marriage to you had a lot to do with your independent mind, and your seeming ability to ride herd on a group as demanding as your relatives. You appeared to be someone who could promise me a placid existence."

"Which would leave me to settle any of my problems on my own, in my own time, in my own way?"

He pretended to think about this for a few moments, knowing that he probably wasn't concentrating as he should — not when he remembered that her bed was only a few steps away, the covers already turned down for the night. "In your own time, in your own way? All right. That sounds feasible."

Abby narrowed her eyelids, glared at him. Remembered the small piece of news she hadn't yet told him. "As long as I don't complicate *your* life."

He nodded once more, his eyes twinkling, his grin making her long to slap him, or kiss him. "Definitely."

"Good," Abby said at last, untying the sash to her dressing gown, shrugging it from her shoulders so that it puddled at her feet, revealed the sheer nightgown — and the outline of her slim body as she stood in front of the light of the fire. "Now, if that's settled?"

He reached for her, snagged her small waist with both hands. "It occurs to me, wife, that we're well suited in our appetites."

"Possibly," Abby answered, as he then lifted her in his arms, carried her over to the bed. "Either that," she dared to tease him, "or I've already got enough on my plate without giving you any reason to embarrass me by taking a mistress within a week of our wedding."

Kipp lowered her onto the bed, followed her down. "Liar," he breathed into her hair. "You couldn't care less if I took a mistress, as long as I show up here several nights a week. Admit it, Abby, you simply enjoy this," he said, kissing her throat, sliding a hand onto her breast. "And this," he continued, lightly pinching at her nipple through the sheerness of her gown. "And this," he breathed into her mouth before molding his lips against hers for a hard, drugging kiss.

He pulled back, smiled as he saw the deep violet of her eyes mirroring the physical arousal she made no effort to hide. "I can't tell you how pleased I am by your honest passion."

She melted against him, an instant heat blossoming low in her belly, her needs immediately awakened, already longing to be satisfied.

"You enjoy being touched," he told her, his hand sweeping down her body, kneading at her hip, feeling the convulsive ripple of her skin as she shivered beneath him. "You enjoy touching. You probably agreed to this marriage so that you could be touched. Held. Pleasured. It wasn't for the money, the position. None of it. Here I was, thinking I'd wooed you with my wealth, my title. But you agreed for *this*. Didn't you?"

Abby couldn't answer him. Refused to answer him. Because he was right. Right, and yet so wrong. Because she wouldn't have married just anyone who asked her — not that anyone would have asked her. She'd seen the good in Kipp, his kindness, his vulnerability.

She'd felt compassion for him, and a kinship with him, because of his heartbreak, because she'd had a heartbreak of her own, even as his physical beauty drew her to him, had fostered many an unmaidenly dream in her head.

She'd imagined what it would be like if she allowed herself to fall in love with him, what their life could be if he ever came to love her in return.

And if she told him any of that, he'd hate her, so she took refuge in ridiculousness.

"Are you really going to keep your boots on?" she asked him as he pulled up her gown, slid his fingertips along the inside of her thigh. "How novel."

"Damn," Kipp said, drawing back, pulling down her nightgown so that it covered her hips once more. How had he gotten so carried away that he'd forgotten he was still in his clothes? "Obviously I didn't come in here tonight to do more than present you with my gift. If you'll excuse me for a moment?"

Abby bit her bottom lip, trying not to laugh. "Certainly."

He stood up, stripping off his jacket, his cravat, beginning to unbutton his shirt.

"And your boots?" Abby teased, already slipping out of the bed and pointing him toward a chair. "I think you might need help with those, don't you?"

"Ah, a wife *and* a valet. What a grand bargain I've made." He sat down, a smile of his own playing around his mouth.

Before Abby could think about what she was doing, she motioned for him to lift his right leg, then straddled it, her back to him, knowing from the nights she'd had to help a drunken Harry off with his boots that she would soon feel Kipp's left boot against her buttocks, giving her a helpful push as she pulled.

Kipp hesitated, his left foot raised, his innate good manners warring with the excitement he felt, the naughty mischief mingled with that excitement. Then he placed his boot square against Abby's hindquarters, waited for her to begin tugging, and straightened his leg.

She landed on the carpet a good six feet in front of him with a breathless *"oof!"* his right boot still in her hands. She tossed it behind her, over her head, so that it clunked on the floor.

"How very dignified," she announced as

she clambered to her feet, brushed her hands against each other, and motioned for him to raise his left leg. "Shall we try that again?"

"Really?" He stuck out his foot, grinned. "I'm game if you are."

"Oh, I am," Abby said, advancing toward him. She took hold of his boot at heel and toe, then yanked hard, so that Kipp, already somewhat off-balance, slid off the chair, his eyes wide with surprise as he landed on his rump on the floor.

"I suppose I deserved that," he said as he looked up at Abby. She stood above him, her hands on her hips, laughing in genuine enjoyment. Her short blond hair and large violet eyes gave her the look of a wood sprite, a mischievous fairy. A very seductive fairy clad in gossamer, her small, pert breasts pushing at that gossamer, a shadowy cleft visible between her thighs. Those firm white thighs, those long, straight, *strong* legs that had grasped him so tightly he could still remember how she had captured him, his delight in having been captured.

He levered himself backwards, sitting up against the legs of the chair as he shrugged out of his shirt, then held out his arms to her. "Come here, wife."

She shook her head, the mop of hair slapping against her cheeks, then settling once more in a sleek helmet that showed her even but quite ordinary features to such extraordinary advantage.

"Uh-uh," she mumbled, backing up a pace, two paces. Giggling like a child, her violet eyes glowing with all the knowledge of a woman.

"But I'm your master, and I command you," Kipp told her, doing his best to be stern.

Abby tipped her head to one side, repeating his last statement inside her head. "You know, I believe I remember reading something very like that. Oh! Now I remember. *The Corsair's Command, Or Tales of an Englishwoman in Travail.* You know, it took me several chapters before I realized that Travail wasn't some exotic foreign country. Wasn't that silly?"

"Rather," Kipp answered, tugging at his remaining boot with all his might, finally succeeding in dislodging it. He had to be more careful, remember not to quote himself in front of his well-read wife. Aramintha Zane was his secret, his indulgence, and he did not feel ready to share "her" existence with Abby. He stood up, clad only in his hose and pantaloons, his chest bare . . . and wondered if he might look at all "piratelike."

"Yes," Abby told him, still backing up, still unable to take her gaze off Kipp's wide expanse of chest, very much admiring the way he'd cocked his fists against his hips as he stood with his feet apart, his blond head thrown back as he stared at her. Smiled at her. Stepped closer to her.

"It — it was Miss Aramintha Zane," she went on, wishing she didn't sound quite so nervous, so defensive. "You know — the author? I remember that line, or something very much like it, from her book about a character named Lucinda Pomeroy. Silly book, entirely too far-fetched and romantic, but there was nothing else to hand, so I read it. It — it was Hermione's book, you understand, not mine at all."

Kipp was careful to keep his expression bland as he thought the lady doth protest too much. Was she embarrassed at possibly being taken for a romantic? Yes, of course she was.

He advanced another step, so that Abby had no recourse but to step back, drawing ever closer to the bed. "I must confess, I don't read novels either. More for women, don't you think? Except for you, of course, as you're not the least romantic. But I admit to some small interest. Tell me, this Miss Pomeroy — she was captured by corsairs?

325

How dreadful for her, I'm sure."

"Yes," Abby said, nodding. "Yes, it was. Except that she was almost immediately rescued by the Corsair — that's all he was ever called, the Corsair."

"Ah, then how wonderful for her. Or not? Please, tell me more."

Abby took hold of one of the bedposts, held on for dear life. She slipped her tongue between her lips, moistened them. "The . . . the Corsair was rather *demanding*," she told him, closing her eyes in embarrassment. A person would have to do much of her reading between the lines of the novel, but that hadn't been difficult for someone with Abby's rather fertile imagination. "He — um — he expected *recompense* for having rescued her."

"Recompense." Kipp's grin turned positively naughty, beyond naughty. "What did he do? Hold her for ransom? Lash her to the mast and have her flogged?"

"No. No, he didn't do that, for at the heart of it, he was a good man. Even a hero, for he defeated the bloodthirsty pirates."

Kipp reached Abby, ran a fingertip down her cheek, traced the line to the base of her throat, came to rest at the pulse he could see beating there. "Ah, a hero among pirates. Even a *good* pirate. Fighting against all odds, routing the evil-doers, saving dear Miss Pomeroy. How boring."

"He *did* carry her off to his island castle as his captive," Abby countered, defending the fictional Corsair, who had fueled more than a few of her dreams, even those which now showed him with Kipp's face.

Kipp teased at the strap of her nightgown. A game. He would play a game. They would play this game together — a thousand times more exciting than a round or two of chess. "Ah, and then he *ravished* her. Didn't he?" he breathed against Abby's ear, nipping at her lobe with his teeth. "*How* did he ravish her? Tell me, Abby. How did he ravish her?"

Abby couldn't move, could barely speak. "I don't know. Miss . . . Miss Zane didn't go into detail. There — there were *hints*, of course, but . . ."

Kipp continued to nuzzle her throat, very much aware of those hints, just how he had phrased them for optimum effect. He insinuated his leg between Abby's thighs, pressed up and against her womanhood. "What did the Corsair demand of his captive? Tell me what you remember."

She felt his hands on her hips as he began to slowly grind himself against her until she opened her legs to him, splayed her fingers against his warm, bare chest.

Abby's ears buzzed. Her mouth had gone dry. Her heart pounded in her throat.

She was Lucinda, Kipp her handsome, daring Corsair. They were alone together, behind the locked doors of his castle, soon to be locked in each other's arms. Brought together in this place, as Miss Zane had written so obliquely yet so tantalizingly, "to know the grand and glorious ecstasy meant to be shared by daring gentlemen and their yielding ladies; the earthly wonderment which they both were soon to recognize as the highest, grandest gift of the benevolent gods."

Abby made one last, feeble grasp at sanity. "This . . . this is silly. Insane."

"Yes, it is, isn't it? But I have brought you games tonight, Abby. Because I believed you might like games. You do, don't you? Now, what did the Corsair do?"

Abby closed her eyes, surrendered to the fantasy. "He — he *said* things."

Kipp's hands squeezed at her buttocks, kneading, releasing. "*Said* things? What things did he say?"

Abby was so embarrassed, so excited, so nearly mortified that she had become so excited. Her fingers tangled in the soft mat of dark blond hair on Kipp's chest, found his flat nipples. She succumbed to the urge to touch them, to squeeze them.

When he responded, the small nubs hardening, she bent forward, dared to lick at him with her tongue. His immediate shudder of response buoyed her, made her more daring. More willing to play.

"*Things*," she repeated, her mind blank except for the sensations she was feeling, the anticipation that broke over her in waves both hot and cold.

"Let me guess, then." Kipp's hands were moving again, this time raising the hem of her nightgown until she was bare to the waist, then concentrating on the buttons holding his pantaloons shut. "Avast, woman. Get thee in that bed yonder and let me ravish ye, my pretty wench."

Abby hit him, boxed both his ears for him. "Oh, *men!* You don't know the first thing about romance!"

Laughing even through his ears were ringing — his wife seemed never to have learned to pull her punches — Kipp lifted her in his arms, carelessly tossing her over his shoulder in the best pirate fashion, then dumping her down in the middle of the wide bed. She was the captive, he her captor. He was careful with her, but not gentle. Just the way the Corsair had been with his Lucinda in all the scenes he had imagined, but had not written. Not if he'd held any hopes of being published.

Abby hit the mattress full on her back. She bounced, twice.

Kipp was beside her in moments, having been slightly delayed when his unbuttoned pantaloons threatened to slide down his legs, tripping him. Silently cursing the real world for not being quite as convenient as the world of fantasy, he stripped quickly, his gaze never leaving Abby as she lay on the bed, waiting.

Pinning her at the hips with his own body, he took hold of her wrists and pressed them against the pillows, high over her head. Adjusted his grip so that he held both slim wrists in one hand, leaving the other free to torment his captive, to tease her, to *pleasure* her.

With a smile he hoped sufficiently herolike not to frighten her, he inserted a hand into the neckline of her sheer gown, then ripped it clean to the waist, and beyond.

Abby felt a sudden need to break the spiraling tension between them. "There's twenty pounds you'll never see again, my lord Corsair," she told him rather sarcastically as he ripped at the gown some more, until it was severed, neck to hem.

Kipp bent his head, chuckled against her breast. Then, remembering his role, he growled low in his throat, as corsairs surely were wont to do. "Not another word from you, my lady. You are my captive now, and totally at my whim, my command," he told her as she wriggled against him, whether to escape him or because she'd willingly stepped back into the role he'd created for her he didn't know. But he'd take his chances. He slid a hand between her legs.

Abby's breath caught on a moan. The gown hung from her in shreds as she lay pinned beneath him. Unable to hold him, her entire body laid bare in the candlelight as he ran his hands over her again. Touching. Probing. Calling for a surrender she knew herself eager to give him.

He lowered his voice to a near purr. "You are my pale English beauty, my sweet slave of love, my bed warmer for as long as I, the Corsair, shall desire you."

"My father will have you hanged," Abby warned him, still struggling against him, knowing full well that her every movement was calculated to excite him. Just as his words were meant to excite her.

"I would die happily, taking the memory of this night with me to my final reward. There is no escape, not for either of us. You are mine, Miss Pomeroy."

His fingers were still between her legs, finding her, opening her, sliding inside. She lifted her hips, pushing against him.

Abby wanted. She wanted so badly. She needed the words. Even if they were not her words. Even if she was not Abigail Rutland, Viscountess Willoughby, but Lucinda Pomeroy, speaking the florid lines of a mere figment of Aramintha Zane's imagination. Hiding behind those words. Freed by those words.

"Yes. Yes, my Corsair. I can no longer fight you with my frail woman's body. Do as you will with me. I am yours."

Kipp bent his head, intent on the game, all the games they had been playing, refusing to consider reasons they both needed to hide behind them, within them. He breathed his next words into her mouth as he nudged her legs fully open. Rose over her, entered her. Filled her. Stared deep into those marvelous violet eyes. "And, until the seas themselves boil, and all the stars fall from the heavens . . . I am yours."

Chapter Seventeen

Abby paced the expanse of carpet in the drawing room as the morning sun poured through the tall windows, playing a game in which she was careful to step only in the centers of the squares, never letting her feet touch on the trellised borders of each delicate grid.

Playing a game.

Games. They had played at games last night, she and Kipp. Small fantasies, stepping into roles, playing out their parts. She as Lucinda Pomeroy. Kipp as the dashing Corsair.

Silly games. Dangerous games.

Why? Why had they done it? What purpose did such evasion serve? Because that seemed the only way they could come together without guilt, without either of them feeling shame, or regret? Remorse?

Because for a husband and wife to share such unexpected passion, without a word of love spoken between them, their only bonds that of a practical, convenient marriage, could only be seen as an anathema to them both?

So that Kipp didn't feel as if he had bought her favors? So that she didn't feel like a bought and paid-for whore?

All of that was possible.

Just as believing they might possibly have feelings for each other could only be considered ludicrous, improbable, probably impossible. Perhaps even unwelcome.

And, if one-sided, most certainly inconvenient for them both.

Two strangers, knowing so little about each other, entering into a marriage for all the wrong reasons. Still keeping secrets from each other.

And not quite as compatible out of bed as they were in it.

Not that Abby hadn't agreed that they keep their lives separate, no impinging on one another. But he could at least have *offered* to help her figure out how to be shed of her relatives, couldn't he?

No, she supposed not. The Backworth-Maldons were her problem, and she'd have to settle it, and them, on her own. Although how she was going to do that without throttling Iggy and then burying his body in the back garden, she didn't know.

Still pacing, and thinking, with her head down so that she could mind her steps, Abby was startled into stepping on one of the grids when Kipp came into the room, saying, "Good morning, wife. Lose something?"

"Lose something? Oh. Oh, no. I was merely concentrating, that's all," she told him, trying not to notice how handsome he looked in his bottle green jacket and buff pantaloons, his highly polished Hessians reminding her of . . . well, of something she'd probably be better off forgetting.

Then her eyes widened as she looked past Kipp, to see Iggy standing behind him in the hallway, grinning and waggling his fingers at her in greeting.

Go away, go away, she ordered him silently, making small shooing motions with her hands.

That, of course, was a mistake, for Iggy's grin only grew wider as he walked into the room, bidding his aunt and "uncle" a jolly fine morning.

"Good morning," Kipp answered, automatically polite, even as his brain struggled to get round the idea that the boy must somehow believe he could claim him as uncle. Which, by God, he probably could, if the posturing idiot had no sense of self-preservation.

After all — Ignatius Backworth-Maldon? And in *his* house? How had that happened?

Kipp looked at the young man, far too handsome, his dress a shade too flamboyant to be considered anything but foppish. The starched shirt points high enough to touch his ears, the cravat an intricate folly, the cut of his coat owing too much to buckram padding at the shoulders and meant to give the appearance of a sapling-thin waist.

Then he looked at Abby, who stood quite still, her hands tightly linked together in front of her, her expression caught somewhere between that of a prisoner about to be led to the block and a hell-and-brimstone minister prepared to launch into a sermon on the Evils of Sin.

"Let me guess. Your nephew is here early, up and about with the vigor of youth, and has stopped by for a visit with his favorite aunt, his only sister?" Kipp offered, not about. to give Abby a scrap of help as he asked for her explanation.

"What? Only visiting? She hasn't told you, Uncle? Dear Auntie, too lost in love to remember such mundane matters as your kind invitation for me to pass the remainder of the Season under your roof."

Iggy minced past Kipp, to seat himself on one of the couches, his left leg crossed high over his right — showing off his ridiculously high-heeled boots, a lace-edged handkerchief lifted to dab at the corners of his mouth. "I slept quite well and my breakfast was, in most part, quite enjoyable. But I would ask, Auntie, that you see to it that the bacon is more *crisp* in future? Thank you *so* much."

Kipp felt his blood beginning a slow boil. "He calls me *Uncle* again, Abby, and I'm going to toss your dear, sweet nephew out of here on his pomaded head," he promised affably, all the while glaring at the encroaching toadstool who, God help him, he now must number among his relations.

"Go away, Iggy," Abby warned the boy, whose cocky smile had faded slightly under Kipp's withering stare. "We have a bargain, and you've already overstepped yourself, so don't expect me to protect you from His Lordship if you open your mouth again to say something else stupid. You really won't look half so fine with your nose spread all over your face, you know."

"We'll speak later, Auntie." Iggy hopped to his feet with some alacrity, and quit the room, the door to the Square opening and closing only a few moments later.

Which left Abby quite alone with her husband.

"There is, I assume, some explanation? More importantly — do I want to hear it?"

Abby didn't really know any feminine wiles. She knew full well that she wasn't the fainting sort. An attempt at righteous indignation would get her nowhere, for she also knew herself to be the guilty party.

That left only honesty, which was entirely out of the question, and evasion, which had its own appeal.

"You told me last night, my lord, that I should settle my own problems in my own way, and without applying to you for assistance."

"I did? I said all of that?" Kipp rubbed a hand across his mouth, attempting to collect his thoughts. "I may have to reconsider, if your only way of *settling* your problems is to have two Backworth-Maldons running tame in my house within twenty-four hours of our wedding."

"They'll be gone soon enough," Abby promised, hoping she was right, that she'd find a way to punish Iggy for his blackmailing heart. "Edwardine will forgive her mother, and Iggy — well, I've promised myself that I'd settle him, one way or another."

Kipp raised an eyebrow. Lord, but he liked this woman. "That sounds ominous. Should I be feeling sympathetic for the boy, or simply thanking my lucky stars you've promised never to *settle* me? Still, I'll leave the details to you, as long as you promise me you will not badger Cook into burning our bacon to a crisp."

"I was thinking some *raw* bacon might be in order, actually, as I don't know if I could stoop so low as to punish a piglet by stuffing it under one of the silver covers for Iggy to discover," Abby said, and relaxed as Kipp laughed at her small joke. "Now, if that's settled, and with my assurance that I will keep both my niece and nephew safely out of sight as much as possible, do you think we might discuss the pile of invitations on the mantel? It seems we've been invited everywhere this evening, and as I don't really know which are important and which are to be declined, I thought you might give me a few instructions on how it's done?"

Kipp bowed to her most formally, agreeable to stepping into the role of social secretary, and retrieved about a dozen invitations as Abby sat down at the small desk in one corner of the room. He drew up another chair, then fanned the invitations out on the desk top.

Remembered how she had looked last night, how she had felt, how she had tasted. Their midnight fantasy.

He mentally shook himself, pushing the memory to the back of his brain. For the sun was out, and the nighttime was another world.

"Those are only tonight's invitations," Abby informed him. "There's piles more here in the desk, but after sorting them by date I found myself not knowing what to do next."

"So you quite rightly appealed to me. Good. We have several ways of doing this, you know," he told her, smiling as their knees touched beneath the desk and Abby flinched slightly, but did not move her legs. Perhaps the night had lingered into day for her as well?

"One," he continued, "we can close our eyes, shuffle this mess a few times, and then pick any three at random. I do that, often. Two, we simply pick all those that are printed on the same size paper, or the same color paper."

Abby nodded, her eyes twinkling, her expression deadly serious. "Or we could take down that sword hung on the wall in your study and toss all the invitations into the air, to see which ones you can skewer before they hit the floor."

"Yes, there is that," Kipp agreed, leafing through the invitations, wondering why each ball, each rout party, each invitation to dine, all seemed so bloody boring when compared to spending the evening at home with his wife, the two of them bent over a chessboard — he had the notion that her strategies would be most intriguing.

Overwhelmingly intriguing.

"Ah, how about this?" he questioned her at last, piling the invitations together and neatly ripping them in half.

Abby's eyes nearly bugged out of her head. She'd scanned the invitations earlier, to see two from earls, one from a royal duke, and another from Lady Jersey herself. Abby might not know too much about Society, but she certainly knew that Lady Sally Jersey was not the sort one snubbed with impunity. "We can *do* that?"

Kipp held out a hand to Abby, helping her to rise, then steering her around the desk so that he could place his hand at her waist, guide her toward the doorway. "We can, and we did. Now, as it's such a fine day, how would you like to have your husband escort you on a walk in the fresh air? We'll avoid the Park, as I'm in no mood for spending my time tipping my hat and listening to inane congratulations on our marriage."

Abby did her best not to melt against Kipp's side, safe in his loose, not quite impersonal embrace. "I think I'd like that very much, Kipp," she told him as Gillett, who seemed always able to anticipate his master's next request, met them in the hallway, their outerwear flung over his arm.

"Is it far to Covent Garden? I walk for miles and miles in the country, but perhaps that isn't accepted, here in town?" she asked as she slipped into the short blue-velvet spencer that contrasted so well with Madame Lucille's palest blue muslin gown — one of the half-dozen already delivered to Grosvenor Square, to be followed by at least two dozen more in the next days and weeks.

She tied a pale blue tucked-silk bonnet on her head, the lace frills framing her face but not impeding her vision as so many bonnets did. "Still, I'd really enjoy seeing Covent Garden. Cook tells me the very best fruits and vegetables are to be had there, and pretty flowers as well."

"Along with other delicacies, and other sights not quite so delectable," Kipp responded, as Gillett frowned, making his disapproval known. "Very well, Covent Garden it is." He motioned for a reluctant Gillett to open the door, held out his arm to Abby. "Shall we be off? Gillett? If we're not back by dinnertime, may I suggest dragging the Thames?"

They stepped outside and stopped beneath the portico, each of them taking refreshing breaths of the cool, spring air. Kipp tucked his cane beneath one arm, offered the free one to his wife. "Definitely a lovely day for a stroll. Probably even healthful, which would send our mutual friend Brady into screeching for his curricle," he told her, as they descended to the flagway, then set off for Oxford Street, thinking it best to take a less direct but safer route from Oxford, to Charing Cross Road, and then to St. Paul's Cathedral and Covent Garden.

No matter what the route, Kipp would never think of taking it at night, not unless in his carriage, definitely not unless he was armed.

"And, speaking of Brady, he sent round a note this morning begging our forgiveness for not coming by to say his farewells in person. It seems he's been called away to his estates for some reason or another — details too boring, he vowed, to bear repeating."

"Oh, that's too bad. We'll miss him." Abby felt genuinely sad that her new friend had gone, but quickly realized that she already had enough on her plate with her relatives without having Brady underfoot, grinning his secret grins, delighting in the success of his plan. Not that he would ever betray her, as Iggy would — at the drop of a hat — but his absence made for one less thing for her to worry about on this fine morning.

"Never fear, Abby. He'll be back soon enough, and probably with a dozen silly stories to tell. Now, what do you know of St. Paul's Cathedral, which is located at one end of Covent Garden?" Kipp asked Abby as they walked along, as he smiled at the way she unabashedly took on the role of sightseer, gawking at some buildings, smiling at others, and giggling outright when a sweeping boy helped them across the street, clearing the way of horse droppings and other offal.

"Ah, that's easy," she replied, patting at her pocket. "I have prepared myself by reading a small touring book I found in your library."

"*Our* library," Kipp corrected, wondering why that clarification seemed important to him.

"All right, *our* library. Thank you. I also took the liberty of bringing *our* book along with us, so that I might be able to identify anything you might not be as familiar with as I would hope. St. Paul's Cathedral, for instance, is the very last large project of Inigo Jones, the favorite architect of King Charles I. Jones created the building in accordance with the then new conception of the Renaissance — which were, of course, only a re- vival of the classical cultures of the ancient world. To some it is the finest example of Jones's work, although Horace Walpole thought the thing atrocious, as he was not enamored of anything that did not have its birth in England."

Kipp was impressed by Abby's knowl- edge, and by her interest. "Anything else?"

Abby warmed to her subject. "Only that Jones remained faithful to the dimensions first introduced by the Ancient Greeks and Romans, including a large stone portico with a triangular pediment supported by pillars, each pillar measuring a third of the width of the church — and many other mea- surements that seemed quite impressive to me at the time. I did not, however, commit them to memory."

Kipp laughed. "Then there are still things for which this humble male can be grateful. But I do have a story of my own, the sort of history that holds appeal for my sometimes romantic soul. Would you care to hear it?"

They were walking briskly, barely a stroll at all, and Abby was having some trouble keeping up with her husband, although she'd rather drop over in exhaustion before admitting as much to him. Still, if she could keep him talking, perhaps he'd have to slow down to catch his own breath. "I would very much like to hear your story. Is it true?"

"Oh, indubitably," Kipp assured her. "A darker part of our history, complete with the requisite hero, one John Rivett, a humble brazier. You see, a statue of poor beheaded Charles I had been housed in St. Paul's and the Parliament ordered Mr. Rivett to melt it down for scrap. No statues of Royals allowed, you understand. But brave Mr. Rivett hid the statue instead, selling small vases and figures he *said* were made from the bronze, then presenting the statue to Charles II when the monarchy was restored. It stands now at Charing Cross — we'll see it as we walk by in just a few minutes. I've always thought the king should have commissioned Mr. Rivett to make a bronze of himself for display somewhere in Covent Garden, but it was not to be, and Mr. Rivett faded into memory, a hero without recognition."

"Well, now I feel silly," Abby said, much impressed by Kipp's knowledge. "Here I was, spouting facts and numbers, and you've come to the heart of the whole thing with that one story. You've obviously a great love of history."

"Only the stranger bits," Kipp told her, smiling down at her, thinking how very nice she looked in her bonnet. Her cheeks had flushed a lovely pink in the brisk air, and her eyes and smile seemed to reflect the sparkle of the sun.

Amazing how pretty she could be, for a woman who could not be termed beautiful. A very extraordinary ordinary woman.

He tried to picture any of his female companions taking such enjoyment in a mile-long walk through London — not all of it through the nicest streets — and failed. Only Merry would have enjoyed such a trek, seeing it as a great adventure.

He waited for the pang of regret that customarily invaded his chest when he unexpectedly thought of Merry, when unforeseen memories of Merry and the life he had longed for caught him off his guard, invaded his heart, clouded his mood.

Nothing happened. No pang. No feeling of regret. Just a small smile as he remembered the child, the young girl, the woman she'd grown to be as he'd stood back, watched as she ran to Jack and her own happiness.

Kipp put his free hand on Abby's as she held onto his sleeve, gave her fingers a small squeeze. "We're almost there. Perhaps we might find a stall still serving lemonade. Would you like that?"

"Yes, thank you, I would." Abby looked up at her husband, saw his smile, saw a new softness in his eyes, and nearly stumbled over a bump in the cobblestones. Kipp quickly righted her and they walked on, now with his arm about her waist.

How naturally they had fallen into casual touches, their nighttime intimacies probably helping to ease them into a physical familiarity that she felt sure they would otherwise avoid like the plague.

She allowed herself to melt against him, loving the warm feel of his palm against her back, sensing that more was in tune between them now than just the steady beat of their matched footsteps. What had just happened? Something had happened. She could feel the change in Kipp, a change so small she doubted anyone save herself would even notice.

Content. Yes, that was it. He seemed suddenly content.

Abby returned her attention to negotiating the uneven flagway, took a deep breath to steady her jangling nerves, and then secretly smiled at the cobblestones. She loved every cobblestone in all of London.

They walked on in silence for several blocks, then Abby spied a sign hanging from one of the tall, narrow buildings, proclaiming it to be *Waterfield's Anciente Book-store, Pamphlets a Specialty*.

"Could we stop and look in the window?" she asked Kipp, then walked to the shop before he could answer.

The small, dirty window held a display of broken-back books and towering stacks of yellowed pamphlets, all of which had to be several decades out of date. Abby cupped her hands around her eyes and squinted through the glass, trying to read the faded lettering on the pamphlet topping one of the stacks.

"Oh dear," she said quietly a few moments later, stepping back from the window. She looked at Kipp, who had been reading over her shoulder. "Is that what I think it is?"

"That would depend, Abby," he told her. "*I* might believe it to be an interesting piece of history worthy of collection for its relevance to the record of Covent Garden. Purely an intellectual pursuit, worthy of my own admittedly skewed view of what makes our history interesting."

"Oh, pooh," Abby said, rolling her eyes. "That pamphlet has about as much significance to history as Uncle Dagwood's collection of unusually shaped horse droppings."

"Horse droppings? You're jesting, aren't you?"

Abby wrinkled her nose. "Just don't ask *him* if I'm jesting," she warned facetiously. She stepped forward once more and squinted through the glass, reading aloud, "'*Harris's List of Covent-Garden Ladies: or Man of Pleasure's Kalendar, for the Year 1773. An exact Description of the most celebrated Ladies of Pleasure who frequent Covent Garden, and other parts of this Metropolis.*'"

She turned, looked at Kipp, doing her best to keep her expression blank. "And it's the second edition, too, so that we may assume Mr. Harris's informative list enjoyed great popularity. Now, husband, having heard what *you* think the pamphlet refers to, do you want to know what *I*, your unschooled country wife, think is enclosed within its pages?"

"I wouldn't dare," Kipp responded, as they continued their walk and he mentally cursed himself for not insisting they take the curricle. "I am already mortified past all bearing."

"No, you're not," Abby retorted, laughing, then looked ahead to where the street seemed to open wide in front of them. She recognized St. Paul's Church bathed in bright sunlight and looking much as it did in the drawing in her touring guide. "Oh, it's lovely!" Then she frowned. "But such a mess!"

"The other side of beauty," Kipp told her, as they walked into the central area of Covent Garden, called the Piazza, a huge area littered with tumbledown stalls, rotting fruit and vegetables, wilting flowers, and more noise and people than Abby probably had ever seen in one place. Dogs so thin their ribs stood out along their sides, searched the debris for scraps, as the morning market had all but shut down, leaving nothing but beggars and scavengers. "Disappointed?"

"Dreadfully," Abby said quietly, shaking her head as she pressed a handkerchief to her nose, hoping to block out the worst of the smell.

Nothing could block out the loud cries of the hawkers.

"Ribbons a groat a yard!"

"Ripe turkey figs! Dumplings ho!"

A man carrying a leg of mutton by the shank calling out, "Who'll 'ave two dips and a wallop for a bawbee?"

"I don't understand. What's he saying?" Abby asked as the man went by, the rankness of the mutton all but turning her stomach.

"He's calling on the housewives along the street to come outside with pails of boiling water," Kipp explained. "For a small fee, he'll dip that joint into the water a few times, supposedly turning it into broth."

Abby watched as two women carrying pails emerged from one of the formerly beautiful houses Inigo Jones had built with such hopes of making Covent Garden the greatest area of London.

"I thought I knew what being poor meant," she said sadly, "but I see I was wrong. Such a lovely idea — the church, the houses Jones designed, the vaulted arcades, the theaters. Do you think any of these people even *notice?* And what would that beauty mean to them, living this dreadful life?"

Kipp opened his mouth to answer her, secretly cursing the duke of Bedford for allowing his ancestors' dreams to fall into such disrepair for the sake of the rental monies he gained from the stalls, when he felt a tugging at the hem of his jacket.

"Buy me dollie fer yore laidie, guv'nor? Jist a bitty one?"

Kipp was already reaching in his pocket for a coin when a large-bellied, blowsy woman appeared behind the child, giving her a rough cuff to the back of her head. " 'Ere now, 'Gina. Wot did Oi tell yer 'bout flash coves? A bitty one? Are yer daft, child?"

She ripped the small doll from the child's filthy paws and replaced it with a much larger one she'd extracted from the wicker basket she carried beneath her arm. "Now, none o'that owt-yenep pittance. Cast-iron Gert walks these treacherous streets the day long fer yer, an' this is the thanks Oi gets? Work m' nabblers to the quick sewin'? Flash this'un, 'Gina. Tell 'im this one fer net-yenep. 'E'll go it fer the doxy."

Abby's eyes had grown round in her head as she watched and listened.

The poor child, no more than ten or twelve years old, unless her sad life had stunted her growth even as it had twisted her small body. Such a sad little face, such a sad little soul. She hadn't even flinched when the woman had hit her, as if she'd become too accustomed to such abuse to react. She had a mop of reddish brown hair that hadn't seen brush or comb — or soap and water — in much too long, if ever.

The child's body, bent into a low and twisted crouch painful to look at, was too thin, clad in rags too small to cover her below her elbows, her knees. Her feet were bare and black as the cobblestones. Her eyes were as gray as a stormy morning, but somehow unfocused, shifting in her thin, gamine face as she

353

kept moving her head at odd angles as if . . .

"Oh, Lord, Kipp," Abby whispered. "Is she blind? Is that her mother? And what is she saying?"

"In a moment, Abby," Kipp told her. "For now, would you like a doll? The small jester is twopence, but the bigger doll is much dearer — tenpence.

Abby was impressed. "How do you know that?"

"Costermonger language," he informed her, not letting out the information that he had studied the cant for one of his Aramintha Zane novels. He also wouldn't tell her that Cast-iron Gert believed her to be his doxy, his kept woman. "They speak some words backwards, thinking no one can understand. Owt-yenep, Abby. Twopence. Net-yenep. Tenpence. Understand? Although none of them can spell *forward*, which makes for some interesting pronunciations."

But Abby wasn't listening anymore. Cast-iron Gert seemed to have decided that little Gina wasn't holding up her end of the begging, and hit her again, so hard the child staggered on her bent legs.

"Shame on you! Touch that poor innocent child again, woman, and I'll see you in the guardhouse!" Abby shouted, causing more than a few heads to turn, more than a few shuffling bodies to melt away beneath the shadow of the arcades, just in case the esclop (the *police,* of course) decided to come see what was causing such a ruckus.

Not that the police would lift a finger to help little Gina, or to attempt to haul Cast-iron Gert off to the guardhouse. The woman had gotten her name by surviving a smashing wallop to her head with a cast-iron pot, then getting up and all but filleting her opponent with a broken scissors.

Cast-iron Gert, obviously aware of her own reputation, growled low in her throat, taking a single, threatening step in Abby's direction before Kipp's malacca cane flashed through the air, its point making a rather prodigious dent in her expansive belly.

"Hold your progress right there, if you please. In fact, I would consider it a major mercy if you were to step back, oh, six paces. Your . . . perfume is rather cloying," Kipp drawled sweetly, swinging the cane up and around with a practiced flourish, then tucking it beneath his arm once more. "Ah, that's marginally better. Now, I believe we were discussing the purchase of one of your dolls?"

"No. No we're not," Abby told him firmly,

already digging deep into the small blue reticule hanging from her wrist. "We're discussing the purchase of this poor, crippled, blind *child*. I've got twelve pounds, *Exisyenep*, as we still have not discussed my allowance. Is that enough?"

"Abby," Kipp said warningly, about to explain a few hard facts to his wife. But the forward thrust of her chin warned him. Her expression stopped him. The tears in her violet eyes devastated him.

And then he opened his mouth again, and amazed himself. "Oh, very well. But allow me to take over the negotiations from here, if you please."

Cast-iron Gert was all but licking her chops, her blancmange body quivering and jiggling as she scented the fortune that surely was to land in her lap at any moment. "Oi cain't be sellin' me own child, yer worship. Not me 'Gina. A regular pet, her is, God's truth. Pore wee blind thing."

"That will be quite enough, thank you." Kipp's tone became steely-hard, revealing his complete and utter disgust. There was nothing else for it, if he wanted to be quit of this place anytime soon — which he most certainly did want. He was about to show Abby a few truths about London not printed in any guidebook.

"One, my good woman, this child's not blind, *or* crippled. Two, I strongly doubt she's your own child, but only a hapless orphan you've hired to peddle your wares to sympathetic ladies like my wife. Or she's your willing *partner* in this chicanery, a thought that makes me cringe. And three, because my lady wishes it, you'll take ten pounds even for her, and we'll have the dolls as well. Now, do we have a deal? You have five seconds to make up your mind."

"Not crippled? Not . . . not *blind?*" Abby whispered, then watched as the child's thrown-back head lowered and her gray eyes, that had been directed toward the sky, suddenly came into focus, looked straight at her. She unbent her crouched body, rising a full half foot taller, her suddenly intelligent expression magically aging her at least another three years, perhaps more. She winked at Abby, grinned.

Dumbfounded by this sudden "cure," this amazing metamorphosis, Abby turned to Kipp in some awe. "My stars, how did you know that? No, no, that's all right. We'll talk about this later."

"Yes, we will. Do you still want to buy this . . . this poor little child?"

"You'd leave her to this life? Of course I

still want to buy her, set her free from this *slavery.*"

"Be it on your head," Kipp said as Abby passed over the money and received the basket of dolls in exchange. "But you do realize that we can't keep her. That drab may have called her a pet, but she is not a pet."

"Of course not," Abby said as Kipp waved down a passing hackney cab for the trip back to Grosvenor Square. "We'll just take her home, give her a bath, find her something to wear beside these rags. Put some good hot food in her belly, bandage her feet. Yes, that will do for starters. Then we can —"

"You said 'of course not,'" Kipp reminded her as Gina climbed into the hackney, then he helped Abby in behind her. "But, even if I were to list two dozen reasons why we can't keep her, you aren't going to listen to me, Abby. Are you?"

Abby smiled at him as he sat down beside her, signaled for the hackney to move on. "Of course not," she then said, winking at Gina.

Chapter Eighteen

Abby had been wrong. Gina had not needed a bath. She'd needed two.

And she had not cooperated.

It took Abby, Sallyann, Mrs. Harris, a giggling tweeny, and the threat of ropes and gags before Gina had finally been coaxed into the tub in the first place. She'd fought the rag, the soap. She'd howled when soap from her hair got into her eyes, "stingin' 'em all hollow," then roundly cursed Abby from head to toe and back again for being worse than Cast-iron Gert when it came to meanness.

But, in the end, Abby prevailed. By the time they'd had the tub scrubbed and refilled for Gina's second bath, the girl had been either resigned to her fate or had begun to enjoy it. She'd played with the bubbles, even blowing a handful of them at Abby, and seemed to delight in the sweet-smelling lotion Sallyann rubbed onto her skin before wrapping her up in warmed towels.

Abby rested now in a warm, quilted dressing gown, fresh from her own bath, and watched, sipping hot tea, as Gina sat in front of the fire while Sallyann brushed the girl's damp copper curls.

The child — no child, not really, not after seeing her stripped to the buff — definitely had calmed considerably, especially once Mrs. Harris had produced a plate of sandwiches and a few warm, buttered scones to fill her belly.

She wore one of Abby's mud brown gowns, inches too long at the hem — as the girl couldn't be much more than five feet tall. Otherwise, the castoff fit her quite well, and looked very much better on her than it ever had on Abby.

She didn't complain when Sallyann tugged at her hair to remind her to keep her head still, those so-intelligent gray eyes active, seeing everything, calculating everything. Probably, as the maid had suggested, estimating the worth of every piece she might be able to pilfer before she made her escape.

Abby had no such fears. She felt well pleased with the accomplishments of the afternoon. She had rescued a poor innocent from the ravages of poverty, and she had learned that her husband, beneath his smiles and easy banter, had the soul of the true gentleman. A caring heart.

And, much to her surprise, Gina had turned out to be quite a pretty girl, probably fifteen or sixteen years of age, with thick, badly ragged wavy hair, remarkably fine features beneath the filth and fake sores they'd peeled from her cheeks and forehead. She had good teeth, straight limbs, and, with care, her poor, battered feet would soon recover from their wounds, leaving her with small, narrow feet worthy of a peeress.

A log fell in the grate, the sound breaking the silence that had reigned for the last quarter hour as everyone tried to recover from the earlier battle. "Yer'd be the Mother?" Gina asked at last, her gaze settling on Abby.

Abby shook her head. "The Mother? I'm sorry, I don't understand."

Gina rolled her eyes in disgust, muttered something under her breath. "The *Mother*," she repeated, louder this time, as if Abby had a problem with her hearing. "The Lady Abbess. The head of this Pushing School. That fella with you, he'd be yer Flash Man, right?"

Sallyann gasped, dropped the brush, and reached around Gina to clap both hands against the girl's mouth. "Here now, shame on you!" she scolded hotly. "This here is Lady Willoughby, and His Lordship is the

Viscount Willoughby. Abbess of a bawdy house and her bully? I've half a mind to fetch back the soap and scrub out your filthy mouth!"

Gina removed Sallyann's hands with the expertise of someone long accustomed to fending for herself, and hopped to her feet, glaring down at the maid. "Touch me again, and I'll wrap your guts around your ears and tie them in a bow," she warned tightly.

She then turned to look at Abby, who had been struggling with both Gina's and Sallyann's statements, finally believing she had properly deciphered them . . . while wondering at the sudden change for the better in Gina's speech even as she'd threatened Sallyann.

"You think this is a whorehouse?" she asked Gina, who was in the process of hiking up her skirts, as she'd nearly come to grief over the hem. "Oh, Gina, I'm so sorry. It never occurred . . . I never thought . . . I just wanted to save you from that terrible woman."

Looping her skirt over one arm, Gina waved off Abby's words and began to pace the width of the large chamber, seemingly deep in conversation with herself. She turned to look at Abby once or twice, then continued on, not seeming to mind the bandages on her bare feet.

Finally, having come to a decision, she retraced her steps and stood directly in front of Abby. Gave an awkward curtsy. Said, "Please forgive me, Your Ladyship. I would not have fought quite so hard if I'd known you weren't fixing me up for some . . . some customer. I — I thought I could do it. I thought, this will get you off the streets for a bit, girl. I've fought it for what seems like forever, becoming one of *them,* but one more day of tying my body into knots and acting the blind fool with Gert would have had me leaping into the Thames and thanking the water for being deep."

"Oh, ma'am," Sallyann moaned, her soft heart touched. She got to her feet, came over to Gina, and gave her shoulders a pat. "I'll be seeing to getting one of the attic rooms fixed up for you, all right?"

As Sallyann left, Abby waved Gina into the facing chair and looked at her for long moments before asking, "How is it you speak so well, Gina?"

"Regina," she corrected, sighing, as she looked around the room once more. "This is another one of my dreams, isn't it? I'm going to wake up at any moment, with Gert's foot in my back before dawn after I sat half the night sewing up those little dolls, with her telling me it's time to go hawking our wares. But it's a pretty dream." She smiled at Abby. "At least I'm clean in this one."

Abby put down her teacup, folded her hands in her lap. She'd been desperate herself, more than once, and knew herself capable of harboring a great affection for this strange young woman. "Will you tell me how you came to be with Gert? Only if you want to, of course."

"All right. I'll pretend this isn't a dream. At least it's nice not having to hide myself behind that terrible thieves' cant. If anyone thought I was trying to be better than myself, or even as old as I am, I'd not have lived out my first day in Seven Dials, you understand. As it was, they took my only luggage the first day, and my shoes, too. I cut my hair before anyone could kill me for it. You won't believe it, but Cast-iron Gert was my savior. *Nobody* dares cross her."

She then eyed the plate of sandwiches sitting on the hearth and gave in to her need for food, rescuing the few remaining squares of meat and bread and then returning to the chair. In between bites, she told her story.

"My aunt and uncle raised me, taught me. South of London, in Little Woodcote, in a parsonage there, on one of the properties of the Kenward family, may they all rot in . . . excuse me, Your Ladyship. As my uncle would have pointed out were he here, I've fallen into bad habits these past months."

"Kenward?" Kipp said, walking into the room, making his bow to his wife. "Forgive me, my dear, but the door was open between our rooms, and I must confess to some innocent eavesdropping." He inclined his head to Regina, who had jumped to her feet and curtsied, then asked, "Are you speaking of the Kenward family I know? Perhaps of George Kenward, Earl of Allerton?"

Regina nodded, much more intimidated by the Viscount Willoughby than she had been earlier, when she'd thought him a well-dressed bawdy-house bully.

"How wonderful," Kipp said, standing behind Abby's chair, his hand on her shoulder. "And so terribly romantic, don't you think? My own lady wife, rescuing the niece of a parson from the bowels of London poverty. Aramintha Zane would be so proud of you, my dear, and then straightaway steal the story and turn it on its head, to make Regina here a stolen princess soon to be returned to her rightful place. Are you a stolen princess, Miss — ?"

"Bliss," Regina mumbled, still not quite able to meet Kipp's eyes. "Regina Bliss. And no, my lord, I am nobody's stolen princess. I'm simply a person turned off after her aunt and uncle perished in a carriage accident, a person who foolishly thought she could come to London and secure a position as nanny to some merchant family. Or, failing that, as a seamstress in some shop. My aunt taught me well, and I'm very good with a needle." Her bottom lip began to tremble. "But nobody wanted me. Nobody but Gert. So I sewed her dolls for her, then helped her sell them."

She raised her head, her lovely gray eyes filled with tears as she looked at Abby, at Kipp. "Six months in London, my lord, my lady, and I've barely kept myself together. Gert was a step up from those first terrible weeks. To — to prostitute myself would have lifted me up another rung. My lord, my lady, I owe you my life."

"Feeling quite the heroine this evening, aren't you?" Kipp asked, taking her pawn with his knight.

Abby sighed, stood, reached her hands beneath her gown. She carefully removed her underpinnings, then smoothed down her gown, sat once more. "I believe *you're* a very nice man for having allowed me to bring Regina home with us, and I am forever in your debt. Now, please, I'm trying to concentrate on beating you into a weeping, moaning shadow of your former self."

Kipp remained silent for a few moments, absorbing the fact that his wife sat across the table from him wearing little more than an underslip and her gown. He'd only laughed when she'd lost her shoes, the laughter leaving him when she'd been forced to discard her hose. Had she really thought it necessary to lift her legs, one by one, and then *slowly* roll down each silken stocking as he watched?

What was she trying to win? Their game? Or him?

Now, damn her, Kipp seemed to be experiencing some mild difficulty in catching his breath, and his mind, far from concentrating on their game, was busy conjuring up ways to maneuver her from the chair to the bed.

"Yes, I know how difficult that must be, concentrating on destroying me, that is. Now, what was I saying? Oh, yes. Quite the heroine, my wife. Brings not a child into our house, but a nearly full-grown woman. The girl speaks well, ergo she must be without sin, and without larceny in her soul. And she most certainly couldn't be lying to us, could she? Not that I won't be sending someone posthaste to Little Woodcote tomorrow, to check out her story. In the meantime, have you warned Gillett to lock up the silver? Never mind, as I'm sure he's already nailed down anything the least movable in the entire house."

"You don't believe her, Kipp? *I* most certainly do, as do both Sallyann and Mrs. Harris. In fact, Regina is already tucked quite firmly under Mrs. Harris's wing, and will be kept quite busy with her needle as well as helping out with various other projects Mrs. Harris has in mind. She's grateful to have her. We have a new *maid*, Kipp. It's not as if we've *adopted* her, although I will admit to feeling rather smug about our rescue. Bishop takes your knight."

Kipp frowned at the chessboard. "By damn, he does. I see I'm going to have to stop coddling you and begin paying attention," he said, peeling off his shirt, as his waistcoat had disappeared three moves earlier. "Husbandly kindness goes just so far, you understand."

Abby lifted the wineglass that sat at her elbow, took another sip. "Ha! Don't try telling me you're not paying attention, sir, for I don't believe that for a moment. I'm just better at this than you are, that's all."

She grinned, waggled her eyebrows at

him. "Are you warm enough, my lord, or shall I ring for someone to stoke the fire? Oh, no. That might be just a tad embarrassing to you, mightn't it?"

She kept her eyes averted as she spoke, knowing she'd have difficulty keeping a level head if she stared overlong at Kipp's bare chest, remembered laying her head against it, feeling his arms going around her, pulling her close. She had to keep remembering that they were playing a game. Every night a different game. . . .

"Edwardine may be moving back to Half Moon Street tomorrow," she informed him, making an attempt at some sort of conversation that didn't have anything to do with their mutual states of undress.

"Really? Well, that is good news. Will she be taking your pernicious nephew with her? No, don't answer. That nasty little leech wouldn't vacate the premises if it were on fire around his ears. Why is Edwardine leaving?"

Abby hid a grimace at the mention of Iggy and answered Kipp's last question instead. "Something about Regina, and all of us being murdered in our beds. She became quite graphic, as a matter of fact, speaking of knives and gore, and heads rolling down the stairs as Regina and her thug friends sacked the house. Oh, and ravished the women, of course. Isn't that lovely? And doubtless spoon-fed to her by her brother, who never misses an opportunity to upset the poor, gullible child. Ah, quite a move, my lord. However, I do believe my rook takes your bishop. May I suggest your pantaloons might find some comfort on the floor, in the company of your shirt, evening slippers, and hose? And your jacket, and your waistcoat, and your neckcloth and . . . well, I believe that's all. So far."

Kipp stood, his hands to the buttons of his pantaloons, daring Abby to watch him disrobe. He looked deeply into her eyes, saw the slight flush invade her cheeks. Grinned evilly. God, but he liked this woman. He really *liked* this woman. "Methinks the lady doth enjoy herself overmuch," he teased lightly, then stepped out of his pantaloons and hastily sat down once more, leaving himself with only one more garment standing between him and revealing his involuntary arousal.

Not that he was about to let her best him at a simple game of chess. Narrowing his eyelids, he surveyed the chessboard, cudgeling his brain as he pondered his next move. He realized that, if Abby recognized it, he had only three more moves before she captured his king.

How had she managed to put him so on the defensive? He'd been paying attention, he was sure of it. When he hadn't been picturing Abby sitting across from him, bare-breasted, trying to act nonchalant, pretending she wasn't as aroused by their game as he was . . . as he most certainly was.

There could be no question. She had him. But he could still take the pawn she had so deliberately sacrificed, and did so, not really to delay the inevitable, but just for the pleasure of watching her divest herself of her gown.

"Rotter. *Some* people, I've heard, play for straws," Abby grumbled, aware that they both knew what he was doing. "Oh, very well," she said, coming over to him and turning her back, exposing the row of buttons she would require assistance in opening. "Do you mind?"

Now here was a dilemma. If he stood up . . .

When he hesitated, Abby bent at her knees, making it easier for him to reach her. He flexed his fingers a time or two, marveling at how clumsy he felt, all his fingers threatening to turn into thumbs.

But he persevered, undoing the buttons one by one, exposing more and more of Abby's pale-skinned back, discovering a small dark mole below her left shoulder blade that had previously escaped his notice.

Without thinking of what he was doing, he unlaced the bows holding her underslip, slowly pulling loose the ends of the ties, uncovering her long, straight spine, catching sight of the matching dimples just below her waist before Abby stood up, grinned down at him.

"Quite the optimistic one, aren't you?" she scolded before shrugging her shoulders free of the gown, intending for it to slide off her while she held the strapless underslip close against her. It was a maneuver that seemed quite reasonable in theory, but she hadn't counted on the weight of her skirts pulling at the underslip, so that, within a heartbeat, she was standing in front of her husband very much *au naturel.*

She shrieked in dismay, covering herself with her arms, one high, one low, and turned her head as if not being able to see Kipp meant he, in turn, could not see her.

"Oh, bloody hell, woman — game's over," Kipp swore under his breath, nearly knocking over the small table as he came to his feet, grabbed Abby in his arms, and headed for the bed.

A week passed. Abby's days were relaxed but full, as she and Mrs. Harris put their heads together over menus and plans for the viscount's second entertainment of the year, this one a rout party numbering no more than two hundred guests.

She spent time with Regina, as the girl proved to be an asset to the household. She did a prodigious amount of shopping, taking the still-in-residence Edwardine with her wherever she went, finding that her niece, always popular, was now being pursued by nearly every unmarried gentleman in London.

That new success, Kipp had told her, had somewhat to do with Edwardine's beauty, and owed rather largely to the fact that he had put it about that he would settle ten thousand pounds on the girl when she married.

Anything to get the Backworth-Maldons out of his house!

Abby's evenings were also filled, as Kipp had decided they should attack Society as a couple, seeing and being seen, stepping into their roles as they had agreed to play them.

This meant that Kipp still flirted rather often, dancing with other women, smiling at them as they flirted with him and whispered secrets in his ear.

For her part, Abby seemed to do very well for herself in her new position of viscountess, especially since Sophie, Duchess of Selbourne, had badgered her husband into allowing her back into Society only a few weeks after giving birth to their son.

Sophie, in Abby's opinion, held the enviable position of being the most popular woman in all of London. As Abby could invariably be seen at her side, it followed that Abby soon became a most important person to know, to court, to claim as friend.

So she allowed herself to be courted, and flirted in her turn, buoyed both by her lovely new gowns and her own natural confidence and friendliness. The drab little widow spending her days riding herd on her relatives and her nights worrying over their meager finances had been set free by her marriage to Kipp, encouraged to fly.

She soared.

All the day long, all through the evenings, Abby enjoyed herself, laughed at Kipp's silliness and turned a blind eye to his flirting. Similarly he never questioned her about her own forays into repartee and fan waving and walks on the balcony with attentive young gentlemen out to flatter her.

Whenever they were in company, Kipp took special pains to waltz only with her, to kiss her hand almost absently as they stood together, talking with friends. Even as he allowed her to flirt, even as he shared a country dance with some giggling debutante, he made sure he looked at her often, and came to her rescue when she found herself cornered by a crushing bore intent on explaining Parliament to her.

She adored his attentiveness. She wished with all her heart that it wasn't just another part of their game.

They arrived at their hostess's parties together. They left together. Anyone would believe them to be very much in love with each other, and content with each other's foibles.

She and Kipp gave each other freedoms they both expected, with no questions, no recriminations . . . because they went home each night with each other, fell into bed with each other. Enjoyed each other.

A perfect arrangement. A most convenient marriage. No real emotional ties, true, but with a firm regard for each other, a genuine liking of each other, respect for each other that seemed to grow stronger every day.

If only he didn't still speak to Lady Skelton.

If only Iggy would stop threatening to tell Lady Skelton and all of Abby's new friends of her cold-blooded bargain.

If only Abby didn't know herself to be falling deeply, passionately, irrevocably in love with her husband.

Still, they were great friends. They never fought.

Could she really ask for more?

Kipp was whistling as he headed for the servant stairs, having decided to visit with Cook in the kitchens and compliment him on last night's meal — a courtesy his mother had taught him, and one of the reasons he was so beloved by his staff.

He'd just put his foot on the first step when he noticed a slim young man coming his way, so that he stood back, allowing the fellow to finish climbing the stairs, a heavy silver tray in his arms.

Besides being slim, the youth was also very slight, the heavy tray nearly sending him backwards down the stairs as he shifted it in his hands. He wore a plain brown suit of clothes, frayed at the cuffs and yet still too large for him — which either meant the boy was shrinking rather than growing or he'd purchased the outfit at some secondhand bowwow shop.

The boy's hair was a pleasant light brown, tied at the nape with a black ribbon, and his face was hairless, which meant he wasn't even old enough to be sporting a beard. Kipp took the lad to be no more than seventeen, rather young to be a valet, if that's what he was supposed to be.

Kipp stopped the boy as he reached the hallway, looking at him intently as the valet seemed to want to drop into a curtsy before bowing as he began quickly backing away, nearly dropping the tray.

"You belong to young Backworth-Maldon, don't you?" he asked, as the youth now trembled so badly the dishes piled on the tray began to clink together. "His valet? How the devil does the little twit afford a valet? Never mind, I believe I know the answer to that. What's your name, boy?"

Regina Bliss stepped into the hallway, her back to Kipp, her arms loaded down with linens to be mended, and nearly cannoned into the valet. "Oh, Lark, I'm sorry. Always so much in a rush, aren't I? I didn't see you. Fetching the master's breakfast, are you? Slipped a few sharp bones in the eggs, I hope? Stop in to see me later, and we'll work some more on your stitches. You really are much improved. What? What's the matter, Lark? You look frightened half to death."

Lark's eyes shifted a time or two, hinting that Regina should look behind her. He then took off for the landing, brushing past

Kipp to race up the next flight of stairs, leaving Regina to gulp a time or two as she curtsied to her employer.

"Good morning, Regina," he said as he watched her cheeks pale, her hands begin to shake. "Settling in nicely, are you?"

"Yes, my lord, thank you, my lord," Regina responded anxiously. "Is there something I can do for Your Lordship?"

Kipp shook his head. "You've done quite enough, Regina, thank you. Carry on," he said, forgetting about his compliment to Cook as he retraced his steps, headed for the main staircase.

He'd put one foot on the entry hall floor before he bellowed: *"Abby!"*

She appeared in the hallway, coming from the direction of the morning room, her brow furrowed, her expression intense. "Kipp? Is something wrong?"

His blood was boiling. He could actually *feel* it bubbling in his veins. "Wrong? Is something *wrong?* My goodness, whatever would make you think that, Abby? Have I given myself away somehow — the smoke coming from my ears perhaps? Come into the drawing room, if you please."

Abby had never seen Kipp really angry. When upset, or nervous or feeling the least bit threatened in any way, he resorted to jolly remarks, an air of silliness meant to deflect anger, to insulate himself from hurt.

But he was angry now. Really, *really* angry. Controlled. Cold. Sarcastic. Frightening.

"Kipp?" she asked as she stood in front of one of the couches in the center of the room, believing she'd be able to think better if she remained on her feet. "There's a problem? Surely not Regina. Mrs. Harris tells me she's quite pleased with her."

Kipp paced the carpet, wondering where he had learned such great self-control. He waved away Abby's words, except to say, "It might be better if *you* were to have a talk with our new housemaid. I believe you could learn a lot from her. Oh, and by the bye — your nephew is keeping a woman in his rooms, wonderfully disguised as a valet."

He paused for a moment, for effect, then continued. "Yes, indeed. Moved himself in, moved in his own light-skirt. Probably made himself quite a cozy little love nest. Damned popinjay has her serving him breakfast, if you can believe that. I can, because I saw her carrying the tray up the stairs. Her name is Lark. Fitting, very fitting. And I'm paying for this, aren't I, at least indirectly? Other wives spend their allowance on clothes, Abby, without finding the need to turn any of it over to their nephews so that they can afford their very own doxies."

Abby didn't know what she'd been expecting, but it certainly wasn't this. "Iggy's keeping a . . . he has a — *what!*" Sick to her stomach, she collapsed onto the couch, would have sat straight down on the floor if she hadn't been close to a piece of furniture. "Miserable ingrate. I'll kill him," she muttered under her breath.

Kipp spread his arms generously. "Oh, no. No — no — no, please. I couldn't have you do that. Really. *I'll* murder him."

Panicked, Abby leapt to her feet. "*No!* You can't — I mean . . . um . . . I mean, he's *my* nephew, Kipp. I'll handle this."

"The way you've *handled* him so far? How? I'd be interested in knowing. Truly, I would. Perhaps you'll withhold his dessert, even send him to his rooms without his supper? No, that wouldn't be much of a punishment, would it? After all, *Lark* is in his rooms, polishing his boots."

Abby began to pace, trying to think, trying to clear her head, trying to decide what to do with her blackmailing nephew that wouldn't land her in the guardhouse.

"Oh, do be quiet, Kipp," she said, speaking without thinking, "I said I'll handle this, and I will."

She took three more steps before her

words echoed in her ears. Echoed loudly in the cold silence.

She thought two things. One, she had succeeded in shutting Kipp up, which really couldn't be such a bad thing, as he had certainly gotten the bit firmly between his teeth and could have gone on being insulting indefinitely if given half a chance. And, two, she'd probably just said the worst thing she could possibly have said.

Then a third thought hit her. He was angry, yes, but he didn't know the half of what was going on — perhaps not a quarter of it. But if he confronted Iggy, cornered him, threatened him, if he frightened that miserable, cowardly worm, he'd know *all* of it.

And he simply could *not* know all of it.

So Abby, with no other avenue opened to her, decided to be as angry as Kipp. Which wasn't that difficult, as the man was being an absolute *pig* about this whole thing. Blaming *her* for Iggy's sins. How *dare* he?

"I mean it, Kipp," she said as she whirled to face him, glared at a spot just to one side of his face, pretending to look at him — she really couldn't look at him. Not right now. "Iggy is *my* nephew. *My* problem. If you don't think I can handle that idiot boy without your interference, then I suggest you think again. Besides, we'd already agreed to stay out of each other's lives, isn't that correct? Wasn't that our *arrangement?*"

Kipp breathed deeply through his nose, like a bull about to charge. "Your nephew is keeping a woman under *my* roof, madam!"

"*Your* roof? Oh, really. So that's how it is, my lord? You make a big noise about *sharing,* about our being friends, about how everything you have is mine — all the little niceties of our *arrangement.* But when one small thing doesn't meet with your approval —"

"One small thing? Christ on a crutch, woman, do you hear yourself? Have you been *listening* to me?" Kipp rubbed at his mouth, started a slow count to ten, trying to get himself back under control. He was *always* under control. Until Abby had entered his life, damn her. Now he was . . . he was . . . well, he damn sure knew he wasn't *happy.*

As it turned out, Abby *wasn't* listening to him. She was looking toward the doorway, at Gillett, who stood there, shaking his head, wringing his hands. Looking like a worried old woman with the posture of a general — an odd combination that warned Abby that something (something *else*) was wrong. "Gillett?" she asked, wincing as Kipp flung himself into a chair, several rather unlovely words slipping out of his mouth.

"Your Lordship, my lady," Gillett began slowly, then rushed the remainder of his speech. "Mr. Dagwood Backworth-Maldon is in the entry hall, announcing that he has disowned his brother and refuses to spend another moment in the man's company. He would, as he has just told me, rip off his own face were that possible, in order never to be reminded of this brother when he chanced to look in a mirror."

Gillett looked rather beseechingly at Kipp, who was in the process of trying to shut his own mouth. "He's brought *luggage,* my lord."

"Of course. Of *course* he has," Kipp said when he could find his voice. He got up from his chair and walked over to Abby, his hands clasped behind his back. Walked all the way around her, staring at her, ending up in front of her, all but leering down into her face. "And I suppose you're going to *handle this* as well? Without my help, as I've told you to settle your own problems. You remember them, don't you? Those problems you said would never intrude on *my* life? Those problems that aren't *my* concern?"

"Oh, stubble it, Willoughby," Abby spat, stepping around him, unable to look at him for another moment. In love with him?

She'd actually begun believing she might be falling in *love* with him? Everything had to be *his* way, to *his* convenience.

Did he ever stop to think that she might want his help, that he could offer his help? Certainly she would refuse him, had already refused him. But at least he could refrain from *gloating* as she sank farther and farther into the abyss, stop belaboring her with *his* upsetment. Did he think she *enjoyed* what was happening?

"Stubble it?" Kipp repeated, grinning at her as he caught her arm, pulled her close against him. Good Lord, but he wanted to kiss her. Kiss her senseless. Carry her upstairs and fling her on the bed, see the anger in her eyes turn to deep purple pools of passion Aramintha Zane could write whole books about without once repeating herself. They'd *devour* each other, in this mood.

Yes, he wanted to take her to bed.

Right after he'd put all her relatives on a boat to America.

He straightened his spine, literally and figuratively, remembering their bargain, remembering that he loved Merry, that all he'd wanted from Abby was a pleasant, uninvolved life and the protection she'd give him from Merry's pity. A friend, if that was possible.

"You're going to move him in here, aren't you?" he asked when Abby returned his stare, that wide violet glare never wavering. "You're going to move them *all* in here sooner or later. Because you hate me, don't you? I don't know why, but you hate me. You want to punish me for some failing you perceive me to have — is that it?"

"*You?* Do you really believe *everything* is about *you*, how it concerns *you?* Of course you do! You're the most shallow, selfish, ridiculous, *insupportable* person I've ever met," Abby declared feelingly. "And knowing my family, you'll realize that's saying a *lot!*"

Kipp stared at her for a long time. Had he really ever believed her a calm person, a basically unemotional person who never lost control of her temper, a person who could most coolly and rationally handle any situation? He'd admired her for her control, her levelheadedness.

But he positively adored her for losing her temper, slipping the tight leash of control she'd formerly only allowed to slip in bed, where she let down her guard, let her passions overwhelm her. She seemed more *real* to him in bed. Now, he realized with some shock, he was finally seeing the real Abby *out* of bed, living her life. Not in control. Not playing a part. Not playing a game.

Even sex had been a game they played together.

Until now. With this argument, this sharp slap of reality, everything had changed for Kipp, and he grappled to understand the why of it, the how.

She wasn't his convenient wife anymore. She was Abby. All of her. They'd moved beyond politeness, beyond passion. They were acting very much like husband and wife. Yes, yes. That was it. They were acting like husband and wife. A *real* husband and wife. Seeing, doing, feeling it all — the good *and* the bad.

So *now* what was he going to do with her? What was he going to *do,* period?

"I'll get out of your sight then, madam. Don't expect me until very late tonight, if then."

"Oh, isn't that *so* very much like you. Keep it happy, keep it pleasant and uninvolved. Why should I have expected anything else from you when you can't even see the nose on your own face? Well, don't rush home on my account, my lord, for I'm in no great hurry to see you again, either."

Then she tore free of his grip and

stomped out of the room before she could fall on his neck and beg him to, for God's sake, *help* her. To, for God's sake, *love* her.

Chapter Nineteen

A distinct coolness invaded the mansion in Grosvenor Square, a thin layer of ice covering each exchange between Kipp and Abby for the space of one long, miserable week, two days, six hours and, as the mantel clock chimed out the half hour, thirty minutes.

They still attended the same parties, arriving and leaving together. They still smiled, and flirted. They still waltzed only with each other. They continued to live up to their bargain.

In public.

But they slept in separate beds.

And they didn't laugh anymore.

On the fourth day, Bailey Backworth-Maldon showed up in Grosvenor Square just in time for dinner, announced through Gillett that he saw no reason his brother should eat better than he, and declared his intention to stay.

And, as Gillett had said concerning Dagwood — Uncle Bailey had brought luggage.

Kipp remained silent, his jaws firmly clenched, although his teeth were beginning to ache from the effort.

Hermione arrived the following afternoon — yes, with luggage — declaring that the whole family seemed to be eating better than she (the Backworth-Maldons based many of their life decisions on food, one way or the other), and she saw no reason not to join them.

She'd already let the Half Moon Street house go, explaining to Abby that she also saw no sense in spending more of her new allowance than necessary as she waited for her ungrateful son and daughter to remember whose body had been gladly torn in two in order to give them life.

Another ice-chipped conversation followed Hermione's arrival:

"Her, too? Is that it, madam, or will you soon be importing Backworth-Maldons from foreign lands?"

"I don't think so, but I have been giving great consideration to going out into the streets and inviting perfect strangers to move into the mansion."

"Contemplating? Ha! You've already done it, or have you forgotten one Miss Regina Bliss?"

"There are four-and-twenty rooms in this mansion last I checked, Kipp, without counting servants' quarters. You won't even know they're here. And don't worry. I'm very close to a solution, at least for Iggy, who is definitely the first to go. He's tried my patience long enough. The uncles may be a little more difficult, however, as they're still set on regaining their fortune."

"Fortune? What fortune?"

"Oh, no. Don't think I'm going to tell you about that, and have you going off again on how I'm bringing my Backworth-Maldon problems into *your* house. You don't want to know, remember? You don't want to be involved. You want me to settle my own problems and not involve myself in yours. That's our bargain."

"It's our bargain as I understand it, but I believe you have another interpretation, madam. For someone who promised me an uneventful life, a life unchanged by our marriage agreement, you seem to have gone out of your way to complicate that life. You're in every nook and cranny, everywhere I turn. I imagine it will only be a matter of weeks until you dismantle my billiards room and turn it into . . . into . . . never mind, blast it!"

"You're impossible! And rather ridiculous, in case you're so sunk in your silly sulk that you can't see the nose on your own face. I said I would fix everything, settle everyone, and I will. I simply need a little more time."

"Time to settle the Backworth-Maldons,

madam, I might remind you. I am *not* a Backworth-Maldon, and I don't *need* settling. I don't much want it, either."

"Of course not."

"Ha! There it is again. Of course not, of course not. Well, don't think I don't know what *that* means, madam. So, please, allow me to indulge myself with a bit of repetition. I do *not* need you settling me."

"No, you don't, do you. You just want what you want, the way you want it. Everyone doing what you want, behaving as you'd want them to behave. Gillett can't retire to Wales because you can't bear to part with him — as if his life is only important as it pertains to your life. I'm surprised you haven't kept every toy from your childhood, even had your first pony stuffed and mounted. You can't let anything go, and you refuse anything new."

"That's nonsense."

"Is it? And isn't that why you married me? So that you could go on being who you were, what you were — holding on to what was instead of looking forward, to see what could *be?*"

"And *that's* a lie."

"No, Kipp. You're wrong there, too. *We're* the lie. Haven't you figured that out yet, either?"

A moment of silence followed, as Kipp watched Cuddles wander into the drawing room, lift his leg against the drapes. Better to concentrate on the dog, on his anger, and not think about what Abby had said, how she had stung him, made him feel guilty. Not that she could be right. She *couldn't* be right.

"I want that thing locked up."

Ignatius Backworth-Maldon also had just minced into the room in his high red-heeled shoes, picking up a full candy dish and taking it with him as he headed for the stairs.

"Who? Iggy? Aren't you being just a tad ridiculous? I've already deprived him of Lark, who's much happier working in Sophie's house. Or she was, until she stole two silver candlesticks and left, probably to find herself another protector. Sophie promised me she wasn't upset, as not every charitable act can be as successful as we were with Regina."

"No. I'm not talking about the twit. Over there. Puddles."

"Hermione's dog? His name is *Cuddles*."

"Perhaps you think so. I, however, believe in calling a spade a spade, madam."

Abby had quit the room before she could betray herself with a smile.

Kipp really was a good man, for all his faults when it came to holding on to the past, refusing to let go of anything, embrace anything — or anyone — new. A kind man. A caring and compassionate and thoroughly wonderful man. He just didn't know it.

Kipp was not about to experience a personal epiphany in which he learned that he was a good, kind, caring — well, everything that Abby thought him to be. Not this morning, at least, that was for certain.

His spirits were lifted somewhat when Brady James, Earl of Singleton, surprised him by showing up in town a full two or more weeks before he was expected. The two, in fact, spent a rather enjoyable hour playing billiards, with Brady ending up owing Kipp two of his estates and his firstborn, before the servant lately dispatched to Little Woodcote returned to Grosvenor Square.

"You met the vicar and his wife?" Kipp asked the man rhetorically, for the fellow had just told him as much.

Brady, taking advantage of Kipp's inattention to halt the progress of the cue ball before it dropped into the corner pocket after his shot, inquired: "What vicar and his wife? Am I missing something here?"

"Quiet, Brady," Kipp ordered offhand-

393

edly. "I'm trying to understand something. Walter, I regret the interruption. Continue if you please."

"Yes, my lord," Walter said, his prominent Adam's apple bobbing as he drew himself up to his full height, prepared to report every last detail of his trip to Little Woodcote. He was a thorough man, Walter Beam was, and it was clear to him that His Lordship desired nothing less than a full accounting.

"I took the stage, my lord, straight from the White Horse, and traveled the miles as an inside passenger — and thank His Lordship for footing the fare, as it rained some once we were out of town and I coulda caught my death as an outside passenger. We stopped at the Crown and Grapes for a meal, and the rabbit was a little stringy, but what can anyone expect from a posting inn, I always say. After relieving m'self, we were off again in an hour, my lord, and —"

Kipp, who had been pondering whether to rub at his aching head or just pound on his forehead with his cue stick, waved his hands, silencing Walter for a moment. "The vicarage, Walter, if you please."

Brady, who sensed that his friend's well-ordered life had got even more complicated during his absence, leaned a hip against the billiards table, and said, "Oh, I don't know, Kipp. Wanted to hear more about the rabbit, myself."

"Shut . . . up," Kipp ordered, and Brady subsided into a chair, sipping at a glass of wine. "Now, Walter, you say you met the vicar?"

"Yes, my lord, that I did. Him and his wife and his seven young ones. Been vicar of Little Woodcote for these past dozen years, he tells me, serving at the Earl of Allerton's pleasure, and never did hear of no Regina Bliss."

"Damn."

Brady lifted one inquisitive brow. "Damn? Why *damn*, Kipp? And who the devil is Regina Bliss? Sounds like a made-up name to me, the sort women use to tread the boards, or worse."

Kipp raked a hand through his hair, wishing Brady anywhere but in the room with him. "Thank you, Walter, you may go now."

"Yes, indeed, Walter, you may go now," Brady seconded, then waited until the door shut behind the man to add, "and now you can tell me what's going on and how Abby is involved, because if she isn't, I'll be mightily surprised. However, before we begin, may I say how pleased I am to see you looking so well, so settled. Married life seems to sit well on your shoulders, old friend. It's what you needed most, a calm, ordered existence, a convenient, complacent wife to smooth your life path, an appearance of domestic bliss that must be all you could have wished for, isn't that right?"

"You know, Brady, I have been fighting my suspicion these past weeks, but I can't seem to shake the notion that you *badgered* me into this marriage of mine, right down to the selection of the bride. I don't know how, because I had truly believed marrying Abby to be *my* idea, but you're entirely too smug about the thing for my comfort. Do you want to tell me I'm wrong?"

"Probably not," Brady acknowledged, grinning. "But admit it, Kipp — when did you last think of Merry or Jack?"

"That's beside the point," Kipp said, then barked: *"What!"* as someone knocked on the door — banged on the door, actually.

The door opened a crack and Uncle Bailey stuck his head inside, soon to be followed by the rest of his body . . . and his *other* body which, of course, was Uncle Dagwood. "Are we interrupting anything, nephew? No, couldn't be. Especially since we've got something important to discuss . . ."

". . . of *vital* importance, truth to tell.

Vital. Right, Bailey?"

Brady delicately sniffed the air, deciding that the Backworth-Maldon twins smelled most like a rotting garden, then leaned back in his chair, crossing his legs at the knee, content to watch the show. As certain as he was of his own hot dinner tonight, he just knew there was going to be a show.

The uncles Backworth-Maldon exchanged conspiratorial looks, then Uncle Bailey smiled broadly at Kipp, patted him bracingly on the shoulder a time or two.

"Kipp?" Brady interjected as the uncles maintained what they surely must have thought was a portentous silence, "I hesitate to point this out, but these two fine gentlemen are wearing carpet slippers. Does that . . . could it *possibly* mean?"

"Yes, Brady, they live here now," Kipp gritted out from between clenched teeth. "Temporarily."

"Good man, His Lordship. Sheltering us all . . ."

". . . Edwardine, Iggy . . ."

". . . Hermione and even Cuddles."

"Cuddles?" Brady interrupted, looking over at Kipp, whose neck had gone an angry red. "My goodness gracious, friend. *Cuddles?*"

"A dog, Brady. A dog." Kipp's terse answer and hot glare silenced him, except for a small chuckle even a mighty glare seemed impossible to suppress.

But Uncle Dagwood was still talking. "Moved us all in, one straightaway after the other. Never ate so well in years. Abby says it's because of His Lordship's great heart . . ."

". . . which is why we're here now, to discuss your great heart, nevvie. You see," Uncle Bailey said, patting Kipp's shoulder yet again, "we've just got wind that Longhope is putting Backworth's Prize out to stud again, right here in London . . ."

". . . probably hurting for blunt, that he'd bring the Prize into the city, to parade him around, show him off and all that . . ."

". . . so that we got to thinking. If you was to call on Longhope, tell him you want the Prize to cover your mares . . ."

". . . you could *borrow* the Prize for a week . . ."

". . . and then give him back another horse entirely. Longhope's a dolt . . ."

". . . won't even know the difference. It's a perfect plan, nevvie. Don't know why we didn't think of it before now."

"Perfect."

Kipp had stood silently throughout the entire conversation — the one between the uncles, for clearly he and Brady were not in-

398

cluded. Finally, when he was convinced they had run down, he glared at them, and asked, much against his better judgment: "What in bloody hell are you two *talking* about?"

Both Bailey and Dagwood opened their mouths to answer, which immediately warned Kipp that he'd made a mistake in asking the question. "Never mind, gentlemen, I'm sure Abby will explain it all to me, won't she?" he suggested quickly, putting a companionable arm around each of their shoulders as he motioned for Brady to jump up and open the door to the hallway. A moment later the uncles were gone and Kipp leaned his back against the closed door, a small smile playing around the corners of his mouth as he looked at Brady.

"They're a little *eccentric,*" he told his friend.

"And Prinny's a little pudgy," Brady answered with a grin. "Do you have the faintest idea what they were nattering on about?"

"That's not the question, Brady. The question is, do I *want* to know what they were nattering on about? I don't think I do. Besides, I promised Abby I'd stay out of her affairs, as she had promised me she can handle her family on her own, without my assistance. All a part of our marriage bargain, you understand."

"And you aren't even the least curious?"

"Oh, I'm curious, Brady. But, as Abby and I aren't speaking at the moment, I suppose I shall have to muddle along quite happily in my ignorance. I mean, think about it, Brady. Do *you* want to know what the devil those two were talking about?"

Brady shook his head. "I think, truth to tell, I'd rather hear about this Regina Bliss person and the vicar of Little Woodcote."

"Too true." Kipp walked over to the bell-pull and summoned a servant he then asked to inform Regina she'd been asked to speak with the master. While they waited for the new maid to appear, Kipp filled Brady in on the events that had transpired at Covent Garden, and later, in Abby's bedchamber.

"Not a child at all? Sixteen or more, Abby says?" Brady asked just as a slight scratching at the door signaled that Regina Bliss was without, awaiting entrance. "And her story — it's a lie?"

"A series of lies is more like it," Kipp said, frowning. "And now I get to sort out those lies and then break Abby's heart by turning the girl off before, as Edwardine has supposed, she murders us in our beds."

"You're not dead yet," Brady pointed out, tongue-in-cheek. "Oh, open the door, Kipp. I really believe I must see this Miss Bliss for myself."

But, instead of the fibbing maid, it was Abby who stood outside the door, patiently waiting for someone to open it for her — as the room, she knew, was Kipp's inner sanctum, and she would no more think to disturb him there than she would consider telling him she missed his presence in her bed. Terribly.

"Brady!" she exclaimed, when Kipp opened the door, flying across the room to launch herself in his arms. "Oh, Brady, how good to see you again!" As she held on to him she quickly whispered in his ear, "He still knows nothing, and if you hold me in any affection at all, you'll make sure he never learns your part in this. Do you understand?"

"You grow more beautiful every day, Abby. Kipp is a lucky, lucky man." Brady dropped a playful kiss on her ear, taking time to whisper, "You're safe as houses, my dear. Especially since I value my own skin."

Kipp stood very still, watching Abby embrace Brady. Watching Brady embrace Abby.

Kipp really was a good man. A kind man.

A caring and compassionate and thoroughly wonderful man.

But if Brady didn't soon let go of his wife, he was going to tear his good friend limb from limb.

Abby kept Brady with them, using him as a buffer between Kipp and herself, even as Kipp took hold of her elbow and led her into the drawing room, telling her that they were going to have a "discussion."

"Am I going to like this 'discussion'?" Abby dared to ask, hoping to see a smile on Kipp's suddenly stern face. "No, I imagine not."

"That would depend, madam," Kipp told her, sitting down on the facing couch, his hands spread on his knees. "You see, I have to tell you that your little *find* of last week, your new seamstress, is not who she says she is."

"Oh good, Kipp, then we are going to talk about this Regina Bliss person," Brady said, pouring everyone glasses of wine. "A seamstress, you say? And you felt it necessary to check up on the background of a simple seamstress? I wonder why. However, I do so appreciate being allowed in on your domestic discussion. It is a measure of your affection for me, that's what I think. Or, on second thought, am I to act as referee?"

Abby's heart did a small flip in her chest, but she kept her expression as calm as possible while trying to ignore the grinning Brady, who she now thought dispensable for the moment. "She's not? Then, who is she?"

Kipp sat back against the cushions, looked at Abby, gauging her reaction. "Who is she? She's a liar, for one. Whether she's anything else is still in question."

He stood up, began to pace, as he couldn't seem to sit still, keep looking at Abby, not when looking at Abby always seemed to mean *wanting* Abby. "I know we've agreed — well, *you* agreed, I must still admit to feeling somewhat fuzzy on the details — that you would handle anything you did not consider to involve me. However, I think I should at least be present when you question Regina, just to satisfy myself that we aren't harboring some criminal under our roof. Gillett has sent someone to fetch her, as a matter of fact, so you might want to begin assembling questions you might want to ask."

"I've got about a dozen already," Brady interposed, then quickly went back to drinking his wine before Kipp tossed him out on his ear.

"A criminal? Oh, Kipp, *really!* How can

you even think such a thing? Regina is a perfectly well behaved . . . I mean, she's certainly given me no reason to . . . oh, dear. I don't understand. Why would she lie to us, Kipp?"

"Perhaps the truth wouldn't be quite so warm and cuddly as hearing that she's a good girl turned off Allerton's property after her aunt and uncle died. Her uncle the vicar, as you'll recall. Ah, here she is. Come in, Regina," he told her, then inclined his head to his wife, allowing her the courtesy of the first salvo.

"My lord, my lady — sir," Regina said, dropping into a respectful curtsy that included everyone. Her gray eyes darted around the large room, resting speculatively on Brady for long moments before finally settling on the carpet beneath her feet. "You wished to see me?"

Abby looked at the girl she had rescued, taken into her house. Kipp's house. Such a pretty girl, now that she'd had several good meals and was dressed in a dark blue dress and large white apron. Young, intelligent, clean. And a liar? "Yes, Regina, we did. Um . . . it seems . . . that is, it has come to our attention that . . . um . . . His Lordship has informed me that . . ."

"Well, this is getting us nowhere," Kipp

interrupted as Abby seemed fated to never say what had to be said. "Regina, you lied to us. I sent someone to Little Woodcote, and that someone met the vicar and his wife, who are both very much alive and who never heard of Regina Bliss. Now, do you have anything to say to us about that?"

So many emotions came and went across Regina's features that Abby began to feel dizzy watching her. Fear. Anger. Apprehension. Belligerence. But definitely not humility.

"I suppose," Regina said at last, "you wouldn't believe I had the town wrong? That it wasn't Little Woodcote?"

"Oh, I *like* this little minx," Brady said, sitting himself down on the facing sofa, smiling at Regina, who cocked her head to one side and smilcd right back at him before quickly sobering, her mobile face taking on an expression of great sorrow and remorse.

"Brady, behave. No, Regina, we wouldn't believe that," Abby said, trying not to allow her exasperation to color her voice. How could she have done this to her, *lied* to her? Was the truth that terrible?

"I'm sorry, ma'am," Regina said, bowing her head. "But would you have taken me in if I told you the truth? I doubt it. So much better to invent the vicar and his wife, so

much better to be the poor orphaned innocent than the stepdaughter running away
from an unhappy home after my mother
died. After all, I couldn't take the chance
that you might send me back, and I'd die,
simply *perish,* if I had to go back to that horrible man and his horrible wool factory. He
— he wanted me to *work* there, ma'am, sixteen hours a day, just as if half the factory
shouldn't have been mine by right, seeing as
how it had been my father's. I couldn't stay
another day. Not with Mama gone."

A single tear ran down Regina's cheek,
dripped onto the bib of her apron.

"You — you've run away from home? A
wicked stepfather?" Abby asked, her tender
heart touched yet again. "And your mother
dead? Oh, you poor dear thing. Kipp, don't
you feel ashamed of yourself?"

"You believe that obvious faradiddle?"
Kipp asked, as close to flabbergasted as he'd
ever allow. "Abby, for the love of heaven . . ."

"I believe her," Brady interjected as
Abby's eyes sent violet sparks in her husband's direction. "Or maybe not. But does it
matter? Clearly she's a good person. Even
you can see that, can't you, Kipp?"

"I look with my *eyes,* Brady," Kipp said
pointedly, knowing that his friend had been
struck by Regina's beauty. "She's not much

406

more than sixteen, by the way."

"Ouch," Brady said, wincing. "Still, I believe her. Wicked stepfathers can be the very devil. Probably has horns, and everything."

"You may go, Regina," Kipp said, totally exasperated, and unwilling to enter into a debate with his wife and friend over the young woman's obvious lies, "but we'll speak again later."

"Yes, my lord," Regina said, curtsying yet again, then all but running from the room.

"She's still not telling the truth, you know, " Kipp told Abby, who realized that another large red brick had been added to the load of problems already resting on her shoulders.

"I know," she answered, sighing. "I'll settle it."

"Of course." Kipp's bark of laughter held no humor.

"You know," Brady said ruminatively as he stood, set down his empty glass, "if I didn't know better, I'd say this Regina girl is someone straight out of one of those silly Aramintha Zane novels all the ladies are so hot for, wouldn't you, Kipp? Mysterious beauty, hidden past, danger in the offing? Abby? You read Miss Zane, don't you? What do you think? I'd say there's an adventure here somewhere. All Miss Bliss needs is a hero. Kipp, what sort of hero would *you* wish for Miss Bliss?"

"Don't you have an appointment with your tailor?" Kipp asked, having decided that his friend was enjoying himself entirely too much, and all at his expense. "Yes, I'm sure you do, just as I'm sure I promised to accompany you, so that you don't end up with another sartorial disaster. Shall we be off?"

Abby remained in her seat as the two men bowed their farewells and quit the room, her mind very much involved in the dilemma of Regina Bliss . . . and the uncles, who had been nattering on about Backworth's Prize again . . . and Hermione, who had just that morning voiced the notion that she expected all of them to retire to Willoughby Hall after the Season . . . and Edwardine, who had formed an attachment for young Lord Wilkins, an impecunious second son . . . and Iggy, who still held a figurative sword of Damocles over her head . . . and Kipp, who didn't know she loved him and would probably hate her if he did know.

What a shame she wasn't Catholic. She certainly did feel a great urge to get herself to a nunnery.

Chapter Twenty

Kipp left Brady at his tailor's, then spent most of the remainder of the day wandering around London and calling himself several different kinds of ass. Stupid ass. Stubborn ass. Juvenile, sulking ass. Holding on to the past and ignoring any thought of the future ass. Dumber than a potted plant ass.

Frightened out of his mind ass.

And he did a lot of thinking about everything Abby had said to him since their first real argument, had accused him of, knowing she hadn't missed her target a single time.

The problem was, he *liked* Abby. He really, really liked her. A lot. More than a lot.

The problem was, what the devil was he going to do about that?

He'd wanted a convenient wife, a shield to hide behind when Merry and Jack returned from America.

What he'd gotten was a friend. A good friend.

A very good friend.

More than a good friend?

Kipp sent his carriage home and walked back to Grosvenor Square from Bond

Street, trying to work all of this out in his head. He didn't pay too much attention to his surroundings, his mind lost in wondering if Abby would run from him if he suggested — only hinted — that perhaps they could be more than just very good friends. More than simply comfortable companions.

That thought immediately did battle with another one, the fact that, after all, Merry had also been his very good friend — and look how that had worked out.

A one-sided love could not last, and Kipp knew that now, accepted that now with all his heart. But, knowing that, could he really risk his heart a second time? Did Abby even *want* his heart? At the moment, it seemed all she wanted was his liver on a spit, not that he could blame her.

Because he'd been an ass.

Several kinds of ass.

They had agreed to live their own lives, put on a grand show of devotion for Society, meet in bed, and otherwise leave each other alone. Stupid, stupid plan.

For a while, it had been rather amusing to watch Abby try to run herd on her Backworth-Maldon relatives, but the time had come for him to step in, find out exactly what was going on — even if it killed him —

and then offer his wife some assistance. Be a hero, like the Corsair, solve a few problems, arise the great man, accept Abby's heartfelt thanks as she fell into his arms and they fell, together, into bed.

Damn, how he wanted to be invited back into Abby's bed. How he missed her. Her laughter. Her silliness. Her passion.

Suddenly, his attention was caught by a couple walking together on the opposite flagway. What on earth were Roxanne and Iggy doing together? Kipp couldn't think of a more mismatched pair of . . . what? Lovers? Ridiculous! But what did that leave? Friendship? Still ridiculous.

Kipp's mouth tightened as another thought hit at him, lodged in his brain. *Conspirators.*

Yes. That made sense, in a twisted sort of way Aramintha Zane would immediately see as quite logical, almost inevitable. Conspirators. But conspirators conspiring to do what? To whom?

No, no, that was a silly question. He knew their target, for there could only be one. Abby. His wife. His wife, who so illogically had allowed Iggy to remain under her roof even after the incident with Lark.

Damn! What an idiot he was, not to have seen it before now. Abby loved her relatives,

411

but she wasn't the sort who suffered fools gladly. Iggy would have been out on his ear in an instant, unless he had threatened her in some way, perhaps threatened Kipp himself in some way, as Abby had made certain not to involve him, had fought with him rather than allow him to help her.

Not that he had offered all that sincerely, if at all.

An ass. Damn, but he'd been an ass.

He'd decided to start small, get over the easiest fences first, then take on Iggy . . . and Abby.

"Gentlemen?" Kipp said affably, as the uncles knocked, then entered the room. "So kind of you to come downstairs so promptly. If you'll just take seats over here, we can get on with it, all right?"

Uncle Dagwood looked at Kipp owlishly as Uncle Bailey visually inspected Kipp's study, a room they had not yet invaded during their capture of the mansion. "Get on with what, nevvie?"

"Don't be a goose, Dagwood," Uncle Bailey said, nudging his twin in the ribs. "The boy's going to help us, of course. Didn't we already ask him? It's your diet, you know. Can't keep a thought in your head past your next meal. And it shows, brother, it shows," he ended, jabbing Uncle Dagwood's ample belly this time, then sitting himself down and folding his arms across the carrot-soup stain on his waistcoat. "Go on, nevvie, how are you going to help us?"

Kipp perched on a corner of his desk, wondering, not for the first time, how Abby managed to keep her sanity around these very *interesting* people. He watched now as the twins fought for space on the small couch, slapping at each other like brats escaped from the nursery, then finally settled themselves, smoothing down their halos of graying hair, pinning expectant looks on their grinning faces.

"Well, first, gentlemen, I'm going to tell you what I have gleaned from Gillett, who is somehow more familiar with your um, *problem* than am I."

"What?" Uncle Bailey sat forward on the couch, all but jumping out of his skin. "Abby didn't *tell* you? Didn't tell you how . . ."

". . . that blighter Harry got himself drunk . . ."

". . . gambled away our Backworth's Prize . . ."

". . . our *fortune*. Don't forget that, brother. Our fortune. All to that rotter, Longhope."

"Can see why Abby didn't tell him, brother. What with how it was her Harry who did us in, ran us aground. Poor child's been trying to make it up to us ever since, not that she's nice about it, pinching at every penny before she hands it over."

"True, true. But now His Lordship is going to get our beloved Prize back for us. Isn't that wonderful?"

Kipp listened to the exchange between the twins, feeling much like a spectator at a rather bizarre game of shuttlecock, then interrupted when he hoped they'd run down, might be ready to listen.

"One, we will leave my wife out of this discussion, agreed? She's been through enough, none of it to your credit, or to mine. Two, *Uncles,* I will *not* ask for stud service from Longhope, then send him back the wrong horse. I don't know why. It's a good plan, a sound plan. I suppose it's just that I don't see myself as being willing to hang, if something were to go wrong. You will forgive me, I hope?"

"Forgive him? What do you think, brother?"

"Can we do that? Forgive someone for *not* doing something?"

Kipp poked his fingers through his hair, having finally figured out how Abby stayed sane around her "uncles." She managed it because she had a delightful sense of the ridiculous . . . and he'd rarely seen anything more ridiculous than the Backworth-Maldon twins.

"Gentlemen, if I might continue? I said I would help you, and I will. In fact, I have already set my plan in motion — *my* plan, which I see no need to share with you — and hope to have Backworth's Prize back in your stables in Syston within the week."

"Splendid!" Uncle Dagwood said, hopping to his feet.

"First-rate!" Uncle Bailey echoed emotionally, pulling out a large white handkerchief and dabbing at his eyes. "You're a grand man, nevvie. A grand, grand man."

"Yes, I know," Kipp said immodestly, then skewered both men with his stare. "But, alas, my heart is not quite as pure as you might believe. I said I *hope* to have your horse back in Syston. I didn't say he definitely would be there, did I? No, I did not. Because, gentlemen, there are a few conditions, a few favors I would ask of you in exchange for helping you. I'm dashed ashamed of myself for being so cruel, but there it is."

"Conditions?" Uncle Dagwood asked, sitting down once more. "What do you want, nevvie — free stud service of your mares?"

Kipp considered this for a moment, then nodded. "All right, that sounds fair enough. But that's not really what I want from you, what I *need* from you."

Uncle Bailey stuffed his handkerchief back into his pocket. "Then what do you need from us?"

"Let's see," Kipp said lightly, tapping a finger against his chin. "How do I say this delicately? Ah, well, perhaps I'll just say it quickly. I want you *gone*, gentlemen. Preferably by first light, and on your way home to Syston. Do you think you can manage that?"

The twins exchanged looks.

"We've already seen the Elgin Marbles . . ."

". . . caught that farce at Covent Garden last night . . ."

". . . could do without Hermione and the furr ball for a while without too much trouble."

"Oh, did I forget to mention that your sister-in-law and niece will be traveling with you? *And* that pernicious little mongrel? Shame on me."

"Take the ladies with us? For Backworth's Prize? I suppose we could manage it, for Backworth's Prize. But it won't be a pretty journey, *that* I can tell you, nevvie."

416

"Will we still receive our allowance?" Uncle Dagwood asked, his eyelids narrowed as he patted a moaning Uncle Bailey on the back commiseratingly.

"Only if you're in Syston to accept it when it arrives every quarter," Kipp told them, and the interview was over as the twins rushed off to pack their luggage.

"Gillett?" Kipp said ten minutes later, tracking down the butler in his private sitting room off the kitchens, finding the man relaxing in his chair, his bunion soaking in a small pot of hot water. "No, no, don't get up, man, for pity's sake. Gillett, I have a question for you. Do you still wish to leave me, go to Wales?"

Gillett, who had stood on ceremony for too many years not to stand on it now, quickly dried his foot and rose from his chair to look carefully at his master. "Leave you, sir? I had thought to leave my *position*."

Kipp's smile was rueful, as he realized, yet again, that Abby had been right. He saw Gillett's retirement as a defection, which was fairly ridiculous. "Yes, yes, of course, Gillett. I chose my words poorly, didn't I? But will you answer my question? I know you offered to stay, help my wife through the first weeks after our marriage, and I thank you for that. But do you still wish to leave . . . my employ?"

Gillett's shoulders sagged, just a slight shift in his posture really, and Kipp suddenly realized how old the man was, how tired he must be, how ready to sit by his own fire in his own cottage. He put his hand on Gillett's shoulder, gave it a squeeze. "Will you consider waiting until the end of the Season, old friend? Just a few more weeks, and then we'll all travel back to Willoughby Hall to gather up anything from your rooms there, and you can be on your way to Wales. Is that all right?"

"Yes, my lord, thank you," Gillett said, his chin lifting a fraction even as it began to wobble, as his eyes shone brightly with unshed tears. "And, sir? You're a good boy, you know, always were. I'm so very happy for you and Her Ladyship."

"Thank you, Gillett," Kipp said sincerely, then quickly left the room so that his old friend would not be embarrassed, and before he, Kipp, possibly disgraced himself.

The door separating Kipp's and Abby's chambers opened in a rush, closed in a loud slam.

"There you are! What in *hell* do you think you're doing?"

Kipp looked up from the book he'd been pretending to read, smiled at his wife. "Reading?" he offered amicably, wondering if the rest of the world realized just how beautiful his very ordinary-looking wife could be when she was in a temper. Even when in a homicidal rage.

"Reading," Abby repeated, all but spitting out the word. "Why is that, Kipp? Did you run out of noses to butt into *my* business?"

"You've spoken to your uncles," he pronounced, nodding.

"Yes, damn you, I've spoken to them. To them, to Hermione — who has taken to her bed, by the way, so don't count on blasting her out of Grosvenor Square anytime soon. To Edwardine, who is delighted to be going home, saying that Society is all very nice but she thinks she'd rather wait another year, and possibly be fitted for spectacles, before returning to London. That was your idea, too, wasn't it? Fitting Edwardine with spectacles. As if I haven't tried!"

"Perhaps you didn't have the right approach, madam," Kipp said, closing the book, setting it on the table beside him. "Perhaps if you had mentioned to her that young Wilkins has proposed marriage to three debutantes in the last week — and been turned down by each of them — and then mentioned to her that it might be easier to see *through* people if she could see them at all."

"Oh, you're so smug," Abby sneered at him, beginning to pace the carpet.

"It's a failing, one of many I probably should have warned you of before our marriage," Kipp agreed, going over to pour each of them a glass of wine. "I wonder if I dare mention that I've also hired a manager for the Backworth-Maldon estate, a man my own manager recommended highly. He should be in place before your family can do any more damage to their finances. As for Hermione, I'll leave it to your uncles to convince her a remove to Syston tomorrow morning is in her best interest. I have great faith in your uncles, and their selfishness."

"They are *not* — oh, bother. Yes, they are. Selfish to the bone. They all are, much as I love them. Well, as much as I love *most* of them," she added, remembering the traitorous Iggy. "But now you probably want me to thank you for settling my problems for me, and I have to tell you, Kipp, that I'd rather swallow lemons, whole."

"I don't blame you," he said as he handed her a glass, motioned her to one of the chairs before the fireplace. "And you will notice, I hope, that I have not attempted to settle

420

your problems with your nephew. I don't know why, but I am confident you will settle him much more thoroughly than I ever could."

He didn't mention Roxanne, and his belief that Abby would also settle his former mistress, because he'd be watching, carefully, ready to step in the moment he decided he might have overestimated his wife's considerable powers.

Abby bit back a smile as she remembered the plan she and Sophie had figured out to punish Iggy the night of the rout party. Her head shot up as she looked at Kipp, hope shining in her eyes. "The rout party. The rest or them — they'll be leaving before our party on Friday?"

Kipp nodded, definitely unable to withhold a grin as Abby sank back in the chair, lifted her glass to salute him. "No worrying about the uncles telling anyone who will listen about how Harry lost their supposed fortune for them. No steering Edwardine away from the stairs and the balconies before she comes to grief. No cringing as Hermione gets herself thoroughly potted even as that damn dog christens every *pot* in the ballroom. Perhaps *now* you'll wish to thank me, wife? I can think of several ways, just off the top of my head."

Abby shook her head, held out her hand to ward him off. "Why, Kipp? Why did you help me, especially after I was so mean to you? I've said such horrible things to you . . ."

"You've said such *true* things to me, Abby," Kipp told her as her voice trailed off and she blinked several times, as if her eyes stung her.

"Well, there is that," she said, smiling again, pulling one leg up and under her as she sat on the chair, feeling so much better about herself, and life in general, now that she and Kipp seemed to be back on their former, comfortable footing. "Who told you about Backworth's Prize?"

"Gillett, mostly, although he knew little more than that your uncles felt Longhope had cheated them out of the horse after your late husband lost to him at cards. Oh, and I also know that your uncles were planning for me to ask for the horse as stud, then return a different horse, which probably would have gotten me hanged if I'd agreed, which I did not. Is there more?"

"Oh, yes, Kipp. There's much, *much* more," she told him, smiling. "If you only knew the number of schemes those two have conjured up between them over the years. Cheating Longhope at cards, stealing the horse outright. Last week they wanted to bracket Edwardine to Longhope's son, until I pointed out to them that the boy couldn't be more than twelve. I felt so sorry for them, especially once I'd decided that they were right, that Longhope *had* cheated them, but I was at a loss as to how to help them. So tell me, how did you get Backworth's Prize back?"

Kipp's grin was positively evil. "Truth? I did something Miss Twelve pounds six probably wouldn't have thought of in a decade. I *bought* him."

She choked on her wine, then looked at him, her eyes sparkling. "You — you *bought* him? My lord, Kipp, you're a genius!"

"I am, I am," he agreed affably. "And good, and kind, and several other compliments that have been tossed at me willy-nilly all day today. In fact, you'd be wise to say something cutting to me in the next five seconds, or risk my head exploding thanks to my overweening pride in myself."

"Idiot," Abby said, laughing.

"All right, that's good," Kipp responded, nodding. "That's good for a start. Because I am an idiot, Abby, very definitely. And I'm selfish, too, into the bargain. As selfish as your soon to be absent relatives. Or did you think I helped them because of my great love for them?"

"Your great love for — no, I suppose not," Abby responded, wondering how much longer she could sit there, so close to him, yet so far away, without disgracing herself by leaping into his lap and kissing him senseless. "So, why did you go out of your way to settle them?"

Kipp stood, held out a hand to Abby so that she would also get to her feet. He linked her arm through his and guided her toward his dressing room. "I wanted our small problems solved, wife, in order to make room in our lives for the larger ones. Because we do still have problems between us, don't we?"

Abby stopped, looked up at her husband. Did he know about Iggy? Roxanne? He seemed to know about everything else, except the fact that she loved him. Did he know that, too? Was he about to remind her of their bargain? "Do we?"

Kipp put a finger under her chin, lifted her face to his. "Yes, wife, we do. But there's nothing that can't wait for the moment, as I have a present for you. Consider it in the way of an apology for my behavior of these past days."

"A present?" Abby asked, caught off her guard again. Just when she thought she knew this man, he surprised her with the twists and turns of his agile mind. "In your dressing room?"

And then she heard it. A slight scratching. A soft whimpering. She looked at the closed door to the dressing room. She looked at her now relaxed, grinning husband. "What on earth? Surely you don't have Cuddles locked up in there."

"Puddles? I should say not!"

"But . . . but there *is* an animal in your dressing room, Kipp, isn't there?"

"Open the door, wife, just open the door. Unless you really want to stand here and ask questions for the next ten minutes."

Abby opened the door.

Out tumbled a fat, fuzzy red ball of fur, four short legs and a wagging tail that looked too long to be supported by the small body. A pair of long, drooping ears. A small snout ending in a velvety black nose. Two large, deep brown eyes that couldn't wait to see the entire, lovely, exciting world.

Dropping to her knees, Abby held out her hands to the puppy, and it came to her immediately, launching itself into her lap and then reaching up to lick her face, her ears. "Oh, you're darling!" she exclaimed, hugging the animal close to her. "Oh, Kipp, isn't she a darling? Is she a she? And what is she?"

"She, as you're correct, my dear, is a dog. A *real* dog. I'm not quite sure of her ancestry, although her fur tells me there's some setter in her somewhere. Do you see the size of her paws? She'll go four stone by the time she's grown, and stand nearly as high as your waist. A *real* dog, Abby. Do you like her?"

"I *adore* her," Abby said, standing up, the puppy still in her arms as she looked at Kipp, tears streaming down her face . . . and being licked away by the wriggling animal. "You're so thoughtful, seeming to know just what I'd like, just how to make me . . . well, *happy.* You know, Kipp, there are times I truly believe I don't deserve you."

Kipp reached out a hand, patted the puppy's head. "You know, Abby," he repeated, using her own words, "all in all, I think I've had a rather wonderful day. In fact, I can think of only one thing that would make this day complete. Do you want to know what that is?"

Abby snuggled the puppy closer against her, smiling inwardly as she kept her expression blank — or at least hoped she did. "A nice hot cup of tea and some of Cook's scones?"

Kipp pretended to consider this for a moment, then shook his head.

"A game of chess?"

He smiled. "Closer, Abby. You're getting closer."

"I know!" she exclaimed, putting the puppy down on the floor. "You're sending my relatives back to Syston tomorrow. Being an inquisitive sort of fellow, you probably want to know something more about Syston. Of course. Well, let me see. Syston is situated in Leicestershire, which is celebrated throughout England for its sheep, its short-horned cattle —"

She giggled as Kipp growled low in his throat, scooped her up in his arms, and all but ran toward his high tester bed, dropping her onto the coverlet and following her down.

". . . and its hunters," she choked out breathlessly, before he covered her mouth with his own.

Abby thought only fleetingly that she had finally made it into Kipp's bed, and wondered, just for a moment, if this meant their relationship had changed in any way.

That was just before her mind went totally blank, just before he lifted his head from hers, looked deeply into her eyes, and said, "I like you, Abigail Rutland. I like you very, *very* much."

When she didn't respond, Kipp mentally

kicked himself for his total lack of eloquence; he, who could be so very eloquent when writing as Aramintha Zane. Where had that eloquence gone? Why did he feel so inadequate, his words so grotesquely banal, if that were even possible to manage at one and the same time?

"Abby?" he asked after a moment, feeling as nervous as a raw youth holding out a crushed bouquet of posies, hoping his sweetheart would like them.

She smiled, with her mouth, with her eyes, those lovely violet eyes, and lifted a hand to stroke his cheek. "I like you, too, Kipp. I like you very, *very* much."

Kipp's body became weightless as his spirit soared, as his heart expanded in his chest, as he knew himself becoming almost giddy even as the notion that he might, by damn, start to cry had him quicky burying his head against Abby's neck.

The passion was there, just as it had always been there, from the first, but this time it was different. He wanted her, wanted her desperately, but not in their usual way. Quick. Rushed. Teasing. Two individuals playing a shared game. Now he wanted her slow, he wanted her gentle, he wanted to learn every inch of her, kiss every inch of her, feel her hands and mouth on him.

Their clothing disappeared, just as if Aramintha Zane had scripted their movements for greatest effect with the least expended effort, and they lay close together on the satin coverlet, Abby's milk white skin glowing against the deep burgundy.

He kissed her. Softly, gently. Saw the question in her eyes. She smiled as he stroked her short mop of hair, traced a finger down her cheek, then rested it against her lips, felt her kiss against his fingertip.

"You're beautiful," he told her sincerely, meaning every word with all his heart. "You're the most beautiful woman I know, will ever know."

He watched the flush of rosy pink begin at Abby's chest, rise up to flood her cheeks with color. "No, I'm not," she protested, suddenly shy, suddenly wishing to cover herself as modesty and confusion — and the look in Kipp's eyes — combined to make her feel like a young bride being bedded for the very first time.

"Never argue with your husband, woman, not when he's telling the truth." Kipp warned her with a smile, his hand now traveling down her throat, finding his way to her breast, capturing one small, perfect mound in his palm. He leaned down to kiss her again. "Beautiful."

Abby sighed deep in her throat, giving in to Kipp in a way she had never done before, despite all their frenetic passion. She melted for him, lay very still as he ministered to her. Kissed her. Touched her. Tasted her.

She felt herself changing beneath him. Being molded into a new Abby, a new woman, a woman who just might dare to think of her husband and love in the same thought.

So gentle. So gentle. A tender worship of her body.

She reached for him, not frantically, but just to hold him, be close to him, feel his heat against her. She soothed him wordlessly, even as she wondered if he knew what he was doing to her, how he was destroying her even as he gave her new life, new hope.

Could he come to grips with the idea that, yes, people can love more than once in a lifetime? Was that what was happening to him, to both of them?

Kipp slid inside her, pushed deep, and then held her close for a few moments, feeling a part of him leaving him, a part of her becoming him. His hands shook, his head reeled. He had never felt worse. He had never felt better.

Could she forget how hurt and betrayed she'd been by that damnable Harry? Could she forgive him for his cold, impersonal offer of a convenient marriage? Could love follow passion, could love build on friendship?

Abby held him tightly, her arms sliding around his back as he kissed her, as he began a slow, steady movement deep inside her, as the world narrowed to include only the two of them, only the oneness of them.

Their passion built, combined, so that they moved in concert with each other, their bodies knowing more than their minds, having already settled this business of compatibility, needing no words to say everything that needed, longed, to be said.

Could she ever love me?

Could he ever love me?

And then it was over, yet not over, as neither of them moved for long minutes, both of them unwilling to let go, to move away, to become separate again.

He kissed her, half a dozen times, and she touched his face, ran her fingers through his hair, pushing it off his forehead as she smiled at him, hunted for words that wouldn't shatter this extraordinary moment and finding none.

Finally, knowing he'd learned a lot about himself, but not yet enough, Kipp kissed the tip of Abby's nose and rolled away from her, intent on getting up, finding his dressing gown for her as the evening had grown cool.

Could she ever love him?

Could he ever love her?

"You'll spend the night," Kipp said. He didn't ask, but simply stated his words as fact. Abby smiled and nodded her agreement.

Their first night spent together in the same bed. Truly a day to be remembered. Truly a very good day.

Kipp slipped out of the bed, put his bare feet on the carpet, and immediately cursed under his breath.

Abby instantly knew what had happened. The puppy, who might not look anything like Cuddles, had made a puddle of her own.

Ah, well, she thought, smiling as she tucked the covers high up under her chin and snuggled against the pillows, *no matter. We're still friends.*

Chapter Twenty-one

The days moved along, finally reaching the night of the rout party that would be Abby's first experience as hostess — as she did not count the ball the day of her wedding, where she had been much too stunned even to consider herself much of a true participant.

She had spent the week either being busy or desperately attempting to look as busy as possible. She played with Hero, her new puppy. She worked with Mrs. Harris and Gillett, considering decorations, food, the musicians who would play, hidden behind screens, as there would be no dancing.

Just two hundred people walking in the front door, to be greeted by their host and hostess, then left free to wander through all the artfully connecting rooms, sip a little wine, have their toes stepped on and their ribs jabbed by others caught in the crush of humanity, and then go away again, to make room for those still waiting on the stairs.

Only a few guests would remain more than a quarter hour, but it would take them an hour for their coachman to get the carriage to the door, followed by a good thirty-minute crush on the stairs, and another thirty minutes or more to stand outside, waiting for their coachman to find his way back to retrieve them.

Abby thought the whole thing a rather silly convention, but she also doubted that anyone had ever looked at London Society and dared to call it anything but wonderful.

Because the party was the least of her problems, and would solve one of them, hopefully two.

Her larger problems, as Kipp had termed them, still needed to be settled. Obviously, as she and Kipp had been as nervous around each other, to quote her uncles, as a mouse who's just discovered a milk bowl on the stable floor.

Abby felt their greater intimacy in the bedroom. She spent the nights in his bed, or he in hers, and they often made love again as dawn broke over the city.

She felt him watching her at odd moments during the day, which only told her that she was watching him just as much. They shared every meal, played chess after dinner, and shunned Society for the entire week. They preferred to stay at home, share their evening meal with Brady or a few other friends, then make an early night of it.

Because the nighttime seemed the only

time there was no need for words.

So, as easy as Abby's life had become thanks to Kipp's successful routing of her relatives, it had become twice as difficult. Now she had no buffer between her husband and herself. There were just the two of them (she most certainly did not count Iggy). If it weren't for Brady, Abby truly believed she might become a quivering shadow of her former self, feeling sure she would ask Kipp one night to please pour her more wine, and end up blurting out how much she loved him and asking did he love her, too?

Brady was their only guest at dinner that night, as Sophie had sent her regrets, saying that it was either the dinner or the party, as she couldn't be away from the baby for too many hours. Sophie hadn't hired a wet nurse, determined to feed her son as she had done her daughter, and if such things were unconventional for someone with the rank of duchess, Sophie snapped her fingers in the face of such silliness.

Abby smiled now, thinking of Sophie, thanking the good Lord for presenting her with such a friend, a woman who laughed easily, delighted in life and, just to make things perfect, had the conspiratorial qualities of a first-rate accomplice.

"Something amusing you, wife?" Kipp asked from the opposite end of the ridiculously long dining table. "Surely it isn't the strawberries?"

Abby looked down at her dessert, her most favorite dessert, then shook her head. "No, I was just thinking about Sophie, that's all. She's promised to be one of our last guests, so that we might actually get to sit and talk with each other for more than a minute."

Brady nodded. "Bram told me as much this afternoon. Made a point out of telling me to linger as well, and said it with a rather unholy grin on his face. Is there something we should know, Abby? Bram mentioned a surprise."

"Now, Brady, you wouldn't want to spoil Abby's surprise, would you?" Kipp asked as Abby sat quietly, having realized that Sophie had, of course, shared their plan with her husband. Sophie probably shared everything with her husband.

Would she ever feel that free with Kipp? She hoped so, with all of her heart, even as she knew that this new gentleness between them, this new closeness to each other, awareness of one another, did not include that most important element — honesty.

She lost her appetite for strawberries,

pushed the plate away from her.

"Forgive me, Abby," Brady said as he exchanged looks with Kipp, who seemed as suddenly solemn as his wife. So, being a friend, and aware that the tension in the room could probably be traced back to him and his very good yet extremely stupid idea of matching Abby and Kipp together in the first place, he stepped into the breach, asking, "So, how is our little Miss Bliss? Still in residence, I should hope?"

"And still very much a mystery," Abby answered, happy to embrace this change of subject. "Kipp is bothered by that, but I see no reason to complain. She does everything I ask of her, including walking Hero when I simply don't have the time. She sews like an angel, has begun teaching some of the servants to read, and believes my nephew Ignatius is most probably descended from wolves. So, yes, we're getting on quite well, even if she doesn't yet trust me enough to tell me her story."

"Not that she doesn't tell enough of them," Kipp put in, reaching for his wineglass. "The girl quotes Shakespeare, Brady, if you can believe that."

Brady looked to each of his friends in turn. "And you're not curious? Not longing to know who the devil she is, *what* the devil she is? My, God, people, you *must* have a lot on your minds, not to be caught up in Miss Bliss and her definite secrets."

"Ha!" Kipp said, rising as Abby rose, so that they could remove to the head of the stairs, ready to greet their first guests. Even though the dining room was to the rear of the mansion, he could already hear the traffic in the Square below them, and knew the nightly rush from party to party was soon to begin in earnest. "You're caught up in Regina's gray eyes, her ridiculous curls. I know you, Brady, remember?"

"Who, me?" Brady grinned. "Ah, you know me so well, my friend. Now, you two go play at host and hostess, all right? I think I'll retire to the billiards room for a while, practice my game. That room isn't part of the party, is it?"

"No, Brady," Abby told him, tipping her head so that he could kiss her cheek. Brady was such a demonstrative person, such an inveterate flirt, such a good friend. "You have my permission to hide there, at least for another three hours. But at the stroke of eleven, I expect you in the drawing room. After all, you wouldn't want to miss my surprise, now would you?"

"Besides that," Kipp said, taking Abby's arm and slipping it into his elbow, "the man needs the practice. From what I hear, he now owes Henry the Crown Jewels, if he can figure some way to liberate them from the Tower."

Kipp knew he was preening as he stood beside Abby, watching her greet their guests, listening to her taking time to spend a few moments with each new arrival, commenting on one's lovely gown, on the other's beautiful daughter, asking about a third's son, who had taken a spill from his horse the previous week.

She seemed to know everybody, this drab country mouse who had become a glorious city mouse, a viscountess, a woman with her own mind, her own heart, her own special way of gathering people to her, making them her own.

A few weeks ago she had blended into the background, dressed in her drab clothes, with her scraped-back hair, her wit only slipping out under duress. Now she sparkled, she glowed. Her smile warmed his heart, her laugh melted his soul.

They'd never know, all these people who curtsied and bowed, who came and went. They would never know the fire of her, the heat of her, the wild wonderfulness of her.

Because she was his. For convenience,

through deception, as a result of a cold-blooded decision that had offered her much and denied her more, she was his.

And not his.

"If I might have your attention, please," Abby said as she stood in the drawing room, having asked the musicians to play a sort of fanfare, which had immediately quieted the three dozen or more guests still remaining in the mansion as the clock struck the hour of eleven.

Sophie stood nearby, so as not to miss a moment of her friend's revenge as Abby called her nephew to join her in front of the white stuccoed fireplace.

"Delicious," she whispered to Kipp and Bram, who stood with her, Brady fighting his way through the crowd to join them. "I told Abby she could count on the most powerful of our Society brethren to be among the stragglers, not wishing to stand on the stairs in order to gain entry. Indeed, hers is a marvelous audience, yes?"

"That would depend, Sophie," Kipp said, watching as Iggy wended his way to his aunt, a wide smile on his face. "There are definitely too many witnesses, if she plans to kill him."

Sophie slapped his forearm with her fan,

then leaned into her husband's side as he wrapped his arms around her. "Your wife's nephew must have been a very, very bad boy, Kipp," Bram commented, resting his chin on his wife's head. "Because, having got a good look at the little twit and, I believe, taken his measure, I'd say he's in for a very nasty surprise. One thing I know for certain — I would never wish my wife or yours out of humor with me."

Kipp looked around, seeing that Roxanne was still rooted to the room, even though she had arrived, uninvited, among the first wave of guests two hours earlier. He'd kept Abby by his side for all of that time, sure that his discarded mistress would not try anything while he was standing near enough to grab her by the ear and drag her down the stairs to her coach. Seeing her still present, and standing with Iggy until he'd been called by Abby, told him the woman had something on her mind. Mischief, no doubt.

But now Abby was speaking again, standing with her arm around her nephew's shoulders, gazing at him with such maternal love in her eyes that Kipp began seriously to fear for the idiot boy's safety.

"Today, lords and ladies, I have the pleasure to announce that my nephew, Ignatius Backworth-Maldon, is one-and-twenty years. A man. Happy birthday, my dear," she said, turning to Iggy, kissing his cheek as the jaded crowd pretended to clap, congratulate this little nobody on finally attaining his majority — as if they cared a whit.

"I've told Iggy that I'd have a surprise for him this evening, a gift he has longed for since he was in short coats, a gift I thought beyond my reach as his loving aunt," she hesitated, smiling at Kipp, "until my dearest husband made my every wish possible."

"Here we go," Sophie whispered, all but wiggling out of her skin. "The idiot's expecting a diamond stickpin and studs. He'll be *stuck* all right. Now please do be quiet, as I don't want to miss a word."

"It's not us who's talking, pet," Bram pointed out, as Brady chuckled quietly.

"And so, my good friends, I am delighted that you are here this evening to share Iggy's joy at having his lifelong wish fulfilled." She looked at her nephew, kissed him again as he blinked in sudden confusion and not a little fear, as he silently mouthed the words "life-long wish"?

Abby's smile became positively beatific, and Kipp grumbled, "Lord, I know that look, too. She's definitely about to strike. Mark my words, the next thing she'll say is *of course*. That, *of course,* just means she's about to do exactly what she wants, and the devil with what anyone else might think. That's how I ended up with Regina, Brady, so trust me to know what I'm talking about."

Abby, who had paused for effect, then stated loudly, "You, of course, must all be wondering what gift this is, what a young man could have longed for all of his life. Dear nephew, I have done it. I have purchased you a commission in the King's army, just as you have always wanted. I thank God we are at peace with most of the world at the moment, although I know how you long to be in battle. But I imagine we'll be angry with someone sometime soon, to make your every wish come true. You leave in the morning, to join your regiment. Isn't that wonderful?"

"Oh, God," Kipp choked out, barely able to breathe as he struggled to contain his hilarity. "Iggy — a *soldier?* I'd as easily imagine you in a church, Brady."

"I resent that," Brady said, grinning. "I'm sure I'd make a very fine vicar. Give a damn good sermon, too, full of fire and whatall."

Kipp watched as Iggy, whose handsome face had gone as white as the mantelpiece, tried to squirm free of Abby's embrace even as several gentlemen — many former soldiers among them — went up to him, congratulating him, pumping his hand until his arm probably felt as if it could become unhinged.

"He has to go, you know. If he doesn't, he'll be branded a coward and will never be able to show his face in Society again. Considering all he's done to *put* himself into Society, he's no choice but to play the hero, go marching off with his regiment for a year at the least. As Abby said, thank God we're at peace. I don't think I could countenance the idiot in charge of soldiers otherwise."

"Absolutely," Sophie chimed in, wiping tears of mirth from her cheeks. "He has no choice but to accept Abby's wonderful *gift*, pretend to be over the moon with joy, yes? Look at him, Bram. I think he might soon have his dinner all over that really ghastly waistcoat. I could almost pity him, if he weren't such a perfectly nasty little boy."

Kipp lingered with his friends, laughing as Bram and Brady wondered aloud how well Iggy would march in his high-heeled boots, until he chanced a look in Abby's direction, to see her peering over the crowd, the light of battle in her eyes.

He immediately knew her target, and tried to push his way through the crowd of well-wishers to reach his wife. But he was too late. She had gone off in entirely another direction and was soon lost to him.

Abby approached Lady Skelton and, before the woman could register what was happening, took her by the elbow, and unceremoniously steered her out into the deserted hallway. "It's all right, Gillett," she said to the nervous-looking butler. "Lady Skelton will be needing her wrap in a moment, but first we'd like a private coze. We'll be in the billiards room."

"We most certainly will not," Roxanne declared hotly, but she was no match for a determined Abby, and soon found herself leaning against the edge of the billiards table as Abby closed the door behind them.

"Now, Lady Skelton," Abby began, doing her best to stand very tall, very still, with her hands linked casually in front of her, "you're probably wondering why I sent you an invitation for this evening's entertainment. The answer is simple, of course. It has come to my attention that you and my nephew have been close as inkleweavers these past weeks. Knowing Iggy to be constitutionally unlovable, I have assured myself that yours is not a romantic interest."

Lady Skelton recovered herself, having momentarily lost her determination in a muddle of wondering if, just perhaps, she had bitten off more than she could comfortably chew in underestimating this country drab. "Your annoying nephew is most certainly not of any interest to me, romantic or otherwise."

Abby smiled. "Now, now, my lady, it isn't nice to fib, especially when we're locked in this room, and I hold the only key. It's time for the truth, madam. What has kept you and Iggy so close? Surely it can't be some faint hope that he'll run to you, telling you that my marriage to the viscount is in a shambles and soon to be ended, so that you can step in to offer my husband your condolences?"

Roxanne's beautiful green eyes became mere slits as she leaned forward, glared at Abby. "You'll never hold him," she gritted out from between clenched teeth. "He was mine before your outrageous marriage, and he'll be mine again. Because I *know* why he married you. I know the whole of it, thanks to your very informative little nephew."

"My very informative, soon to be *gone* little nephew," Abby pointed out casually. "I would keep that in mind were I you, my lady. You say Iggy has told you, what — the *whole* of it you say? Then may I assume that he also has told you I am not a very nice person when I believe anyone I love to be in difficulties? That I have never stepped back from a battle, and that I don't necessarily follow the rules when I do take up cudgels against anyone I consider an enemy? There's a cheating greengrocer in Syston, as a matter of fact, who probably still trembles at the mere mention of my name."

Roxanne backed up a step, once more leaning against the billiards table. "Love? Is that what you said?" Her sneer made her ugly, made her older than her years. "Are you saying Kipp *loves* you? My goodness, does he know his convenient wife suffers from delusions?"

Abby was careful not to let her dismay show on her face, but Roxanne's barb had hit its target. She was too angry, that she'd so recklessly let the word *love* slip past her lips. "Better you should concentrate on what *you* know, my lady," she challenged the grinning woman. "And what you do know is that I'm aware of your hopes, your plans, and that unless you like bloody fights, you'll step away from this one."

"He's mine," Roxanne declared, her smile leaving her as she stepped forward again. Abby wondered if the woman had misunderstood her, taken her literally, and now wanted nothing less than a biting, kicking, hair-pulling match that would have Kipp disgusted with them both.

"*Yours?*" Abby shook her head. "I live with him, I sleep with him. I wake with his arms around me. How is he yours, madam?"

Roxanne turned a reflexive flinch into a rather elegant shrug. The woman was beautiful, there was no getting past that. Abby wondered, not for the first time, how Kipp had told her *she* was beautiful. Abby wasn't stupid. She knew she couldn't hold a candle to Lady Skelton when it came to physical beauty. Hanging on to Kipp's seemingly sincere flattery of these past weeks was perhaps yet another hopeful rationalization that, yes, the man might actually be falling in love with his wife.

"Well, madam," Abby persisted as Roxanne remained silent, "how *do* you explain that?"

Roxanne touched the diamonds at her throat, seemed to take much pleasure in the gesture. "He's always been a *lusty* man. I imagine he'd mount any mare he could ride. But I knew him first. I *had* him first," Roxanne told her, beginning to breathe heavily in her agitation. "He was *mine*, until you came along. Until I made a mistake, a slight misjudgment, and frightened him into this ridiculous marriage. I'm smarter now, and willing to bide my time, but he'll be back. He needs a woman in his bed, not an insignificant, *homely* creature like you. You'll see. Within another month at the most, he'll be showering me with jewels again, just as he did before. Jewels like these."

Abby grinned. She couldn't help herself. She grinned. And then she laughed, and went in for the kill now that Roxanne had so considerately opened the door for her. "Jewels? Is that what Kipp gave you? Oh, you poor dear thing, he *used* you, didn't he? Men can be such wretched beasts when their hearts are not involved."

"Oh, really?" Roxanne came closer, so that Abby could smell the wine on her breath. "And what great gift has he given *you*, that you know he isn't *using* you?"

Abby shook her head, sighed, looked at Roxanne with real pity in her eyes, knowing no woman could be so thick as to misunderstand what she next said. "He gave me a *puppy*, my lady. My very own puppy. I'm sorry, but if you know anything at all about my husband, you'll know that yours was a gift from his pocketbook, while mine could only come from a man whose heart is involved in his choices. And now, I do believe Gillett has your coach waiting for you."

As Roxanne, cheeks pale, mouth agape,

stared at her, Abby fished the key out of her pocket and unlocked the door. She watched as Roxanne began to walk out, her steps dragging like those of an old woman.

Lady Skelton stopped, looked at Abby for long moments. "A dog. That's not at all like Kipp, not at all."

"You're wrong there, my lady. It's very *much* like him. You just never really knew him, did you?"

"Why? Why did he marry you? Iggy was wrong, I see that now, probably leading me on because he's as crafty as you are, you horrible Backworth-Maldons, and enjoyed my small gifts to him. Iggy in the army? It's almost laughable, and probably serves him right. But I still don't understand. I'll never understand how he could choose you."

She straightened her shoulders, gathering her dignity about her like a silken cape. "I never loved him, you know. And now he'll probably swell your belly every year and turn himself into the most boring and dull man in creation. I pity both of you."

Then Lady Skelton continued out of the room. Out of the mansion. Out of Abby's life.

Leaving her free to worry about the "larger problems" Kipp had referred to, and that she probably knew better than he.

She waited a few minutes, mentally collecting herself, then left the billiards room, just to run into Iggy — quite literally, as he had been hunting her down the past five minutes, longing to choke her.

He settled for another threat. "How could you have done this to me? What would I want with the army? Damn you! And now I have to go or else be handed the white feather. And Mama will probably knit me socks and send me boxes of stale, crushed cake and tell everyone that her son is now a man. Damn you, damn you, damn you! I'm going to tell everyone, Auntie. I just wanted you to know before I go back into the drawing room and tell everyone everything I heard that day at the stream."

Abby smiled, shrugged. She'd known he'd say this, and had her answer planned. "You'll do what you want, Iggy. I really don't care."

That stopped him. "You — you don't *care?*"

The smile became a grin, a real one, wide and happy. "Nope. Not a whit. Oh, and you just missed Lady Skelton, as she suddenly found it necessary to leave. Poor woman, she appeared rather shaken."

Iggy wasn't nearly so handsome with his lips all white and compressed, with his eyes wide, giving him the look of a person expecting a sugarplum and mistakenly biting into a sour lemon. "You routed her? How?"

"Does it matter, Iggy? Isn't it enough that you know I have, and for you to consider what that might mean to you?" Abby asked, patting his arm. "Now, I really think you should be thinking about packing up your fine new wardrobe purchased at my expense and sending most of it back to Syston. Just think, by tomorrow evening you'll be with your — what do they call them, *mates?* Within the next fortnight you'll have your new uniforms as another part of my gift to you. I imagine you'll look quite the hero in your uniform, as you're a handsome little monster. Yes, yes, your uniforms, a nice quarterly allowance as long as you behave. India and no allowance if you don't. My friend the duchess of Selbourne says India can be arranged quite easily. Just a whisper dropped in the correct ear . . ."

Iggy leaned close, bearing down on her like a man brought to the brink of physical violence, yet knowing it would not be worth it to him to cross over the threshold. "A parting gift, Auntie," he whispered gruffly, as Kipp had just stepped into the hallway, and was bearing down on them. "Look in your husband's desk, Auntie. The one in his private study. You think you know the man? I doubt you do."

He then laughed out loud, gave Abby a hug that edged beyond hearty and into hurtful, shook hands with a fairly startled Kipp, and bounded up the stairs.

By the time Kipp had led Abby back to the drawing room most of their guests had departed, off to repeat their waiting, standing, mingling, standing, waiting, in some other mansion in some other Square.

Sophie and Abby hugged, Sophie still ecstatic at their success, Abby definitely more subdued, as Iggy's parting words rang in her ears. He was a nasty little boy. She'd always known that. But that didn't mean he was stupid. If he had poked his nose into Kipp's desk, and found something there sure to upset her, she was only surprised he had waited this long to tease her with it.

Threaten her with it.

He certainly wasn't stupid enough to try to threaten Kipp. Even a Backworth-Maldon with the stamp of his uncle Harry all over him had more sense than that.

So, after accepting everyone's congratulations, and while still able to feel good about having routed Lady Skelton so easily, Abby bid her last guests a good night and climbed the stairs, Kipp's arm around her waist . . . and tried not to think about how she might be able to sneak downstairs once more and take a peek inside her husband's desk.

"You're rather quiet for a woman who just routed the enemy without firing a single shot," Kipp said as he followed her into her rooms, shooing Sallyann away so that he could play at maid to the lady of the house. He stood behind her, undoing the latch on her diamonds, then pressed a kiss against her nape. "A true Aramintha Zane heroine."

Abby shut her eyes, collapsed against him. "I'm no heroine, Kipp," she told him. "I could be sending my nephew to his death, you know."

He took her by the shoulders, turned her around to face him. "No, you aren't. Sophie told me Iggy's assignment, and the boy will be lucky if he ever gets out of Dover. Boring, Dover is, but the Crown feels it must be defended at all times. He'll spend a lot of time staring out to sea and, if I know your nephew at all, making himself rich by pretending not to see smugglers."

"He threatened to tell everyone who would listen that we'd entered into a marriage of convenience," Abby blurted out, unable to keep this particular secret a moment longer. "He saw us heading off to the stream that day, followed us, and heard every word we said."

She bent her head, looking down at the floor. "He had particularly committed to memory what I said about not being a virgin."

Kipp's hands tightened on her shoulders as he contemplated leaving his wife where she stood, climbing the stairs two at a time, and throwing Iggy out his bedchamber window. But then he relaxed, remembered that Abby had at last confided in him, and pulled her close, saying, "It's over now, wife. I wish you had told me, as I've been subsidizing the bastard this past month, but you've certainly paid him back for bringing his mistress into our house, for threatening you. The way Lady Skelton threatened you?" he ended, feeling Abby stiffen in his arms.

She pushed away from him, looking up at him in surprise. "You knew? How did you know that?"

He decided they'd had enough truth for one evening. "How did I know? Madam, might I remind you? I am the Corsair. I know everything."

Abby smiled weakly, really trying to banish her stupidly somber mood. For the little bit of truth they'd shared tonight, they were still playing games. Still hiding behind those games. "And I am Lucinda Pomeroy, heroine extraordinaire," she told him, then laughed as he scooped her up in his arms and headed for the bed.

Chapter Twenty-two

Kipp woke slowly, putting out his arm to draw Abby to him, speak to her without words what he still feared to say, had spent half a lifetime believing he'd never say. He stretched his arm across the mattress, moving it back and forth, then opened his eyes, saw the other side of the bed empty.

That wasn't like Abby. She was always there when he woke, sometimes still sleeping, sometimes wide-awake, propped up against the pillows, watching him sleep.

He sat up, pushed a hand through his hair, and looked around the room.

"Abby?" he said, seeing her standing at the bottom of the bed, fully dressed and wearing a frown that was anything but loverlike. "What time is it? What's wrong?"

"Wrong? What should be wrong?"

Kipp shook himself fully awake, hearing an edge in Abby's voice he'd never heard before, an edge that told him she was hanging on to her composure by a very slender thread. He slipped out of bed, shrugged into the dressing gown his valet was always careful to leave over a chair in her ladyship's boudoir, tied it at the waist.

"What's that?" he asked, looking at the pack of papers Abby held clutched tightly in her hand. "Have you been making lists? My mother adored making lists, just so she could cross off every accomplishment."

"Indeed," Abby said, her voice as cold as the bottom of a well. "Then I suppose I should be crossing an item off my list, shouldn't I? Who is your husband, Abby? That's the question now answered. I should write the answer behind the question, then cross it off my list. My husband is Aramintha Zane!"

She threw the papers at him, and he automatically caught at them, finally recognizing them as the first chapter of his latest effort — the one in which he'd planned a marriage of convenience, a bit of derring-do with nefarious foreign spies, and a very happy ending. He turned over the first page and saw his own handwriting: *Love's Long Journey or, The Ascension of Angeline Bolton, by Mrs. Aramintha Zane.*

"Damn," he breathed, tossing the pages onto the bed. "Abby, I was going to tell you . . ."

"Really, Kipp? And when would that have been? When you were entirely done figuring out the plot and knew the ending? After I've stupidly given you more material for

Angeline? After you'd *used* me long enough as . . . as *fodder?*"

He raked his fingers through his hair. "It isn't like that, damn it," he protested, knowing it was very much like that. He had been writing their story, in a way, writing it down and giving that story a happy ending. He'd been writing happy endings all his life, finding ways to comfort himself that, at least in his mind, nothing was impossible. "Abby, I can explain. . . ."

She began to pace the carpet, her arms flailing, her head moving back and forth as she tried to deny what she'd learned. "Games. Always games. Did you steal downstairs to your study after you left me — to write down everything I'd said, everything I'd done? And why didn't I see it before this? It's all so clear to me now. You were the Corsair, stealing another man's intended bride and making her your own. Wishful thinking, Kipp? Is that how you kept Merry hugged close to you — by becoming Aramintha Zane? And now me. Who am I, Kipp? Some new heroine, or just another version of Merry?"

Kipp, who had been in the midst of composing a very abject apology, suddenly stiffened, his every sense alert. "What did you say?"

Abby skidded to a halt, slapped both hands over her mouth as she looked at Kipp, her eyes wide. Her stomach dropped to her toes as she realized what she'd done, how cowhandedly she'd done it.

"You *knew?*" Kipp said accusingly. "How did you know? How? And *when,* damn it." He punched at his own forehead, punishing himself for not seeing the obvious. *"Brady!"*

Abby suddenly found herself on the defensive, even as she'd been about to strip a very wide slice off Kipp's insensitive hide. "That isn't important, Kipp," she told him. "But, yes, I knew. You did send Brady to find you a wife, didn't you? Well, he picked me. And so did you, if you'll recall."

Kipp rubbed at his abused forehead. "And he told you. Of course he did. He told you all about Merry, about Jack, about my poor pathetic broken heart. I can see it all now. Very worthy of romantic fiction, madam, I congratulate you both. Putting you in my way everywhere I turned, with you knowing all about me, knowing just how to gain my interest. I'll kill him!"

"Why?" Abby countered hotly, truth spilling from her lips almost faster than she could form the words in her mind, she was so eager to have the last of her secrets exposed and have done with it. "I never had the chance to approach you, propose a marriage between us once you'd realized that Edwardine was no longer a candidate."

"Brady was going to have *you* propose to me? My God, this just gets worse and worse, doesn't it? Where the devil was my head, that I didn't see through such a ridiculous plot?"

"I never seriously believed I could do it, Kipp. Besides, you beat me to it, remember? Or was that Brady with me that day at the stream, and I'm simply confused? But now it's all out, spread out on the table, so to speak. I knew. Yes, damn it, I *knew*. And you lied. About your reasons for marrying me, and most definitely about your being Aramintha Zane. That's a lie of omission, of course."

"*Of course.* Well, madam, that tells me I'll get nowhere from this point unless I want to go in the circles you draw for me. I'm going out," Kipp stated flatly, already heading toward his own bedchamber.

"Good," Abby pronounced with a sharp nod of her head. "You do just that," she called after him, then threw herself on the bed and wept as if her heart would break.

Except it couldn't break. Her heart had broken the moment she'd opened the drawer and pulled out those damning pages.

It had shattered into a million small, jagged, hurtful pieces when she had thought back over the nights she'd spent in Kipp's arms, so many of them playing at games. Always at games.

And now the games were over, and it was time for her to go.

Kipp and Brady were sitting at their favorite table in the Bond Street club when Bramwell Seaton, Duke of Selbourne entered the room and joined them.

"Both still alive, I see," Bram said as he sat down, signaled for one of the servants to bring him a glass. "That's more than I expected, actually, although Sophie promised me that you're too sane, Kipp, and Brady's too lovable, for you to actually tear out each other's throats. And, if it's any consolation, Sophie had some explaining of her own to do to Abby, considering that she'd only invited her to our ball because Brady asked, and originally only became her friend so that she could watch the fun. They've cried friends again, however, so I felt safe in leaving them to bring you this note."

"Note?" Kipp eyed the folded piece of paper as if it contained the news of his method of execution. "From Abby?"

"No, from my cook," Bram said, handing

over the note as Brady did his best to be invisible, as his interview with Kipp had not been an easy one and he could only hope Abby had not written his good friend a letter of good-bye.

Kipp took the single sheet of folded paper, opened it slowly, only to realize it was the first time he'd seen his wife's handwriting. It was so like her. The letters nearly straight, with no hint of flourish, the strokes dark and bold. There was no salutation, as she went straight to what she saw as the heart of the matter:

"*We have disappointed each other terribly. Lied to each other in what we've said, what we have not said. We are a pair of fools, Kipp, a fine pair of fools. I shall be staying with Sophie for a few days at her invitation, as she tells me Constance has a small fever and I can be of some use to her, but then I will be returning to Syston. I'm so very sorry. Kipp. So very, very sorry. A.*"

"That was Sophie's idea, by the way," Bram said when Kipp folded the note again, tucked it into his waistcoat. He finished his drink, stood up, motioned for Brady to join him. "Constance is right as rain, the little angel. But you know Sophie, always managing everyone's life in what she sees as their best interests. She's given you three days at the most, my friend. I don't believe I need to suggest that you use them well."

Brady stopped just behind Kipp's chair, bent down to speak to him quietly. "Did you ever tell her you love her?"

Kipp shook his head, sighed.

"Don't you think it's time, old friend?"

Kipp touched the hand Brady had laid on his shoulder. "It's time for a lot of things."

Abby sat on the drawing-room floor of the Portland Square mansion, rolling a brightly colored ball to Constance, who then giggled and rolled it back. She'd fallen very much in love with the pleasant child with Sophie's same mop of curls, Sophie's beautifully rounded features, and wondered, not for the first time, how a child born to her and Kipp would look.

Would she have his softly waving blond hair, or her own thick, poker-straight tresses? Would she mirror her father's physical beauty, perhaps choosing to borrow her mother's eyes or complexion?

Abby had been at Sophie's for two days, not that it had taken her more than a few moments in Constance's company to learn that the child was many things — sweet, intelligent, pretty . . . and most definitely *not* ill.

She smiled as she considered what Sophie

had done, how she had fibbed most blatantly in order to keep Abby from hiring a hack to take her to the nearest posting inn and a retreat to Syston.

Sophie had harangued her rather mightily that first afternoon, pointing out the differences between Kipp and Abby in her own sweet, manipulative way.

Kipp had quite a temper, even if he hid it behind a smile, his droll wit. But, then, Abby had a temper of her own. So, the way Sophie saw things, they must both learn to think about what the other said, agree in principle to each other's conclusions, and then do this one very important thing . . . remain calm, cool, and most definitely composed under all circumstances.

Screeching at each other, as Sophie had so baldly put the thing, could only be considered a fruitless waste of energy and Abby had to agree. People nearly always found they had to agree with Sophie.

"You're the best of friends, Abby, which is above all things wonderful, and quite rare," Sophie had pointed out to her as they'd shared a cup of tea in her private sitting room.

"From what you've told me, desire is rather much a game you two play between you, sometimes energetically, sometimes gently, but always successfully," she continued, as Abby felt her cheeks go red at her friend's bluntness. "And that's what you found in his desk, dearest. A love story, written for you by your husband, full of all his hopes for the happy ending — a happy *beginning*, I should say, yes? — that you're both too silly and stubborn to realize you've found. My goodness, you found it that first night when he took you to bed. Now, now, don't go all missish on me, my dear. I have told you I was raised in the art of pleasing my husband, and myself. There is nothing wrong with enjoying each other, yes?"

"I think I talk too much when I'm weeping. No, I *definitely* talk too much when I'm weeping," Abby had said, and Sophie had dissolved into giggles before becoming serious once more.

"The problem, as I see it," Sophie had persisted, "is that you both entered into this marriage for reasons that wouldn't have mattered unless you fell in love with each other, yes? But, now that you have, these problems, these deceptions, seem almost insurmountable. But they're not, my darling Abby, not if there is love. You just stay here, allow Kipp's temper to cool and his pride to heal, and you'll see. He'll be here soon enough, and you'll talk, and then you can both be as happy as you deserve to be. Trust me in this, Abby, for I am never wrong. Not when it comes to love."

So Abby had allowed the deception, hoping against hope that Sophie was right, that Kipp would read her note and come running to Portland Square . . . to yell at her, to accuse her, to let her yell at him, accuse him . . . to tell her he loved her.

But it was not to be. He hadn't come yesterday. He hadn't come today, and the mantel clock had just struck three. If he didn't come by the next afternoon, Abby was determined to leave London. She'd allow for some stubbornness in the man, she'd give him time to, for pity's sake, realize what she already knew, but she would not just sit here, useless as a wart on Prinny's nose, waiting for him forever.

There came some small sound of activity in the outer hallway, and Abby put out her hands to Constance, who immediately crawled across the floor in her crablike fashion and snuggled in her lap.

Abby winced inwardly, knowing she was shamelessly using the child as a shield. But if that was Kipp's voice she'd heard, and she believed it was, she'd rather be sitting on the floor, her arms full, so that she wouldn't be tempted to run to him, hug him to her.

Then the doors opened and Kipp was striding into the room, his hat and gloves still in his hands. He stopped just in front of her, and she had to relax her grip on the suddenly squirming Constance, realizing she was holding her too tightly.

"Madam," Kipp said with maddening calm, going down onto his knees in order to chuck at Constance's chubby chin, "when are you coming home?"

Abby hadn't known exactly what Kipp would say if and when he appeared in Portland Square, but it certainly hadn't been this. "I'm enjoying myself quite mightily, visiting here with Sophie. Hero is thrilled with Constance, so much so that Sophie has declared she's going to add a few fat puppies to her menagerie. Besides, as I told you in my note, I am leaving for Syston anytime now."

She watched as a small tic began in Kipp's cheek. "No, you're not. You're coming home."

"Why?"

"Because you're my wife, damn it," he blurted out, inwardly cursing himself for his utter stupidity. He'd thought so long and hard, planned his every word for a night and a day, and then taken one look at Abby and reverted to his former ridiculous self.

Abby handed Constance to him, then rose, walked over to sit on one of the couches. "That's not enough, Kipp," she told him, watching as he sat down on the facing couch, Constance still in his arms. He looked very natural with a baby in his arms . . .

"No," he said after a few moments. "You're right, Abby, it's not enough." He allowed Constance to stick her fingers in his mouth, then took hold of her small hand, kissed it. "My father died just when I'd become old enough to appreciate his presence in my life," he began without further preamble. "My mother died when I'd barely attained my majority. In their ways, Merry and Jack left me, too."

He shook his head, uttered a short, wry laugh. "Even Gillett. I even saw his retirement as a betrayal, as yet another person I loved leaving me. Keeping my secret about Merry, about Aramintha Zane, about . . . other things . . . are only important in that, if I'd told you the truth once it became important for you to know the truth . . . well, you would have left me, too. You did leave me."

Abby surreptitiously wiped at her moist eyes, did her best to keep from dropping to her knees in front of Kipp, laying her head in his lap. So much truth. He was giving her so much truth he'd never shared with anyone before, probably not even with himself.

"I've made a fine muddle of things, haven't I, Abby? I married you for all the wrong reasons. I made you agree that we'd live our own lives, feel free to live our own lives. But I don't *feel* free, Abby. I feel shackled by my own selfish stupidity."

"I didn't exactly marry you for altruistic reasons, Kipp," she was able to say at last. "Brady waved you in front of me like some grand and glorious prize, a rescue from circumstances that had become nearly unbearable, and I leapt at it, and you, with both hands. And then, once Iggy began badgering me, I didn't have enough faith in you, or myself, to come to you, tell you the truth. To very necessarily tell you that I had purposely set out to trap you into marriage. We're neither of us heroes in this, Kipp."

He stood up, brought Constance to her. "No, I suppose not." He bent down, kissed her cheek. "How did we get so lucky, and so unlucky, at one and the same time? No, don't answer that. Not yet. I've intruded long enough, Abby, so I'll leave you alone now."

She nodded, then buried her face in the child's hair, biting back a sob as he left the room.

Sophie appeared not a minute later, fairly bouncing into the room to flop herself down on the same cushion Kipp had sat on just a moment earlier, a lifetime ago.

"Well? Don't just sit there watering my daughter with your tears. Did he tell you he loves you?"

Abby looked up, barely able to see her friend through her tears. "Yes. Yes, Sophie, he did."

Kipp sat on a chair in the billiards room as the clock struck six, bent forward over his knees, holding one of Abby's favorite fans in his hands. Opening it, closing it. Opening it again.

How had it happened?

How had she entered his life courtesy of such a cold-blooded plan, and ended up being so indispensable to his happiness?

He knew so much more about her now, having spent a few hours with Gillett, learning all the things the butler knew and he had not known. Had not bothered to ask.

He knew about Harry, *all* about Harry, and how difficult the marriage had been, how even more difficult the years had been since his rather ignoble death.

And he wondered how Abby could ever have the courage to love again.

He wondered how he'd find the courage to go on if she couldn't love him.

How would he open his eyes in the morning if he knew it wouldn't be to see her lying beside him?

He could have told her that he loved her, told her that afternoon, but he'd been afraid to chance it. Harry surely had told her he loved her, and then used her shamelessly and just as surely tossed her aside once she'd served her purpose.

Kipp recognized his dilemma. How could she believe that he loved her, if he'd only said the words once she'd left him? After all the lies and deceptions between them, there could be no worse time to confess his love and hope she'd believe him.

Kipp looked around the room he'd stripped so ruthlessly, trying to hide from his memories of his mother. Stupid, stupid, stupid. He'd never forget his mother, didn't want to forget her. But he'd been losing so much. Merry. Jack. So he'd stripped them all from his life and entered wholeheartedly into the silliness that was London, ever aware of the shadows in his life, always trying to banish them.

He smiled ruefully. He could burn this whole damn pile to the ground, and not be able to forget Abby.

The way her eyes smiled when she was happy.

The way they darkened in passion.

Her way of answering his questions with questions of her own.

Her loving heart, that could expand to hold all the Backworth-Maldons, all of London Society, every servant in the mansion — even a conniving doll seller she'd made a part of their household.

Her courage, her resilience, her proficiency at solving unusual problems in most unusual, inventive ways.

Her ability to stand on her own two feet, dare down the world . . . then melt in his arms . . . flame in his arms . . . play and laugh and tease in his arms.

He folded the fan, pressed his forehead against it.

He'd loved Merry, that was true enough. But not in the way he loved Abby, never in the way he loved Abby. Merry had been a boyhood dream, an unrealistic fantasy, perhaps even an unspoken competition between himself and his best friend, Jack. He saw that now, so very clearly.

Merry had been his childhood.

Abby was his life.

"I've been looking for you."

Kipp squeezed the sticks of the fan so

tightly they snapped between his fingers. He looked up, saw Abby standing in the doorway, Hero in her arms, a bandbox at her feet.

She was home. She'd come back to him.

"Abby?" he breathed, unable to believe his own eyes.

He nearly stumbled as he got to his feet. "I've been looking for you, too," he told her, walking around the billiards table, stopping a careful three feet in front of her. "I've been looking for you all of my life."

She bent down, allowed Hero to climb out of her arms, then stood up once more, looked at him closely. "Is there anything else you might want to say to me, Kipp? Something you didn't say earlier?"

He swallowed down hard over the lump in his throat. The words seemed so necessary before, so unnecessary now, almost paltry. He was momentarily amazed that poets had gotten away with such banality all these centuries.

"Yes," he said at last, smiling at his wife. "I wonder if you would consider putting this room to rights, putting it back the way it appeared when my mother was alive, then taking it as your own. Gillett will help you, I'm sure, as he knows just how it was." He smiled again, rather sheepishly. "Brady can't play worth a damn anyway."

Abby's bottom lip began to tremble, her heart so full she didn't trust herself to say more than, "Of course," before launching herself into his waiting arms.

Epilogue

*I have great hopes that we shall
love each other all our lives
as much as if we had never married at all.*
— Lord Byron

Not quite two weeks later, Abby watched in mild amusement as a blur of sea-green gown and glorious red hair sailed into the Grosvenor Square mansion drawing room and directly into her husband's arms.

"Kipp!" the apparition exclaimed, hugging him, being hugged in return. "Oh, how we've missed you! And Gillett has just now told us that you've married! How wonderful!"

Jack Coltrane entered the room behind his wife, shaking his head affectionately as he watched Kipp lift his wife and spin her around several times before putting her down.

"My lady?" he inquired, politely bowing to Abby. "Please forgive my wife's restrained and sober entry. She tries so hard to appear enthusiastic, but it has always been so difficult for her to express her emotions."

"Yes," Abby replied as she stood up, held out her hand to Kipp's childhood friend, doing her best to be serious herself. "I can see her problem. Welcome home, Mr. Coltrane. We've been expecting you these past weeks, Kipp all but champing at the bit to see you again."

"Jack, please, if that's all right with you," he said, as Abby took in the great height of the man, nearly that of Kipp's. Hair as black as her own, eyes as green as emeralds. A fitting foil for his wife.

At one time Abby would have felt intimidated by all this physical beauty, but Kipp's love had given her confidence in her own appearance and, although Abby didn't realize it, she had actually become more attractive, her love for her husband softening her edges, giving her a glow that only a blind man could not see.

"Jack!" Kipp exclaimed, crossing the room to embrace his friend, the two of them slapping each other's backs in that hearty way men have of pummeling each other when they meet again after a long absence. "Our note of invitation reached you at the docks, I see. You will stay with us for a few days before returning to the country, won't you?"

"That we will. These old legs of mine still

think we're bobbing up and down in the water like corks and need a few quiet days to comprehend that we've made the transition to solid ground. As our own mansion is in dustsheets, we'd be fools not to accept your hospitality, dear friend," another voice, a very deep, full-bodied voice supplied as an even taller, broader, darker gentleman came into the room, carrying a small blanket-covered bundle in his arms.

"Walter!" Kipp said, shaking his head as his grin nearly split his face. "You magnificent savage, you look bigger every time I see you. Abby, darling, this is Walter, Jack's business partner, mentor, and very good friend. You remember me telling you about him?"

"That I do, that I do," Abby said as Merry took the bundled baby from the American Indian's arms, then stood beside him, looking very much like she'd just stepped into the comforting shade of a tall, sheltering tree. "I'm very pleased to meet you, Walter." Abby spread her hands, grinned. "To meet all of you."

"Not half as pleased as we are," Merry said, being her usual forthright self. "We had begun to wonder if Kipp here was destined to become a crusty old bachelor, tending to his hounds and drinking entirely too much port after dinner. Would you like to see our son, my lady? His name is John."

"And I'm Abby, please," Abby said, as she and Merry walked over to one of the couches. They sat down as Merry unwrapped the small scrap of humanity that had begun to make his presence known with a few lusty yells. She looked down at a chubby, round-faced cherub with eyes as blue as his mother's, a short, thick mop as dark as his father's own hair. "Oh, he's darling!"

Kipp gestured for Jack and Walter to join him at the drinks table; wine for Jack and himself, a glass of lemonade for the Indian. "God, but it's good to see you." He handed them each a glass, smiled. "So, tell me, how was Philadelphia? Do you two own all of it yet?"

As Jack and Walter took turns speaking, and as Kipp listened with half an ear, he watched his wife and Merry, the two of them fussing over the infant now cuddled in Abby's arms, and seeming to be quite content in each other's company. They'd be good friends as well as neighbors, he was certain of it. Abby was very good at making friends.

". . . and then we bought Independence Hall and turned it into a bakery shop."

Kipp's head whipped around, and he stared at his friend. "*What* did you say?"

Jack threw back his head, laughed. "I wondered if that might get your attention. She's lovely, Kipp. You're happy?"

"Very subtle, Jack," Walter said wryly, sipping lemonade. "I'm so gratified to claim you as my student."

"Happy?" Kipp shook his head. "Happy doesn't begin to describe how I feel, my friends, just as saying that I'm lucky doesn't come close to telling you how fortunate I am." He looked at Abby once more, envisioning her with their own child in her arms. "We're both very lucky men."

"They're gone? Just this morning, you say? Well, that's a disappointment," Brady said as he kissed Abby's cheek, then accepted the glass of wine Kipp offered him. "That will teach me to go jaunting about the countryside on a whim, won't it?"

"That's all right, Brady," Abby told him, patting his arm. "You're still planning to join us at Willoughby Hall for Christmas, aren't you? You can meet them then."

"I've already met Jack," Brady reminded her, "during the time he was banished from his family hearth, I believe. Good man, if a shade intense. Is his Merry beautiful?"

"Very," Abby said, smiling at Kipp, who winked at her in response. "Now, do you have any more questions, or are you ready to tell us just where you were *jaunting* about this past week?"

Brady shrugged. "Nowhere in particular. Just a gentleman off on a small tour of the bucolic countryside." He looked at Kipp. "Stopped in Little Woodcote for a few days, made some very discreet inquiries about your Miss Bliss, that sort of thing."

"You didn't," Kipp said, shaking his head in disbelief. "You're like a dog with a bone about our maid, aren't you? I keep telling you, Regina's sixteen, couldn't be more than seventeen, not that I'd believe her no matter what she might tell us if we asked. Much too young for you. Besides, Abby here would have your guts for garters if you attempted to make the girl your next mistress."

"Mistress?" Brady pressed both hands to his chest, exaggeratedly expressing his shock at Kipp's words. "As if the thought ever entered my mind. I'm just curious, that's all. Is it a crime now, to be curious? Besides, you can't fool me. You're both all a-tremble, wondering what I found out, aren't you?"

"No, we're not," Abby answered firmly.

"Pity," Brady said, his smile meant to be maddening, "but that's all right. I'll just take it up with Miss Bliss herself. With your permission, that is."

"Permission granted," Kipp said, sighing, shaking his head at his stubborn friend. "And I hope she ties you up in so many lies you can't fight your way free for a week."

Later that same evening, Sallyann left the bedchamber as Kipp entered it, knowing her services would not be required. They rarely were, not with her master and mistress billing and cooing all the time like lovebirds, wanting to be alone together more than would probably be considered proper for married couples in some societies.

Abby turned her back to Kipp as he undid the clasp on her pearl necklace, then eased her gown from one shoulder and kissed her warm skin. "Brady can be so impossible, can't he? Do you really think he went to Little Woodcote, Kipp? That he actually did learn something about Regina? Perhaps we should have listened to him."

"Absolutely not, darling, as the last thing I want to do is encourage the fellow," Kipp told her as he worked at the closings on her gown, expert that he now was in the quickest way to disrobe his wife. "Besides, I think we've had enough intrigue of our own for a while, don't you? We'll just let Brady amuse himself. You'll see, it will come to nothing."

He took her hand, led her toward the bed. "I'd much rather talk about how I'm planning to take you back to Willoughby Hall in a few weeks, then keep you there as my captive. In the bedchamber, I believe."

Abby turned, melted into his arms. "Hmmmm, I like that. Tell me. How would you keep me captive? Would you come to me each night, intent on stealing my innocence, only to find yourself falling madly, deeply in love?"

Kipp's smile melted her toes. "Something like that," he purred as he pushed the gown completely from her shoulders, so that the fine silk puddled at her feet. "But I do believe I need some small assistance with the plot, as it's still rather thin. Perhaps if we adjourned to the bed . . . ?"

"I love you, Aramintha Zane," Abby told him as he lifted her in his arms.

"And I love you, wife. I don't tell you enough, I know, but I do love you with all my heart and soul."

"Idiot," she whispered throatily, keeping her arms around his neck as he eased her onto the mattress. "Don't you know? You tell me every day. . . ."

The employees of Thorndike Press hope you have enjoyed this Large Print book. All our Large Print titles are designed for easy reading, and all our books are made to last. Other Thorndike Press Large Print books are available at your library, through selected bookstores, or directly from us.

For information about titles, please call:

(800) 223-1244
(800) 223-6121

To share your comments, please write:

Publisher
Thorndike Press
295 Kennedy Memorial Drive
Waterville, ME 04901